For Liz
I appreciate you
enjoy!,

MW00627567

THE FLOOD

A NOVEL

MEGHAN O'FLYNN

PYGMALION
PUBLISHING

THE FLOOD

Copyright 2019

Distributed by Pygmalion Publishing, LLC

ISBN (paperback): 978-1-947748-85-9

For those who hunger for more.

ALSO BY BESTSELLING AUTHOR
MEGHAN O'FLYNN

STAND-ALONE THRILLERS
The Jilted
Shadow's Keep
The Flood

~

THE ASH PARK SERIES
Salvation
Famished
Conviction
Repressed
Hidden
Redemption

~

SHORT STORY COLLECTIONS
Aftertaste
Listeners
People Like Us

~

DON'T MISS ANOTHER RELEASE!
SIGN UP FOR THE NEWSLETTER AT
MEGHANOFLYNN.COM!

PROLOGUE

SHE AWOKE to her brother making a wet sound with his mouth, the horrible smacking that always made her want to punch him even if Mom said hitting wasn't allowed. She thought about sneaking, though, hitting him in places where it wouldn't bruise, where Mom couldn't see. The way he did to her.

Was that wrong? Maybe she was a bad person just for considering it. That's what her brother would say, if he knew.

She squeezed her eyes closed, hoping to drift off to sleep again, though she couldn't see much—the darkness had come with the tornado and stayed. A power outage was one thing, but the terrible roaring collapse of the house above them had blocked out the windows. Black, black, black. She squeezed Dad's lighter, letting the metal bite into her palm, imagining her dad was still awake to make it work.

She hadn't heard his wheezy breath for a long time, that low whisper from the other side of the room. Somewhere in the darkness, a tiny noise pinged through the air—*A bell? A chime?*—but it vanished just as quickly. Maybe she'd imagined it. Then another sound, definitely not in her head: that horrible smacking again, a wet gooey noise, like her brother was eating gummy worms. Was he? The thought should have made her hungry, but that painful twisting ache in her belly had mostly gone away after a few days down here—or maybe a few weeks, she wasn't really sure on the time. She only knew that her insides felt numb, her feelings and her guts. All hollow.

And they *were* hollow, weren't they? She'd cried as much as she ever had before, until the tears stopped and her muscles ached. Maybe her stomach was eating itself and that's why it didn't hurt. But Dad was the one who knew about science and he wasn't awake to ask. He always said she asked more questions than anyone he'd ever met. That he loved this about her, her...*precociousness*. That word always made her brother scowl. Then again, anything she did well made him unhappy.

She strained her ears; nothing from the other side of the room. Nothing but pitch blackness and her own brain. But she could still imagine both her parents sitting there the way they'd been since the house fell—Mom pale in the flickering lighter flame, face all squished up with pain, her head on Dad's shoulder, her legs under the roof beam, the same beam that was on top of Dad's ribs. He'd been smiling like it didn't hurt a bit. She'd seen blood coming out of his ear, though, and more on his chin and she thought he had blood other places even though he wouldn't let her see—he'd covered his belly with an old towel. But she shouldn't think about that, should she? Especially since it might be her fault. Her brother hadn't said it down here yet, but he blamed her for everything else, so often that now she automatically heard his voice when she made the slightest misstep. And she'd just listened to the smacking while her brother ate up that last bag of bread, her tongue frozen in her mouth, not saying a word. She'd let Mom eat that old jar of peppers too, hadn't she?

Somewhere in the distance, that little chime rang out again—*ching!*—bright and harsh, but her body was too heavy to jump. *What is that?* She strained her eyes but saw only the dark, black like the velvet of her father's Halloween costume last year: a spider. She had gone as a fly. Her eyes prickled like she wanted to cry again, but she blinked and the feeling vanished. Numbness returned. The dark spun, around, around, around.

Ching!

Was someone out there looking for them? Finally, finally, *finally* ready to blast them out of the rubble and into the sky like superheroes in firefighter outfits? But it didn't seem to be getting closer, that noise—maybe it was farther away. She strained her ears. The water dripped once, then silence. Was this what it was like being deaf? Being blind? All she had was her nose, really, and she wished she could give that one up. It smelled real bad down here, like puke.

And she didn't like all that jumping around happening in her chest, the way the air had thinned out. Mom had said not to worry, before she passed out, said that God didn't want them to suffer more than they had to, and that the hunger would come back when they needed it—when there was food again.

She inhaled through her nose and coughed at the smell—sour. Thick. Rotten. Really, really bad, like old nasty eggs. But worse.

"How long you think it's been?" her brother said from his little spot on the dirt floor, and this time, she did jump, pulling her feet up toward her gut, away from his voice.

"I don't know. And..." She wanted to tell him she was scared, to tell *someone, anyone* so they'd make her feel better, but she bit her tongue. He wasn't scared. He was never scared. He was almost twelve, four years bigger than her, practically a grown-up, and he'd slapped her in the mouth when she'd tried and failed to squeeze through the crevices in the rubble. But his shoulders were too broad to squeeze through the cracks himself, and he was not strong enough to lift the mounds of brick that blocked the stairway. Or that big wooden beam that had fallen on Mom and Dad. That was the one time Dad'd shrieked, screamed like a yelping puppy, when she'd tried to free him. *Just leave the beam alone, baby,* he had moaned in a high-pitched way that had terrified her. *Just let it be.*

Smack, smack, smack.

"Shut up!" She wanted to yell it, but it was barely a whisper. She pushed herself to seated, every muscle in her body aching with effort. Her tongue tasted grainy, like sand. The bell she'd heard outside rang again—louder, and not from outside. The noise was in the cellar with them. From over near her brother.

Ching!

Her brother's laughter rang through the demolished cellar along with the bell, bouncing off the rubble. How did he have the strength to laugh? Just squeezing the lighter in her palm took every ounce of energy she had left.

The chime came again. And the smacking, the smacking, the smacking.

"Stop making that sound! Mom always tells you not to do it, and you're doing it on purpose for no reason!" The words exploded from her and when the last one left her lips, her chest heaved. Dizziness tugged at her. Her eyelids dropped closed.

"Well, Mom's not here," he said and that punched her hard in the guts. "Besides, I'm not doing it for no reason." She heard him moving in the dark, closer, closer, and she opened her eyes again, saw only blackness. Pulled her knees to her chest.

"Here, give me your hand."

She sat on her fingers.

"Seriously, I'm your brother. I'm just trying to help you."

She didn't want to, but when he moved to walk away, she extended her hand, palm down. He grabbed it and prickles like electricity jittered up her back and—

"Ouch!" Something sharp had bitten into her arm.

He held fast to her hand. "Sorry, accident."

No it wasn't. Was he trying to cut her arm off? Then she recognized the round clinking bells bouncing against her wrist bone: the handle of the old stone blade that Dad'd gotten after Grandpa died...what had Mom called it? *Ceremonial.*

She couldn't breathe, and though she yanked at her arm, he would not release her. Mom wasn't there to help her. Dad was asleep. *Why is he still sleeping?* But she didn't want to think about that.

"Watch the tip of the blade—it's old, but one side is still kinda sharp." He turned her hand over and took the lighter, and something wet slid into her palm, onto the little sore spot where the lighter used to be. He let her go. Her shoulders relaxed.

"Eat it," he said. "We need to keep up our strength or we'll die before they find us."

It felt slimy and cold and gross, but then...

Her belly rumbled. Mom was right, the hunger was coming back. Her hand lifted all by itself, toward her mouth. But...how did she know it wouldn't kill them, like that thing Mom ate? She sniffed—didn't smell like much. Maybe her nose was broken after all. "What is it?" she asked.

"Don't worry about it. You're hungry, aincha?"

Yes, she was, suddenly she was, the pain roaring back,

twisting her belly in knots, and the emptiness became a dagger, like she'd swallowed that knife right down into her guts. Her hands shook with need, desperation to put the thing to her lips. She squeezed it tighter in her palm and it… squished. Just a little, like the slimy red clay they used to find out back. Her mouth tingled. "What if it makes us sick?"

"I've been eating it since yesterday…or I think yesterday. If it was going to make us sick, I'd be sick, right?"

Right. He was almost twelve and he knew better and he'd worked hard to catch…whatever this was. He knew what he was doing. She put the chilly thing to her lips. Yes, slimy. And super chewy, like the alligator meat Dad had made her try once, but this tasted like metal. She didn't care—it wasn't half as nasty as the water burbling up from the dirt floor.

"Do you really think they'll find us?" she asked him now, and her voice seemed to shrink, vibrating against the rock and wood before vanishing into the dirt walls.

"They will. They have to, right?" His voice was high. In her belly, the metallic meat rolled around in there, angry—bitter. She gagged. Swallowed it back down. "We're gonna get sick."

"We'll be fine." But his voice still wasn't right, not at all. He sounded happy. How did he always sound so happy? But she knew; because he wasn't a downer like she was. "Stop being so pessimistic, too," he said. "It's a real bummer." He sniffed. Their toes were touching. Her chest hurt.

"Want more?" he said.

"Is there more?" Electricity lit up her chest, not worry this time—it felt like Christmas morning. Her belly burbled.

"Yeah." He was farther away now, his absence loosening the tightness that had crept between her shoulders. The lighter flicked, one harsh *chssshh*, but it failed to ignite.

"How much more?"

The lighter flicked again, *chssshh, chssshh, chssshh* then caught and the room lit up with yellow. "There's enough."

Her brother was over by Dad now, crouched by the roof beam, his dark hair blurring in the hazy light and hiding the pale skin of his forehead—it looked like someone had taken a bite out of his skull. He had put a sleeping bag over their parents' heads so she couldn't see them, but Mom's hand was on the floor of the cellar. Skin dark. Green or purple maybe. Dad's arm lay on top of the enormous wooden beam...bone, it was skinned to the bone, all the flesh gone, all the meat...

She couldn't breathe. Or move. Or speak.

Her brother turned to look at her. He smiled. His teeth were red with blood.

CHAPTER ONE

VICTORIA COULD ALMOST SEE IT: the way the cotton pillow would pucker around her fists as she clamped it over his face, how the misshapen lump beneath would wriggle as he tried to force air through the goose feathers, how everything would lapse into silence, nothing to break the stillness but her hushed exhale of relief. On any normal evening, at least. Now, the night breathed wetly, almost as loudly as he did, a thick swooshing against her eardrums. Viscous. Raindrops *plink, plink, plink*-ed against her soaked hair. The shingles caught the skin on the backs of her legs sharply no matter how she tried not to move, like being slowly ground to dust by sandpaper, and water stung in every scrape. Victoria inhaled in the soupy night, stifling her gag reflex when the musky, acidic stench of shit hit her. Her muscles cramped harder. The sound of the rain against the lake of sewage around them was a constant reminder: they were going to die.

Three days they'd been stranded so far, sitting on top of Chad's family home, separated from the nearest dwelling by a mile of farmland and animal pastures. Three days of not eating, of her belly twisting and angry. Three days of filling her hands with rainwater to avoid dying of thirst.

Three days on the roof with the husband she'd been planning to leave.

The forecasters had said it was a long shot, the storm hitting here, and an even longer shot that the enormous storm systems out in the Atlantic would build in strength and aim themselves at their little low-flood-plain section of Louisiana. *That would be ridiculous*, they'd insisted, *unprecedented*. And they'd all been wrong, especially that twit on the news with his gray hair, his eyes an odd purple-blue that didn't exist in nature—"Probably won't be more than a category two, and a little rain the week after," he'd said. Bullshit. And now all the people who'd stayed were fucked. Totally, one hundred percent fucked. *We should have left*. That would have been the rational thing to do, *honey*, the logical thing.

Her heart seized, her stomach cramping too, a burning knot of hunger. Her lungs were far too small. But panicking made you stop thinking clearly—it could only make things worse. She forced air through her mouth as loudly as possible, drowning out the sound of the storm and Chad's equally labored breath. But not his words.

"Are you okay, Vicky?" He said it in a high voice, almost sing-song, the kind of voice he'd use to ask one of his students about a skinned knee.

Victoria wiped her wet hair from her forehead and tried to relax the painful knot in her guts. Raindrops tapped against her flesh, incessant, like a petulant child. The gray of Chad's irises seemed darker than usual in a world haunted by yesterday's storms and pregnant with electricity and anticipation of the second hurricane. She wished they had a radio, a cell phone to check the status of the upcoming storm, but their electronics had been impossible to keep dry. Their phones were sitting on the roof somewhere near the chimney, useless. *Why the fuck did I listen to you?* She turned away from Chad. Couldn't stand to see the guilt in his eyes, like she was supposed to make him feel better.

Chad always felt awful if he gave someone bad advice—he'd once teared up when he realized he'd given a stranger the wrong directions—but he had this way of convincing people not to bitch at him by making them feel guilty or sorry for him. That wasn't going to last. If they stayed on this roof much longer, he was going to get an earful.

In her peripheral vision, off the edge of the roof, the shitty, brackish water rippled like the skin of an enormous serpent, oily scales shivering with the anticipation of finishing them off. Half a block down, the broken post that used to hold their street sign stabbed through the surface of the filth. And to her other side loomed the muscly bulk of the chimney, topped with the grate she'd installed to keep the animals out, now ripped open like snapped metal ribs—some creature had been at it. Maybe whatever had clawed it apart was still there, lurking in the brick tunnel, drowned and bloated, tenderizing in the sea of bacteria.

Her throat closed. She forced it open. Her black leather work boot tap-tap-tapped against the soggy shingles. She tugged on her cut-off shorts, then the hem of her favorite black T-shirt, so dark she couldn't see the film of dirt and wet. The water was still rising, the red of the shingled roof so dark it looked like drying blood, and some of it probably was —Chad had a gash across his shin from a torn aluminum gutter. Behind Chad, the expanse of sky darkened, threatening, and the rush of rain on water seemed suddenly louder; she felt sure he wouldn't be able to hear her unless she yelled. But she said nothing. There was nothing to say.

If only they lived somewhere else, somewhere higher, somewhere the earth wasn't perpetually soggy from April to August, somewhere with some semblance of civilization. All they had in this section of Fossé, Louisiana was the community college, but that was over an hour away by car—and the levees had failed, leaving the paved roads leading to the college impassable by car or truck. The college itself would be underwater too before the week was out, especially if this storm didn't move on, or the second hurricane hit as hard as they'd been saying. And if the next storm hit while the citizens of Fossé were on their roofs… The winds would rip over the flooded streets, tearing shingles and people alike from the tops of their homes, flinging them against the treetops, impaling them on the remains of fences or drowning them in the sewage from overflowing septic tanks. Even if it did pass quickly, the water table was so high that people would be stuck for weeks. No power. No food. No drinkable water once the rain stopped. These might be her last days on this earth, and she and Chad should not be living their final hours together.

They'd been inhabiting their own little worlds for months now, independent planets merely circling the same sun. Even now he was staring out over the water, waiting passively for someone else to come to their rescue, though for once, she had no other ideas herself. They weren't going to swim twenty miles, and the waste products from the farmland—pig and chicken shit—were rife with E. coli and salmonella and other antibiotic-resistant bacteria that would spread through their injuries into their blood before they got to safety. Sepsis. That'd be a fun way to go out. Better than drowning though—she'd done that once, and once was enough.

The rain spit, water on water. The wind howled, an angry beast bellowing from the sky. The expanse of water pulled her gaze, but she refused to look at it, like it was a monster that could only exist if she let herself notice. Victoria shivered.

"Is there more peroxide?" Chad said.

"It's gone."

She sat back on the gritty shingles and turned away from him, squeezing her eyes closed, forcing the sound of the rain and the image of the storm from her mind. But in the blind starbursts of light behind her eyelids, she saw her parents' Chicago apartment and the square of afternoon sunlight that hit the living room floor when the sun snuck between the neighboring buildings. She and her twin brother Phillip used to sit on that little spot whenever they could, which wasn't often—usually the room was occupied, her father out there screaming at her mother, or screaming at Phillip for stealing money, and later for taking their mother's painkillers. Once she'd tried to help and ended up in the emergency room with a broken rib. Phillip had held her hand the whole way there, sung her songs, refused to let go even when the nurses came to ask her questions about her "fall."

Why the fuck am I thinking about this now? But she always thought about Phillip when she was stressed. He was like…a teddy bear, the memory of his voice somehow comforting. Illogical, sure, but everyone was entitled to one foolish, illogical thing. Better than Chad's foolishness—his was going to get them killed.

She leaned back, resting her head against the sandpapery shingles.

You're going to be okay, Victoria, you know that.

Her brother had said that just before he left Chicago for good. That was why she'd come to Louisiana in the first place, Phillip's last known address—she'd hoped their twin connection would help her do what a PI couldn't. She'd been wrong, yet she'd stayed—too long. Ten years now, fourteen since she'd seen her brother. She did get occasional postcards from him, pictures of historical spots around Louisiana, little notes on the back like "I hope you're doing well. I'm still working on 'well'. See you when I manage to get there."

Those cards ripped her wounds open every time, kept her up hearing the words in her brain, his voice whispering to her while she tried to sleep. She could help him. If he'd just fucking *call*.

"Hey!"

Her eyes snapped open. Chad scuttled to his feet, the grating sound ringing through the night as he slid on the gritty roof tiles. The sky was pitch as tar, not even a glimmer of haze on the horizon. Oh god, how long had she been out? Was the next storm here? She'd slept through the last dregs of light leaving the sky. But she didn't feel the harsh gusts of wind, didn't see flying debris, only Chad's silhouette, and she'd not have seen him at all were it not for...

The light.

Far out over the water, a hazy circle swept first one way, then the other, the rippling muck glittering like yellow diamonds in its wake.

Victoria pushed herself to standing, but the roof was slick despite the grit; her foot slid from beneath her and she went down hard on her knees, scrabbling at the tile with her fingernails, cursing under her breath at the wretched shingles.

"Hey!" Chad cried, waving his arms. "Over here!"

The light glided back and forth, back and forth, and only then did she realize the whoosh of rain was muddling the noises around them. She'd become so accustomed to the patter and slap of rain that it had all but vanished from her awareness, but now, looking over the water...the night was *loud,* the wind screaming, the rain hissing into the muck around their little island of house. They'd disappear into the landscape if they couldn't overcome it, and...the water was higher than it had been just hours ago, the ripples licking at the base of the gutters. A few more hours and the nasty water would creep over the shingles, and then—

"Help!" she yelled, still on her hands and knees. The roof and the water went black again as the light swept away off to her left, then to the far side of the boat—the opposite direction. *They can't hear us.* She planted her feet. *Stand up, stand up! Yell louder!* She inhaled once through her nose, put her hands on her thighs, and heaved herself to standing. "We're out here!"

"This way! Hey, help us!"

"Over here!" Her throat ached, her eyes stinging with rain and unshed tears, but the light swept toward them once more. The beam hovered—and stayed. The sound of a motor cut the night.

They were coming to help. Hopefully, they had a place to ride out the storm.

CHAPTER TWO

BLACK RAIN BOOTS came into focus in front of her, haloed in yellow, then indigo jeans as the girl stepped toward the vinyl bench where Victoria was sitting. Above the hazy glow of the light, dark curly hair peeked from under the hood of the woman's green rain slicker and plastered itself to the side of her face. She smiled, her bow lips pulling back to reveal perfectly straight teeth, the kind that belonged in a toothpaste commercial. No wrinkles. Twenty-three maybe. And she had her own boat? Shelter? Her brown eyes reflected the yellow light from the flashlight, making her irises glow like a cat's. But there was no mistaking the optimism in her gaze—hopeful. "I'm Windy." A hand slid into the yellow beam from the darkness beyond the flashlight fast as a snake striking at prey—fingers like talons. Windy's black wristwatch, bulky, masculine, glowed in the dim. Beside Victoria, Chad had gone completely still, a statue poised on the floor of the boat.

The dark jeans vanished, the feet stepped away. Victoria lurched to her right as the boat rocked beneath her—one heavy jolt as Windy shoved the boat off the house—and then they were moving, Windy back behind the wheel. Rain splattered her face and the *thunk, thunk, scrape* of the boat against the gutter was replaced by the ticking of the rain and the throaty growl of the motor.

Victoria steadied herself, her fingers clamped around the low vinyl bench, barely bigger than a single chair, that probably served as a cooler during fishing trips—the boat was low and flat, the kind used for fishing on a glassy lake. If only they were off on some jungle expedition, an archeological dig, anywhere the rushing of the adrenaline in her veins would be a prelude to excitement instead of horror—and the real possibility of death. There were no railings around the perimeter of the boat, no walls save for a foot-high fiberglass ridge. The bench was the only thing protecting her from falling off the edge if they hit something, and if the driver hit a building that lifted one side, even hit a sign or a fence, they'd probably flip.

VICTORIA GLANCED BACK toward the house—everything she owned—but it was too dark to see much beyond the glint of the boat's running lights off the gutters. Just as well.

She was ready to start again. And she would.

Was this how Phillip had felt the morning of their twentieth birthday when he headed for the bus station? Had he focused on what he was leaving behind, or had his mind been full of possibilities for the future? It was hard to tell from his postcards, and it'd been nearly two years since the last one. She dragged her gaze to the dark water and though it was impossible, just for a blink, she swore she saw his fingers reaching from beneath the black waves, clawing for the sky. They'd both gone under, that day when they were five. They'd both drowned. She'd held tight to his hand until the waves took her own breath, but it hadn't been enough. If someone else hadn't seen them...

"How long do we have before the next storm hits?" Victoria hated the way her voice shook. She hoped no one could hear it over the rumble of the motor. Gooseflesh prickled on her arms, though it wasn't really that cold, like her nervous system was going haywire. And her mouth was dry. Did Windy have any bottled water? *A fucking steak would be better*. Hunger awoke in her guts, gnawing at her, turning her stomach inside out.

"About forty-eight hours, I think? And it's going to be a doozy. Category five."

Five. Even worse than the last update they'd heard—worse than the first hurricane. The woman's voice was strained, but not agitated—just trying to be heard over the rain. Then, as if Windy had heard her thoughts, she reached below the wheel for...*a plastic bottle*. Oh god, and a granola bar, the cellophane glittering in the hazy yellow light. Windy passed them back.

Victoria's whole body shook as she tore off the wrapper and shoved the granola bar into her mouth. Oats, honey, it was the most delicious thing she had ever tasted, second only to the bottled water. Both were gone far too quickly.

"You're hungry, huh? I'm sorry there isn't more food here." Windy smiled over her shoulder. "Don't worry though, there's plenty more food at the shelter."

More food at the shelter. "So, two days...are the shelters full to capacity?" Either way, it'd be fine—not like the shelter organizers would leave them in the rain when the actual hurricane was on top of them. They'd be dry—cleaner, hopefully. Better than on that roof, at any rate.

"Well, two days until the storm, but it'll take longer than that to make it to Mayfield and the shelters. Everything between here and there is underwater, and I don't have the fuel to get you to a dry road—not that you'd be able to drive anywhere if I could. The bridge to the highway is totally flooded. I'm afraid we're stuck in Fossé."

Victoria balked, clutching the seat, Chad grabbing his knees beside her, both bracing against the shuddering boat. Stuck in Fossé? She'd assumed Windy was taking them to safety, somewhere outside this godforsaken town. "Stay here? You want us to—"

"I have a place you can stay dry, tough enough to weather the hurricane. There are provisions there, food, water, blankets. Do you like card games?" She glanced back and her profile was sharp, almost bird-like, haloed with the flashlight she was aiming out at the water. "Might be boring, but we'll make it until the storm lets up, and once the water recedes some, we can use the boat if we have to—if it hasn't blown away." She shrugged. "We'll make do. Got enough provisions to last a month."

Victoria's belly rumbled around the granola. Her mouth watered. A month in a shelter was doable, but assistance would surely come—the Coast Guard, the National Guard— well before that time. Cool rain pattered against her hair and soothed her skinned knees. "What about first aid?"

Windy's shoulders tensed, just a little. "Yeah, I wasn't expecting to use the shelter so soon, so I don't have every- thing, but at least I've got bandages and stuff. That'll get you by, right?"

"Where exactly is this shelter?" Chad asked, and his voice sounded shaky too, but that might have been the strain of trying to be heard. The boat vibrated with the jittering of the engine and the rippling waves.

"Next town up, but it'll take a while in this old girl." Windy patted the steering wheel like she was patting a dog. Tendrils of hair escaped from around the sides of her raincoat and plastered themselves to the outside of her green hood like curling brown vines. "We'll have to go slow," she said.

"Sift through the wreckage, be extra careful we don't capsize."

Capsize. Victoria opened her mouth to catch the rain on her tongue.

The woman was still talking: "The chimneys can be hard to see even with the flashlight, and the higher the water gets…" The rest of her words were drowned out by a gust of wind that sent Victoria's own dark curls slapping against the side of her face. Her eyes burned. "We'll be there by dawn," Windy said. "A few hours. Then I can refuel and go back out, see who else needs help." She kept her gaze on the water in front of the boat, and Victoria peered that direction, at the subtle blue glow beneath the flashlight's beam—the thin band of neon lights that illuminated the water directly in front of the craft. A hundred feet out, the world was completely and utterly black.

"That's awfully altruistic of you," Chad said from the floor beside Victoria, and this time Victoria turned to look more closely at him. His face was shrouded in shadow but his mouth was tight and not in the way of someone frightened or embarrassed. He looked…suspicious, like he couldn't believe anyone in their right mind would offer assistance to complete strangers. And though Victoria's own face probably looked like that on the regular, she had never seen an expression like it on Chad's. She squinted, and the play of light and shadow morphed his flesh, cheekbones remolding like a shapeshifter—she barely recognized him at all.

Then Windy moved the flashlight and he was back. No more suspicion. Just exhaustion.

This storm is messing with my brain. She usually prided herself on being the rational one, the pragmatic one. She just needed sleep. A real meal.

And dry land.

"So, you've been out here doing this alone, Windy?"

Victoria asked. "It's a pretty big job for one person. Dangerous too."

"Nah, my boyfriend is out here somewhere. We've collected quite the little community. I think...five people now?"

Heat prickled the back of her neck, and she raised one hand to scratch at it. If Windy's boyfriend was out here, that meant they had two boats—hopefully one would make it through the storm intact.

Windy craned her neck to look back at them. "Can one of you take this flashlight, keep an eye open for houses, chimneys and stuff? Just holler if you see anything, and I'll steer us through the debris." Through the debris to safety on a little fishing boat in the middle of a lake that used to be a neighborhood. Only a thin membrane of fiberglass separated them from the sewage below. At least she couldn't smell the pig shit anymore—little miracles.

Victoria reached for the flashlight, but Windy stretched past Victoria's open palm and handed the light to Chad. Victoria frowned as the world around her went dark. The water off to her right—Chad's side—lit up in the flashlight's beam.

"Here." Windy twisted forward once more, this time reaching around the wheel to grab something in front of the steering pedestal; something large and orange wedged near the floor. A five-gallon bucket. She hauled it out and rolled it in Victoria's direction, and now Victoria could see the floor of the boat, see her feet sloshing in at least two inches of water, held back by the foot-high lip of fiberglass around the perimeter. Chad was sitting in it. Soaking in it. *That better be from the rain*. And the boat was rocking. Rocking. Rocking. Her stomach turned, the granola suddenly unhappy with the rolling waves and the burbling in her guts. She gagged and swallowed hard.

"You okay?" Chad asked, eyes—and flashlight—still on the water.

She smiled weakly though no one was looking her way. "At least I'll have a place to puke." She nodded to the bucket.

"I'd throw up over the side," Windy said, her form shrouded in the raincoat, haloed in hazy green from the blue neons mixing with the jaundiced flashlight. "We'll need the bucket."

"For what?"

"Bailing."

Victoria was still staring at the water rising around her ankles when the deluge came, rain splattering like frying bacon, hissing and angry. Soon she could no longer see beyond the few feet in front of them. She bailed the water with frantic movements, muscles screaming, her hair sticking to the sides of her face, clothes plastered to her skin. Rain dribbled down the backs of her bare legs. Her scrapes stung. And her guts—it was like someone was trying to wring out her entire abdomen. She fasted when she traveled, but never like this. One hundred calories of granola going into day four was far too little. Acid etched holes in her lower esophagus, or felt like it, and just heaving the bucket to and fro was sapping the last of her energy.

The sky lightened from pitch to a dreary gray then faded to a murky white, the rain ebbing, then falling harder again. The horizon darkened to steel. Victoria collapsed onto the bench and anchored her calves against the vinyl, her knees aching—one was bleeding. She closed her eyes, pretending that she was back in Chicago, that she'd never moved down to Louisiana, that the closest she'd ever gotten to this lake of sewage was the pool where she'd practiced swimming every day. She'd thought it would make her less frightened of the water, but the moment she went in, every time, she'd felt Lake Michigan, frigid on her face, over her head, filling her chest, stealing her breath. Felt Phillip's limp fingers clutched in hers. They'd thought they were going to swim away from their house. From their father. She should have known better.

The engine sound died, and Victoria startled, the sudden absence of it hitting her ear like an air horn. She squinted through the driving rain at the greenish-brownish-gray of the water that stretched before them to nowhere. The boat knocked against something, almost tumbling her from her seat, her feet clambering for purchase on the slick floor in front of the chair. *Shit, we're going down, this is it,* and she was five again, her brother on her back, and he was scrabbling, panicking, pushing her head down, down, down, under the frigid waves—

She sat straighter, staring past the hull of the boat.

Land.

Hills rose above the dark expanse of water, the thick brown surfaces pockmarked with sparse, scraggly trees. They'd made it, oh thank god, they'd made it.

CHAPTER THREE

VICTORIA SCRAMBLED from the boat before Windy had finished securing the craft. Her feet slipped on the grass, boots sinking in the muck and squelching crudely—the sound was music to her ears. The landscape rose toward the sky, obscured by dark lines of storm along her left side, black and green. Tornado weather. Spindly pines leaned sickly toward the rising water. No cars, the water was too high for that, but every few feet near the shore a wooden post stood visible, with carved wooden caps sporting battered fleur-de-lises. Were they in someone's backyard? A hairy lump of sodden gray fur floated past the post nearest her, the flesh bloated, tongue lolling from between pointed white teeth, and bumped against the shore near the boat. A cat, a dead cat —along with what might have been a used diaper. She winced.

Windy was still working on the rope, Chad beside her now, leaning over to help her fish the end from the murky water. Victoria stumbled a few steps up the hill, but her legs were rubbery and the world around her suddenly seemed unstable, as if the hill itself was made of some gelatinous material that might give way at any moment. Below, Windy had finally finished tying the knot and stepped onto the grass, one corner of her mouth turned up. And then they were heading uphill. Victoria opened her mouth, ready to say something like "Thank you," but Windy brushed by her without a word and strode up the slope.

"Where is she going?" Chad muttered as he and Victoria fell into step behind her. The squelching of their shoes was barely audible now under the hissing from the sky.

"Probably going to the shelter." *Duh*. But when she followed Chad's gaze, she saw no sign of a building, only the gentle slope of green grass, up, up, up, higher than any hill she'd seen in the time she'd lived down here. Beyond it, the horizon stretched, shimmering with rain and the misty film of early morning. There were lots of hills now that she was looking, though not all as sparsely treed as this—most were covered in pines and lower hanging oaks. Were they in a historic district? Shame to lose pieces of the past. But she didn't see any houses in the filmy morning light. They might have been tucked inside the foliage.

Chad shrugged, and when she turned to him his brow was furrowed, his gaze locked on Windy. But then he met her eyes and smiled. Calm. As always. She'd miss that dependability, the nice-guy quiet, the way he never said the things she—or anyone—didn't want to hear. *Chicken shit*. But right now, she was glad of it; some discussions led to panic, and that was the last thing she needed.

Victoria stretched her arms to the sky, muscles aching. Sleep. Food. A blanket. Maybe a bath, though she doubted she'd get that lucky.

Thhhhwwwaaaaattttch–Victoria jumped. Then a squeal. Windy stood at the top of the hill, her hand resting on a round door with an enormous hinge at ground level, the door so tall the top nearly reached her waist. The shadowed walls of a tunnel came into view, a dark hole sunk into the earth, a chain link ladder glinting dully in the meager light. A deep baritone laugh rumbled from below. Victoria's heart accelerated, throbbing with the same biting pulse of the hunger in her guts.

The shelter was below ground? She'd thought Windy had some cement room on top of the hill, or a high-ground new construction, bricks and steel, complete with those fancy hurricane panels, but not…this. "This is the shelter?"

Windy smiled. "It isn't much, but there's food, water. Enough for everyone."

The food won't help us if we drown. "It'll leak—we can't climb *down* to get away from rising wat—"

"It's an old military bunker, built to withstand bombs. It'll be fine with a little water—or a lot. We're above the waterline anyway." She glanced into the tunnel. "You ready?"

"But—"

"Listen, I lost my family during hurricane Gabriel." She leveled her steely eyes at Victoria. "They didn't die from the hurricane winds, or in a storm surge—the tornadoes afterward took them out. When I was old enough, I used part of my inheritance to renovate this shelter, make it safe in case that happened again. And I've never been more glad I did it." Her gaze had softened. "My house is gone. Everything I own is ruined. But I'm safe, right? I'm just trying to help you."

From the hole, that low voice drifted up again, grumbling like thunder below the hissing rain.

Victoria looked back toward the shore—the flooding. They were high enough here that the water level shouldn't submerge the top of the hatch, and if the walls were made of cement, they should hold out even if the water rose. It'd be like a house with a leaky basement foundation—dewy walls but not over-the-head water, and if it did get too high, they could climb back up and sit on the hill.

Windy raised an eyebrow. *Come on, let's go.* Victoria's feet were frozen to the ground, toes slippery inside her boots. Her eyes lit on Chad's leg, the gash on his shin a finger-width rope of crusty black, bloody rainwater trickling down toward his ankle. But Chad stared toward the expanse of water beyond the left side of the hill, where blackness simmered off into oblivion. Here and there, a telephone poll stabbed from the waves like relics from a half-sunken city of Atlantis.

Windy glanced at the water too. "Look, I know it's weird, maybe? I mean, who uses a bomb shelter to escape a hurricane? But no matter how afraid of water you are, nothing is getting through those walls."

Victoria narrowed her eyes. Had she told this woman she was scared of drowning? From the hole in the ground, the murmur of voices rose and fell. Rainwater trickled down her face and into her ear, blotting out the noises of the storm. *This is just another work adventure, another excavation. Like all the trips you took during graduate school, to distract yourself after Phillip took off.* She was being ridiculous. Her motto had always been: The more treacherous the assignment, the better—the jungle, the mountains, everything except islands...or any kind of water. The room below was probably twice the size of the smaller underground dig sites she'd explored.

"Hey, shut the door!" someone called, a deep voice, maybe the one that went with that baritone laugh. "Things are getting wet down here and not in a fun way!"

Windy held the hatch door like a giant metal Frisbee against her hip. The entrance yawned like a gaping mouth ready to swallow them. "Listen, you can wait up top until you make up your mind, but the door needs to stay closed, okay? And I'm running out of time to find anyone else."

Chad stepped toward the hole. "You coming?" he said over his shoulder, but he didn't turn to face Victoria. His hand was on the hatch now. Touching Windy's fingers.

What am I doing? Everyone below was laughing. Joking the way she and Phillip used to when their parents were fighting, keeping each other distracted—and safe. And suddenly, she could hear Phillip's voice in her head: *Get down that ladder, dumbass.* Phillip had always been the one to say things she didn't want to accept—unlike her husband—and sometimes she needed to hear those things. Sometimes she needed actual advice.

Chad's feet were already on the ladder, the thing hanging from two silver bolts that did not look strong enough to hold it, his fingers clasped on the top lip of the hatch. His shoulders bobbed ever so slightly as if he were having trouble getting his footing. *Now or never.* Victoria squared her shoulders and watched him descend into the darkness, then started forward.

"Wait a sec." Windy held out her hand, and Victoria froze: a knife, curved blade just larger than her palm, the top edge glistening sharply in the meager light. The blade was aimed at her belly.

She's going to stab me—

Then in one motion, Windy slid the blade into a leather case and flipped it, extending the handle to Victoria. Its weight was comforting in her palm, like the knife she'd carried on an archeological dig in Brazil—though she'd used it for guava instead of self-defense. But she had stabbed a man in India, slashed him across the abdomen with a trowel of all things when he tried to take her wallet. Cut him deeper than she'd intended—far deeper. Victoria slipped the weapon through the belt loops in the back of her shorts, beneath her T-shirt, as Windy said: "You might need it. There's Spam and stuff down there, but no plastic knives."

Victoria took a deep breath and followed Chad down into the darkness, one step, then another, the flimsy ladder wiggling every time Chad moved. She looked up once more at the circle of gray sky...and Windy's face smiling down at her. And then Windy shifted backward and the hatch turned the disk of sky above to a gibbous moon of gray, then to a crescent, a sliver. Then the gray vanished altogether, plunging the tunnel into darkness.

CHAPTER FOUR

WINDY

WINDY STOOD in the sudden silence, feeling the gentle smattering of rain on her face like the mist after a sneeze. Warm, almost oily. Was it weird, thinking of it that way? Maybe. She'd never been the smartest, but at least she'd asked the questions. Was still asking them.

Precocious. Dad had loved that about her.

She appraised the thick murk of the shoreline, then the fenceposts that marked the border of her property, not that she needed them—the next neighbor was usually over thirty acres off, and even farther now. The world was soaked in a stillness that leaked into her soul. Had she forgotten anything? No. She'd made lists, and she'd checked every box. Was this the right thing to do? Of course it was. But the tension between her shoulder blades would not relent.

The sky grumbled at her, the storm just spinning above them, dumping massive amounts of water instead of moving on. "If you want to see the sunshine, you have to weather the storm." Her voice vanished beneath the mounting agitation from the clouds. Her father used to say that, and never had it felt more appropriate, more prophetic, than when she was watching him die.

But weathering a storm led to epiphany, if you were strong enough to act. Strong enough to let the pain flow from you like a raging river over a waterfall, the angst flinging itself into the atmosphere on each droplet of mist. No matter what you believed yourself to be, crisis had a way of rearranging your psyche. It made good people do bad things.

Her gaze dropped to the surface of the hatch, smooth and dusky green, more like a scuttle hatch than a bunker door. Her father had been in the Navy—she used to love visiting the docks with him, climbing down those round tubes into the bowels of the ship, the passages a human ant farm crafted of metal. The hatch door, all of it, was an ode to him. Even this plot of land—though neglected until recently—had belonged to their family for over fifty years. Her Dad's blood and sweat and tears were here as much as hers were, which made what she was doing all the more cathartic.

She'd asked the hard questions, decades of questions. Hopefully she'd finally get the answers.

Windy kissed her fingertips and bent to press them against the sick-looking metal. So cold. The sandpaper grain of the door ground against her fingernails, the hissing rain *shh*-ing against her eardrums, and a memory—her brother's bloody lips, his bloody teeth—flashed in her brain, then dispersed into a million tiny droplets of mist—unrecognizable. Above, the charcoal clouds that had skirted the horizon as she'd maneuvered the old fishing boat toward the bunker had turned darker. Threatening.

This is my last chance. It was a pessimistic-downer thing to think, but that didn't mean she was wrong.

Windy closed her eyes against the weeping heavens. Victoria had the knife; the others were anything but trustworthy, but they wouldn't break Victoria. She was a survivor, a *winner*. The rain dripped over her lips and onto her teeth like tears.

Windy pulled out her keys, the brash sound tinkling through the air above the growling sky. Chose one. And slid it home.

CHAPTER FIVE

THE TUNNEL SEEMED to go on forever. Victoria's boots on the metal rungs squealed loudly, making her grind her teeth, as did the clanking of the ladder against the cement wall above, the occasional burst of pain when she smashed her knuckles against the tunnel sides. But what was most disconcerting was the absence of other sound. The *whoosh* of wind, the muted *tap*, *tap*, *tap* of rain that had rattled her eardrums… these background noises had become so much a part of her the last few days that the sudden quiet left her head feeling empty and dull, hollow as her stomach.

Ten shudderingly unstable ladder rungs down, and she was swinging in open air. She shivered. The room had cooled as they descended, and now it took on a slight antiseptic tinge. Bleach? The blackness of the tunnel had lightened to a hazy ash, but it appeared no brighter when she focused on the room beneath her feet. Were there no lights down here? *And, shit, how tall is this ladder?* She blinked, trying to force her eyes to adjust. Chad was already on the floor and she felt him release the ladder, the bottom swinging beneath her like a goddamn rope swing. She skipped the last three rungs, one long, stretching step to the ground. Her heels slid on the wet tile. She grabbed the ladder to regain her balance, and then a voice that sounded like her brother: *Wouldn't it be just perfect, sis, to make it this far and crack your head open on the floor?*

Victoria stepped away from the ladder into a square room, 400 square feet or so, similar to a bomb shelter she'd seen in England, but that one had been full of heavy furniture and dark wood paneling. This room had painted cement walls, higher ceilings than she had at home though it was too dark to see exactly how tall, and linoleum floor tiles shining beige in the yellow beam from a flashlight. *Whose flashlight?* She peered through the glare. The only other meager illumination leaked from a row of LEDs that ran around the perimeter of the room and under the long wall of shelves at the back—shelves of food. She could make out the silhouettes of boxes and canned goods, and clear bottles that had to be water glittering in the blueish LED haze. Yellow sleeping bags, too, and white towels. Someone—too cocooned in their own yellow sleeping bag to tell if they were a man or a woman—lay curled on their side facing the left wall. Definitely seemed to be enough supplies to get them through the next few days—or a week—of storms. Victoria blinked.

The flashlight lowered to the ground as if the person holding it had only now realized she was squinting. A young black man, unlined features, maybe college age though it was hard to know for certain in the dim light, stood with the flashlight just outside the puddle of water at the base of the hatch. Someone had tossed a towel onto the mess, but the floor remained shiny—slick. They'd need another towel. No wonder Windy had been anxious to close the door.

She glanced toward the shelving again, and her shoulders tightened. Another man sat against the far wall near the shelf with the towels, hidden in the shadows where the light didn't reach. But his outline looked big, like a wrestler, or a construction worker.

Three others. But...hadn't Windy said five? And it was so *dark*. But if she needed light, she could climb back up the ladder. For now, she was exhausted and thankful for the dim.

The big man in the shadows stood and stepped into the bluish haze from the LEDs, and the college kid swung the flashlight beam his way. Tall and sinewy, with a head full of John Stamos hair, and smiling like he was amused. How was he smiling? Sure the danger had passed, but they'd all lost everything. Chad had spent the first hour on the roof crying over his mother's old quilts, and she suspected most people were like him about their things.

The man cocked one perfectly sculpted brow and extended his hand, eyes on her face. He didn't even seem to notice that Chad was there. Where was Chad, anyway?

"I'm Nick." His grip was warm and soft, too soft for a construction worker. He had some cushy job that didn't involve manual labor. She was suddenly aware of her own callouses, hard-earned from years of digging, brushing, excavation. These days, she spent most of her time cataloging antiquities for Charles Dinwater and Sons or teaching at the university, but at least once a year, Dinwater sent her somewhere exotic on approved grants, or had her travel to examine goods for the museums they contracted with. "I'm Victoria."

"You guys are up early," Chad muttered—behind her. She should have known. He wasn't an introvert, he was just plain shy, except around kids.

"Eh." Nick shrugged one muscular shoulder. "Without windows it's like living in a cave. Not that the time matters much with mother nature acting like a whore."

Victoria didn't have to turn around to see Chad frowning as he said: "Acting like a—"

"Because she's blowing. Rather indiscriminately." Nick grinned again and Victoria stared, stunned, as the man with the flashlight chuckled, the light shifting just enough for her to see him better. Yeah, he was definitely younger, twentyish, an earring in one ear, and a short black afro dyed blonde at the tips. The kid stepped beside Nick and Nick gestured to him —"Carter." Beads of sweat glistened on Nick's forehead, but her own skin felt chilled. She had to get out of these wet clothes.

"How long have you been down here?" Chad asked.

Nick finally drew his eyes to Chad. "Five days."

So he'd come down before the storm hit. Must have known Windy ahead of time.

"And you?" Chad asked the kid.

"Same." The kid, Carter, looked down at his T-shirt, a tie-dyed smiley face, the word "Smile" stenciled in purple. "Is the storm over yet? I mean, you're here, so it must not be, but…"

"Should hit in the next forty-eight," Victoria said.

"Man, this first one's been sitting over us *forever*."

Victoria nodded—it was insane, really, two hurricanes back to back, rotating so slowly, sticking around. Between that and the goddamn levees…

"At least the second storm has to knock out the rain, right?" Carter continued. He breathed a sigh that sounded like relief. "We're getting close to freedom, Nick!"

Nick clapped him on the shoulder and they both laughed. *Nothing like five days in a bomb shelter to build camaraderie.* Well— she glanced at Chad—at least for some of them.

Nick had settled, but Carter was still chuckling, maybe a little hysterical. Stressed. There was something familiar about him, even if Victoria couldn't put her finger on it— though with that slouchy-cocky young-adult walk, that loose hippie vibe, he could have been any of a hundred students she saw on campus the one day a week she taught her archeology course. If only she made more doing cultural resource management for Dinwater and Sons, but the work would pad her resume once she was ready to relocate. Chicago. So many museums there, so many opportunities. And now she didn't even have to move her things.

"You guys want food?" Nick said. "Water?"

Victoria wrapped her arms around her chest and shivered again. Her biceps were sticky. "Is there a place to clean up down here first?" The thought of touching food with grime on her hands—the sewage water—turned her already queasy guts, but her belly rumbled anyway. She'd better hurry before instinct took over and she started snatching Spam with her nasty fingernails.

Carter raised his chin and it took her a moment to realize he was gesturing at the wall to her right. At…a door. "We've got a composting toilet back there. Just turn the handle on the side to open the bottom and let everything go down the hatch." *Sounds delightful*. But better than the accommodations in half the places she'd traveled. "No running water," he continued, "but we've been using that bucket for washing hands and whatnot." He pointed to the side of the bathroom door, where she could just barely make out a five-gallon bucket against the wall, the same type she'd used to bail the boat. She frowned. They were supposed to…share the wash water?

"It has a bunch of bleach to keep it less gross, and there's washcloths and a garbage bag too." He gestured to the corner, a little nook where the shelves stopped short of reaching the far wall. "Hopefully the rain cleaned you up better than it did me." Victoria glanced over in time to see Carter wrinkle his nose. "I still smell a little like that shitty water."

"You mean you don't always smell like shit?" The tall guy...Nick.

Carter frowned. His T-shirt grinned.

Nick raised an eyebrow. "Too soon?" Silly, crass, but something about him struck her as honest.

"I should go get dried off," Victoria said.

"Well what fun is that?" Nick dropped his eyes to her chest and winked at her.

Chad stiffened, yet said nothing. He was probably smiling, uncomfortably but amicably. Victoria didn't look his way, even when he followed her toward the back wall. She grabbed a towel from the shelves, which, now that she was closer, did not appear as well-stocked as they'd looked from the front—lots of empty spaces behind the front packages. No way they'd make it through the month as Windy had promised, but at least they'd be fine through the storms.

"We're going to be okay, you know," Chad said quietly.

She nodded, though she wasn't sure she believed him. If Phillip had said it, she would have taken it as fact.

Chad touched her elbow. "If you want to see the sunshine, you have to weather the storm, right?"

She squinted at him. Where had he picked that up? "I guess." *Stop talking, Chad.* Leave it to her to get caught in a deluge with her soon-to-be ex-husband, who was more likely to quote Winnie the Pooh than whoever he was referencing now.

She turned to the rest of the room. "Is the first aid kit around?"

Carter dropped his flashlight, and gaze, to her legs, maybe looking at her skinned knee. "Tiny one, real basic. But we'll need to save it in case anything really bad happens." He was probably right, but her knees itched anyway.

"You go first," Chad said. "I'll clean up the floor out here." She nodded, refusing to meet his eyes. Her soul felt scooped out, a hollow ache. *No, at this moment, I'm missing food, not affection.*

Bells tinkled above her head as she shoved the door open. The bathroom was barely big enough to turn around in, one tiny LED over a toilet with a huge white tank attached beneath it. She'd seen composting toilets before, but most had a smaller tank on the front side for urine. This one…all the excrement appeared to go down the same hole. Weird, but at least they could close the hatch to keep the smell down.

She undressed quickly, untying her boots, peeling off her sopping jean shorts, her socks, hanging her soggy T-shirt over the empty towel rod. Gooseflesh prickled her skin. She paused with her fingers on her underwear, then stripped them off too and hung them beneath the other pieces. One night hiding in a sleeping bag, and her clothes would be dry. And it sure wouldn't do to get a yeast infection or some other ungodly thing while they were down here. Even after the storm, who knew when the drugstores would open again?

She wet the washcloth, trying not to think about how many others had used this same water to clean the filth from their bodies, and wiped herself down as best she could. She should climb back up the ladder to the hill, shower off in the open, in the rain, but… *Later.* Exhaustion suddenly weighed on her shoulders, pulling her bones toward the earth. Even her skin felt heavier than usual. She wrapped the towel around her breasts, and paused with her hand on the door.

Now or never. Just like the tattoo on the inside of her elbow, a mere smudge in the dimness now, but she knew what it looked like: "Now or Never" on the crest of a wave. Her brother had the same tattoo in the same spot. Sitting side by side, tattoo needles buzzing against their flesh, he'd told her it had always been the two of them against the world and that with her going off to college, well… That was the night she realized he intended to leave. She didn't blame him for not staying, for wanting to make his own way. But it had never occurred to her that he'd just...vanish.

She stared at the tattoo for a moment in the dim blue light, willing the ache in her chest to lessen. Willing the nausea to ease—she suddenly felt like she might vomit. A side effect of starvation? Maybe she should wait to eat until the cramps subsided; she couldn't afford to lose the few calories she had in her stomach.

Sleep. Food. Later on—or tomorrow—a rain shower, once she felt well enough to climb. That was logical. Everything would be easier after she ate. And rested.

She turned back to her clothing, where the knife was still secured in her belt loops. It might rust if she left it with her wet clothes, but if she were being honest, the thought of keeping it close *did* make her feel safer. Ridiculous, no one was going to mug her for her wallet, but she slid it from her shorts and hid it beneath the edge of the towel at her navel, holding onto it with her right hand. The leather was cold against her belly.

Victoria padded from the room, bells above the door ringing in her ears. She scanned the wall of supplies as Chad ducked into the bathroom.

"You see the bandages?" Carter said from somewhere on the other side of the bunker—he'd turned the flashlight off. "I put a bag of cotton balls on the shelf there."

The cotton glowed hazy blue, dimmed by the stark shadow cast across it from...*huh*. A crowbar sat against the far wall, directly in front of one of the LEDs.

Carter's footsteps tapped on the linoleum. "Who's ready for some breakfast?" As if on cue, his stomach grumbled loudly enough to pull a chuckle from Nick, who was already standing beside the long shelf. But Victoria's stomach was oily, sour, and her eyelids were dragging themselves closed without her permission, each eyelash weighted. She yawned.

"Why do you think I'm over here, bro?" Nick reached for a box of cereal, hesitated, then moved his fingertips to a smaller box: toaster pastries.

Victoria shook herself awake, her knees itching. One more thing to take care of before she could rest. She grabbed the cotton balls but remained standing, hand fisted around the towel—and the knife—and set to work dabbing her skinned knees with a bottle of rubbing alcohol she'd found near the paper products. Her wounds weren't bad, no swelling—yet—but she'd look at the abrasions more closely in the morning. Or...afternoon. Sometime later on. How late was it, anyway?

But she didn't care, not really. Every movement was like slogging through mud. She found the garbage bag hidden in the back corner behind the shelving unit, near where Nick had been sitting, and slipped the dirtied cotton balls inside, then laid a sleeping bag out in the corner across from the bathroom near the shelves. Her body...so heavy. Used. And though it had to be raining still, had to be storming, the shelter was a bubble, insulated from everything including the wind—even when she strained her ears, she could hear nothing but Nick and Carter murmuring about which packages to open, what to eat. She slipped into her bag.

Then the LEDs went out, and they were plunged into total darkness.

Victoria shot to seated, sleeping bag falling from her shoulders.

"Hey-O!" Nick said, but she could barely hear him over the blood thundering in her ears.

Was it the storm? Generator fail? She grabbed the bag again to cover herself, but it didn't matter—she couldn't see her hand in front of her, and the absolute silence of the underground bunker made it feel like they were in outer space. She could almost imagine she'd been sucked into a black hole where nothing existed but her—well, her and the knife beneath her thigh. The hilt pressed hard through the leather. Her flesh ached.

She forced a breath deep into her lungs and exhaled slowly. They were okay. Even if the lights didn't come back on, they were dry, and that kid, Carter, he had the flashlight.

The moment she thought it, a dim light blinked on in the corner...a night-light? But weaker, dimmer even than the hazy LEDs. Then another, and another, five total along the wall under the long bottom shelf, small and very close to the floor, like the lights on either side of an airplane aisle.

"Who turned off the lights?" Chad called—he was still in the bathroom.

"Our omnipotent dictator," Nick said with a lilt that sounded like he was smiling, though she couldn't confirm or deny that. Only his feet caught the night-lights, fleshy appendages so pale they were practically glowing, but that wasn't what drew her attention. Tattoos? Yes, definitely images inked on the bare skin around his ankles, though she couldn't tell what they were. Victoria jumped as something hit her bag—cellophane—then a heavier *thunk* against her foot. A package of toaster pastries. And...*Oh!* She snatched the bottle Nick had tossed and emptied it within seconds, the water warm and sweet as it filled her belly. Her guts clenched, then accepted the liquid. Then clenched again. The package beckoned.

Her mouth watered despite the bile in her throat. She tore the cellophane open with her teeth. God, sweet relief. But it was momentary. Within a minute, the package was empty, and the raging aching hunger in her guts had intensified. How much food would it take to quell it? They'd have to ration the rest tomorrow, see exactly how much they had. She squinted at the shelves, invisible now in the blackness.

Chad poked his head from the bathroom, the bell jangling. "Excuse me, but is there a way to...turn the lights back on?"

"Nah. They go off and on at fixed intervals," Carter said. "Got one mode for day, one for night, and the other for dawn and dusk, as close as Windy could estimate. Should help to keep our internal clocks balanced." The kid sounded like he was proud of her for considering this, but Victoria's stomach curdled, and it wasn't just from the churning sugary-acid mix. They'd arrived at dawn. Shouldn't the lights be going *on* now? Unless it was because of her and Chad—Windy had to know they were exhausted. She listened to Chad padding his way closer along the shelving, probably using the airline lights to orient himself, and she could almost hear his limp, so minor she didn't usually notice it. He had a pin in his toe from one of their softball league tournaments, a bad run-in with the catcher when he tried to steal home. He'd always been so confident out there, but only because it didn't matter, same reason he taught grade school: second graders thought you were great so long as you were fun. And he was. Chad shuffled to his sleeping bag. She should probably tell him to clean the wound on his leg, but she was tired, she was so, so *tired*. Luckily, she'd learned to sleep anywhere: on planes, on busses, through the distant *pop, pop* of gunfire, through the long, brilliant days in Switzerland that had forced her to surrender to sleep even when the sky was blazing.

She slouched down in her sleeping bag, the itchy warmth of it cocooning her. Her skin still felt damp.

From near the shelves, a foil package crinkled. "Fucking flaxseed crackers? Whose idea was that?"

Finally, with Nick's chuckle in her ears, she slept.

CHAPTER SIX

VICTORIA AWOKE TO MEN LAUGHING—DREAMING, she was dreaming. She buried herself deeper under the covers, pulling the blanket over her face. But why was her bed so hard? Wait...the bunker. She was in the bunker. And her hip was swollen, sore, like she'd slept on a rock.

Awesome. She ran her fingertips over the sandpaper grit of her skinned knee, but it wasn't hot to the touch, no swelling that she could feel, and the minor scrapes had already scabbed over. She finally dragged her eyelids open, registering the brilliant white of the painted ceiling, the neon yellow of the sleeping bag beside her. The airline-aisle night lamps had been replaced with the blinding glare of fluorescents that snaked around the perimeter of the ceiling. It was like staring into the sun. Even the cement walls were painted white, sterile like a hospital or a doctor's office, and *reflective*, everything conspiring to beam the light straight back into her retinas.

She eased herself to sitting, clutching the sleeping bag against her bare chest, and squinted at the two men sitting against the wall by the bathroom. Nick was smiling, a great deal taller in the light, his gray T-shirt stretching over a broad chest. He worked out. A lot. But so did the man beside him, and that guy didn't look near as happy: scowling, white hair buzzed close to the scalp, shoulders high and tight. Probably ex-military. Who was he? Had he been here last night? He scratched his cheek with a scarred index finger, that and the thumb the only two fingers on his right hand—a crab's claw, ready to pinch.

Nick shook his head, but his eyes twinkled. "I'm just saying—"

"You're trying to get my goat, is what you're doing," the older man barked. The gruffness felt at odds with the southern drawl that trickled through with every word, the sort of accent you could only find in New Orleans, where the As draw out lazily as if they yearned to be words all their own. "And it'll work, son, keep it up." He finally noticed Victoria and narrowed his eyes at her. "How many people y'all got down here?"

Victoria glanced at the wall directly across from her: two more sleeping bags filled with lumps that looked like people. Long, dark hair spilled from one—another woman? The thought made her feel weirdly relieved. "You make six." She shivered, a faint stink like rotting vegetables in her nose, and glanced down at her black shirt on the floor. Someone had laid her dry clothes beside her bag, boots to the right, under-wear on top. She snatched the pile, sniffed her shirt—musky. Sour.

The older man averted his eyes. He frowned at the floor.

Victoria slipped back down under the cover of the sleeping bag, clothes in her fist. The shorts were stiff, harsh and irritating against her thighs, but now that they were dry they were...looser. Or she'd already lost weight. *Nothing like the flood starvation diet*, Phillip's voice whispered, *haha*. She wriggled the T-shirt over her head.

"Did you find your clothes?"

Victoria jumped at Chad's voice and eased herself to seated against the wall. His sleeping bag was pressed against the wall behind hers, as close as he could get without touching her. Respectful. He was handsome in his way, that little curl of dishwater hair plastered to his forehead, but it was what he lacked that had drawn her—none of the meanness she'd always seen in her father. Chad didn't have a mean bone in his body, but even that quality, his best quality, made him meek. Wishy-washy. Victoria wouldn't miss the wishy-washy when she finally left him. "Yeah. I found them." Her belly rumbled—hot and achy.

The older man shook his head. "I didn't know there'd be so many of y'all."

Nick smiled and scratched his bicep, and beneath the cloth of his T-shirt blinked a flash of vibrant color. It vanished when he lowered his arm.

"You have a bunch of other great prospects right now?" Nick said, smirking. "Some handsome man waiting on you at home?"

The older man rose to his feet. "Just what in God's—"

"Oh, I doubt God likes you much." Nick winked at Victoria. Chad cleared his throat but said nothing as the older man stepped away from Nick, toward the shelving.

Idiots. They didn't need to be arguing, not when they were all hungry and stressed, in close quarters. Twelve hours and these men would be at one another's throats. A day and they'd kill each other over a toaster pastry. Besides, she didn't want to listen to this all day...or for the next two.

The older man stood at the far side of the room now, back against the little nook behind the shelves, as far as he could get from Nick without leaving the room entirely. "Listen here, I swear on all that's holy—"

"Okay, okay, how about we figure out breakfast," Victoria

said. Her eyelids felt like sandpaper. She scanned the walls—no clocks. *Huh.* What time was it? Had the storm hit yet? Beneath the ladder, the tile was dry now, littered with little bits of grass.

Nick stood. "As much fun as it is talking to you, sir, I'm going to have to insist on food as well." He wiped a hand over the bit of stubble on his chin and started for the shelves, and in the brighter overhead lights Victoria could see instant coffee and packets of oatmeal, raisins. The wall behind the shelving seemed to glare at her between the boxes of cereal and stacked jars of jelly. In the corner opposite the shelving—on the bathroom wall—sat the garbage bag, mostly full, surely where that faint rotting-vegetable smell was coming from. But hadn't the bag been in the nook behind the shelving before? She was too tired to recall. Whatever, they'd take it up after breakfast, toss it out with all the dead cats and old diapers now floating downstream.

Rustling sounded from the wall across the way. Victoria glanced over to see Carter pushing himself to sitting, rubbing his eyes with his palms as if his yellow sleeping bag was blinding him. Sparse curly hair peppered his chin—she hadn't noticed it in the flashlight beam last night. But did she know his face from somewhere? Not that this was any great feat in a town this size, but...

Another rustle. On the floor between Carter and Victoria, the black-haired woman was pushing herself up too: early twenties, with hooded eyes and a thin mouth, the edges now turned downward. A string of dirty pearls hung around her neck. She scooted closer to the wall, resting her back against it as Victoria had done. "I am Olivia," the woman said in a soft voice with a melodic intonation, the accent familiar. Something she'd heard in the Philippines? And her presence was calming somehow, friendly. "Sleeping together...it smashes the ice, yes?"

Victoria raised an eyebrow.

"You mean it breaks the ice," Carter said, yawning. Nick was rummaging through the packages on the shelves to her left, ignoring the exchange.

Olivia kept smiling. "If you say so. Neither makes more sense than the other."

Victoria liked her immediately. She grinned back, stretching as she climbed from her bag. One of her best friends in Chicago had immigrated from Cuba as a teenager and had loved nothing more than to make her laugh by purposefully butchering common English phrases. She'd never realized how ridiculous the things she'd grown up saying were...until she had tried to rationalize them. Glass houses? Whether you're inside or outside, the rule should simply be "don't throw rocks."

Olivia climbed from her sleeping bag too, and made her way toward the bathroom. The bells above the door jangled, little round bells, like the ones you see on wreaths at Christmastime. And below the bells...were those hash marks? Yes. Six of them. Victoria had spent her first three days of this flood on a roof, and now it was day four for her...four days since she'd had a real meal. A few weeks from now, this would all feel like a bad dream while she stuffed her face with chili fries and a bacon cheeseburger...a *double* bacon cheeseburger.

Nick followed her gaze. "Like my fancy timekeeping?" He snorted and moved a box of cereal to grab some other package behind it.

The older man looked over at the marks on the wall, too. What was his name?

Victoria cleared her throat and addressed him. "I'm Victoria."

His scowl did not relent. He nodded to Chad. "He with you?"

Chad's eyes widened, but he did not answer the question.

Well this is going to be great fun. "Is there a problem?" Victoria said.

Nick paused in his rummaging to point at the older man. "Yeah, you can't tell her what to do, Daddy Earl, she's not thirty-four anymore."

Earl. That was his name? And…she *was* thirty-four. She was *exactly* thirty-four. Most people thought she looked younger, but maybe the stress had forced the years to catch up with her. A dull ache throbbed in her guts in time to her heartbeat. She headed for the shelves, for the food, leaving Chad sitting on his sleeping bag, blinking like a four-year-old whose mother had woken him up too early.

"You okay?" Nick raised one of his perfect eyebrows at her, but he wasn't looking at her face—his gaze was locked on her chest…no, her arm. Her tattoo.

"I'm fine—well, as fine as can be expected under the circumstances."

"Like the ink. Have some special meaning?" His eyes had narrowed in a way that wasn't exactly friendly.

Yes. "No, I just liked the design."

He frowned, lips tight, like he knew she was lying. But it wasn't his business. She wasn't shy about her own shit, but about Phillip she was…protective. Every time Chad pursed his lips about Phillip's addiction, his long absence, she wanted to punch him in the face, though he probably meant the look to be one of understanding and not judgment. Some subjects were just off limits. She laid her hand against her arm, covering the tattoo.

"So, how'd you get here, Nick?"

He turned back to the shelves and shrugged. "Windy picked me up after a show. I drove in from my place upstate, didn't even know a storm was coming, though I did think it was weird how dead the bar was that night. Owner said the only reason he was there was because his place was too close to shore, but I just thought he didn't want to drive drunk." He chuckled.

A show? She dropped her hand—her tattoo felt suddenly hot. "What kind of show?"

"Comedy."

"You tell jokes?" Carter said, approaching the shelves. "Who'd pay for that?"

Nick chuckled again, his deep bass grumbling around them, same noise she'd heard up on the hill. "Anyway, I was up there with a buddy of mine, getting ready to do my set— got stoned as shit. Later, when things started blowing around outside, she said she had a place. I went with her, figured it was better than sitting around the bar. Lots of liquor to pass the time, but I hate those bowls of peanuts."

Victoria frowned. How was it even possible to have no idea about the hurricane? "You didn't wonder why there was literally no one else out? That's just..." *Unbelievable.* "Your friend should have at least asked where you were going for the storm, right? I just—"

"We aren't close, okay? He...he brings my pills. For my set."

Not a friend, then. "A dealer?"

He shrugged. "Whatever he is, I don't pay attention to shit that doesn't concern me."

"But it *does* concern you."

"The drugs help me ignore my concern." He grinned, and when she did not smile back, he said, "Hey, comedy isn't easy. I'm shy." He winked, and not in a shy way at all. Her eyes lit on the sheen of sweat on his forehead. Was he in withdrawal? *Great.* Now they'd be stuck down here with a junkie unable to get a fix. Her brother usually wanted to be alone when he was jonesing, but there were things you did for your twin that you'd never do for anyone else, and patting their forehead with a towel while they puked acid onto your lap was one of them. Nick was on his own if it came to that.

Nick sniffed. "Anyway, she showed up, watched ten minutes, and left. Then came back an hour later and brought me here." He shrugged, eyebrows raised in a way that said it was hard for him to believe that anyone would want to miss his joke-telling genius. "Then she left again, got Carter and Olivia"—Carter nodded—"and the rest is history."

So he did a show for what, two people? It didn't add up. But maybe shitty comics always played small crowds. And if Victoria herself were trying to locate people without proper shelter, she might go where she knew the stoned idiots would be.

"Maybe she left because she figured out that you aren't funny," Carter muttered.

Nick elbowed Carter and grinned wider. "Oh, you're wrong there, my friend. I'm hilarious." His face fell. "But she didn't smile once."

The bells jangled, Olivia wincing at the sharp ringing above her head. "Sorry. Loud enough to wake dead people, yes?"

Victoria smiled. "Yes." The bells were attached by wire, easily removable if they got too annoying. She squinted at the hash marks, just below the bells…six days. Her skin crawled. So long to be in this little room. But they'd only be adding a few more before the storm was over.

When Victoria looked back down, Nick was crouched by the shelving, so close to where she was standing that he could have reached out and grabbed her knee as he examined the rows of boxes and cans. Instead, he grabbed something wrapped in plastic—a loaf of bread.

Olivia sidled up to Carter and squeezed his arm, and the way she edged nearer to him, chest against his shoulder, was anything but platonic. Were they a couple? Did everyone here know each other? Up close, the young man looked exhausted —his eyes were bloodshot, his face drawn.

"Where'd you guys meet?" Victoria asked her.

"We have been friends almost five years. Met in freshman English."

Carter nodded, his expression far more mechanical than the adoring, almost hopeful look in Olivia's eyes. *What does Chad see when he looks at me?* But she couldn't ask him now— Chad was ducking into the bathroom, the bells marking his departure.

Nick pulled out two slices of bread and shoved one unceremoniously into his mouth. "How do y'all have things rationed out?" Earl asked gruffly, standing by the bathroom door—staring.

"We don't," Nick said around a mouthful of bread. "There's plenty of food, not like we're going to be here forever."

Exactly. Another day, maybe two if they couldn't get a boat ride out. But the waters would recede sooner than later. Provided it stopped raining.

"You never know, son. The storms could take the grocery stores out for weeks, a month even, and with them foreigners taking all the space in the shelter—"

"Foreigners? You need a tinfoil hat to go with all that conspiracy?" Nick scoffed.

Victoria almost smiled—after all, they'd be here two days, maybe three tops—but Earl was the last to arrive; maybe he knew something they didn't. "What have you heard? About the storms?"

"Power's gone for miles. There ain't nowhere to get more food." He shook his head. "Those damn weathermen said we'd be safer stayin' here instead of trying to make it north on the freeway. What a joke."

"Probably a funnier joke than any of Nick's," Carter said, and Nick guffawed.

"That's the spirit, kid."

Carter gave him a wan smile. "We would have been okay if the levees hadn't failed. Government kinda screwed us over."

"Wasn't our government," Earl snapped. "Someone tried to blow it sky high last week, probably that damn Al-Qaeda."

Victoria had heard about that. A series of homemade bombs had weakened the structural integrity of the levees, causing a large area near Fossé to fail when the storm surge came—not that the levees had been in great shape to begin with. The police had called it a random malicious act; why they always shied away from "domestic terrorism" she wasn't sure.

"Al-Qaeda?" Nick snorted. "You think they're running around here in Louisi-fucking-ana blowing up levees?"

"Sure as shit wasn't someone who lived here, son. And those bastards don't care where they hit, as long as they're taking down infidels."

"You're right—screw New York and London. Let's mess with the ten people who live in Fossé."

"What about the next storm," Victoria said, turning her attention back to Earl. "Anything changed?"

"Not that we should trust 'em after last time, but they're thinking the second round of storms will be worse than the first. Last one ended up clocking in at a four—they think we'll get a five this time, and because it's already so flooded…"

He didn't have to finish. With the rain still coming down and without a faster way to drain off the already flooded landscape, any additional flooding, let alone hurricane winds or tornadoes, would devastate the town. Most people would never return home. And…this was the end of day four for her, wasn't it? The second storm must have slowed if it was still two days out. That was what had happened a few days ago, too; slow moving storms took longer in the Gulf, then stuck around and killed you with the rain.

She sighed. "Earl's right," she said to Nick.

"Not you too," Nick groaned, shaking his head. "You seem like the least likely person to get into a truck with a confederate bumper sticker and go fight an imaginary terrorist threat—"

"About *rationing*." She gestured to the bread in his hand. "There's hardly enough bread for one person for more than a couple days, let alone six adults."

"Yeah, we only have one box of toaster pastries left," Carter said.

Olivia squinted at the shelves as if in search of better—healthier—provisions, but Carter actually looked worried, as if their survival hinged on crappy sugar explosions. Then again... Her mouth watered at the mere thought of the pastries. She eyeballed the bag of bread in Nick's hand, and her stomach rumbled greedily. Once the storm passed, they'd be able to open the hatch, wander a little in search of nourishment, berries, plants, whatever they could find on this hill, but they might be stuck eating what they had here for the next week. And Victoria's body was already slowing down; even her hunger was no longer quite as painful as it'd been in the first days of the flood. Fasting was a matter of routine on her overseas trips—parasites and viruses and food-borne illness would put you out of commission faster than anything else—but usually when she fasted for two or three days, she felt revived, rejuvenated. Alert. Now, she just felt worn down. Dizzy, too, though her body was used to the process—the others would feel that pain more intensely and would eat more, putting everyone in danger. "It's only logical to be prepared for the worst-case scenario," she said. "And we don't know who Windy might come back with. We could end up with eight or even ten people to feed here."

Nick shoved another slice of white bread into his mouth and chewed slowly. He kept his gaze locked on her, the little hairs on the back of her neck prickling until he swallowed. When he finally turned away it was like an invisible wire had been severed. "Fine. We'll take everything off the shelves, each pick a spot for our rations, and reorganize them."

"We don't need to do all that," Earl scoffed, producing a small silver box from his pants pocket and shaking it open— carved silver top, intricate, though he flipped it closed again too quickly for Victoria to get a good look. It pinged a little bell of recognition, though—maybe it was an antique.

"We can eat every meal together, make sure ain't nobody takes more than their share." Earl tossed a few small white pills into his mouth. Oh fuck...did they have two addicts down here? Not like anyone kept aspirin in a carved metal snuff box.

Nick was waving the loaf around, the bag swinging below his fist. "So I have to eat the same thing as you for every meal? Thanks, but no thanks."

"But what if someone else comes down?" Carter said. "They'll need rations too, and if we've already parceled it all out—"

Earl sniffed, jaw working. The bells above the bathroom jangled again.

"If more people come down, we can reorganize again," Nick said. "Each of us give them the shit we don't like...if they seem cool." He smiled. "We'll need something to do anyway. There's only one deck of cards back there, and only one of you I'd consider fucking." He glanced at Earl and winked. "Okay, maybe two."

Nick tossed the loaf of bread onto the floor—the only one, already three quarters gone.

"Watch it," Earl barked, agitated, but the edges of his voice were softened by his accent, a melodic wave of vowels with unexpected peaks and valleys. People down here rarely sounded angry, really angry, to Victoria. Not like in the cold north where saying "Hello" on a crowded street earned you a suspicious look instead of a wave. At least up there you knew what people were really thinking.

"I am watching, old man. That'll be the pile for things we need to open," Nick said, his back to Earl, eyes on the shelf. "Unless it was meant as a threat, in which case we should probably hug it out."

Carter joined Nick in emptying the shelves, and Olivia staked out a spot on the kid's right. Victoria stepped up too, Chad beside her. Earl watched their progress from his spot against the wall, his fists clenched at his sides.

CHAPTER SEVEN

HER EYES BURNED WITH EXHAUSTION, but the work went quickly. For the first time since the storm, Victoria found herself relaxing into mind-numbing monotony, her focus on the task and not on the what-ifs—if only for a few minutes. They took bread and jelly and peanut butter from the shelves and stacked them on the floor. They removed pull-top cans of beans, bottled water, canned meat, crackers.

"What are these?" Carter asked, holding up a palm-sized package, one of three—candy?

"You should know," Olivia muttered.

Victoria glanced at her. "Why should he know?"

"I helped Windy carry all this stuff down," Carter said. "No biggie." He shrugged, but Olivia's eyes remained tight.

Nick snatched the package from Carter. "Razzles! Oh man, I haven't see these since I was a kid!"

Victoria hadn't either…had she *ever* eaten a Razzle? Were they old? Expired? Probably, but candy was just sugar and preservatives in an airtight bag.

"This might be bad," Olivia said, shaking a container of hemp milk. "Sounds kind of clumpy."

Nick scoffed. "She got the bullshit bargain brand, that's why."

Earl shook his head, muttering: "Ungrateful, ain't nobody got appreciation these days."

Victoria neatly set a jar of strawberry jelly on the floor. It felt like she was packing her belongings the way she had when she moved into Chad's house in the boonies. For a time she'd felt more at home there than she'd ever felt in the stuffy Chicago apartment she'd grown up in, where you could smell your neighbor's microwaved ravioli through the vents. When she and Chad fought—or rather, when she yelled at him—she never had to worry about what the neighbors a mile away were thinking. But at some point, the fighting had stopped. She'd always been the only one with any fight in her.

Victoria put the lone package of toaster pastries onto the pile and stepped back, narrowing her eyes at the empty shelves. As in the tunnel the day before—*no, this morning?*—it was the absence of the things she'd grown accustomed to that made the new reality stand out so starkly. Strange how it tugged pieces of memory from her—the sleeping bags, the canned goods, it was almost like camping, really. Reminded her of the time she and Phillip had gone to Camp Blue Lake and he'd sat on the shore with her instead of swimming with his friends for the whole month. She blinked at the floor, at the corners of boxes jutting up at hard angles like the spines of a porcupine.

Should they eat after this? It had to be close to lunch, maybe even dinner if she'd slept a full eight hours. No wonder her arms felt like they weighed a thousand pounds. And her throat was gritty, dry; she needed more water. As soon as they arranged it, she'd drink up.

"Ladies and gents, stake out your spot," Carter said, waving one arm toward the shelves like a ringmaster, his face matching the grin on his "Smile" T-shirt. Victoria and Chad could put their stuff together—not like either of them would let the other go hungry. So long as she didn't tell him about the lawyer...or the divorce paperwork now floating in her dresser drawer.

"And don't go thinking you're gonna be taking more of that bread," Earl said, drawing Victoria back. He aimed a scarred index finger at Nick. "What's left in that bag belongs to the rest of us."

Nick rolled his eyes. "Like it's really going to matter. But okay, fine."

"We should make a section for Windy," Carter said, patting the shelf directly in front of him.

"Maybe one for her brother too," Nick said. "Brooke said he might be coming."

"Who said their brother—?"

"Windy, not Brooke. Sorry." Nick shook his head and turned back to the empty shelf. "Kinda reminds me of someone I used to know."

But Windy had said her boyfriend was looking with her, hadn't she? Would he be down here too? A brother, a boyfriend, Windy herself...that was three more mouths to feed. "Are you sure she said brother? Windy said she had the place built after storms killed her family." Victoria stepped backward, her elbow jostling Olivia's arm, and she turned to see Olivia clench a jar harder to her chest. "Oh, sorry, Olivia." Victoria's nose itched with the woman's perfume, something flowery.

Olivia didn't seem to hear the apology—she was shaking her head. "Not her whole family. Her brother is alive, right, Carter?"

Carter's eyes had tightened. "I...think so, yeah."

Earl frowned. "Even if he is alive, there's no way it's her

brother up there with her. She doesn't want nothin' to do with him."

"Yes, he is bat-shit crazy." This phrase, Olivia had gotten right.

"Why, what'd he do?" Victoria asked.

"He's a damn fool," Earl barked. "A liar and a thief—took all the cash out of the collection one Sunday."

"I heard he molested little kids." Olivia nodded, knowingly.

Nick was shaking his head. "No...that isn't right."

Carter turned to him. "Why's that so hard for you to believe? What'd she tell you?"

He shrugged. "Well...nothing, actually. We didn't have time for a family history on the way over. It just seems strange that she told each of you a different, but equally extravagant story."

Victoria watched Nick's face, his furrowed brows—*confused?*—then Earl's agitated stare. Earl knew Windy's brother, knew he'd stolen from the church. Windy might have lied about her brother, or maybe he really was a bad guy, but either way she wouldn't bring him back to hang out with the people she'd talked to about him; or put him down here with Earl who would probably go on the attack. "You sure she said he was coming?" Whoever he was they should plan accordingly—he'd need to eat too, and she'd rather not argue about who had to give up what in front of him. Especially if any of the things the others had heard were true. She glanced back at her sleeping bag. Where the knife lay hidden.

Nick nodded. "I'm sure. And I'm sure she said brother too—not boyfriend."

Earl's nostrils flared, spots of color rising in his cheeks. *Well, that's going to be awkward.*

"She told us it was her boyfriend," Victoria said, and here Earl nodded. Carter shrugged as if Windy'd never mentioned anyone at all. At least she had Chad on her side—why wasn't he saying anything? She turned. Three feet behind her, Chad's eyes were focused on the cereal box in his hand. Avoiding her eyes? Avoiding any hint of conflict? Fucking figured.

She sighed. Maybe Nick had misunderstood. In times of stress, people didn't pay attention to things that weren't matters of life and death.

"Back to the chalkboard," Olivia said.

"The drawing board," Carter said.

Olivia shook her head. "You can write on both, Carter, do not be silly."

Victoria's throat was tight—dry. "Let's do this so we can eat. We'll start by dividing the cans, okay? How many are there?" She reached for her cans mindlessly, lined them up on her shelf. Chad stood at her side, stacking his things beside hers, a perfect uniform space between them. Together but separate.

EARL FINALLY STAKED his claim on a section of shelf on the far side of the room as they divided up the water. They each got six plastic bottles. That wasn't near enough, but they should make it—they could always climb up the ladder and collect rainwater.

They moved on to the cardboard packages. The work kept her hands busy for a few minutes, arranging, counting: six boxes of cereal, brilliant yellow packages with cartoon characters grinning slyly from their cardboard covers; five containers of jelly total, red raspberry, grape, orange marmalade; one lowly box of brown sugar toaster pastries. Instant oatmeal. Crackers. Plenty of food for a day or two, but the uneasy feeling in her guts did not relent. Earl muttered to himself under his breath every time Nick called out the quantity of each item so they knew how many to take. Once, Victoria thought she heard Earl mutter "damn Yankee" though she couldn't be certain. But she was certain something felt wrong here—she could feel it in her blood with every shuddering pump of her heart. But what good would it do to worry in this moment? None. She let the anxiety steady her hands and force her on. *No use panicking. Fucking fight.* Or find something better to focus on.

"So, do you have family, Earl?" she asked as she passed a box of cereal to each of them—exactly one per person. "A place you can stay after the storm if you can't return home?"

"No." No explanation, just no. Maybe he had a family he'd rather forget. Maybe when she moved back to Chicago she'd forget Chad too, cut him from her mind as cleanly as clipping a fingernail. She stooped to open the last container of toaster pastries. How many individual packages—enough to ration? She slid her nail under the flap and glanced at Earl, but he kept his gaze on the shelf. Olivia caught her eye and smiled, though it was strained.

"What about you two?" Victoria asked. "You have a place high off the ground?"

"We have an apartment," Olivia said. "Third floor."

"Ah," Nick said. "So you two…"

Olivia's eyes lit up, but Carter shook his head. Earl was staring at Olivia. "What about that ring you got there?" He gestured to Olivia's hand, where a tiny diamond caught the light.

Olivia raised her hand to her throat—to those dirty pearls. "He…died. And now Carter rents the room."

"Pretty young to be a widow," Nick said, eyes narrowed. He was right—Olivia looked to be about the same age as Carter. Twenty-three, tops.

"He was not as…young."

"That's how y'all get in the country." Earl shook his head. "Taking advantage of law-abiding—"

Olivia's mouth tightened. "I do not care what you think, I loved Lenny and—"

"Peanut butter next," Nick said. "Should we smear the rations on each other? Maybe glop it right on the shelf?" Olivia's lips were still a hard line, but her flaming cheeks had cooled, and she turned back to the shelf. Away from Earl.

Victoria gestured to a section near the middle. "We can just put those containers here. We'll eat together when it comes up, make sure it's fair."

Earl was still glaring at Olivia—at the gold band on her finger.

"Where did you say you were when Windy picked you up?" Victoria asked him.

"I didn't." Earl paused over the single container of peanut butter, then resumed his collecting, more fervently than before. "But it was my roof. Same as you."

Had they talked about this already? "How do you know where Windy found us?"

Earl shrugged. "I'm assumin'. She said everyone south of the highway had to be on the roof. I'm just lucky she started out in the boondocks, that she knew I was stayin'—knew right where to find me."

Olivia bent for a box of crackers, but wavered and grabbed the shelf instead. Carter touched her arm. "Let me."

"Everything okay?" Victoria asked. She watched him set the crackers on Olivia's shelf.

"I am fine," Olivia said, righting herself.

"You aren't fine," Nick said.

Carter nodded and rested his hand on her back. "He's right, Olivia. You've been asleep for two of the last five days. You slept almost the entire day yesterday."

"It is from the trauma. The stress." But she yawned as she

said it, shook her head, and slid a package of instant oats onto her section of the shelf.

"Y'all can take these." Earl waved his hand over a package of seaweed crackers. "I don't like that foreign shit."

"Oh, fuck you, they were probably produced in Milwaukee," Nick said, but his eyes were on...Victoria. She glanced down. Oh. The toaster pastries. She opened the box top and set it on the shelf to distribute the packages inside. But... *No, that isn't right.* Instead of the shiny crinkly foil she'd expected, she pulled out...a small piece of cardboard.

"What the fuck is that?" Nick snatched the box from the shelf, dumping the rest of the contents onto the floor. Five equal pieces of cardboard, all cut very precisely into pastry-sized rectangles.

Earl's face had gone red. "Which one of y'all ate 'em?" He turned on Carter. "Your little freeloadin' ass—"

Carter put his hands up. "I didn't touch them!"

Now Earl turned on Nick. "Well, y'all came down here before the rest of us."

"Where the fuck would I get the cardboard?" Nick snapped. "I don't even have a pair of scissors."

Who cared about scissors? Someone had cut the cardboard and then glued the box back together so anyone shaking the package would hear what they expected to. Who would do that? *Why?*

She reached for the nearest box of cereal, but Olivia was already tearing open the box flaps with her lithe fingers and yanking out the plastic bag, a bag full of tiny shavings of...wood?

Victoria's heart thrummed wildly in her temples.

Earl's nostrils flared, his eyes hard and sharp—twin daggers aimed at Carter. "You helped her bring this shit down, you—"

"I just carried the packages down and put them in front of

the shelves while she lined them up. I didn't think anything was wrong with them!"

The silence stretched. Then they were all tearing apart the boxes, peeking into the packages, popping the tops on the cans.

"This one is okay," Chad said behind her, holding up his own box of cereal, the package ripped down the front. Nick opened a jelly jar and Victoria gagged—the smell was putrid. Awful. Like rotting meat. The cans of beans were full of something hard that looked like bits of resin.

"What the fuck is going on here?" Victoria whispered, mostly to herself.

None of them answered. Then Earl said: "Maybe she bought the food out in front of a store. Got scammed."

"Yeah," Carter croaked. "Maybe she couldn't afford everything she needed, bought it on the cheap."

"What is wrong with you?" Olivia sputtered, but not at Earl…Carter. "You are a…a…"

"Look, as long as we have water, we'll be fine," Chad said. He waved to the shelves.

Victoria frowned. Nick stared at the bottles. And grabbed one, twisting the top off—the cap clattered to the tile.

His face changed, nostrils flaring, lips turned down. Bright spots of pink rose by his cheekbones. Fear? Or fury?

"What?" Carter said. "Is it water?"

"Vodka." Nick put the cap back on and opened the next one. Grimaced.

"Why would she—"

"She obviously thinks we're going to have a party down here."

"With no food and dozens of bottles of alcohol?" Victoria snapped. "And how do you know it's vodka and not just rubbing alcohol? They smell the same." And rubbing alcohol would kill them.

"It was a scammer, had to be," Earl said. "Some thug trying to profit off the supply shortage, sellin' rotten food." He looked pointedly at Carter as if the kid was precisely the "thug" he was referring to. "All them grocery stores were slammed for the week before, wasn't nothin' left—but we'll still make do."

Nick frowned. Shrugged. But his eyes…he was watching Victoria again, eyes narrowed at her tattoo. She crossed her arms once more and looked at the tiny section of shelf that contained their remaining provisions—the few boxes they still needed to open. Meager. Even if it was all real, it was barely enough to survive.

CHAPTER EIGHT

THE LIGHTS WENT off again just as they opened the last package. Hemp milk, but it wasn't. Something horrid and sour and sick: glue.

Of the original provisions, they had a single box of cereal left, three slices of white bread, and twelve bottles of water, two apiece. All the good food—the *real* food—had been lined up in front so none of them would be the wiser...until it ran out. Even the candy had been fake. If they hadn't rationed the provisions, they'd have eaten all the real food today and by tomorrow they'd have been stuck with nothing but bottles of rubbing alcohol, or vodka if you believed Nick. But Victoria wasn't going to find out. Rubbing alcohol was denatured with methanol—made it poisonous so it wasn't subject to liquor laws. They wouldn't have an issue cleaning wounds, but if they drank it, death was likely.

"Maybe it's just a mistake," Carter said in the dark.

They'd all made their way to their sleeping bags soon after the lights clicked off. Had it really been a full day already? Probably. She could believe she'd slept from dawn to dusk after days of trying to rest on the rainy roof, and her exhaustion was palpable now, a weight on her back, her brain foggy. Confused. Even her eyelids were heavier than they'd been when she'd awoken, and the muscles in her neck were threatening to give way if she didn't rest her head.

"This was no mistake," Olivia said.

"Even if it was on purpose, don't mean Windy did it." Earl, from over by the bathroom.

Victoria's jaw dropped. "How can you—"

"I still think it was someone tryin' to take advantage of her, selling her stuff that wasn't—"

"Why would someone trying to make a buck put alcohol in water bottles?" Victoria said, stretching her legs out on top of her sleeping bag. She closed her eyes longer than a blink, and it hurt to drag her lids back open. The air burned her eyeballs, needling her skin.

Carter sighed. "Maybe they looted a store and there was lots of liquor but all the water was gone."

"Then where did the *bottles* come from?" Nick said, and from the direction of his voice, he'd moved his bag closer to Carter, away from Earl.

"I don't know where the bottles came from, son." Earl's gruff drawl sounded lower, thicker, as if the accent came out more fervently in times of stress. "I'm just sayin'…"

The drone of the men's voices buzzed in her head, punctuated by Olivia's higher pitched and occasionally ardent whisper: "She wanted to trick us."

But why? Why would Windy try to make it look like she'd stocked more food than there was? That was just…illogical. It wasn't like they had better options up on top. They'd have come down without any food at all just to get out of the storm.

Olivia kept on: "She has pulled the wool onto your face, Carter, you just do not see it."

"The wool over my eyes, and she hasn't—"

"It was in the way she talked to you, smiling and flirting, but the second she turned away, it was gone. She was faking."

"Olivia, just let it—"

"She wanted something from you. Maybe just a pet, someone to push around, but she wanted something. And because she did not want anything from me, she treated me like sand."

"Dirt."

"Maybe she was jealous of you," Nick said to Olivia. "First the Asians came for the tech jobs, and now they're after the good men, am I right, Earl?" Earl grunted. But he didn't disagree.

A cramp tightened Victoria's guts and she wrapped her arms over her abdomen. Not as painful as the cramps had been those first few days, but the sudden darkness came with a bone-deep weariness; her muscles had been reformed in lead. Victoria crawled inside her sleeping bag and eased out of her stiff shorts. At least her injuries showed no signs of infection—cool to the touch, no swelling. The chilly water bottle was a balm against her skin. Her remaining bottle and a half of water would only last a few days, but she could always refill it. A little rest, and she'd climb the ladder to the top. Even without food, they could survive for months so long as they had water—the rain would sustain them.

"I think we ought to sleep on it," Nick said from somewhere in the blackness. "Get some rest before those fucking lights come back on."

He was right. There could be other explanations she'd see clearly once she'd slept. *Just be logical.* Phillip used to whisper it to her when their father was screaming at their mother so Victoria wouldn't go after him and get a beating for her trouble. It had made her feel better then and made her feel stronger during her travels. Now it slowed her racing heart.

Logic and panic rarely paired well, especially when you threw exhaustion into the mix. Everything ached.

She snuggled deeper into the bag, letting the pain inside her stomach ground her, easing the anxiety still burbling in her chest—she was too weak to react to it anyway. The heaviness had leached into her blood.

"Things do look better at dawn," Olivia said, but her voice shook.

CHAPTER NINE

CLANK, clank, clank.

Victoria awoke to the sun shining directly into her eyeballs. No, not the sun...

She yanked the sleeping bag off her head, the fluorescents nearly blinding her, that weird clanking sound ringing in her ears—remnants from a dream? Her hips and elbows ached and she inhaled steadily, slowly, trying not to show the others her discomfort. Carter was staring at her—*damn, he looks familiar*—the whites of his eyes practically glowing pink. Bloodshot. Had he slept at all? Nick's eyes were red too as he peered at her from inside his sleeping bag on the far wall, so cocooned in the neon yellow that he appeared like a very angry—or very exhausted—cartoon sun. She rolled toward them and winced. If she had just one gloriously fluffy down pillow instead of the goddamn cement and a towel...

Clank, clank, clank. She squinted; the noise was real. *What the hell is that?* There was another sound too, she realized, someone mumbling words she couldn't discern, but the rhythm...they were repeating something. A female voice. High. Tense.

Victoria heaved herself to sitting, rubbing the soreness from her neck. The noise was coming from the tunnel—*the ladder*. Feet emerged from the hole, descending from the hatch. Then bare calves, shorts. Her heart leapt. *Windy*.

Victoria pulled her feet from her sleeping bag and struggled into her shorts, hurrying too much to care about the others seeing her underwear beneath the hem of her shirt. Windy was *back*. Victoria could put all this unease to sleep, could quell the tightness in her chest. They could ask her about the fake food, because there was a reasonable explanation—there was always a thread of logic even in the most bizarre situations. Victoria had survived hanging on to that thread enough times to know.

Why was everyone still sitting there? Carter and Nick sat side-by-side across the room now, both frowning in her direction. Earl was looking at the floor, hunkered down in the same corner where the shelving unit and the bathroom wall met—the little nook behind the shelf. And Chad...was he still asleep?

Dizziness tugged at her. She stumbled for the ladder and grabbed the nearest rung, her bones vibrating with anticipation. "Windy?"

But it was Olivia's slight shoulders that emerged from the tunnel, then her shiny black hair, though it seemed a little less glossy than yesterday. Victoria's heart sank. Tension she didn't realize she'd lost hardened her shoulders once again. Not Windy. They were still alone down here with a wall of fake food.

What time was it? She stepped back from the ladder and glanced at the hash marks near the bathroom. Someone had added a seventh. The start of her...second day down here, five days since she'd been stranded on the roof. And though she knew she'd slept, she'd never felt more exhausted—the hard floor and lack of food weren't doing her any favors. Her eyelids prickled like they were full of slivered wood.

Olivia climbed off the ladder and met Victoria's gaze, her lips trembling. *Crying?* "I did not mean to wake you," Olivia said, and her voice was hoarse but pressured, as if she were trying to whisper but the anxiety was amplifying her words. Victoria recognized the panic—she'd lost a good assistant in Syria to it. Poor guy freaked out listening to the bombs in the distance, went home the next day. Not that Victoria was immune, but she'd pushed it down, then let it make her... angry. More aggressive. Focused. *Useful.*

Olivia sniffed. Victoria's insides twisted, nerves mingling with the dry, brittle ache of thirst. One thing at a time. She'd climb up, get some more water—hell, they could even dump the alcohol and fill those bottles too—then she'd take a fucking nap. Might be berries out on the hill somewhere. Could they eat grass? Leaves, maybe. Probably healthier than cereal and a half loaf of white bread.

Olivia was watching her, the woman's clasped hands a tight ball at her sternum. "I wanted to walk, to get out, to just see...I wanted to *see*..." The last word exploded from her lips like hot ash from a volcano, her breath the sighing exhalation of a million pent-up nerves. Hysterical.

Victoria inhaled deeply, willing Olivia to breathe, to calm down, but the tinge of something rotten stung her nostrils—the trash. "We should take the garbage out," Victoria said, and she didn't recognize her own voice. Her tongue was a sticky weight on the floor of her mouth.

"Can't," someone said: Carter, sitting on his bag, Nick on one side, the rumpled remains of Olivia's makeshift bed on the other. "We have to wait for Windy."

Victoria peered back up at the hatch—the dark tunnel above them. "I'm sorry?"

"It's locked," Carter said, and now he pulled his legs from

his sleeping bag and rose to his feet. "You need a key to get in."

Victoria wracked her brain, but she could not recall Windy using a key—then again, she'd been tired, hungry and…Windy had been handing her a knife. But that wasn't the problem—was Carter saying they couldn't get out? Had Olivia said…

Her heart throbbed against her breastbone. "Wait…we're stuck in here? Locked in?" What if Windy didn't return?

"It's fine. The hatch does lock from the outside, but it's just a safety measure to protect all the stuff down here from looters. It'll protect us too," Carter said, keening, almost whining. "Never know what desperate people might do if they find us. Best case, they'd take our food."

"They'd take our three slices of white bread? One shitty box of cereal?"

A shuffling from behind her: Chad pushing himself to sitting on his bag. Watching. Not contributing a goddamn thing. She turned back to Carter. "That doesn't explain why it would be locked to us from the inside."

"There are only so many kinds of locks for these doors. They either lock or they don't."

That wasn't true at all—Victoria had seen bunkers and cellars alike with adjustable locks, where you had a choice from either side—and in any case, there was no reason to opt for the lock. Looters? Who was left in Fossé to loot a store, let alone stumble across some hidden hatch in the middle of a hill? A padlock would be a fine safeguard during times of disuse.

She stepped onto the ladder, rungs swaying beneath her feet, her thighs burning in protest as she climbed—fifteen rungs off the ground, then into the dark.

There was no reason to put fake food down here, no reason to lock them in the bunker. None.

The ladder clanked. *Four rungs in the blackness, five.*

No reason at all. At least no good, healthy, trustworthy, non-psycho reason.

Her hands ached. *Six rungs. Eight.*

She pushed against the hatch—smooth. A perfectly smooth circle of metal. No latch to even grab on to. She gripped the top rung harder, muscles aching, and heaved against the hatch door with her other hand, the why scratching in the back of her brain, whispering that Windy needed them to think there was food, needed them to think that everything was fine…until she got them down here. Why? Why, why, why?

Her face burned. Her arm was on fire. The dark of the tunnel grew heavier, like it might suffocate her. She dropped her hand and descended, the clanging of the ladder ringing in her ears above the pounding of her heart.

This makes no sense. That more than anything rocked her foundation. Thinking rationally, finding the logic even in the worst of things, had always been her one piece of normal when the world was in chaos. Phillip had taught her that, and now…now…

Victoria stepped back onto the tile. No one else had moved. Olivia had remained beside the ladder, staring into the tunnel; Chad sat in his sleeping bag; Carter stood against the wall, arms crossed; Earl glowered from his half-hidden corner; and Nick leaned against the cement wall, legs still in his sleeping bag, shoulders relaxed like he didn't have a care in the world. But they were locked in a fucking bunker while the world outside fell apart—they were trapped. With just over a bottle of water each.

"Vick?" Chad. Who had convinced her to stay in Fossé to ride out the storm.

Why the fuck did I listen to him?

Victoria took a deep breath. *Save your strength.* Because

when her reserves ran out, when the water ran out… The air was still too thin and her body was too heavy and her heart was beating too fast. Fuck Windy in her stupid fucking face, *goddammit*. Even if it was some weird misunderstanding, she was going to punch that bitch square in the teeth.

Chad was watching her, face pink—had it been so red before?

She straightened her shoulders, trying to expand her rib cage, trying to force air into too-small lungs. "I just don't… the idea of being trapped here…" Her fists clenched as she scanned the others—lots of red eyes, worried faces. Chad was chewing on his cheek. Olivia's chest rose and fell in little agitated bursts. "Does anyone have an explanation for this?"

"I think the word you're looking for is 'motive'," Nick said, dark eyes glittering. And for once, he did not smile.

Olivia rubbed her hands up and down her arms as if she were cold. She was shivering a little, too—was she actually cold, or was the hunger getting to her? Or fear? "Maybe because…well, she got stuck in a storm when she was a kid, maybe she wants other people to feel that also?" She almost looked hopeful.

"Why would she want other people to feel stuck?" Carter said. "She's always been so nice to me, always seemed to care…"

But Nick was nodding in agreement. "People are twisted, man. Misery loves company, right? Maybe she just wants to see what happens, you know? See what we'll do."

Victoria could barely hear them, as if she were listening underwater. *Just be logical. Just…* She frowned at the ceiling. She'd once excavated a shelter that had dated from the Cold War. The owner had used it for his collection of Syrian and Egyptian antiquities, almost all of them imported illegally—hence cementing over the original door when he realized the English government was on to him. But her team had found a second way in by digging around the entire structure: a hidden hole in the roof of the bunker. "Even if all we do is look around...I can't just sit here waiting to starve to death." Victoria eyed the ceiling now, but saw nothing out of the ordinary. No lines that might indicate another exit, even a now-sealed one. *Fucking Windy. I should have shoved her overboard and stolen her fucking boat.*

The rage, the thrumming in her chest...it centered her. Cleared the cobwebs from the edges of her brain, letting her think. Even if they had good reason to panic, it wouldn't help, but being pragmatic might.

"She's right," Chad said. His face was still flushed.

"I am with you," Olivia said, her smile kind. Far more trusting than the dark glare she was getting from Carter, Windy's personal errand boy. Why the hell was he so loyal to that woman? Even Nick had climbed from his sleeping bag and was staring at the ceiling as if he could penetrate it with the sheer force of his gaze.

"Let's work our way around," Victoria said. "Look for any divots in the walls and ceiling, or lines from doors that have been filled in. Even cameras." Someone so big on security, someone who'd lock the doors, surely had other safeguards. Victoria squinted up at the ceiling, eyes tracking back and forth. No divots, no tiny lenses, no little red lights. She knocked on the wall nearest her, to the right of the bathroom —solid.

Nick peered at the wall to the left of the bathroom, running his fingers around the doorframe, tinging the little bell with his pinky as he examined it—the only one of them tall enough to reach it. He left the door open as he ran his hands over the bathroom walls, floor, then picked at the LED above the toilet. It released with a muted *shhhhh* like it was stuck on there with tape or glue. "Wireless, remote activated," Nick said, bringing it back into the room. "Might be a camera in one of the lights, but I'd think the glare would be too bright to see much, and at night…" He shrugged. "I'll take one apart and see."

Earl was still sitting in his nook behind the shelves. Maybe this was a fool's errand, but what was the alternative? Not like Earl had shared any better ideas. Besides, the thought of sitting still made her want to strangle someone—namely Windy. Maybe she'd do that anyway.

Victoria inhaled, trying to focus on the wall down the way from the bathroom, but her vision blurred, a headache slowly taking root in her temples. She knocked on the next section of wall—smooth, flat. Solid. An emergency escape could be anything from a tunnel to a stairway, but most likely, it'd be a catch in the ceiling—the lock would release from inside, a pile of dirt would fall onto the floor, and they'd have to climb up. Like the one in that English bunker. But this ceiling looked solid, and it was so *high*. Twelve feet, maybe even fifteen. She'd noticed that before, in passing, but…damn. They'd have to stand on the top of the highest shelf to get anywhere near it. That wasn't normal for a bunker, not at all.

She dropped her gaze to see Carter pacing below the hatch, Olivia wringing her hands at his side. "I wish she'd just left the door unlocked," Carter said. "It made sense when she told me about it, and I keep thinking she would have told me a way out, given me instructions or something, but I—I can't remember."

I can't remember. That brought Carter's face back, but in her mind, he wasn't in this room—he was sitting in her Introduction to Archeology course, and… Her chest heated. He'd missed the final. *I can't remember everything. Sometimes dates…they slip by me.*

And he had failed the course. Victoria had failed him.

Carter was still frowning at the ceiling tunnel. Did he

remember her? Had to—you don't forget the woman who gave you a failing grade just last year.

Nick had given up on the light. Victoria didn't like what she saw in his face, though she could not initially identify why—*oh*. That bleary bloodshot look, hard and smiling on the outside, but the terror behind it…she'd seen that in her brother's gaze on the nights their father came home drunk, even if Phillip did put on a brave face. For her.

"I'll go take another look at the one door we know exists," Nick snapped. Victoria blinked, trying to clear her vision—the crowbar, Nick had the crowbar in his hand, clutched like a baseball bat. She startled and stepped backward, but he brushed past Carter and Olivia and disappeared into the hole in the ceiling. Her eardrums vibrated as the metal ladder clanged against the side.

"Why an escape ladder?" she mumbled. Bunkers usually had more permanent ladders with metal rungs attached to the wall. But the only reply was the ladder clanging against the tunnel as a series of dull thuds rang through the bunker —Nick pounding on the door. Then nothing. The silence stretched.

"Dark up here," Nick called down. "Carter's right, no way out unless she opens it from above. This side is completely smooth like a dead baby's ass."

"Why a dead baby?" Carter said.

"Why not a dead baby?" he called back. "They're quieter. And easier on the nose."

What a fucking whacko. Olivia met Victoria's gaze with wide, horrified eyes.

Clong, clong, clong. Nick's crowbar on the hatch door, then on the walls of the tunnel. *Please let it open.* But her chest was still too tight, her shivering muscles on the verge of snapping if she dared allow panic to gain so much as a toehold. She couldn't just stand there and wait to find out if he succeeded.

She resumed working on the wall where the bathroom was—knocking, kicking, using her fingers to palpate the cement. Work, just work, just another excavation. Floor to ceiling, ceiling to floor. Smooth, smooth, smooth, the paint making the walls cold and slick like textured glass, or the patterned china Chad had taken from his mother's house. The only keepsake that woman ever asked about, all the dishes now locked in their cupboard, unused. Underwater.

Locked up—like them.

Clong, clong, clong.

Next she made her way along the wall behind the sleeping bags, stepping carefully over Nick's things, Olivia's, Carter's, looking for anything that might indicate an exit, even a tiny camera lens to show they were being watched, because why lock people in a room if you couldn't see what they were doing? Psychos liked to watch the pain they caused, and though she recognized this thought as sensational, it didn't feel like an overreaction—just fact. She knocked harder. Squinted. Nothing but smooth white paint.

"I will help you." Olivia was beside her, eyes twitching with anxiety, but determined nonetheless. "Two hands are better than one, yes?"

Victoria might have smiled if Olivia's face wasn't streaked with tears. Nerves stung at the base of her skull, like they were trying to devour the remaining threads of her resolve. What would Phillip say? *Get it together, sis, or both of us are gonna get hurt.* Victoria took a breath. "Yes. Two hands are better than one."

Clong, clong, clong, clongclongclongclong.

They made short work of the sleeping bag wall, Victoria taking the top, Olivia working her way along the bottom. Searching. A cemented over crawlspace. A crack in the façade. *Anything.*

"This reminds me of our apartment," Olivia said.

"Yours and Carter's?"

"Well, before Carter. It is…an old mansion, yes? A planta-tion that they converted. My husband and I spent one weekend looking for hidden passages after we saw *The Skeleton Key*." She smiled, but her lip trembled. "Times like this…I miss him more."

They got to the corner and slid over to the wall that ran behind Victoria's things. "What happened to him?" Wait… maybe that was the wrong thing to bring up right now.

But if Olivia minded, she didn't show it. "My Lenny…he had a heart attack. Only fifty-six, but he was a big man." She leaned back on her heels and held her hands in a half circle in front of her belly.

"Where'd you meet?"

"He lived in my building growing up, taught me English." She glanced up at Victoria. "It is not what everyone thinks— he never looked at me before I was grown. And he was the nicest man I ever met."

The nicest guy…like Chad. Victoria peered up the wall toward the ceiling, at the fluorescent lights…so high they couldn't reach them. Her eyes burned, head throbbing. They couldn't turn them off even if they wanted to. Why would Windy need control over the lights? How could that possibly benefit her? A switch would have been easier and cheaper to build than whatever bullshit she had going on.

Clongclong, clong, clong.

"What about…" Olivia nodded to Chad, who was standing at the middle of the shelving wall between Victo-ria's sleeping bag and Earl's corner. Peering through the shelves. Not even touching the wall.

Her fists clenched, But she forced them to relax. "We met playing softball."

Olivia cocked her head, and Victoria smiled, though it hurt her face. "I know," she said. "It was right up the road from my work. Figured I'd try it. The first play, he hit a ball almost to the fence and no one was there to scoop it up—would have been a home run. But he ran into the first baseman and knocked him over. Spent all his time making sure the guy was okay." In his favorite yellow Converse, bright as their sleeping bags. He'd taught her how to swing the bat that day while she squinted at his blinding yellow feet.

He always just wanted to have fun.

"Sounds like my Lenny," Olivia said, fingering her pearls. "A soft soul."

Victoria's arms ached. She'd thought the same. But who cared whether Lenny and Chad were soft or sweet or fun—what did it matter now? Lenny and Chad hadn't locked them all down here. And if they couldn't find a way out... Victoria inhaled deeply, forcing her lungs to expand though her breath wheezed in her throat. She coughed and met Olivia's gaze. "Windy isn't a soft soul, is she?"

Olivia shook her head. "Carter...he does not believe it. But I know better. I think she is crazy."

But was she "human social experiment *haha* what a great joke" crazy or "you're all about to die" crazy? "Do you think she'll come back, Olivia? To let us out?" How well did Olivia know her? Most of what she'd said so far made them sound like strained casual acquaintances, connected only by Carter. Still more extensive than Victoria's interactions with their captor.

Olivia pursed her lips, eyes flicking to Carter, who was still staring up toward the hole in the ceiling. She leaned toward Victoria and lowered her voice. "I do not know. Everyone else down here...they say she will return. They trust her, but I cannot figure out why." She met Victoria's eyes. "And I do not like Nick. Or Earl. Not at all."

Neither do I. She hadn't overtly considered that before,

perhaps she'd been trying not to, but now the thought hooked itself into the meat of her brain—those two weren't to be trusted. Something about them felt wrong. Victoria let go of the wall, temples throbbing in time to the pulsing cramp that had taken root in her guts. At her feet, her water bottle glistened. Her throat ached anew, arid and prickling with heat. She snatched the bottle up, hands shaking, and sipped. But only once. Putting it down was agony, every nerve in her mouth tingling, yearning for more.

Don't think about it. Olivia had headed for her own sleeping bag, probably to get her water bottle too. Only Chad still seemed to be actively working, just a few feet away in front of the shelving—more initiative than he showed at home, and the fact that she didn't have to nag at him softened her shoulders...just a little. He'd already moved the boxes, real and fake, to the floor. Her stomach turned. They should eat. They should. But who knew how long they had to make this last? And it took water to digest food, so maybe it was better not to eat until they were more...desperate.

Chad stepped in front of Earl and grabbed the shelf, sliding it over the tile with a deep grinding noise. Earl moved from his little nook and headed for the garbage corner. Above, the *clong, clong* grew louder, then a *shhhh, clank, shhhh, clank*, not like the crowbar smashing against the hatch this time—more of a scraping followed by a crash as if Nick were trying to pry at the door but kept slipping and hitting the side wall.

The clanging subsided, and Nick reemerged through the ceiling. "Yeah, it's solid. No give at all." He set the crowbar on the tile beside the bathroom door.

"Told you," Carter muttered from the far wall, on his sleeping bag again, his eyes on Olivia who was sitting beside him, their knees touching. Had they just...given up?

Chad was crouched at the section of wall behind the

shelving now, running his fingers over the paint. He stilled, one hand against the wall. But even when she stepped closer, she could see nothing behind the shelves, just painted cement. "What are you doing?"

"You can feel a little divot here." He stood and ran his fingers up the wall in a straight line until they were in front of his face, then made a sharp ninety-degree turn. And then she saw it, faint but visible, the tiniest protrusion in the wall...in the shape of a large rectangle.

A door—at least it used to be.

"Is it—"

Chad knocked in the center—like punching rock. He moved his fist to the spaces surrounding the outline and tried again. Same. Someone had filled the only other escape route with cement...no, not someone. *Windy*.

"We are trapped," Olivia breathed from behind them. "She...she trapped us here, locked us in, and we are out of water! We are almost out of water!"

But that wasn't entirely true. Victoria let her gaze drift to the bathroom, to the bucket beside the door, just a few feet from Earl's nook. Gritty, dirty, bleached water, but it would save their lives until...until what? Maybe they should put it in the middle of the room, where they could all keep tabs on it. Earl hadn't shown a tendency to take more than his share —yet—but hunger did funny things, and he'd already isolated himself from their little group. No one to see him sneak an extra bite here and there. She turned back to Chad, to the cemented over door. "Can we dig through it?" They had the crowbar—she had the knife. Not exactly the perfect tools for digging through cement, but...

"Come on now, ain't nobody diggin' through a thing." Earl crossed his arms and finally pushed himself off the wall. *Lazy asshole, of course he wants to have an opinion when he's been doing jack shit to help.* "Besides, might be dangerous—she probably keeps a generator back there, maybe air filtration or it'd smell a lot worse."

"What would make you—"

"I just know about these kinds of structures."

"How?"

He glared. "How what?"

"How do you know—"

"Military." He sniffed, looked away. "I was an engineer."

Maybe he was right about the air filters. Victoria inhaled —stale, but not horrendous despite six people without deodorant for…she glanced at the hash marks again, as if this time they would have dwindled to a more rational and acceptable "two."

Still seven.

She breathed slowly, thinking. Dangerous or not, there could be a way out; if Earl was right about the filters, the generator, surely there was a way to access the equipment, and you couldn't get to it from this side. There had to be another entrance. And exit.

Yes, they should dig. With whatever they could.

"I sure as shit wouldn't mess with it," Earl said more gruffly, and she turned to see Chad picking at the paint. "No one would block it off without a reason."

"A reason? Like that she's a fucking psycho?"

Olivia was nodding, her lips pressed together in a thin line.

Earl's nostrils flared. "Might be it leaks. If we crack it open and the other chambers are already full of water, ain't no way we're getting out of here before this place fills up."

"But if the water can get in, then there is a way out too," Olivia said.

"I thought your kind were supposed to be smart."

Your kind?

Earl narrowed his eyes, but one corner of his lip curled

up. Smirking. How could anyone find this funny? And then he was reaching for his little metal box again, shaking it. The few pills he had left pinged around; he was getting light.

Olivia crossed her arms. "We are high on the hill, and I am just saying—"

"Y'all don't know how high the water is outside, and you're assumin' we can fit a human into the spaces water can flow through. Even if it were just dirt out there, if anything beyond this wall is flooded, we'd have a hard time diggin' out with a backhoe before we drowned—and all we've got is a crowbar."

There might be something to that. She'd once done an excavation in Egypt where a tunnel had collapsed even without the added pressure from rising water. Her assistant had broken his foot and she'd half-carried him nearly two miles out the other side—if the tunnel had been full of water, the displaced liquid would have drowned them before they could escape. Shit, had it really been four years since then? Life had gotten a little boring until this week. Maybe she preferred boring.

Earl brushed at the air between them like he was shooing off an annoying fly. "We ain't got energy to waste on fool-headed nonsense."

"Watch it," Carter said, brows furrowing. "You're no better than anyone else."

"I don't think I'm better'n anyone." Earl glowered.

"Always with the comments about minorities, and we don't have to take it anymore, you know? A long time has passed since slavery."

"I've got a bit of a grudge, son."

Victoria peered at the shelf. Chad was still fiddling with the line in the cement, as if there were a secret passage that would open if he happened on just the right spot.

"I'm not your son, or your boy, or your negro," Carter

snapped. "And she's not your girl, or *your kind*, or whatever the fuck you said."

The wall blurred. Victoria turned back to the others. *Shut up and let me think*.

Nick chuckled, framed by the open bathroom door. It was darker in there, no fluorescents, just the LED Nick had removed. She hadn't even seen him replace it. "Earl likes his spot at the top of the white-boy food chain, isn't that right, old man?"

"Everyone makes everything about race nowadays. Maybe I just don't like morons." Earl scowled, his fists clenched at his sides, arm muscles coiled, biceps hard as rock. "Back in my day, we called it like we saw it, and you"—he jabbed a finger in Nick's direction—"ain't no good. And I'm gonna call it like I see it from now on."

The air buzzed with electricity and ill-spent agitation. Victoria's stomach growled, heat blasting through her guts and up into her throat. Bright. Burning. "For fuck's sake," she said. "Just stop. Yelling at each other is pointless."

"So's what you're doing with these walls." Earl's posture had softened. "Whatever she did, whatever she covered over, she did for a reason."

"The reason is that she is crazy!" Olivia practically screamed at him.

"That girl saved your life. Mine too." Earl shook his head. "Fucking ungrateful generation, I'll tell you what."

"Then you are crazy too!" Olivia shouted, her voice high, her cheeks pink with fury.

Earl grunted.

"Olivia's right," Victoria said. "No one fills a shelter with fake food without some kind of agenda. Windy's not simply trying to keep us safe." Her head pounded with each beat of her heart, and she closed her eyes, listening, willing it to subside. *Thud, thud, thud*. The pain did not relent.

Thud, thud.

As if on rhythm, a *thwack* sounded from the back wall. She opened her eyes in time to see Chad slamming the crowbar against the cement.

"That's the spirit!" Nick shouted.

Earl's eyes widened. He ran for Chad and grabbed his shoulder, yanking him from the wall by his shirt, the shelf wobbling, a jar skittering across the floor and shattering—should have been jelly, but the stink was sulfuric, repugnant. Victoria gagged. The room spun. She'd gotten so used to it, the spinning, that she had stopped registering it, but now the fuzziness was making the world unstable.

Beside her, Nick cocked his head, watching her with a raised brow. And then he was stepping toward Earl instead, grabbing the man's shoulders, the muscles in his own forearms taut and hard. Earl swung at Nick with his fist, but Nick outweighed him—he tossed Earl against the wall beside the bathroom as if the older man weighed next to nothing.

"Why are you so certain that digging through the wall will end badly?" Nick demanded, one thick forearm across the man's throat—did he have military training too? "If the generators were underwater now, the lights would have blinked off already, right? Now's the time to dig—now, before whatever's back there really does flood." He released Earl with one final shove and snatched up the crowbar from the floor where Chad had dropped it.

Chad. He was watching Earl, his expression more hurt than angry.

"And if we can't get through here," Nick said, "if it is flooded, we should be able to tunnel out the top"—he glanced up—"if we can reach it."

"I'm telling you, boy, ain't no use."

Nick paused with the tip of the crowbar pressed against

the painted cement wall just above his head. "How can you be so sure?"

"Because I'm the one who cemented it off."

The air stilled, the hushed silence before a lightning strike, and then the room exploded into questions, so many that Victoria couldn't keep track of who was speaking.

"You've been down here before?"

"What's behind the wall?"

"You worked with *her*?"

"Why didn't you tell us?"

"Why the fuck should we believe you now?"

Then Earl: "I'm stuck here too, same as you."

The world was a confused jumble. And still, Victoria's belly grumbled, feral, animalistic, hot, and her heart, her head were pulsing, pulsing, as she snapped: "But not the same as us because you've been down here before and you know her and you helped her build a *fucking dungeon*."

Earl held up his hands—one scaly pink claw, one normal. The good one was bloody. Had that happened in the scuffle? "Listen, if y'all want to know, I'll tell you. But I'll only say it once." He paused and lowered his hands, gently, slowly, as if he were pulling a lever that would calm his whole body down. "There used to be a single room back there, that's all. No exits. She hinted that there were generators, but I never saw 'em."

Carter crossed his arms. "Why wouldn't you tell us that?"

"Y'all think everything is a big deal. All I did was help her reinforce a fallout shelter. The ceiling was collapsin' back in that room there, and she thought it was easier to fill it than to try to fix it. Once the tunnels start cavin', you don't want to risk it unless you know you have good support. And the supports in this room"—he knocked on the wall nearest him —"these walls will withstand an earthquake. Steel reinforced, not just steel beams. Steel panels. Solid. Can't get through 'em with the crowbar even, and if you did, you'd flood us out —them walls are the only thing between us and the water table risin' outside, and hill or not, you can bet that water is looking for a way in right now."

A way in. Victoria swallowed hard and tried to keep her voice from shaking. "You better tell us everything you know about this place, and fast."

"Ain't nothin' else to tell. All that matters is, there ain't no other exit."

Was he lying? She couldn't think of a reason for Earl to hide things now—like he'd said, he was stuck here too. "Why didn't you tell us before?" she said. "You flat-out lied about it, pretended you had no clue—"

"Y'all needed something to do. To keep your minds busy." He sniffed.

"That's not good enough." The only reason to keep what he'd done a secret was that they'd suspect him of working with Windy, conspiring to get them down here, and turn on him. Maybe they should suspect him.

Earl's chest was expanding quickly, like he was panting— hyperventilating—though his voice stayed even. "Havin' an idle mind, when there ain't no way out…" He frowned, shook his head. His breath slowed. "It's a good way to lose yourself. Ain't a single one of you know what it is, the demons that come out when you're at war, when your time slows up and the world stops spinnin'…"

Victoria stepped closer, her eyes locked on his. "Are we at war, Earl?"

He looked away. But they were.

The lights went out.

CHAPTER TEN

THEY SET up their sleeping bags in pairs, Olivia and Carter on theirs against the far wall, Victoria and Chad by the shelves, Nick sitting cross-legged between them. Earl sat all the way over on the other side in his little corner, the nook half hidden now that they'd moved the shelf back. Almost sneaky. Appropriate, perhaps, for the man who'd cemented the room off, who'd maybe helped Windy trap them here.

Victoria relaxed her fists, but they clenched up again, the word *trapped* echoing in her brain. Nick had set the flashlight on the floor in front of his bag; the ladder cast stark shadows that looked far too much like bars. She cleared her throat before the thoughts could take hold. Surviving—that was all that mattered. They had to get out.

"Y'all wasting the light," Earl barked.

Nick sniffed. "You'll have to fight me for it, Earl."

Silence. Then Earl scoffed, "There ain't nothin' to get worked up about—it's only been a couple days. And she saved all y'all."

"She's a fucking *stranger* to me," Victoria snapped. "How are you so sure this is all fine?"

"She's a *woman*," Earl said and Victoria balked—even Nick's eyebrow rose—but before she could protest he continued: "And she ain't no stranger. I've known her for years, from church." He shook his head. "She'd never hurt no one."

"I think...I trust her too," Carter said. "Once the storm hits, I'm sure she'll head back down here. We just have to be patient." He shrugged. "If you want to see the sunshine, you have to weather the storm, right?"

Victoria squinted at him, the phrase pinging a little bell of memory at the base of her brain. "What did you just say?"

But Olivia was already huffing: "That is what you said about the first storm! Where was she then? And this room is full of fake food, food as fake as her smile!" Olivia's voice was rising, and in the space between her words the long high zzzzzzzzzzzz of Nick's sleeping bag abraded Victoria's eardrums until he'd zippered himself inside.

He lay on his belly, facing them, chin on his hands. "If the lovers are going to scream, I should at least get a better view," he said, yawning. Olivia pressed her lips together, and dropped her eyes.

But Victoria's mind was not on them. Windy hadn't been here during the first hurricane, so she had another shelter somewhere. And... *If you want to see the sunshine, you have to weather the storm*. She'd heard that before. From Chad. "Carter?"

He met her gaze, the dark behind him melding with his skin.

"Where did you hear that phrase?"

Carter said nothing, but Olivia said, voice softer now, "Windy says it all the time."

Victoria turned to Chad. He was a lump between her and the shelves, hidden beneath the flaps of his sleeping bag— she hadn't even heard him lie down. She resisted the urge to kick him awake. He had said it before they'd come down, the phrase Windy said "all the time"—did he know this woman who'd picked them up? No, it had to be a coincidence, maybe from one of those shows Chad watched while she was reading in the other room. *Forget it*. But her guts still burned —hunger and nerves. They were trapped. *Trapped*. Her eyes blurred as if her brain couldn't simultaneously process the images in the room and the thoughts in her head. She blinked hard.

Olivia wrung her hands. "The next storm should have hit by now, and we are still here and she is not."

Carter shrugged. "I trust her," he said again. "She's been through some horrible shit and—

"I am telling you, she is off her rocking chair." Olivia crossed her arms.

Nick nodded. "On that, I have to agree. She's always been a little fucked up."

Always? Victoria stared. "I thought you first met at a bar when she showed up to rescue you."

He swung the light back to his own face and positioned it beneath his chin, grinning ghoulishly. "I'm just saying she seemed off."

"No, you said she '*always*' seemed off."

Nick shook his head. "It's a figure of speech—not like I knew her before this. I just meant…you know. She was weird from the get-go."

"And you still followed her down here?" Then again, they all had. And everything had seemed fine until they realized they were locked up and starving, holding bags of fake food that someone had purposefully planted to trick them into complacency.

Victoria leaned her head against the cement wall and massaged her aching temples. Carter and Olivia knew Windy from school. Earl knew the woman from church. Chad had used that phrase, the one Windy said "all the time"—did he know Windy too? And Nick...he was one of the original three, but his story, about not even realizing the storm was coming...something was wrong there.

What the fuck is happening? But she had no idea. And her head was killing her, throbbing in time to her heartbeat so powerfully that even the fillings in her teeth pulsed with white-hot pain.

On a dig, she would collect data. Then she could decide what to do with it.

CHAPTER ELEVEN

THE LIGHT SEEMED HARSHER TODAY. Or else her eyes were just more tired.

Chad lay in his sleeping bag between her and the shelves, chest rising and falling steadily at half the pace of Victoria's pulsing heartbeat. How could he sleep now? They should be trying to escape, trying to get out of there, but the mere thought of wasting energy pounding on a hatch that wasn't going to open turned her stomach.

Across the way, Nick and Carter and Olivia sat in a row against their wall. Carter's eyes were on the shelf where they'd put their meager rations; Olivia tugged on her dirty pearls; Nick glared at Earl, who was doing sit-ups in his little corner.

Victoria felt hollow and spent. Her instincts—*fight! fight!*—had waned as she slept, easing the flood of adrenaline that had kept her single-mindedly focused on seeking an escape. Now, with the morning came new clarity—they should know their enemy.

This was war. On that point, Earl was correct.

"So, Windy told us all conflicting stories, right? Maybe we

should go through them, see if we can figure out what's true." The words came out raspy. Victoria tried to swallow, but there was nothing in her mouth, and her tongue was dry. She grabbed her water bottle—one last sip in this one. It was gone too fast but helped soothe the fire in her throat.

"Why does it even matter?" Nick said. "You think it'll get us out of this place?"

"It's good to know who we're dealing with. What we're dealing with."

Nick sniffed. His lower face was dark with facial hair, but it was coming in haphazardly, as if he'd splashed mud across his jaw.

"You have other plans?" She tried to smile, though heat was creeping into her neck. It was just a conversation. What did he care?

Nick smiled—or smirked. "We should ask Carter. He's the one who's in love with her," he said in a higher sing-song voice. Olivia frowned and Carter snorted, but the kid hung his head. Shame?

"I used to have a thing for her," Carter said, "but I'm not like...into her anymore."

Nick laughed. "Only took her locking you in a cement dungeon, eh?"

Victoria tried not to wince. Her throat was burning again, and with the influx of water had come a rumbling deep in her guts—*ignore it, ignore it*—but just the thought of the bread made the acid in her stomach burn brighter. Olivia's hand clutched her own belly. They'd have to eat soon.

"I met her through Carter," Olivia said in response to Victoria's raised eyebrow. "Only saw her at school when she came around him. As for the stories, there was something in class, genetics, and she told me her brother...that he hurt kids. I suppose now I am not sure exactly what she meant, and she refused to say anything else about it because"—she glanced over at Carter—"you came. To class. So she put on that smile for you, like she always did. She never told me anything else about herself or her life. I just know she is *crazy*."

Carter sighed. "You don't know that."

"I saw her every week, watched her with you, Carter. She is not right. You just do not believe it because you want to hit her."

Nick cocked his head.

"Bang her," Carter muttered, and Nick grinned.

Olivia did not. "And you remember why she left school last semester, yes? Got kicked out. For stalking that teacher." She puffed up her chest, triumphant.

"Do you have a thing for her too?" Nick asked Olivia, but he kept his eyes on his own hand, squishing his water bottle with a plasticky crackle. Squish, crackle, release. Squish, crackle, release. *Water, water, water.*

"Can you fucking stop that?" Victoria snapped.

Nick's eyes widened, but he set the bottle down. And the outburst had eased the burbling in Victoria's belly, helped her forget the grit on her tongue, the dryness that was edging its way across her lips. Earl grunted from the corner. Was he still doing sit-ups? His face shone pink, and from here, she could smell him too—musty.

"We all love the stink of pheromones, Earl," Nick said, wrinkling his nose, "but you're turning Carter on a little too much. How about using all that energy to bust open the hatch?"

Earl muttered something, then grunted again. "Won't do no good. That's military-grade steel, son." He huffed through another set. "And I'm not about to waste my time looking for a way out when she'll be back any day."

"*Exactly,*" Carter said, nudging Olivia. But Olivia didn't look any more convinced than Victoria felt.

Earl wiped his forehead. He couldn't be sweating—none of them had enough fluid in them to sweat. Victoria closed her eyes. Maybe she should stop looking for a logical explanation to a psychopathic problem.

Don't panic without a good reason.

There's a reason, her rational brain said in Phillip's voice. He was right. Day eight according to the hash marks, and she was ready to dig through the walls with her fucking fingernails. Why weren't they?

Was she overreacting? No. And even if she had been, Phillip wasn't here to talk her down, wasn't here to sing her his made-up songs, even if she could almost hear the lyrics. *Now or Never*. She traced the tattooed letters with her index finger. Her skin was hot and dry.

Earl rolled himself to standing and toweled his face. Then he reached into his pocket for that box again. That box, that little carved snuff box. Earl chewed the pills, jaw working overtime. Jonesing? At least Nick seemed fine now, no signs of withdrawal. *Unless he has a secret stash to take the edge off, like Phillip used to*.

Earl pocketed the box once more.

"Earl, you said Windy had you working on this place before the storm?" Victoria said slowly. "Where do you know each other from again?"

Earl tossed the towel over his shoulder. "Church."

"Since when does she go to church?" Carter muttered. But they were in the deep south—what church you attended was the first thing people asked after your name. Which was why Victoria hadn't had many friends here. Not everyone took kindly to folks who spent their Sundays eating takeout egg rolls instead of eucharist crackers.

"Well, she don't go much anymore, but her daddy was a good man, went every Sunday before he died. Like that one ought to." With a final glare in Nick's direction, Earl headed for the bathroom. The bells jangled.

"Weird," Carter said.

"What?" Victoria asked.

Carter nodded at the closed bathroom door. "It's just... she never mentioned Earl to me, and that's a long time to have known her. I mean, before her Dad died? That's like twenty years ago."

Nick shrugged. "Old fucker like that, small town, smaller church communities...not that strange."

And with that kind of history, maybe Earl knew the truth about the stories they'd heard. Was Windy's brother a child molester or a thief? Victoria could have sworn Windy said her brother was dead too, but the others seemed to think he was alive. And...the boyfriend. There was a boyfriend up there too, right? *So...* She wracked her brain, but the memory would not resurface. "She told us she lost her family in a hurricane," she said finally. "I wonder if Earl knows about it."

Carter sniffed. "Hell, everyone knows about that."

They stared at him. The silence stretched.

"Well?" Victoria said.

Carter glanced at the bathroom door again, then sighed. "I guess he'll tell you anyway. It was a hurricane. Tornado afterward trapped the whole family in their collapsed basement. Windy and her brother were nearly dead when they were discovered, and they had to...do things to survive. Eat things not normally on the menu." He dropped his eyes, shoulders slumping, almost...embarrassed.

Eat things like what? Phillip whispered in her ear and she shook her head. Dizziness made the room spin.

"Squirrels?" Nick guessed. "Though I hear Earl's kind does that on the regular." He glanced at the door as if hoping Earl had heard, but the older man was still in the bathroom. "Or maybe it's bugs. Mushrooms grown in her own shit?"

Carter frowned. "That's a thing?"

"Stop being vague," Victoria snapped. Her heart was throbbing too fast—painful.

Carter leaned closer as if confiding some secret. She supposed he was. "Her parents died down there and no one found her or her brother for over a month—she'd spent all that time prying the debris away, finally managed to shimmy through a gap and wedge herself up just high enough for someone outside to hear her screaming. But the only way she was able to find the strength to start climbing was that her brother..." He looked down. Scraped at the cuticle on his index finger with the opposite nail.

"Her brother what, Carter?"

"Yeah, man, the suspense is killing us!" Nick said, but the glitter in his eyes was not his usual tease—the corners had gone tight.

"I guess..." Carter finally raised his head. "He kinda tricked her into eating their father."

Olivia's face went green. Carter had never told her? Nick cocked his head, eyes equally shocked.

Carter leaned back against the wall once more. "Her dad...he took a long time to die. She and her brother were mostly starved by the time he finally did, and her brother sawed the guy to pieces with debris. Fed the meat to her in the dark."

Victoria tried to keep her voice even. "You just thought to bring this up now?" And Earl...he had to have known too, if he'd known the family that long, been friends with her father for Christ's sake. Something like that would have been sensational news in a small town. *Why the fuck are they protecting her?*

Earl was sitting on his bag again, though Victoria hadn't heard him return. She focused on him—his crossed arms. "Did you know about this?"

"I knew they died in that tornado. The rest was just rumors." No expression, the blue in his eyes a steely gray.

"But this isn't the first time you've heard the story?"

He frowned. Coughed. Shook his head. "I didn't think… well, who'd believe a thing like that?"

Carter certainly did. She whirled on him. "If you thought it was true, why would you keep it from us?"

"I…it's hard to explain."

"Fucking try."

Carter dropped his gaze. "I've always been a little…restless. No reason for it, really, I just didn't feel like I fit anywhere. I was filing at my uncle's law firm with no idea what to do with my life when she showed up. Windy treated me like a brother. Helped me figure out a major, even— accounting." He glanced Victoria's way and half-smiled. "It sure as hell wasn't going to be archeology. I just…I don't know why we're here. Why I'm here."

Because she's a fucking psycho? But if Phillip went insane, would she believe it? Probably not. And she'd have kept her mouth shut about it too, not said a word about him or about their past…about them lying in bed in the dark, whispering their fantasies of all the ways they might kill their father. Pain bloomed behind her eyeballs, throbbing and angry and insistent.

"She did stop asking you to come over last year," Olivia said. "No more dinners, nothing. Maybe she does not think of you the same way any longer."

Carter smiled but it was strained. "She had her own life, it wasn't like…she dumped me or something. She just…"

"She liked you more when you did things for her and did not ask why."

"Well, you gave her enough shit for everyone. I think she was just trying to get over her fucked-up brother—she said he sent her pictures for years from his foster homes, like that plane crash in the Andes? Like he was studying…eating people. And he'd send her letters, too, joking he wanted to do it again." Carter shook his head. "How fucked up is that? And she was totally traumatized the first time—eating your dad at eight years old, anyone would be. But people who've been hurt…those are the least likely people to hurt anyone else, right?" He dropped his gaze. "Because they know how it feels."

But abuse ran in patterns too. In families.

"I think people who've been hurt want to spread that pain around," Nick said slowly.

Olivia nodded once, but pressed her lips together, perhaps not wanting to give credence to Nick's words, though she clearly believed them. Because if Windy was spreading pain around, then hurting them, even killing them, was more likely than some terrible social experiment. Was there any part of Victoria that actually believed that's all this was? A part that thought Windy would come back and let them out as if it had never happened? Olivia grabbed Carter's arm and squeezed, and he patted her hand kindly. Like a brother.

Earl snorted. Skeptical. *Just rumors*, he'd said.

"You're positive these stories she told you are true?" Victoria asked. Eating your dead parents seemed like something you'd take to the grave.

"I mean, not the brother thing, I guess, but the rest, yeah. My uncle is a lawyer, worked on her case," Carter said. "There was some trouble with getting her property back or something because she changed her name. That's where we met for the first time, actually, but we weren't friends until later on."

Her head, god, her head. It was like being stabbed in the brain with a letter opener.

"What about her brother?" Nick asked Carter. "You and Windy seem pretty tight. Did you ever actually meet him?"

"I read a story about him, said he fell off the face of the earth the year after their parents died. No one's heard from him since then except Windy." Carter scratched nervously at the back of his neck. Nick's lips were a tight white line. "Not one photo either. He changed his name too, like she did. No one wants to be known as the Fossé cannibal."

A vanishing brother. *Just like mine.*

Carter shifted, picking at his cuticles again. "I might have seen him from afar once, though. I think, anyway. I was coming over for dinner at the house, and this guy was getting into his car while I was walking up the drive. Long hair, not at all what I expected."

Nick frowned. "Why do you think that was her brother?"

"I'm not positive. But she said she was seeing her brother that day, so I figured…" He shrugged.

The others had gone blurry. Victoria blinked hard and her vision cleared in time to see Nick shift on his bag. He was staring at her…no…at the body on the floor behind her. Chad. Her husband was still on his back, but his eyes were open, gaze glued to the ceiling, face pink. Embarrassment? Did he know Nick was looking at him?

"Where do you know her from, Chad?" Nick said. "You know Windy from church too? Or from your lawyer uncle?"

Chad didn't turn Nick's way, but his expression hardened, subtle, but Victoria knew his face the way she knew her own body. Whatever he was about to say was a lie. "I don't know her."

"You seem awfully familiar to me." Nick looked at Victoria. "What about you, Vicky?"

Her name, edged in red.

Victoria shook her head. "Never met her." And it seemed she might be the only one.

Chad was steadfastly staring at the ceiling.

"Are you sure about that?" Nick raised an eyebrow and

glanced over at Carter who furrowed his unlined forehead into chaste ridges. "She mentioned you, Vicky, when we were driving over here. Said you went way back, that you were practically sisters."

What the fuck? "I'm positive. The first time we met was when she came to collect us off the roof."

Nick grunted. "If you say so." But Carter was eyeballing her now, suspicious. Even Olivia's face had tightened.

"Victoria doesn't know Windy," Chad said.

Nick turned back to Carter and...did he just roll his eyes? Carter crossed his arms. And glared. At her.

Her chest tightened, but not from hunger. *Thank god someone has my back.* She glanced at her husband as if the explanation for Nick's sudden change in demeanor might lie in his face. Why was Chad's skin so pink? Like a lobster. Not right, not right at all. She brought her gaze back to the others, the tension in the air palpable, needling her skin.

Nick was trying to...alienate Victoria, but if he really thought she was in with Windy, if he thought they were friends, he sure as hell would have brought it up before now. He'd only decided to mention it—maybe make it up—because...she was asking questions. Whatever these people knew, Nick didn't want her to find out about it.

Illogical. But nothing made sense anymore—nothing.

Chad grunted, and she looked back in time to see him wince, hand on his leg as he climbed out of his bag. The line of sticky black on his shin was puffier than it should have been, the skin around the wound swollen and angry. No red lines she could see, nothing to indicate sepsis. But...his cheeks. So flushed.

Carter was still glaring at her. Olivia had dropped her gaze to the floor.

She put her hand on Chad's arm, his skin far too hot. "Chad, did you clean that out?"

He nodded. "Yeah, twice, it just...still hurts." He pushed himself to standing and limped toward the shelves—for the bottles of alcohol. At least he could still walk.

And cleaning it out...that was really all he could do. One actionable item when they seemed to have no more left.

CHAPTER TWELVE

CSSSSSHHHHH, csshhhh. Water crashed around her with enough force to steal her breath. Phillip held tight to her shoulders, and she paddled, frantically looking for the shore, but the only hard surfaces were the rocks—enormous jagged boulders spiking from the sea like teeth. *Tick, tick, tick* went the droplets of water on her face. Any closer and they'd be thrown against the rocks. She'd have to hear their bones break before they drowned.

Then the blue took her, sucking her down beneath the water, silence, then reemergence—*cshhh, cshhh*—waves moving faster, throwing her, twisting her as Phillip's wriggling, worming body slipped from her back and brushed against her leg as he sank— *cssshhhh, cshhhh*—spindly arms flailing, desperately trying to grab hold of her— *shhhhhhhhhh-hhhh*—but then she was swimming away from him, pushing him off, shoving at the water, clawing toward the sky—killing him.

Victoria opened her eyes, gasping for breath. No water, only the small room hazy under blue LEDs. A dream. But the rush of water in her ears remained, the steady hiss of waves punctuated by the roar of water on rock and the ticking spatter of droplets against her face.

Cssshh, tick.

She blinked her burning eyes. Had she slept at all? She'd lain silently with Chad the night before while the others played Crazy Eights—they hadn't asked her to play. Refused to even respond when she'd told them again that she didn't know Windy. But Nick had been whispering, Carter staring at her. God knew what they thought. She'd finally closed her eyes with the fluorescents still glaring down at her, her body too tired to move, brain exhausted. Even now she couldn't put two thoughts together into a cohesive whole.

Victoria rolled over, her body one giant bruise, and squeezed her eyes shut tighter to block out the world.

Cssshh, tick, tick, cssshh. But…the sound of water in her ears —those noises were *real*. Her heart leapt into her throat, closing off her airway. She squinted. Then she bolted from her sleeping bag, the world wavering as she stumbled toward the ladder. Tiny glistening drops fell from the tunnel, glittering in the misty blue lights. Was Windy back? Had Nick managed to get the hatch open? But there was no roar of wind, no thunder, not a hint of breeze. And *no water*. The floor was completely dry. She was seeing things. *Shit.*

Cssshh, tick, cssshh.

Was she hearing things too?

Victoria's guts clenched, pulsing with that familiar hollow pain—but less sharp than yesterday. She was more worried about Chad. His wound was definitely infected. She'd had sepsis once herself, in Uganda, and she'd never forget the incessant shivering, the way the world had spun and twisted, the hallucinations of Phillip sitting by her bedside, stroking her hand, talking to her like he had when they were kids. *Suck it up, Vicky, no point in feeling bad for yourself.*

Cssshh, tick. Cssshh, tick.

She turned, squinting at the wall behind the shelving. Someone had moved the shelf out again. A hunched figure sat along the back wall, backlit by a yellowed glow—the flashlight— shoulders flexing as they did something beyond her line of sight. But the noise…what was that sound? She stepped around the side of the unit.

"Chad?"

He did not acknowledge her. Maybe he'd found something.

Please let him have a way out, please, please, please.

The flashlight he'd positioned at his feet cast eerie shadows on the floor and the walls, making his laboring silhouette into a hulking thing, a hunchback. A monster. *Tick, tick, scrape, cssshhhh.* His shoulders and back hid his hands from view as he worked, arms moving from one side to the other, right to left, over and over.

She reached the wall. "Chad?" Her voice was strained, higher pitched than it should have been and it seemed to echo around them like a scream in a cave though she was sure she'd whispered it.

He finally raised his head and sat back. His fingers and knuckles were slashed open, striations of dark red and brown smeared across the wall from his bloodied hands. And glinting between his palms, the crowbar. "I thought I could… maybe dig enough to…I don't know…" Wheezing, he was wheezing. She peered past him at the long scratches in the cement—barely deep enough to be called gouges. Yet.

"I mean it's fine, it's probably fine…"

Probably fine? Nothing was fucking fine. And when she touched his shoulder—dry, but hot, so fucking hot. He was burning up.

He swiped an arm over his flushed forehead, though his skin wasn't the least bit damp. "The generator has to be working from somewhere nearby, and there isn't any reason to think the tunnels are flooded. We could get out if we make a hole big enough to squeeze through."

The back of her neck prickled and she glanced over at Earl, down the way in his little dark corner, exposed now that Chad had moved the shelf again. The yellow light bounced off the whites of his eyes and glittered in his silver hair. He was silent. Watching. He hadn't wanted them to dig but he wasn't doing anything to stop Chad. He knew they couldn't break through.

"Has to be better than staying here," Chad was saying.

But he'd always been fine staying in one place.

He whipped his head back as if she'd slapped him. Why was he looking at her like that? Oh shit, had she said that out loud? From the look on his face, she had. His hands shook, metal tapping the wall, eyes still on her face, then a dripping sound that irritated the back of her brain because it wasn't real, she knew it wasn't real, and yet her body was responding as if there really was a bucket of water for her to drink. Her stomach roiled. Her mouth itched and burned.

Chad sniffed and turned away. "Meaning I didn't want to move forward with you, right? That's what you want me to say?"

"I don't want you to say anything." It didn't matter anymore, did it? Chad was the one person here she was still on speaking terms with—she didn't want to lose her only ally. Though, watching him scrape at that wall in the dark, trying to get them out of there, reliable, dependable even during this bout of fevered madness...maybe she didn't want to lose Chad. Maybe there was something to be said for comfort. She pushed the thoughts back down.

He sighed. "I'm sorry, okay? I'm sorry for everything, if I was absent, or didn't talk to you enough, if I just...wanted things to stay the same. I didn't want to tell you I was unhappy, at least not until I had a better plan—a way to fix it."

He'd been unhappy? She sat beside him on the cement. "Why didn't you say something?"

"You weren't happy either." He met her eyes. "I thought it was because of your brother, that you followed him down here but never found him. Then I realized...he was all that was keeping you in Louisiana." Chad faced the wall again, raised the crowbar. *Scrape, csshhh, tick, cshhh.*

"Chad?"

He dug at the wall, harder, faster. *Scrape, csshhh, cshhh-scrape, csshhhcshhh.* Refusing to meet her eyes. Because he knew she'd see something he didn't want her to? This wasn't just about their relationship. *He knows Windy. Doesn't he? Am I crazy?*

"Chad!"

The crowbar stopped mid-stroke. Chad drew his gaze back to her and before she could say anything he blurted: "I lied to you, okay?" His voice cracked. "The PI...a few weeks before the storm hit, he called the house. Told me Phillip was dead. I didn't want to tell you. I knew you'd leave—you sure weren't going to stay in this little town for me."

Phillip. The room was spinning, blackness tunneling her vision. Dead, weeks ago. And he'd... "How could you not tell me?"

He gripped the crowbar tighter, wincing, fingers sticky with blood. "I'm sorry, Vick, I just wanted to wait until...I thought we could figure things out, that maybe you'd talk to me about whatever was bothering you, but you were just so distant." And then she met his eyes...hurt, not only sorrow or grief or guilt—anger. *He was all that was keeping you here.* Had he found the divorce papers?

"How long have you known?"

"That you want to leave me? I'm not an idiot, Vick. You

don't even want to be in the same room with me." He shook his head. "She was right."

"Who was right?" *Like it matters now. Phillip's dead, he's fucking dead.*

"Windy." His lip trembled, but no tears came.

Windy. The tunnel she'd been looking through closed. Red clouded her vision. She'd thought it illogical, insane even, that her straight-laced ever-dependable husband had known this woman and hadn't said a word about it. She'd been wrong. Her rib cage was too small. "Did you start fucking her before or after you found the divorce papers?" she said quietly.

His head snapped up. "No! I mean..." He sighed. "Okay, I found the papers in the drawer. I was looking for a pen—"

"Answer the question. Did you start—"

"We met...maybe six months ago, over at Delaney's."

"The diner? What does that have to do with—"

"I was in counseling at the building across the street. I used to go there after my appointments." His hands shook. "She saw me leaving the office, and she walked with me to the diner, asked if we could sit together. She seemed so sad, I didn't have the heart to tell her no..." He dropped his eyes. "It just kinda happened and—"

"It just happened? You were just walking by and your dick magically *fell* into her?"

"I didn't sleep with her!" he cried. "We only had coffee at the diner like three times, all right after therapy if we happened to be leaving at the same time. That's it."

The room was still spinning. *Why the fuck did he lie about therapy? Are Nick and I the only ones who don't know Windy? I should have just divorced Chad, I'd be in Chicago now.* And Phillip, how could Chad keep that from her, how fucking could he? *Don't think about Phillip, don't think about your sweet brother, dead, dead, dead.* What mattered right now? Windy. Chad knew something about the woman who'd locked them up. "And what about her? What do you know—"

"She told me she was in therapy because she felt lonely. That she didn't really have anyone except her brother, and she wanted things to get better between them so she could… feel better I guess. She seemed like she had low self-esteem. Kinda confused."

"Why would she want to work on her relationship with a monster?" *Because she's a monster too*, Phillip's voice whispered, then her own voice: *He's dead, my brother's dead.*

Don't think about that now. Think about it later. But her chest hurt like someone had put her heart in a vise.

"If someone says they want to fix their family, you don't ask them why," Chad was saying, bringing her back. "And really…that's all I know. She didn't talk about herself all that much."

Victoria inhaled hard through her nose. "If you're just friends, only friends, you don't hide it. And you don't hide that you're going to therapy from your wife." But the divorce papers now floating in their dresser did not make her a paragon of truthfulness.

"She thought you might be upset."

"*She* thought? And you listened to her?" Too bad he hadn't told her he'd made a new friend who listened better than his wife. She wouldn't have been in town to get stuck on the roof in the first place—she would have been in fucking Chicago.

Chad kept talking as if he hadn't heard her. "And I did ask you to go to therapy with me, remember? You said no." His lip trembled. "You and I were…in a bad place. And you didn't want to help me fix it."

Victoria frowned. He had asked. Asked on the day she was supposed to leave on a dig, and she'd forgotten all about it. But he'd never asked again.

Because Chad wasn't the fighter—she was.

And now they were locked in a little room and Windy knew everyone here except for her. *Unless Windy thinks she knows me too.*

"What did you tell her about me?" she said slowly.

"It was small talk at first. But pretty soon I was talking about how I missed you." His lip trembled—embarrassed? *Ashamed.* "How I worried you'd leave me."

Her fists were so tight she could almost hear the tendons rubbing together. But...was he telling the truth? Did she care? The more she considered it, the more she realized she wasn't upset that he knew Windy, or that he'd gone to therapy; she was upset because Chad was the reason they were down here. No one would be out in the boonies on a tiny boat unless they knew where to look. And Phillip, god, Phillip was—

"Did she know we were staying home? During the storm?"

He could not meet her gaze. His hands clenched and unclenched around the crowbar.

"She told you she had shelter if you needed it, didn't she?"

He nodded.

"Do you know why she chose us? Why we're here?"

He shook his head, eyes glassy. Her nice guy husband had killed them both. And suddenly she could think of nothing else to say.

Chad went back to the wall, shoulders flexing, breath coming rapidly—*scrape, csshhh, csshhh*. Across the room, one of the others shifted with the hiss of fabric on fabric. The shadows around them remained amorphous mounds in the dark, but when she squinted she could almost see Phillip's silhouette, bloated, hunched, and rotting, skin blue the way it had been the day they'd drowned. This time, no one had been there to bring him back.

Is this a nightmare? That idea seemed as logical as anything else.

Victoria made her way back to her sleeping bag. Her mind spun. She closed her burning eyes, feeling for the knife that was still tucked beneath, praying for just one opportunity to use it, imagining slitting Windy's throat.

I'm dead, Phillip whispered in the blackness, and he didn't sound like himself—he sounded furious.

CHAPTER THIRTEEN

OFF. On. Off. On. Off. On.

On.

She blinked hard, trying to force the room into focus, but her eyes were sandpapery, drawing themselves closed despite the brilliant florescent lights. Without a watch or any other way to keep time, the lights had become her only frame of reference; every time the room snapped back into existence, the next day dawned in her brain. Nine hash marks. And her nerves…

Victoria's chest was tight in a way that felt like anxiety, but it wasn't, or at least it wasn't only that—exhaustion too. She hadn't eaten since they'd divvied up the food. She wanted to cross the room to her sleeping bag, pull the flaps over her eyes, and sleep for a month. Maybe it was grief. For Phillip or for herself? Probably both.

Victoria pressed her back against the wall. The cement was cold, but it felt nice. Her skin was hot and itchy, not from her stiff clothing this time, but from the energy of too many bodies too close together. All of them in a single line against this wall. She wasn't a fan of people on her best day, but the people she was sitting with now...they hated her. Maybe Chad did too, though she wasn't sure how she felt about him—her grief, that steady, lonely ache, had overridden her fury at being lied to.

Olivia leaned back against the cement wall beside Victoria, her eyes bloodshot. Waiting. Carter's eyes were glassy too, the hollows of his cheekbones angular and sharp against the round curves on his smiley face T-shirt. On her other side, Chad's elbow was hot enough to burn, but his leg wound didn't appear near as swollen.

Victoria sighed, hating the way it shivered past her lips. Time was definitely lagging, a slow crawl toward eternity.

Nick fingered the deck of playing cards, then the bag of bread sitting in front of them. "Should we do this?"

They all nodded. And watched as Nick opened the bag, watched him break each slice in half, listened to the rustle of the plastic, the steady hiss of their own breathing. Nick laid the pieces on the now empty sack.

"I still don't think you oughta get any," Earl snapped at Nick.

Carter shook his head. "We can't just let him starve. He hasn't eaten in days."

And the extra half slice of bread split between the rest of us wouldn't do much. But her belly rumbled as if in protest of that thought, hot and angry. Greedy.

"He ate more'n his share, we sure as hell—"

"You're outvoted," Carter said. "Let it go." They had an alliance, Carter and Nick. An alliance Earl wasn't part of—Victoria and Chad were on the outside too.

Earl glared at Nick, but pinched the bread between the index and thumb of his scarred hand, his skin pink and rough as a boiled crab claw. Then he retreated back to his little spot in the corner. Through the spaces between the shelves, Victoria could see the steel beam and the metal sheeting

Chad had managed to unearth with the crowbar: dinged but unbroken. They weren't going to escape through the wall. Earl had been telling the truth.

Earl shook his head at the gouged cement and muttered, "I told y'all," as he climbed onto his sleeping bag. Chad took his half a slice back to his bed too—"Tired." Her arm was cold where he'd been sitting, his absence thick, heavy, like her tongue.

Nick shoved his bread into his mouth, and Carter did the same. Olivia nibbled hers. Victoria's slice lay soft in her palm. Her salivary glands tingled, but there was no fluid to wet her mouth. She tried to swallow but failed.

Earl still had his eyes on the metal beneath the crumbling jags of cement.

"What about the ceiling, Earl?" Victoria asked, her voice far too harsh, but not from anger—raspy. Painful.

He sniffed. "All steel. I put that in myself."

"Why should we believe you?" Nick said around his slice.

"Y'all don't have to, I guess," Earl muttered. "Go ahead, waste your time and your energy, you can't hurt nothin' up there."

Victoria raised her bread to her lips, no scent, and she realized she hadn't been able to smell anything in days. Not even the rotting garbage, and that had to stink by now. She licked her cracked lips. Her belly clenched.

The half slice stuck to her dry tongue like glue.

Victoria gagged, then sipped her water, one glorious, delicious, perfect sip. Forced herself not to chug what was left in the bottle—her last bottle. Forced herself not to think about the single box of cereal that was their last source of food. They needed to save it as long as they could. Not only were they unsure how long they'd be down here, but digestion required fluids, and they had none to spare. She glanced at the bottle in her hand. Half a bottle more—it'd be gone by tomorrow. And what then? Their bleached cleaning water? But even that wouldn't last forever.

A steady *thip, thip, thip* cut the air—Nick dealing cards straight down the line, one pile in front of each of them. No one looked her way. But he'd…dealt her in. She picked up her pile, and when Olivia stood to sit across from Carter, Victoria followed suit and sat beside her, their backs to Chad. Maybe the others had realized that whatever Windy had told them about her—that they were like sisters—was a lie. There was some relief in that, but not enough to quell the awful aching hole in her heart.

"How do you guys feel about Beyoncé?" Carter said, looking at his cards.

Victoria balked. Nick cocked his head. "What?"

"That singer, you know."

"I know who she is, just…"

Carter grinned, and for a moment his smile matched the one on his tie-dyed T-shirt. "She has that song, about freedom or whatever. I was thinking that if I get out of here, I'll sing it to Windy. Like, after I kick her in the tit or something."

They all stared at him. Then Nick laughed, loud and long. Victoria and Olivia looked at one another, frowning, but the vibrations in the room, Nick's insane giggling bouncing off the walls made Victoria's belly contract around that bread, and soon she was chuckling, then full on snort-laughing despite the discomfort in her chest. It wasn't that funny, not really, and her brother was dead, her husband was a liar, and the world was falling apart, but the noises were exploding from her mouth, from everyone's mouth, filling the room with brilliant, bright, hysterical laughter.

Hysterical. Absolutely mind-numbingly hysterical. But she couldn't seem to stop—she was choking on it.

Nick wiped his eyes. "Only a guy like you would want to serenade his captor."

Olivia panted: "What makes you think singing to her will help?"

"No, it's like...to make a point."

"And what point would that be?" Nick asked, but Olivia said, "Yes, Carter, why would singing to her lend a helping foot?" But she was grinning so wide...she'd made the error on purpose. She was fucking with them.

Victoria's sides hurt, her face hurt from smiling, and for a moment she could have been at home, with Chad. The whole first week after they moved in together, they'd spent every night watching stupid movies and cackling like idiots.

She glanced back at her husband—sitting on his bag. He was smiling at her, though it was tired, strained. His lip trembled. But he scooted closer and reached out his hand anyway, tentative as if sure she'd spit on it.

She paused—*You lied to me*—but there was a piece of her that didn't care. He'd always been so wishy-washy, and though he'd lied to her about Phillip, though this was a grievous sin, it was perhaps the single most decisive action he'd ever taken in defense of their relationship...that and his secret therapy. *He was all that was keeping you here.* Chad's face fell and he started to pull his hand back, but she took it. And squeezed.

Clank.

Nick stopped laughing.

They all froze.

Thunk.

The hatch.

Victoria dropped Chad's hand, and her cards. Windy was back. They were getting the fuck out of there, were going to go sit on top of the hatch, watch the water rise inch by inch knowing that they weren't trapped in this fucking cement room with no way out. She rolled onto her knees, pushing herself up. Dizziness tried to drag her down.

Nick was already up and grinning ear to ear, hustling for the corner—for the trash bag? Victoria clambered to her feet along with Olivia and Carter, her chest light. Another squeal rang out from above, and with the creak of the door came the roar of wind and water—*Water!*—sprinkles, not a deluge, pattering onto the tile at the base of the ladder.

"Tally-ho, out of the way!" Nick was already at the bottom of the ladder, the bulging trash bag in his fist as he climbed up through the ceiling. His thighs vanished up into the hole. His knees disappeared. Then: "Hey! Fuck, wait, hang—"

Nick yelled something unintelligible, and the garbage bag dropped through the opening and landed with a sick *thunk* on the tile. Then Nick himself tumbled through the ceiling to the slippery ground, grappling at the ladder to break his fall, and above him came someone else's feet, then pants, then shoulders, and...another person.

"Oh shit," Carter whispered. Victoria stared. Olivia had gone still beside her. Only Earl moved, edging closer to the ladder as Nick landed on top of the garbage bag, eyes wide to the ceiling. A blond man lay facedown on top of him, arms splayed to either side of Nick's shoulders as if he'd fallen asleep on Nick's chest, almost romantic looking if not for the nasty gash on the back of the man's skull. Blood oozed down the back of his neck. Beneath Nick, oatmeal dribbled like vomit from the ruptured trash bag. For a beat, the rain *tap*, *tap*, *tap*ped on the plastic, on the back of the man's head, on Nick's face. Then the rain was eclipsed by another sound—a squeak.

She's closing us in again.

Everyone moved at once, Earl heading toward Victoria, or maybe toward Nick, but Victoria didn't wait to find out; she grabbed the ladder, swinging her leg up over the figures still lying at the bottom, and for a moment she saw light, gray sky, and then the hatch squealed again—*screeeeeeeeeee!* The circle of sky shrank to a crescent moon.

No.

"Wait!" Carter yelled from the room beneath her.

"Let us out, we need to get *out!*" Olivia.

Victoria's hands ached. Her thighs burned. She climbed, foot on rung after rung, her breath wheezing from her cracked lips, eyes focused on that sliver of gray. Beneath her, the voices reverberated through the tunnel, but they were muted as if the storm itself were tamping them back down, forcing them into the room below. *Almost there.* She reached up toward the sky—*almost there, almost*—raindrops cool and delicious on her fingers, wet dripping down her cheek. Then the crescent of gray blinked out as the hatch slammed shut. The roaring wind went silent as if it had never existed.

Victoria couldn't breathe. She hauled herself up the last two rungs and pushed against the door, the metal ladder wriggling like a serpent under her feet. *Stuck.* She drew her hand back down to steady herself, but kept her eyes on the hatch, expecting the crescent to reappear and expand into that perfect disk of silver—*She's coming back, she just didn't want to get rain on the floor.* But the silver sky did not return. "Who's in denial now, sis?" She whirled around so fast she almost lost her grip on the ladder, convinced she'd somehow see Phillip there, floating in the tunnel at her back.

"Goddammit, help! Help us, let us out!" Victoria was screaming, throat burning, head throbbing, one hand beating on the hatch, smarting as bone and skin met metal. Below her, someone moaned. Loudly. In pain. No sounds came from above, not the slightest hiss of rain or a low growl of thunder. The door was sealed.

Windy was gone.

I watched the hatch close, and she could hear us, she knew, she knew… The hatch was tucked away, camouflaged by the hill; in the spring and summer, it was surely covered by the thick caterpillar grass that meandered over walkways and manhole covers and everything else like prickly green snakes. And in the aftermath of the storms, no one would find this place for weeks, maybe months. Maybe never.

Victoria's hands shook, her fear brightening into rage. *That fucking bitch. What is she doing?* But the why didn't matter, not now. *Just be logical. Think. There has to be a way out of here.* And if she ever saw Windy again, that bitch would be sorry she'd given up that fucking knife.

CHAPTER FOURTEEN

DEAD. Was he dead? The guy's face was buried in Nick's throat, the back of his yellow T-shirt stained red with blood. The gash that bisected his blond hair was as red as his clothes. Iron cloyed in the back of her throat, sickening her with its metallic sweetness.

Victoria reached for the man's hand, but righted herself as Olivia cried: "Do not touch him!"

"Get this motherfucker off me!" Nick croaked. Olivia approached from the other side of the room—the area where she'd stowed her sleeping bag—snapping on a pair of latex gloves.

Where had those come from? They had cotton balls down here, alcohol, and a few bandages, but she hadn't seen gloves among the provisions.

Olivia knelt at the man's side, just outside the puddle of wet oats. How much food had these guys blown through before she'd gotten here? *Five days' worth.* "He could have a neck injury," Olivia was saying. "We need to—"

"If you don't get him off me, I'll give him a fucking neck injury." Nick pushed at the man's shoulders again just as

Olivia cupped the man's head, her palms on either side, over his ears. "Do not try to roll him yet," she said, voice soft but firm. Blood dribbled from the man's head wound onto Nick's gray T-shirt, a fat crimson worm trying to wriggle away from the injury.

Earl crossed his arms. Why was he just standing there? And where the fuck was Chad?

"I will get his head. Carter, can you…" Olivia gestured to the man's feet.

Victoria crouched beside Nick, careful to keep her knees off the bloody floor, her hand on Nick's arm, staring down at his face: pale, cracked lips pulled back from clenched teeth. "We're going to get him off you, and the less you move, the less of a mess you'll make. Throwing him around…" Nick's eyes widened, the implication clear—*the more you move, the more he'll bleed*.

Nick finally stilled. Olivia held the man's head steady as best she could as Carter dragged him down Nick's body until the man lay belly-down on the linoleum tile.

Wheezing, Nick crab walked backward, his shirt soaked with blood. "Oh fuck me, fuck this, goddammit." He scrambled to the bucket, scrubbing at his arms with handfuls of the bleached cleaning water…*oh shit*. Pink fluid sloshed on the floor.

Olivia's mouth dropped open. "You cannot use that water, it is—"

"The hell I can't! That bitch threw a dead guy on top of me!" He dunked his arms into the pail to his elbows.

The only other source of water they had. Bloody now. Bloody and bleached.

"Use the fucking alcohol!" Victoria yelled, as Olivia said, far more calmly, "There is a first aid kit, yes?"

Nick was panting. "You don't need first aid for a dead guy." His eyes—she could see the whites all the way around the irises, like his eyeballs were about to pop from his skull. A vein in his neck throbbed. But he backed from the bucket and snatched a bottle of alcohol off the shelf near where Earl stood. Gooseflesh prickled on Victoria's back. Earl's blue eyes were cold as a glacier…too calm. Apparently dead guys weren't worth his concern.

Dead guys. Was he really dead? Nick had said he was. The new man's face was planted on the tile, the gash on his head glaring, a brilliantly red chasm in a sea of blond. And he wasn't moving. But wait…oh, there, the tiniest expansion of his rib cage.

"Here." Chad strode from the bathroom, first aid kit tucked under his arm, and extended it to Olivia. Heat burbled in her chest—*He's a liar, no, he was trying to save us*—but this wasn't the time to consider that, not with a bleeding man lying at her feet. When was the time? There were too many things to consider and none of them seemed to matter. Nothing mattered if Windy had doomed them all.

Nick dropped the now empty bottle of alcohol and wiped a rag over his neck, staining it. "We're going to fucking die down here," he said, eyes blazing—shock? Or perhaps it was finally sinking in that they were fucked.

Olivia set the kit on the linoleum at her knee: one tube of antibacterial cream, five bandages. She shook her head. "It is not much. I will have to use all the bandages."

"Don't waste them," Earl said. "Make sure he's worth it."

Victoria forced air through her too-tight windpipe. "Worth—"

"Make sure he's got a chance."

Olivia frowned but nodded, and snaked her fingers beneath the man's jaw, pressing her fingers to his carotid artery. "Weak pulse, but there." Blood dripped from his head into a puddle on the floor. The red pool was small, but it was expanding, already a fist-sized amoeba of crimson. "Bring me the cloth," Olivia said to Nick, her slight shoulders rigid, face drawn in concentration.

"Wait...he's alive?" Nick's eyes widened. "Like...for sure alive?"

Olivia glanced up. "Yes, just unconscious. Now can you..." She waved to the bloody rag slung over the lip of the bucket.

Nick frowned but complied, setting the bucket and rag behind Olivia as if he had suddenly decided he'd rather move the entire bucket than touch the soiled cloth again. He set a bottle full of alcohol beside it.

They watched Olivia pour the alcohol onto the cloth and then swab it across the man's neck, then higher, just below the wound, carefully dabbing to avoid pulling clotting blood from the surface. The sharp bite of alcohol and iron stung Victoria's nostrils. She looked into the bucket, at the pinkish-gray water. Contaminated. "Is there more bleach somewhere?"

Carter shook his head. "Nah, she took the bottle back up with her."

Of course she did. "Where did you get the gloves, Olivia?" Victoria asked. If she let herself think, let herself lose focus... she'd lose more than her grasp on logic. She'd lose her fucking mind.

Olivia patted her hip pocket. "I am in nursing school. I use the gloves for my clinicals, still had a pair from class when we came down."

"You have gloves but no backpack?"

Olivia turned her gaze to Carter. "I was told there would not be room for bags. And that we would be out and home before I even needed new clothes." She frowned as another bloody drip sluiced over the man's ear. He moaned.

"Can you hear me?" Olivia asked softly.

Silence.

Olivia laid one hand between his shoulder blades, the other carefully moving aside his hair. If that wound was as deep as it looked, Victoria didn't need to be a doctor to know he'd probably get an infection. Or worse.

"We will need to apply pressure," Olivia said, eyes still on the man's head. Then she laid the cloth against the wound, and slid her other hand beneath his forehead. The muscles in her forearms coiled. The man went rigid, sucked in a breath, and mumbled something.

"Do not move." Olivia's calm voice was every bit the patient physician. "I need to stop the bleeding."

"What are…where…" He tried to heave himself up, but Olivia pressed harder on his head and he moaned again.

"Stay still. You passed out, and you have a head injury. You might have a neck injury." Her eyes darkened as she said it. If he had a spinal injury, he was screwed. Then again, maybe a quick death was preferable to the slow agony of starvation. *How had Phillip died?* Victoria forced the thought away. *Think about that later.* If there was a later.

The man wriggled again, pushing against the floor so hard that Olivia faltered. Her bare feet slid in the blood as she tried to stay upright. "Sir, just let me get the bleeding under contr—"

He moved suddenly, ramming his hands beneath him and shoving, violent and quick. Olivia fell back against the bucket. Pink water spilled over the tiles—oh god, the water, the *water*! Time stalled. The water in the bucket, those few last precious inches…

Victoria dove, fingers slipping then finding purchase on the lip of the bucket and she righted it. Too late, it was too late for most of the water, but a few mouthfuls still sloshed on the bottom. Better than nothing, but if she'd had tears, she would have sobbed.

Carter and Chad jumped back as the man staggered to his

feet and stumbled against the ladder, hand gripping his side. Was he injured beneath his shirt too? All that blood... He lurched forward drunkenly, pressed his back against the nearest wall, eyes wild, frantic—a cornered animal. His wound had leaked, tracing over the flesh of his cheeks, his nose, his temples, turning his face into a city map, each street drawn in blood. But none of those bloody streets would lead them out of there. He met Victoria's gaze, blinked again, then lowered his head. "Who are you? Did she kidnap you too?"

Kidnap?

"She...kidnapped you?" Carter said.

"From my roof."

Earl leaned his shoulder against the cock-eyed shelves, glaring. "You wanted to stay on that roof? You got a death wish?" As if they wouldn't die down here. But Earl's voice was kinder than she'd heard thus far. "What's your name, son?"

"Ken. And I just wanted to save my dog. The shelters won't take him." He scratched at the brown crust around one eyebrow, his voice a monotone. They'd made it through the first storm okay, but the rain had done them in, he said. "The first floor is underwater, like everyone else's here, I expect. But the house is rated for a category five and this next hurricane is already weakening." He grimaced. "This morning, before the radio batteries ran out on me, they were sayin' it'd be a two when it made landfall, and I knew I was safer there than..."

Victoria could barely hear him over the rollicking of her own heart. How could the other storm not have hit yet? When they came down, it was only two days out, and even if it had slowed, she'd been here for...four days? That couldn't be right. Bile rose in her throat. The danger above might be abating, but if Windy was going to let them out, she'd have done it before she threw this man down the hole.

Victoria glanced at the hash marks on the wall, but caught Nick's gaze instead—was he smelling his fingers? He crossed his arms.

Ken wheezed, and his hand tightened against his ribs. "Brutis...my poor dog didn't deserve this."

"What happened, exactly?" Victoria asked.

The man groaned and leaned back against the wall, dropping his chin to his chest and for a moment Victoria saw a bloom of gore haloing his head, as if the back of his skull had exploded, painting the cement in blood and bone. But when she blinked, the wall was clean and he had raised his head once more. *Hallucinating, I'm hallucinating. Just stress, it'll be okay.* "Yeah, stress and no water," Phillip said, and she whirled around, again expecting to see her brother behind her. Chad squinted back. She shook her head at him—*I'm fine, definitely not hearing things*—and refocused on the bloody man at the wall.

"I was just sitting on the roof. Looking at the sky." He winced, pressing his hand against his rib cage, and little spatters of blood hit the tile when he shook his head—like hot grease spitting from his wound.

"Brutis was barking at her, and she had an oar, just swept him right off the roof, raised that oar up again, and then..." *Windy.* Had to be. But why hurt the dog? Just so she could get to Ken? Nothing made sense. He sighed. "Don't remember much after that." He touched the back of his head and stared at his bloody fingers as if he had no idea who they belonged to. Maybe he didn't. But he hadn't walked himself to the hatch, and there was no way she'd carried this man up that hill alone. "Who'd she have with her?"

He frowned. "Maybe...I think ...some kinda sled?"

A sled? She'd dragged him all the way up here on a toboggan? But with the wet grass and this man already incapacitated…it was possible. Blood dripped from his earlobe onto the floor.

Victoria drew her eyes to the tile where the droplets were joining together to form sticky little puddles. Below the hatch, pink water pooled, soaking the scattered cards. Someone had already thrown a towel down to keep it from spreading, but they didn't have an unlimited supply of towels either.

Olivia must have been thinking the same. She approached Ken, cloth in hand, and raised it to show him. "You need help. You are still bleeding. Like a stabbed hog."

"A stuck pig," Carter said, but no one acknowledged him.

The man's jaw softened, his shoulders going slack. He nodded. "Yeah, I'm pretty dizzy."

"You need to sit," Olivia said.

The man eased himself down the wall. It left a smear of red against the white.

Victoria's head throbbed, but the ache was waning, the world clearer—sharper. She crouched beside the man as he bent his head forward so Olivia could apply the cloth. The wound appeared to be bleeding less, but it was still leaking. Too much. Not good.

"Okay, now," Olivia asked, pressing the cloth harder. "What is it like out there?"

Ken told them, his voice muffled by his hands and the angle of his head and tight with pain. Water-choked streets, sewage at dangerous levels, dead animals. Still raining, but slowing. If you believed the radio, people were looting everywhere that wasn't underwater. "New Orleans wasn't supposed to get hit as hard as it did," Ken said. "Hundreds dead so far, probably thousands. They've never seen anything like it before. And with the next storm on its way…"

No way the storm had slowed *that* much—were they

wrong on the time, the days? She was opening her mouth to ask when Olivia peeled the cloth back. *Oh.* Nasty-looking gash, still bleeding in thin trickles of red that mostly soaked into his collar before they could make it to the ground. But beneath him, the puddle was still growing, despite the stemmed flow from his head wound.

Ken's face twisted in pain as Olivia slicked his hair with antibacterial goo.

"Sorry, I am trying to be gentle," she said.

"No, it's my gut...and my chest. Feel like I'm having a heart attack."

If he was having a heart attack, they couldn't help him. Hopefully, it was a panic attack. He didn't look that old—thirties, maybe forty—but it was impossible to tell for sure beneath the blood.

Olivia frowned and put her fingers to the man's throat again. "Your pulse is fast, a little weak, maybe, but..."

"He dyin'?" Earl barked as he approached, shoulders ramrod straight, surveying the scene like a drill sergeant. Definitely monitoring something, probably their use of bandages, maybe even towels. Rationing them in his brain.

Ken looked at Olivia pleadingly, and she smiled at him, but it was forced. "You will be fine—maybe you are in shock." But her voice was tighter than she probably intended, like she was trying to convince him of something she didn't believe.

"But my chest..."

Olivia paused with the bandage in her hand. *Uh oh.* "Do you have...um...hemophilia?"

Blood was trickling down his arm—the wound on the back of his head must have opened again. Victoria squinted at his hair. No, the blood didn't appear to be coming from that wound. Was he injured somewhere else? His face was soaked with blood, too sticky to identify other injuries. But the puddles on the floor…

"Nothing like that. Got hurt on the job last week and it healed up right away."

"What line of work you in?" Earl asked.

"Trucker."

Then he raised his face. Olivia stiffened. Blood sluiced over his bottom lip and down his chin and he moaned, doubling over with his arm around his gut. He wasn't bleeding from the back of his head at all—it was dripping from his mouth.

Oh no, please don't let this be what I think it is. Her father had died flat on his back in the bedroom, Christmas Day the year after Phillip left. Alcohol abuse, mixed with too many blood thinners, and over time…internal bleeding. They hadn't even had time to call an ambulance. Not that she would have. "Olivia…"

Olivia put the bandages back into the first aid kit. "Can you open your shirt and show me where it hurts?" Like he was a five-year-old. *Show me where it hurts, and you can have a lolly.* But candy had never comforted her—Phillip was the only one who'd ever helped her feel better. Who'd ever really tried.

And now he's dead. *Dead, dead, dead.*

Ken leaned back and hissed in a breath as he unbuttoned his shirt. Olivia gasped.

"Fuck, man," Nick said. For once no jokes. No smiles. The right side of Ken's body was covered in a horrific bruise, maroon and purple and blue. Olivia knelt and bent her face closer, and when Ken looked up and finally registered Nick, his brow furrowed. Confused. "What did she do to me, what—" He touched his side. Winced.

"Did you get stuck with something?" Olivia pointed to a spot just below his ribs where the skin was darker—black in the center, like a bullseye. Like he'd been...stabbed. But it was so tiny—

"What did she do to me?" Ken said again, more moan than question.

Olivia shook her head. "I do not know."

But his words rumbled around in Victoria's head. *What did she do to me? Did she kidnap you too?*

"Probably got stabbed with a stick when she had to pull him into that boat." Earl scoffed.

Olivia shook her head. "He has massive internal bleeding. There is no way we can..." A tiny tremble formed at the corner of her lips.

"No way we can what?" Carter said, voice shrill. "What?"

Ken looked at Nick again, and again he frowned. But when Olivia touched his shoulder, his gaze shifted to that of an injured dog, maybe similar to that of his own dog, pleading for help after being struck by Windy's oar. Ken wanted Olivia to tell him that he was going to be fine, that he was going to live. And Olivia wanted to—but she knew it was a lie. They all did.

Olivia waited until he dropped his gaze. Then she closed up the box of first aid supplies. "We need towels," she said. Nick took off for the back wall, and Victoria watched him, trying to blink away the images of the bloody floor.

"Help me," Ken panted. "Please...god." He clutched his bruised belly, as if doing so would stop the blood from silently filling his abdominal cavity. He slumped back against the wall, his harsh sobs barking against the tiles.

Nick passed Olivia a folded towel and she pressed it so hard against Ken's head that he yelped. "Hold it tight, yes?" Her words were dull, monotone, but her chin vibrated as she drew back to the half circle that had formed around him. They all took a step backward, edging away, past the ladder, stepping carefully around the mess of trash, toward the other side of the room—as if they were trying to separate themselves from the truth, trying to move where they could not hear this man whose breathing was strained with pain and terror.

"I just wanted to save Brutis," he wheezed, closing his eyes. "That old boy better have found a dry place to land, or I swear to god…" He broke into open weeping, earning a grunt of disapproval from Earl, and a hissed inhale from Chad as if he were in pain himself. Probably was. Chad had had a cat when she met him, and he'd loved that thing like a child, had sobbed like a child when it died. Oddly, that was when she'd known she'd marry him. She'd figured if he could love a cat like that, there was hope for her.

Olivia whispered, "If she does not come back soon…"

He will die. She didn't have to say it. Even if Windy came back now, he would probably die anyway—not like they could get him to a hospital.

"We should have been waiting up there when she came back," Carter said.

"There is no good way to stand up there—nothing to hold on to," Olivia shot back. "No one has energy to wait on that ladder for days, Carter."

"Have a better idea?"

Chad cleared his throat. "What could do that to his stomach?" He glanced at the man over Victoria's shoulder, then said, lower, "Did he get stabbed or—"

"No, there would be a wound—there is only a little dot, a pinprick on his belly." Olivia swallowed hard. "Blood thinners can cause internal bleeding if you give too much. That on top of being kicked around…"

"You on blood thinners?" Nick called, but Ken did not reply. Nick frowned and shoved his hands in the pockets of his jeans. His shirt was plastered to his skin with Ken's blood. Why was he still wearing it?

Olivia ignored him. "I do not know what to think here, and it does not matter. He will die without a hospital. If Windy had not attacked him, maybe—"

"You think that girl beat him like that?" Earl stalked over from the corner, eyes spitting fire, his melodic drawl flattened now by volume and agitation. "He's gotta outweigh her by fifty pounds."

"Earl, he has bruises," Victoria said as Ken groaned again. "Clearly someone hit him, probably with an *oar*." The air was too thin, and heavy with iron—she was choking on it. She swallowed hard, inhaled through her nose, but the pressure in her throat did not relent. "Olivia, the little black dot in the middle of that bruise…the pinprick…could it be from an injection?"

"Yes, could be." Olivia nodded slowly. Ken slumped to the side, breathing shallow—the towel was already soaked through.

Windy could have injected him with anything once he was unconscious. And she clearly knew she couldn't convince anyone else to climb down. Now that everyone in this bunker realized she intended to starve them to death, any new arrival would hear screaming—and they'd try to escape.

"She did it on purpose." Victoria could almost see Windy's fishing boat as she drove Ken to the bunker, the rainwater in the bottom stained crimson. Had she bailed it herself, pouring this man's blood over the side like it was nothing?

"What's wrong with y'all?" Earl drew himself up to his full six foot two, his white hair an angry bristle in the over-heads, and each consonant he spoke now had its own sharp peak, as if each word was trying to prick them. "She saved him from the storm. Just because he was too stupid to get off his damn roof…"

Denial was one thing, but Earl had to be delusional to

believe the things he was saying. Or in on it. *He cemented over the only other exit.*

"You're not worried about him getting off his roof, old man," Nick said, voice low and threatening. "You just don't want to admit that something fucked up is happening here. Because if you admit that the woman who got us all to follow her down here Pied-Piper style isn't who she appears, well, we all have to worry, don't we? She could gas us all, and then you'd shit your pants, tough guy, like the rest of us."

Carter was shaking his head. "I just don't...I mean, why lure us underground in the middle of a storm when we'd have died sitting outside? Why fight a guy twice her size just to toss him down here to die anyway?"

And why give me a knife? Why give Nick a crowbar? Maybe Victoria didn't want to know. *Why does Daddy drink? Doesn't he love us?* Knowing the why was only useful if it helped you solve a problem.

Olivia said, "She does not need a reason."

But even psychopaths had a reason. Sometimes the reason was to cause pain.

"There could still be an explanation, now," Earl insisted.

Fucking delusional bastard.

"Yeah, there's a reason—she's nuts." Nick's eyes were wary, tight. Teeth bared. "She's playing with us. It's a game. You didn't see her fucking eyes, it's a—" He glanced down at his shirt, stained with another man's blood. His mouth dropped open—"Oh shit"—and then he stripped off his T-shirt and tossed it to the ground, and...*whoa*. His skin was brighter than the blood—elbow to shoulder, across his back, over the top of his chest, all of it painted with tattoos: blue waves, red skulls, black tribal patterns. "It's all a fucking game!"

Earl's eyes were locked on Nick's arm, the half sleeve of

ink…the large cursive R in a circle of pale flesh on his shoulder. "That boy ain't right," he muttered.

Nick snatched up another towel, the last towel on the shelf, and scrubbed at his flesh. Victoria was too tired to care. All the provisions were scattered about, the room a mess of fake food containers, cock-eyed shelves, crumpled sleeping bags that reeked of their own musk, all of it accented with Ken's blood—the pink on the floor. The smears on the wall. The ruby-speckled garbage beneath the ladder.

A game. *A game, a game, a game.*

From the far wall, Ken groaned, curled up in a fetal position now on the bloody tiles. His hand loosened. Victoria watched his ribs rise and fall, rise and fall. Shallow.

Earl grunted, then retreated to his little isolated corner between the shelves and the bathroom without so much as glancing in Ken's direction.

"Guys…" Olivia's eyes were locked on Ken. "We need another towel."

CHAPTER FIFTEEN

VICTORIA'S BREATH whooshed in her ears as if the dark void around her needed to be filled with something. She pressed her back against the cold cement wall and turned her wrist, back and forth, listening to the *swish, swish* inside the plastic bottle clutched in her fist, feeling the water move—too light. Two sips left.

Hunger wracked her insides. Soon they'd finish their sparse provisions, their one box of cereal, the water in their bottles. Maybe in the morning. Or…afternoon? What then?

"How many days do you think it's really been?" she said into the blackness.

"Ten." Nick's voice echoed from somewhere on the other side of the room.

"That's impossible."

"We've been keeping track."

Yeah, with your bullshit hash marks. "We'd have died of thirst by now."

"I tried to tell you the lights were wrong," Olivia whispered from her spot by the bathroom—by Ken. Ken's breath hitched, then settled. Wet. Phlegmy.

Had Olivia told them that? Victoria couldn't recall, not that she would have listened before. Who cared about the lights when they had no fucking food? Her guts twisted, cramped hard, and she winced, glad that no one could see her in the dark. "She has to be shortening the days." *Why? Why would she do that?* "How long did you say you were here before we came, Carter?"

"I thought it was five days," Carter said, "but..."

"Had the storm already hit when you arrived?" She hadn't thought to ask that—she'd just assumed they'd come before the hurricane.

"Assumed! You're an ass!" Phillip's voice sang. She ground her teeth to avoid looking around for him. *He's not here, he's dead.*

"It was just starting to bear down when we got here," Carter said. "I was surprised she left, to be honest."

"We were here three days after the storm," Victoria said slowly. If the others had arrived as it was starting, they'd been down here a day or two, tops. Not five. "She probably cut the days in half with the lights...or thirds." But they had no way to tell exactly, and there was nothing to say that the rhythm of the lights was uniform. Maybe there was no rhyme or reason—maybe Windy was just screwing with them.

"That explains why you slept so long, Olivia," Carter said. "Your body was like...trying to stick to your schedule."

Olivia sniffed. Was she crying? "She wants us to be crazy." And no one offered a more reasonable explanation. Maybe there wasn't one.

Victoria stared through the blackness toward where Olivia was sitting with Ken, but it was hard to see with the dim LEDs, even with the light over the toilet casting a faint square of blue onto the bathroom floor.

Wait.

Something was back there, near the toilet...something

had *moved*. She squinted, breath trapped in her throat. Tall and thin, wispy tendrils hanging from its gangly arms, scuttling like a giant insect. Watching them. Her heart stalled though she was too weak to run, too weak to react, but when she blinked again, the scuttling thing was gone. She pulled her gaze to the ceiling. To the hole. Losing it, she was losing it. The only real, palpable things were the electric bite in her guts, the ache in her muscles, and the fear, cold and sharp as a Chicago winter. And the fact that she was going insane.

"A nurse, eh?" Nick.

"I wanted to help people."

"You do," Carter said. "You do help. You've always helped me."

"That is what friends do," Olivia said, her voice almost a whisper.

"I thought Windy was your bestie," Nick muttered.

"Used to be. I guess." Carter chuckled, but there was no humor in it. "I mean, even before...Olivia, I didn't tell you, but she wanted me to drop you. Like move out and never talk to you again."

Olivia gasped. "Carter, that is—"

"I know, I know. She never seemed angry that I didn't listen, just kinda...pulled away." He sniffed. "I still can't believe she'd put me down here. I really thought she cared. I wanted to do more with my life, you know? I really did."

Oh shit. Was he giving up? Victoria tongued the sore spot at the corner of her mouth, tasting the metal where her lip had split.

"You have time," Nick said. "Unless that old redneck bastard decides to kill you in your sleep."

Earl grunted—first time since lights-out that he'd made a sound—but he didn't argue.

Chad's breathing cut through the room, the raspy sound of dried snot and the subconscious growl of pent-up terror.

"So what's going to happen to us?" Carter asked. "Like… from a nursing standpoint."

"We're going to die." Olivia said quietly. Victoria could almost see her tugging on her dirty pearls. Was Ken's head in her lap? Was she stroking his hair, easing his transition from this world?

"No…before that. With not having water and all."

"Headaches," Olivia said, her voice hollow.

Check. Victoria remembered most symptoms from her travels—had to be careful of your hydration levels on a desert dig. But this time…

"Confusion, irritability. Dry mouth," Olivia continued.

Dear god, her tongue stuck to her teeth like glue, and her lips were cracked, literally peeling from her face.

"That's not all though. Right?" Carter's voice was a disembodied echo in the blackness.

"Lethargy. Delirium." Olivia's sigh hissed through the dark. "Hallucinations."

The insectile creature in the bathroom, the explosion of blood around Ken's head. Her brother's voice, that up until this week had always sounded a little more like her conscience—now it was more than that. She'd *heard* him. Her lungs clamped shut. Perhaps her dead brother's chiding would be the measure upon which she could gauge her steady decline into delirium.

Olivia had gone silent, but Victoria knew the rest. Their blood would thicken, their organs would shut down. Shock and seizures. Coma. Death.

Death.

Chad shifted in his sleeping bag, and Victoria could almost see the lake of blood around Ken widening, creeping, engulfing their sleeping bags in red. If Chad had never met Windy, the woman wouldn't have been paddling her boat out that way. You had to know the house was there. Victoria could be sitting on her rooftop now, getting rained on. Or maybe she'd be stranded in a fucking tree, but she'd rather risk sepsis or blunt force trauma from flying debris than die locked in a dungeon. *Stop.* They'd have died out there too—it was this or drown. But she'd drowned before; this was worse. This was…slower.

She eased onto her back, feeling the hardness of the knife beneath her hip. The smooth plastic of the bottle that contained her final life-giving drops of water. The room had quieted, everyone settling for sleep, but Ken's breath hitched every once in a while, and sometimes he moaned. Mostly he just lay still. It wouldn't be long now. The only thing keeping her sane, the only thing she could cling to, was that saving a group of people just to leave them to starve…it made no sense. Victoria had studied in war-torn regions and traveled in places where machine-gun wielding gangs made a habit of kidnapping tourists. She knew what psychopaths looked like, and she was certain that a psychopath would want to watch them squirm.

"You don't know everything," Phillip said.

She closed her eyes.

"Remember that little diner next to the fire station?"

Victoria jumped, banging the back of her head against the floor. "Shit!" Someone had taken her towel-pillow to mop up the water…and Ken's blood.

"Hey, sorry, I didn't mean to scare you." Chad rolled toward her and pushed himself up on his elbow. She fought the urge to kick his arm out from under him.

"Of course I remember," she snapped, and sat once more, rubbing the back of her head with her fingertips —tender.

Chad's breath was a warm, steady pressure against her knee, even through her sleeping bag. How long since they'd been this close, had actually looked at one another? His eyes were unreadable in the darkness, but his breath…faster than usual?

"We should go back there again," he said. "Once all this is over."

Was he kidding? She almost laughed. But the thought of being free, going to that little diner again… Twice, Victoria had almost died trying to swallow pulled pork just as a siren went off next to the window. They'd laughed so hard each time.

Their house had been full of laughter once too. She used to wonder if their cackling would wake the neighbors. But things stopped being funny when she realized her whole life would be wasted there, stuck in that house—stuck like her own mother, who'd been too old or scared to bother walking out. Victoria had thought if they moved…but Chad just couldn't move on, sentimental bastard, even if that very trait helped him understand her fears for her brother—her need to find him, to help him.

They should have kept laughing. Should have kept trying.

But it was too late now.

Her eyes burned, though no tears came, and words of reassurance caught in her throat. She knew what he needed, but she didn't want the last things they said to one another to be lies.

She pressed her cracked lips together, a lump rising in her throat.

Chad sighed. She felt it all the way up her arm this time, smelled his sour breath, and with that scent came the reek of rotting vegetation, the metallic tang of blood cloying in her sinuses, and she exhaled hard through her nose, trying to force the smells away. They'd cleaned up the floor beneath the hatch, but the stink had remained.

"Vicky?"

She forced her lungs to work. *He lied to you.* About

Windy...at the same time she'd been lying about the divorce paperwork. But Chad's other lie hurt worse. "You should have told me about Phillip." Her chest heaved. No tears came.

"You're right. I should have. I was...scared. And I guess I wanted to wait until I had the rest of the information."

The air vanished. "What do you mean?"

"Like...how he died. Or if we had to arrange things for a funeral. They said they didn't have a body."

She straightened, heart leaping. "No body? How do they even know he's dead?" *He might be alive, he could be—*

"Found his stuff down by the Gulf, and a...note."

"Oh." *Oh.*

"You'd have driven yourself crazy until you dragged him out of the water yourself. You still have those dreams about drowning—I didn't want your thoughts of Phillip to be... about that. Until we knew for sure."

Looked like he knew her just as well as she knew him. She listened to his breath again, his soft, steady inhales. Felt his heat on her leg.

"What happened to us, Vick?"

She leveled her gaze at him, though she could barely see him in the blackness, just the subtle outline of his blond hair. *No more lies.* "You were content to live in that house forever. I guess I wanted more."

"More than here, in this town? Or more than me?" His voice wasn't angry—he sounded hurt.

"Both." Her throat burned, but she swallowed hard and said, "But it doesn't matter now. All that matters is finding a way out." That felt like the truth. They were allies; Windy was the common enemy. As long as she stayed calm, she'd be fine. Experience had taught her that. She'd stayed calm in the cave, managed to walk herself and her assistant out. She'd panicked in that lake with Phillip—look where that had gotten her.

"Convince yourself," Phillip whispered from the darkness. "Convince yourself you aren't going to die."

Chad cleared his throat. "I love you. I don't know when I stopped being enough, but I'll change, do whatever it takes. Can we just work on it? I'll even agree never to ask you about kids again."

A dull throbbing ache spread through her chest, a giant bruise from clavicle to sternum. Her grandmother once said the only thing that kept her and Victoria's grandfather together was that they had never wanted to leave at the same time. That had left a tiny flicker of hope burning inside Victoria, the same aching hope that was now expanding into her throat. It was why she hadn't told Chad she was moving out. Why she'd hidden the divorce papers.

He was still waiting for an answer, but her mouth was sticky, dry. She stared into the blackness and coughed, but it sounded more like a sandpapery wheeze.

"Here." He passed her a bottle—his bottle. Water. *Water.*

She winced. "I can't—"

"I want to talk to you. You can."

I can. God, she could already feel the water on her tongue.

"Please, Vick, for once set aside that stubborn independence thing and take it."

A sip went down like nothing, because it was nothing, a few drips, but her lips, her throat, all of it rejoiced, sucking the liquid into her flesh like a sponge.

He took the final swallow and set the bottle aside, but turned at a gasping, choking sound from across the room: Ken's breath shuddering through the darkness, one long quavering exhale. *Oh shit. He's dying, right now, he's dying.*

Chad whispered, "Are we going to be okay?"

Phillip laughed in her brain—meanly—and her heart

slammed against her ribs. She shifted her attention to Ken's raspy breath. No, they were not okay. "The water…it's not going to last much longer."

"I don't mean that, I mean…us. Are *we* going to be okay?"

They were locked in an underground bunker, a dying man mere feet from them, and he was worried about whether they would stay together? Was he that sure they would both get out? She put her hand on his arm, fingers tingling uncomfortably. "Nothing we say matters until we're talking about it in the open air."

He sighed and it almost sounded like a sob, long and shaky. "I love you, Vick. And I'm so sorry."

Her heart throbbed, dully. Painful.

"We should have had this conversation a long time ago," he said. His skin was too hot against her legs. Victoria pulled her feet from the sleeping bag and the zipper let out an irritated buzz that echoed through the silence of the room. The silence.

Silence.

She squinted at Olivia and Ken, amorphous shapes in the gloom, until their bodies fused into a single hulking creature —zombie-like, half-dead limbs still dripping blood onto the tile. But as she blinked her eyes into focus, she could just barely make out Olivia's head. Aimed at the floor? And then she heard the tiniest of gasps, and a long hiccupping sob.

Victoria stood slowly, every muscle in her body screaming with tension, but there was nowhere to go, nothing to do. "Is he…" she finally whispered.

Olivia sniffed.

"Olivia?"

"Yes."

They were locked in a cement room with a dead man.

CHAPTER SIXTEEN

WINDY

THE WATER WHOOSHED outside the half-open front door, the sound and feel of it so substantial, so close, that Windy was almost certain if she looked down she'd see the water there too, just beneath her feet. But the floor was wood like always, dark as the paneling that covered every inch of the cement walls. An aboveground bunker turned cabin. She leaned back on the loveseat and propped her heels on the wooden coffee table. Her foot wouldn't stop vibrating. And from the next room came a steady *clank, clank, clank* like metal shutters hitting the side of the house.

She peered at the iPad. At the view of the little room. The dead man. She'd agreed to let her brother choose one—Ken had hit his car a few months back—and she'd kept her word like any good person should. Though she hadn't killed Ken first like she'd promised—couldn't. But he'd died quickly enough.

Her brother would forgive her for that, wouldn't he? But why should she care? She hated him.

On the far bottom of the screen, Olivia—the girl who'd

taken Carter from her—was dragging Ken's body to the corner. A smear of crimson marred the tile.

Windy's throat tightened, and she sipped from the bottle of water on the side table, trying to cool the guilty ache around her heart. *It's okay, you're a good person.* Her brother had tricked her, he had. But even after she'd known what she was eating, she hadn't stopped. Didn't good people do horrible things when they had no other choice?

Her brother's teeth flashed in her mind's eye, a smile dripping with their father's blood. Did guys like him go on without a second thought? Did he think about how he'd destroyed an entire town? The storm would have been enough, she'd thought, until he'd come by with plans for the explosives. He'd blown the levees sky-high and watched the fallout on the news, smiling that same smile.

Clank, clank-clank.

On the screen, Olivia settled Ken—what used to be Ken—in the corner, lowering his legs inch by agonizing inch, and the guilt pulsed hotter through her ribs. She resisted the urge to turn the screen off. *Watch. See what they do.*

Windy peered at the screen: Carter's arms around Olivia —*that bitch*—Olivia shaking.

Had it been long enough? They hadn't had time to get to know Ken, she'd made sure of that. And she'd cycled the lights, trying to make them think they'd been down there longer, make them desperate, but so far they were more calm than she'd imagined.

Clank, clank, clank.

Her brother might forgive her about Ken, but he could never absolve her of the other. Too callous, indifferent. Too hardened. The only person who could absolve her was someone just like her. It was one thing to harm a person when you had no soul—psychopaths couldn't really be blamed for what they were—but her? Oh, she could be blamed for her sins.

And so could Victoria.

But if Victoria was willing to do what Windy had been tricked into, if Victoria could justify it, if she could look her husband or her new friends in the eye one day and cut them apart the next...

Well, Victoria was a good person. A sure person. And she was strong, too; she had the knife. She'd live long enough to act, and then they could both be forgiven.

She set the iPad aside and glanced at the big red door across the hall from the living room.

Clank-clankclank-clankclank. Metal on cement.

Her brother was angry. But he could moan and clank his cuffs all he wanted, she wasn't about to give this up now, and there was no one around to hear him—not even Victoria. They were miles from the hatch door. You'd never know the two were connected.

CHAPTER SEVENTEEN

THERE WERE NO FLIES. Maybe that shouldn't have seemed odd to Victoria; it made sense, being in the bunker, and she was certainly thankful she didn't have to listen to the incessant drone. But she'd seen death before, and the absence of flies, as the absence of pattering rain, the unknowable time, were far more disconcerting than the presence of any of those might have been. It was as if without bugs the death wasn't real, as if the man on the floor was just sleeping, dreaming away in a lake of blood. She grimaced when her gaze caught the red streaks on the tile where he'd been lying before someone dragged him away from the bathroom. *Wet*. It should have dried by now. Ken had long since stopped bleeding.

The mere thought of wetness, of liquid, tripped her salivary glands into overdrive—tingling but no moisture, despite her sip from Chad's water bottle the night before. Across the room, the bucket, a few mouthfuls of bloody, bleached water beckoned. Would the bleach kill enough of the germs? Would it sterilize the blood Nick had rinsed from his arms? But they'd still be drinking Ken's fluids. She licked her lips and the flaking skin caught the sensitive underside of her tongue. *Think about something else.*

Victoria blinked, trying to force her eyes to adjust. Day... ten? Eleven according to the hash marks—no way in hell. Chad's breath grumbled from his mouth beside her. Snoring. The others were asleep, too, Earl still in the nook though the shelves had been pulled out, the rest of them quietly stirring mounds against the wall, as far as they could get from the body in the front corner. She blinked again and her eyelids rasped against her corneas. The heap of flesh that used to be Ken lay prone, one hand open to the sky as if waiting to receive some offering, his head covered in stained towels. She frowned. Was it better to see his dead, glassy eyes, the sleepy, slack-jawed death mask that came after those final breaths? Would she believe it then? Maybe not, but it was far more disconcerting to have his face covered. Anything could be happening under there, anything at—

The towel moved, shimmering as it fell from his face. *Olivia was wrong. He's alive!* Her heart leapt, but something wasn't right; his mouth *was* slack, his eyes *were* open in a death mask, but *his eyeballs were moving*, vibrating, and from his tear ducts maggots erupted like trails of tears and puddled on the tile. She tried to cry out, tried to stand. Ken blinked his wriggling eyelids. Turned his head to look at *her* with those maggot eyes, his face still red and shiny with blood, opening his mouth—maggots there too, pouring from between his lips, a living pile of vomit. Victoria choked, and finally her feet were her own once more and she shot to standing—

The towel was still. Ken was dead.

"Hallucinations, check!" Phillip cawed. "Delirium, coma, here we come!" But Phillip could laugh about the situation all he wanted, same way they'd wisecracked about their father—*if it weren't for the olives in martinis, he'd never eat a vegetable, haha*—but this time they were, no, *she was*, dying. Slowly but surely. And Phillip wasn't here to hug her goodbye any more than she'd been there to hug him in his final moments on the shore. At least last time they'd drowned together.

She slid deeper beneath the sleeping bag, covering her eyes with her arm. The handle of the knife beneath her makeshift bed dug into her thigh. She inhaled deeply, exhaled harder, trying to get comfortable, but her stomach was tied in knots, one giant cramp in the middle of her abdomen, and she was *thirsty*. The water bottle held one final sip. But she could hold off just a little longer—she had to.

Her mouth burned. Victoria could still see the bucket behind her eyelids, the few inches of lifesaving water, brown despite the bleach. Not enough bleach, or too much…blood. Her belly clenched. Her heart raced.

No more about Ken, not another thought about his eyes or maggots or bloody water, no more wishing she could say goodbye. She breathed deeper and felt herself sinking into sleep, but her brain drew her back. No maggots, no flies, but would there be rats? There were always rats in tunnels; she could almost hear them clawing at the cement, *scrape, scrape, scrape*, and the sound was deceptively like the noise of Chad dragging the crowbar down the wall.

Victoria inhaled slowly through her nose and focused on the knife. The handle. She licked her peeling lips, tasted iron. But…her mouth *was* wet. And when she bolted to seated, her plastic water bottle slid from her hand and clattered hollowly to the floor—empty.

Oh no. She'd taken her last drink. She didn't recall doing it, but she had, she must have. *What now?*

"At least it's one less mouth to feed."

Victoria heard the words, but for a moment could not understand them. Across the way, in the corner behind the bathroom in his nook, Earl sat on his sleeping bag with his shoulders against the wall. Was he happy Ken was dead? What did that mean for the rest of them? She focused on the knife. The cement, cold against her back.

A hissing buzz cut her shocked silence and she turned her head. Nick stood glaring at Earl, tattooed chest all the more vibrant in the bright light. The trail of thick, dark hair that led beneath the button on his jeans was almost invisible in the cornucopia of greens and blues and reds. "Jesus Christ," he snapped. "If you'd rather a man die than have to share your food with him, why don't you fucking eat him yourself? We've got some sporks in the back there."

Eat him? She gagged, and closed her eyes—longer than a blink—and opened them again to see Nick wrinkle his nose. But his eyes had calmed, his shoulders relaxed. How the fuck did he switch it off like that?

Nick was still frowning like he smelled something bad, but Victoria couldn't tell if that was true—her nose wasn't working. "Who farted?"

"Probably shit," Carter said, rubbing his eyes sleepily from his bag near Nick's. Olivia was sitting on her bag now, too, knees tucked under her chin, arms around her shins, eyes wide and vacant. How long had Olivia been up? *Did I fall asleep?*

"Bodies lose muscle control in the hours after death." Olivia's voice was a monotone, as if she were reciting from a textbook; she had to be in shock. *Is it weird that I'm not freaking out more?* But Victoria knew how to turn off her panic, even if she wasn't as fast as Nick. Not like you could do your homework if you thought your father might hurt you—not like you could work if you constantly worried about getting shot at a dig site. It was a well-honed coping skill, that was all. She wasn't losing touch with reality. She was not losing her mind.

But hunger, thirst, those would make her lose her mind

too…eventually. Soon, now that she'd drunk the last of her water. She was already seeing things, hearing things. Hearing Phillip, and not just in that "little voice in the back of her head" kinda way. Really hearing him.

Her throat tightened. She couldn't breathe.

Someone touched her back. Chad, that patient, gentle way he had of stroking along her backbone. He used to do that while she cried about Phillip—silent, unwavering support. She'd done the same for him when his father died. But this wasn't grief, not only grief, and through all the fear, despite all the pain, rage tensed her shoulders and tightened her fists.

"You okay, Vicky?" Again with that fucking six-year-old voice. *Do you have a boo-boo?* And more than annoyance, above the pain in her burning guts, her brain screamed: *Do I fucking look okay?* Fight, flight or freeze—she always fought. The other reactions were worthless.

She was shaking. *Fuck this. Fuck all of this.*

"I know, Vick, I know," Chad whispered.

She blinked through the sandpaper grit of her dry eyes at the dead man on the floor, the stained towels, the crimson of his blood, drying brown at the edges. Soon, his skin would bloat—he'd start to stink. And apparently none of these assholes were going to do a thing to prevent it. She drew her eyes upward to the glittering silver bells above the bathroom door. They hadn't rung in a long time—no one had enough fluids to pee.

"We need to…I wish we could get him out of here," she said, her agitation fighting desperately against the panic that still pulsed fervently around her heart. *Stupid.* If they could get Ken out, they would all be leaving. Olivia moaned from her spot on the floor—still sitting on the sleeping bag, Carter at her side. Eyes dull. Vacant. Did they all look like that?

"You'll be nose blind to it soon," Earl said from his little corner. Earl, who had been relieved that Ken was dead—*one less mouth to feed.*

"We have. To fix. This." Victoria lowered her hands and stared hard at Earl, then at her husband; Chad dropped his eyes to the floor. Chad always wanted to help, because he was a nice guy…and now he was too nice a guy to tell her she was losing it.

Just be logical.

Okay. She inhaled hard. Exhaled harder. What options did they have? Was there any hope, real hope, that wasn't just a pipe dream?

She glanced at her husband—lying in his sleeping bag once more, facing away from her. If anyone outside this room knew Chad was involved with Windy, maybe they could trace him to this place? Victoria herself really didn't have friends to speak of, just a few work colleagues, and with the university in ruins, they'd never know she was gone until it was too late. Maybe she should have made more friends. Had a kid, even, though she'd never had that desire before. As it was, when she was gone…no one would care.

Victoria put her fingers to her temples, wishing she could ease the pulsing in her head. "Did you guys tell anyone where you were heading? Before you came down here?"

Carter shook his head. Olivia stared at the wall. Earl sniffed: "No."

"Nick?"

"Comedy club, remember?"

"What about the bartender? Or your dealer friend?" Her heart lightened. Surely one of them—

"I lied."

"What? About which—"

"All of it. There was no bar, no show. I went to buy drugs, she told me she had a place, I took it."

Windy was his dealer? *Fuck.* So, no trail that might lead

someone to look for them here. But... "Why would you lie about that?"

"Who wants to be locked up with a junkie?" Nick dropped his gaze.

But he wasn't a junkie. He hadn't done drugs the whole time they'd been down here or one of them would have noticed he was stoned. And she knew what withdrawal looked like—unless his dependence wasn't as strong as Phillip's was. *Had been.*

Nick ran a hand over his forehead. Carter was worrying his cracked lower lip with his teeth, the curls of his facial hair wriggling like tiny caterpillars, his smiley face T-shirt grinning obscenely.

Olivia's eyes were haunted, hollow. She had watched Ken die, held his hand while the rest of them were tucked in their sleeping bags.

Victoria climbed from her bag and settled down beside Olivia, Carter following her every move from his position on Olivia's other side. "You okay?"

No response. Victoria resisted the urge to snap her out of it—some people broke if you applied too much pressure. Like Phillip. He'd taken his broken pieces and run off and never come back, and now...now he was—

"I was learning how to take blood." Olivia finally drew her dull gaze to meet Victoria's, her voice a soft monotone—numb. "Learning all the basics," she said. "Books do not tell you..." Her breath shuddered from her lungs and she pressed her forehead against her knees.

Victoria nodded.

She had watched Phillip die. And watched him come back to life. But Ken was never coming back, and if any of the rest of them died down here, they weren't coming back either. *A person, he was a person, and now he's a sack of rotting flesh.*

Victoria put her hand over Olivia's and the girl turned her palm up and squeezed, but it was feeble, shaky. "He is dead."

Victoria nodded. "Yes. He is."

"There is a presence here. Evil." Olivia's eyes cleared. "Do you feel it?"

Victoria pressed her back against the cement wall and watched Chad's resting form, the steady rise and fall of his ribs, up and down and up and down. She swallowed hard. "No."

"What if this is like…that movie where the killer is inside the room the whole time?"

"What, like a Jason movie?" Carter said.

Olivia squeezed her hand harder. Victoria sighed. "No, Jason wasn't—"

"Michael Myers," Chad muttered from his sleeping bag.

Victoria balked. "What the—"

"Dracula!" Carter shouted, eyes wide.

Nick laughed, but his voice was shrill, too high. On edge.

They all went still as the laughter dissipated into the air. The silence leaked into Victoria's brain. *He's losing it too. We're all going to die.* She turned back to Olivia, but Olivia was peering past Carter at the body, the stained towels over Ken's face finally drying from crimson to black.

"We'll need to do something with that body if we want to keep it from stinking," Victoria said quietly.

"We must get out of here." Olivia's words spilled from her lips, frantic, tripping over one another like rats pouring from an infested cupboard…maggots from a dead eyeball. "After everything I have been through, I cannot have this be the way it…ends." The last word was a whispered squeak.

CHAPTER EIGHTEEN

NICK WIPED the fluids that had seeped onto the floor during Ken's final hours. The fumes from the alcohol made Victoria's head spin—no way it was vodka. And beneath the antiseptic stink in the air was blood, Ken's blood, metallic and bright. Her stomach clenched with each pass of the rag. The linoleum remained stained, off-color with diluted blood and remnants from the trash: here the fine yellowed crust of something unknowable, there a fleck of grass, dried and brown. Nothing edible in that garbage bag—they'd checked.

Her muscles coiled with anticipation, but weakly; she had to wrap her fingers around the ladder to keep the dizziness at bay. The brilliant fluorescents made the flesh of Ken's arms glow a cool blue, almost translucent looking, muddied by congealing blood. She winced, but still she watched the body. There was something grotesquely intriguing about it, like the way one stares intently at a horrific crime report. It isn't merely the serial killer or the hit-and-run that attracts the attention, or the human interest story hidden beneath the outer layer of flesh and bone—it is the knowledge that one's own life lacks this horror, the brokenness, the flashing lights and screaming loved ones. Humanity is tenuous. Life is tenuous.

So is sanity.

What would happen in the coming days? Would one of them fall ill? Who was next to be entombed in garbage bags? They were all one bad injury away from being cold and dead on the tile, wrapped in bloody towels, on display like a carnival attraction.

Adrenaline zinged through her veins, preparing her for a fight, tunneling her vision, but there was nothing to attack, not now, and her waning strength made attack impossible anyway. Nick's demeanor had changed too: his muscles were taut, flexing and shivering as he snapped plastic bags from the container. He met her eyes, scowled, then dropped his gaze once more. Her back tensed. It seemed survivors should be allies, play nice, yet Victoria had never felt more alone. This would become her tomb if she couldn't think her way out.

Victoria waited for the panic to set in, the tightening around her chest, but her lungs stayed open—even her vision was more focused, the colors brighter, Ken's blood deeper than it had been just moments ago. And the blue of Earl's eyes was more vibrant too, the indigo of his jeans deep as the night sky as he approached Ken's body.

Nick looked up from his position behind Ken, fist clenched around the handful of white plastic garbage bags, his back to the wall as if he were worried something might sneak up behind him. But all he said was, "The bags have that weird scent stuff in them. Odor blocker or whatever. That'll be good."

"Smell can't hurt you, anyhow," Earl scoffed, kneeling beside the body opposite Nick, his back to the room. He wasn't afraid of someone sneaking up on him the way Nick seemed to be.

Victoria peered up into the tunnel. Black. Empty. Silent.

"I don't need your help," Nick said.

"Y'all will use twice the materials you actually need." Earl nodded to Nick's hands, each wrapped in its own plastic bag: makeshift gloves.

"I don't care what you say, I'm not getting a dead man's shit on my fingers. Just because you get your jollies off playing in—"

"It also takes more than one person to move a dead man —dead weight ain't like tryin' to move the living."

"Play with a lot of dead people, do ya?" Nick gingerly tugged the first bag over Ken's shoes with his plasticized thumb and index finger, then gripped it harder in his fists, grimacing, and slid it up past Ken's calves, hands as far from the body as he could keep them. "Oh fuck, his knees..." He inhaled hard through his nose, then pulled harder, shimmying the bag with the other hand, first one side, then the other. Victoria couldn't be sure, but she thought she saw him shudder as he cinched the top of the bag at Ken's thigh. He licked his lips.

"War makes you do things you'd never thought you'd do," Earl said. *War—this* is *war*. Earl shifted his weight and reached down toward his foot—no, his ankle—and... *Oh shit.* The knife he pulled from the holster gleamed, and not the Swiss Army kind, but some sort of tactical weapon, longer than her hand and curved wickedly like it was smiling at the prospect of slashing. He grabbed another bag with his other hand, his injured hand, pinched it deftly between his two fingers, and sliced cleanly through the seam.

Olivia gaped. "You have a knife down here?"

But that wasn't really so unusual. And Victoria had a knife too—the knife Windy had given her lay tucked neatly beneath her sleeping bag.

Earl sniffed in response and finished cutting the bag.

Nick was frowning, his knuckles white. "I think you need to put that up somewhere, man."

"I ain't the only one with a weapon," Earl said, and Victoria's shoulders went rigid, but Earl looked pointedly at Nick instead—*ah, the crowbar*—and spread his plastic bag out in one long strip. "And you won't get my knives until I'm good and gone." He grabbed the next bag and snatched up the knife again.

"Wait…knives with an s?" Olivia stepped closer, shoulder to shoulder with Victoria, her breath whisper-soft. "I will just stay away from you and stick with Victoria." But what would Olivia think if she knew about the blade Victoria had hidden beneath her sleeping bag? Olivia pursed her lips, but Carter asked: "What other weapons do you have?"

"Ain't *weapons*. Just tools." Earl slid the lip of the intact bag beneath Ken's head, then pulled it down over the man's face, tucking the soiled towels inside it with his bare hands, then cinched the opening at Ken's throat and tied it—quick, efficient. How many times had he done this? "And that's not your concern. This here is a crisis situation." He shoved the knife back in the holster and pulled out his little silver box, then shook a pill into his bare palm. Only a few left from the sound of it. He tossed it back, like he didn't care about the nasty death bacteria on his hands.

"You should probably ration your drugs," Victoria said, softly but firmly.

Earl raised an eyebrow. "Drugs? Ain't nobody—"

"That silver box? It's a little fancy for ibuprofen."

"Fancy…" He turned it over, flipping it into his injured palm, his missing fingers all the more apparent against the shiny metal, not because they were gone, but because of what they'd left behind—rough skin, reptilian.

But that was not the main thing drawing her gaze. Engravings—triangles, one right side up, the other upside down on top of it. For the first time, she could see the box clearly, and now she knew exactly what it was. In her line of work, it was to be expected that some vase, or a dish, or a piece of pottery might look familiar, but Victoria committed an entire week each semester to the Freemasons.

"It ain't mine," Earl said.

"Whose—"

"Windy gave it to me on the way over. Said there ain't no smoking down here, and without a pack of cigarettes or nicotine gum, I'd be a hell of a lot meaner." He shoved it in his pocket once more and leaned over the body.

The others were still talking, but Victoria could no longer make out their words. Nicotine gum came in a box already, didn't it? Little foil packets? And Windy had given him the metal container just before sending him down here, a box that Victoria would recognize. But had Windy known that?

She felt suddenly raw, her nerve endings prickling with familiarity, with knowing. "May I?" Victoria said, arm outstretched.

Earl raised one bushy white eyebrow. "You don't seem like the smokin' type," he said.

"I'm not, but I studied a piece just like that box once. I'm an archeologist." She shifted uncomfortably. "Might as well do something while you guys…finish."

Earl grunted and passed it back. The metal was cool in her hands, but her arm tingled, hot, the tips of her ears on fire as she traced the engravings on the top, and the feeling of those subtle indentations beneath her finger…yes, she knew this piece. From the university collection. Had Windy stolen it?

Olivia had crossed her arms, undaunted by the box exchange. "What if you decide you are going to take over?" she asked Earl. "That you want all the food for yourself?"

Food. *Ah*, there was the hunger, a dull throb in Victoria's belly that exploded up through her abdomen and singed her throat. The cereal on the shelf practically glowed. She could hold out a bit longer, but soon they'd have to eat. And the countdown to their deaths would begin.

Earl did not look up as he tucked the cut plastic around Ken's shoulders. "I went a month without food in the war. I'm better equipped than…" He nodded to Nick.

"What war?" Nick shot back.

"You wouldn't understand." Earl's voice was so hard, so sharp, that Victoria was suddenly convinced he was moments away from snapping. She stepped back toward the shelves, her eyes on the metal box.

Inside were the tiny white squares of…gum? That's what Earl had said. But she was more interested in what was hidden from view. She ran a fingernail around the inner edge of the top lid—solid metal. Windy couldn't have known she'd recognize the piece. Could she? But Victoria couldn't stop her fingers from moving. Though the outside of the box top was curved, the bottom of the lid was flat, leaving a concave hollow on the inside—the secret compartment. Victoria closed the lid again and drew her fingernail just behind the front latch, seeking the lever, something hidden in the—

Click.

Across the way, Earl snatched another strip of plastic from the floor and set to work wrapping it around Ken's chest, the way you'd wrap a mummy. But the outline of Ken's face and the towels beneath the white plastic made him look less like a mummy and more like a child playing ghost for Halloween. Maybe he *was* a ghost, haunting them, agitating their emotions—like her brother. *Her dead brother*. The air thinned. "You're going mad," Phillip said in a voice that wasn't unlike her own. Had she said that aloud?

She dragged her gaze from the body back to the box in her

hand. Gently she pulled the lid up—hollow, like she'd thought. And it wasn't empty.

Bile rose in her throat. Her mouth was stuffed with cotton.

Now or never. The words stared back at her, searing themselves into her skull, block letters in thick black ink riding on the crest of a wave. She traced the letters, written on something too soft to be paper. Something with tiny indentations. And was that...hair?

Not paper.

Flesh.

From the other side of the room, a familiar odor hit Victoria's nose, like a port-a-potty sitting in the sun.

"Oh god, there's something wet here," Nick moaned.

Victoria gasped, choked, but not from the smell.

She was looking at Phillip's tattoo.

"Can you hear me, sis?" Phillip's voice blasted through the room, so close and real that she snapped her head around, seeking him out. Nothing. But those words...he used to say them all the time when they played the whisper game in the treehouse.

Victoria couldn't hear him anymore. She was touching his fucking skin, but he wasn't there, he was dead.

He's dead.

The room blurred.

There was no rational explanation for this, none, except as a way to...mess with her. And in that moment, she was certain that Chad hadn't been the reason Windy was out paddling near their house. This had all been planned, the whole mess aimed at Victoria as sure as an arrow to her heart. She'd known Victoria would recognize the box. She'd known Victoria would look at it, too, because who wouldn't look at it to pass the time in a bunker? And Windy had first approached Chad to go to that diner—had she been planning for this long? But the storm…she hadn't planned the storm. Or the levees.

Victoria stared at Phillip's skin, torn from his body. Did Windy have something to do with Phillip's death? Did she plant the note on the beach? Was he…still alive? Was any part of what Chad told Victoria true? Maybe the PI who called had been someone working with Windy, perhaps her brother or her boyfriend.

What is happening?

Olivia was still talking: "Earl, if you have a gun, we can shoot at the hatch, get out of—"

"A shelter like this is made to withstand blast pressure; you shoot at that hatch, the bullet will just ricochet, and one of y'all will end up dyin'." Earl raised his head, as if waiting for Nick to say something contradictory, but Nick's eyes were cast down at the body, his hands…in Ken's pockets?

"The fuck you doin', boy?"

"Just making sure he doesn't have like…food or something." But Nick's face twitched as he said it, and then Earl was sighing, tying another strip of plastic around Ken's thighs. "I don't have a gun," Earl finally muttered to the corpse.

But he seemed like the kind of guy who would. What military man didn't carry a sidearm, especially in times of emergency?

As if he could hear her thoughts, Earl turned back to Victoria. "You done yet?"

Earl, with the knife, with who knew how many weapons. She closed the box slowly, suddenly terrified. What might the others do if they figured out there was a connection between her and the flesh Windy had hidden in the silver box?

Everyone down here was suspicious of everyone else. Earl was suspect for cementing the wall, Nick had lied about how he'd ended up here, no way he'd been completely oblivious to the storm, and then there was Carter, a kid who Victoria had failed in her class, who had stocked all the shelves himself, who knew Windy and defended her at all costs despite what she'd done to them. Chad, Victoria's own husband…he'd hidden his relationship with their captor. And even now, after everything that had happened, they were all too calm, as if they all thought things would be okay, that Windy would come back. *What the fuck am I supposed to do now?* Nick had already cast suspicion on her—*said you went way back, that you were practically sisters*. They'd all stopped talking to her then based on that one sentence. If they saw this, a skinned tattoo that matched her own, she'd be in trouble. Nick had a crowbar that Windy had given him—Earl had his knives. Even with Chad on her side, she'd be no match for a room full of people who thought she was somehow the target. Maybe Windy wanted her dead. Had Phillip and Windy…been a couple? Had he made her mad, the way Carter had made Windy angry? Would Windy let everyone else leave once Victoria was dead like her brother? Unless all of them were here for a specific reason, but Victoria had no idea what that reason was.

"So you can all die, like me," Phillip whispered.

Her usual severe rationality, the thing that had gotten her through digs in war-torn regions, that had kept her collected in the jungle…it was failing her. She was lost. Alone. She made her way back to the others and held the box out to Earl, hoping he didn't notice how much her hand shook.

CHAPTER NINETEEN

THE FLUORESCENTS HAD LONG since shuddered off, turning the place into a dark, vast cave until the weak blue night-lights clicked on. The water in the bucket was gone, gone to replenish everyone's bottles, the liquid cool and crisp and deliciously wet though it smelled like bleach and just a touch of iron. Blood in it, blood from Ken's head; they all pretended not to notice.

Nick and Carter attempted small talk, Carter about Comic-Con and Nick about some new horror movie, but neither seemed to know what the other was blathering on about. Victoria certainly didn't. And the silence between each new conversation made everything worse, the lack of discussion, of common ground, prickling like needles.

They could play a game. Charades. Even Rock, Paper, Scissors had to be better than sitting here waiting to die. Her muscles ached fiercely, sore with the lack of nourishment, and hydration only seemed to intensify the hunger that had subsided in recent days. Now the hot, painful churning was back with a vengeance, tearing apart her guts from belly to rib cage. She pretended she was on a dig, focused on nothing but the work, but her thoughts ran around and around in her brain like a frantic child in a corn maze. Was she here for a reason beyond random chance? Windy had taken the trouble to leave Phillip's skin, hidden as if it were…a clue. But was it a clue that could lead to escape? It wasn't as if there was a door she was missing, some way to get out even if she could figure out what it all meant. She glanced at Chad. Sleeping again…or still. He seemed to be faring worse than all of them, but her sympathy was dampened, and not because he'd lied to her. The only feeling she could identify outside blistering hunger was…numbness.

Olivia's words rang in her brain: *Confusion. Disorientation. Death, death, death.*

She had to sit tight, regain as much strength as she could with the meager rations remaining. If there were no exits except the hatch, their best chance of escape was someone else coming along and seeing the door. It was a long-shot, but worth holding on to—a little shining sliver of hope, like the tiny sliver of light she'd kept swimming toward the day she and Phillip had drowned. Just keep going, *now or never*. The only other option was…well, Windy coming back. But last time, Windy had tossed down a dying man.

The urge to urinate struck in the wee hours, or what she assumed must be the middle of the night. For the first time in days, she emptied her bladder in the dark bathroom, the tiniest of trickles, holding an empty bottle gingerly between her legs. Piss dribbled down behind her knee. She crept back into her sleeping bag and tucked the bottle beside the few sips of bleached water she had remaining, strangely ashamed of herself.

Sleep did not come that night. No matter how she tried to force her brain to inconsequential things, no matter how she tried to sink into herself, to vanish into rest, it eluded her. At least the sharpness of her hunger eased once the water had been digested, mellowing to a dull ache that tugged her from her half-sleep at odd intervals, reminding her to fight, to try, to seek out some source of nourishment. Even the bottle of still-warm piss did not disgust her. And had her mouth watered, just the tiniest bit, at that piece of flesh in Earl's box? *No, fuck, no.*

Her muted fears rolled around in her head like marbles, silently tripping her heart rate into overdrive.

Had Phillip been alive when Windy cut that tattoo from his arm? And if Windy had killed him, if all of this was about making the people below suffer, making *her* suffer by hiding his flesh here... Windy wasn't the kind of psycho Victoria was familiar with, one who relished every scream they goaded from their victims. Perhaps the knowledge of her victims' pain was enough, Windy jealously hiding her own secret evil like the last bite of chocolate. And then Windy didn't need to come back down, didn't have to see their suffering face-to-face. She'd get as much twisted pleasure looking down on their corpses.

Victoria ground her teeth, inhaling deeply through her nose, watching the darkness, gaze flicking past the bathroom door...*oh shit*. Dark in there, but the silhouette was enough: gangly, insectile, the creature she'd seen scuttling before, but now it stepped closer, into the light, a skeletal hand sheathed in blue flesh emerging from the shadows as she watched, transfixed. A sunken hole of a mouth appeared, deep, black and full of all the things she didn't want to know—

"Victoria?" Phillip's voice.

She blinked. Nothing there. No *one* there. Victoria let her air out slowly. *It's a game,* Nick had said. They were playing Risk, like Victoria used to with Phillip, and Windy owned the whole world while they were all trapped in Australia, *g'day, mate*. Laughter burbled up in her throat and she fought to keep it contained. More bad things were coming. *Hallucina-*

tions. Delirium. Was any of this real? She was struck by the sudden desire to stalk to the corner and peel the plastic from Ken's corpse—perhaps he'd never been there at all.

∼

SOMETIME LATER, Earl awoke. She heard him huffing and puffing his way through sit-ups, then recovering on his sleeping bag, a hulking shape in the corner where even the night-lights did not reach. He had to have some hidden reserves—how else was he able to exercise? He'd come down a day later than she and Chad, and she'd been three days without food when Windy had picked them up, but still. It made no sense. Maybe he figured he'd outlast them all, with his arsenal and his ability to survive on very little: *I went a month without food in the war. I'm better equipped than you.* Or maybe Earl was the man on the inside, and when the rest of them were dead, Windy would let him out. Was *he* the real killer, the sadist? Relishing every moment of their slow, painful deaths?

Like that movie where the killer was inside the room the whole time.

Ridiculous. Minutes passed in silence. Hours. It could have been days for all she knew. More days, weeks, months in the blackness. Eventually, the others roused themselves and clustered around Nick's sleeping bag on the other side of the room, the flashlight in the middle like a campfire. They did not discuss it, did not bother. It was time. They all knew it.

Their last meal was dry and tasteless, though there had to be enough sugar in her cereal to choke an elephant. It settled hard in her belly, her insides twisting and jumping excitedly, too excited—her guts clearly didn't realize that no more food was forthcoming. And it made her *thirsty*. But she couldn't do

anything about that, she had to wait, to ration. Prolonging a
life that might end anyway.

Nick seemed to be thinking the same—he stared at his
water bottle but did not bring it to his lips.

Carter drank the last of his water, muttering about how
eating had only made him hungrier—his voice cracked like he
was crying, and then he was, hiccupping and moaning,
though no tears streamed down his cheeks. Olivia crinkled
her bottle, over and over, as if she were trying to silence
Carter's dry sobbing with the plastic, maybe wishing she'd
silenced him before he asked her to come. And even in their
agony, their unlined faces in the flashlight's haze reminded
Victoria how *young* they were. For a couple college kids,
they'd been remarkably quiet about their suffering, but she
saw it on their faces now—Olivia's eyes tight with pain and
fear; Carter doubled over as if putting pressure on his guts
would ease the rumbling.

Their last meal. The countdown to death started now.

The cereal eaten, they clicked the flashlight off and made
awkward small talk in the dark. Chad wondered if his mother
would be able to plan a funeral. Nick said he'd always wanted
to be a magician. Olivia missed her husband. Carter mostly
cried, guttural and hoarse.

None of them mentioned the body. Ken had been reduced
to a pile of wrapped flesh, all but forgotten in the corner, but
they wouldn't be able to forget him for long. No matter how
many rolls of plastic they wrapped him in, eventually he
would putrefy. And which of them would be next?

Victoria felt certain they knew her brother's flesh was
hidden in that little silver box and that all this was somehow
connected to her. Unless they each thought the same.
Perhaps all of them had found some clue from their captor,
an item to convince them they were the victim she was really
after. Maybe Windy had chosen each of them for a different

reason and was taking pleasure in torturing them. Because that's all this was, torture. Quiet and questioning and *patient*, but the simplicity of it made it all the more poignant. Windy had contemplated this, collecting piece by piece the things that would unsettle them the most—just like she'd meticulously cut out each cardboard toaster pastry. Then she had waited for an excuse to get them down here. And the flood had provided the perfect opportunity. Windy—ah yes. Not her real name. She could just as easily have called herself Stormy or Tornado…Hurricania. *Very funny, bitch.*

Laughter bubbled up from her guts and she bit her dry tongue, suppressing the urge. Nothing was funny, nothing at all; the others would think she was insane. They'd come after her. Watch her at least. And she didn't want any of them watching her. Nick was cracking at the seams, and Earl and Carter…their loyalty to a woman who clearly wanted them dead, who was holding them all hostage, was disturbing. If any of the others were in on this bizarre savior-kidnapping scheme, they weren't going to admit it.

Carter said something, more moan than statement. Olivia answered. They quieted again.

Eventually, the others stopped speaking altogether and retired to their beds, and with each moment of silence, the darkness weighed heavier on Victoria, a sweater made of granite. Her stomach ached, twisting, fiery, the dry cereal writhing at the base of her esophagus—threatening. She swallowed it back down, swallowed everything back down, including the panic that was trying to climb into her throat along with her half-digested meal. *She skinned him, she tore Phillip's skin right off his corpse.* Had *she* written the suicide note? Had he wanted to live?

Victoria crawled into her sleeping bag, the cloth sliding too easily over her shoulders. Her skin felt slick, greasy, and her hair was weighed with oil.

She closed her eyes. And finally let the night take her.

~

"WHAT TIME DO you think it is?"

She jumped at Chad's voice, her muscles stiff and tight and sore as if she'd been lying there for hours. Her abdomen was a ball of molten stone—burning. Though she could see nothing but the glitter of his irises in the night-lights, his voice was the low measured tone he used when he was nervous. Like the day she'd arrived at his school for lunch and all the kids had construction paper letters: *WILL YOU MRARY ME?* Chad's lip had trembled while he struggled to get the ring out of his pocket. She'd never seen herself married so young—she'd never believed in marriage at all— but there with him...saying yes had been second nature, like breathing.

Like *eating*. A sharp pain radiated out from deep in her belly up through her throat, wrapping her rib cage in agony. *I shouldn't have eaten that cereal.* It was a ridiculous thought, but the hunger had started to abate before that. Now the fire in her belly was raging and she did not have enough spare water to put it out.

"Sorry if I woke you."

"You didn't." *I don't think.* She fingered the sleeping bag— what if she pulled the stuffing from the middle, swallowed it down just so there was something in her guts to absorb this pain? But even as she thought it, she knew she'd choke. She dropped the bag and reached for Chad's hand instead, found his arm in the dark, squeezed it. His skin was hot. "You okay?"

"Yeah. I just missed you." Quiet. Sincere. Anxious.

She coughed, her belly still twisting—oily and bitter. She pushed herself to sitting, and leaned back against the wall.

They both turned when a rustling sounded from the corner where Nick's sleeping bag had been before the lights blinked out. The zipper squealed as he emerged.

"Oh don't mind me," Nick muttered, yawning. "Just gotta piss. You guys can use the bathroom after I'm done, get your kinks out." Though she could not see his face, she thought he might be winking. He definitely sounded like he was smirking.

Nick shuffled toward the restroom, but slowly. He tripped and staggered when he reached the spot in front of the bathroom door. Victoria could barely make out his silhouette as he caught himself against the far wall and below him—was someone sleeping in front of the bathroom? For one horrible moment she thought it was Ken, that the man had awoken and crawled to the bathroom, oozing blood and fluids from beneath the hem of the bags that mummified him. But that wasn't logical, that wasn't real. Maybe Earl? But he always slept beyond the night-lights, in the corner nook. Her belly cramped so hard it stole her breath, and she wrapped an arm over her gut. *Fuck*.

Day...twelve? Only if you believed the lights. And she fucking didn't. But even seven days was too long.

"Jesus Christ, the love is everywhere this morning!" Nick said, then, when no one replied, "Listen, you know I can't really see, just move back from the door so I don't step on you."

Again, no answer. Chad shifted in his bag, his leg brushing hers. She shifted closer to him and wrapped an arm over his shoulder, hand on his chest, and he put his hand over hers—the gentle pressure of camaraderie. Love. The way they'd slept nearly every night for the first three years they were married. When had it changed? When exactly had she rolled to the opposite side of the bed and started dreaming of a life away instead of a life with him? And dear god, why hadn't she just…talked to him? Opening your mouth was what got you hurt—she'd learned that growing up. Sometimes the best gift a partner could give was silence. But sometimes that silence ate at the web that strung the relationship together—a web that was too easily torn.

Nick sighed. "What the fuck man—"

The lights snapped on and Victoria buried her face in Chad's shoulder, momentarily blinded. Was Nick talking to them? She raised her head, squinting, enough to make out Nick's blurred form, his hands over his eyes, standing near the wall next to the bathroom. He cursed under his breath, but not at her. Victoria laid back down.

The silence stretched. A prickling sensation raced up her arms—gooseflesh. She blinked once more and sat up fast.

"Guys…" Nick's voice was tight. He stared down at… Carter and Olivia. They did not budge. Olivia's head lay on Carter's shoulder, their eyes closed, their mouths open in sleep.

Nick swiveled his head in Victoria's direction, eyes wide with panic. "Guys!"

Wait, he *was* talking to her and Chad? Chad eased himself onto his elbow. Still no response from Nick's side of the room; Olivia and Carter hadn't even heard him. They were still sleeping.

No one sleeps that hard, not sitting up like that. But then… Olivia moved. Stretched her arms to the sky. But Carter…

Victoria shoved the sleeping bag from her legs, Chad emerging from his own beside her.

Earl was rising in his nook now too, eyes narrowed. "What's goin' on?"

Nick knelt beside Carter, but the kid remained still, jaw slack, one palm open on his lap, the fingers of his other hand lying limp on the floor. Was he breathing? Victoria approached, hurriedly, shakily, tripping past the ladder, Chad at her heels. White light glinted off Carter's lips...no, not a reflection of the fluorescents. There was something on his mouth—crusty, dirty white, a shade lighter than Olivia's pearls. Vomit? Earl knelt by the kid on the floor before the remaining pieces came together, locking into place, solidified by fear. The water bottle at Carter's side, tipped over. It smelled of rubbing alcohol even from where she stood. A still-full container of hemp milk that was really glue. The light glinted off the metallic liner of a bag stuck down between Carter's thighs. Olivia's eyes had gone wide, though the rest of her hadn't moved. Staring, just staring.

"Olivia, what—"

"We were just sitting, we just...he was hungry, and I..."

Earl pressed his fingers against Carter's neck just below the jawbone. Looking for...oh god, a pulse. He stood, shaking his head. Olivia scrambled back, gaze darting from Carter to the body behind her, Ken's body, and then she skittered forward again, toward the ladder, hyperventilating.

Carter was dead? He couldn't be dead. Victoria's belly rolled again, twisting and sick with oily rot.

"What in the hell happened?" Nick spluttered. "How could he just...die without us knowing?" He whirled on Olivia, who stood with her back pressed against the far wall, holding herself, rocking, rocking. "Without *you* knowing?" Nick turned back toward Victoria's side of the room, eyes glittering darkly—suspicious. "If he was sick, he'd have said something, right? At least to her. She was sitting *right there*."

"Not if it happened fast," Earl ventured. "You'd be surprised at what ya can sleep through."

Earl's voice faded in her ears. Carter's lids were at half mast, a crescent of glassy white peeking from beneath his eyelids, and that crescent was so much like the sliver of gray sky above as Windy closed the hatch that Victoria had to clench her fists to keep from running at the kid, prying his eyes open as if she could climb to freedom through his pupils.

"You're losing it," Phillip whispered.

Just think, just be logical. Her throat was a desert. She swallowed and failed, but rasped, "You'd think it would take more than a few minutes for his body to go from perfectly fine to just...dead." But bodies did give out that fast. One moment she'd been holding Phillip's hand in the water, and the next it was limp, wasted muscle. And then her vision had gone black too. If someone hadn't been there to save her, she'd have died before she registered what was happening behind her panic. Dying made your logic fuzzy.

As did denial.

"You were right there," Nick repeated. "Sitting next to him. You'd have known if he was sick or gagging. You had time to say something to us, at least. Unless someone injected him with something or strangled him..." Nick turned to Earl. "You were over on this side—your sneaky ass could have hurt Carter without the rest of us knowing."

There might be a thread of truth to that, but why leap to the conclusion that one of them was guilty? She was no doctor, but wasn't it more likely that he'd just eaten something spoiled?

Earl's nostrils flared. "Watch your step, boy. She was the one sittin' by him all night."

"If I don't watch my step are you going to poison me? Stick me with something? Or are you going to use that fancy knife of yours?"

"Come on, guys, we're all upset here," Chad said in a low voice, calming—steady. Chad *had* been a calming presence in Victoria's life too, easing her fears, telling her it would be okay each year on her birthday when she missed Phillip most. How had she forgotten?

The men remained stiff, glaring at one another.

"Maybe the dead guy had...an illness," Chad said, and now his voice was raspy as her own. "Like a virus?"

Ken, his name was Ken. Rage and panic burbled in her already twisting guts.

"Carter didn't even touch him, and I used fucking garbage bags." Nick stared at his hands, then back at Chad. "I'd say the fact I'm still here is a damn good sign."

Victoria couldn't keep her eyes from the packages littered around Carter's—

—body, his body—

—the fake food. The water bottle, the one that contained alcohol, tipped over. The hemp milk, still full of glue. But between his legs, that singular cellophane bag...wasabi peas? Empty now, but where had it come from? Had Carter hidden it before they rationed? Any of those could have made him sick.

"Did you eat some of this, Olivia? This hemp milk"—*glue*—"or the peas?"

Olivia shook her head. "No. I heard him here, opening things, but the peas were gone by the time I sat with him. I do not know exactly what he ate."

Either the peas were poisoned, or Carter had lost it and eaten things that weren't food—*deliberately or accidentally?* But even glue shouldn't kill that quickly. Rubbing alcohol wouldn't put you out of commission without any symptoms of distress.

"Maybe he just wanted to see if it was vodka," Nick said. "And you know what they say: curiosity murdered the puppy." He smiled at Olivia. Fucking *smiled*.

Earl glared at him. "You're on a fast track to Hell, son."

"What, too soon? God seems to like a good joke anyway. Have you ever seen a sloth?" Nick raised an eyebrow.

Is he fucking insane? But he was, wasn't he? They all were, *should be* by now. Victoria opened her mouth to speak, but a flash of movement caught her eye: Earl, kneeling again beside Carter's body, his injured hand on the kid's throat, and the other hand…in one swift movement of gleaming silver, he had a knife. The blade on Carter's clavicle.

"What the fuck, what are you—" Victoria shot forward, hand out, ready to grab him, hit him, do anything to stop him from cutting the kid, but it was too late—Earl was already drawing his blade down over Carter's neck. *Oh god, he's slicing his throat, why is he slicing his throat?* To make sure he's dead? Was he here to kill them all?

She couldn't breathe. Maybe Earl was the one who sliced her brother's tattoo from his body. Earl was definitely the one who had Phillip's skin in his pocket.

Nick reached for Earl too as if to pull him off, but he stopped short, his hand a claw on the man's shoulder.

"Get off, boy."

A ripping noise cut the air as Earl freed Carter's collar and drew the blade lower, across the "Smile" T-shirt, the grinning face ghoulish against Carter's bare, dead flesh. Nick let go and backed up. *The blood, where is the blood?* Earl tore the smiley face down the middle, then re-pocketed the knife and pulled Carter closer to peer at his back. He eased Carter against the wall once more, picked up the kid's hands, checking between his fingers, and then peeled one of the boy's eyelids up. She recoiled at the too-gray death stare.

"What are you looking for?" Nick asked, squinting at Carter's face. Earl moved on to Carter's silent chest, turned the kid's head to one side, then the other. Victoria looked away. Carter's eyes…like her father's eyes the day he died, devoid of all color. Her stomach clenched so violently she could barely keep her nausea at bay. She breathed through her nose, deeply—sweat and iron, the musk from the bath-room, the sour of urine, and something that could only be death.

"I don't see nothin' on him. No wounds. Ain't nothin' else it could be but gettin' greedy, hoardin' food—musta ate somethin' bad."

"Greedy?" Victoria sputtered. "Because he had an extra package of wasabi peas?" But she was allergic to wasabi—if she hadn't been, she'd probably be pissed as hell that Carter had hoarded food. Even now she was jealous. Still she said: "He was starving to death. Dying of thirst."

"So am I, girl." Earl shook his head.

"Fuck you," she spat.

"Maybe he killed himself on purpose," Nick said.

That smile, that shirt... Even if Carter had broken down crying, he hadn't seemed suicidal, had he? But someone could have killed him for hiding food.

"He did not kill himself!" Olivia suddenly screamed. Sitting on the floor now. Fists clenched at her sides. Her lip had split down the middle, but nothing leaked from the wound. "He was there for me after Lenny died, he was there, he was the one who told me to keep myself together. Saved my life. He was the one. He never...he never would have..." She collapsed into hysterical sobs, face on her knees.

Victoria wanted to go to her, but her legs were made of lead.

Earl's nostrils flared like an angry bull's.

Then Olivia rose in slow motion, realization written all over her face. She pointed at Nick. "You told him to...you said..."

Nick frowned at Olivia. "Told him what?" he asked.

"You told Carter to hide the peas."

Jesus Christ.

"You thought I was asleep," Olivia said, "but you ...you said no one would notice."

"You're crazy! Maybe you dreamed it! You were the one—"

"I know what I heard!"

"No, no, no." Nick ran his hands through his greasy hair until it stuck out on the sides. "This isn't about the peas. She's trying to make us do it again."

She…Windy? "Do what again?"

"Windy wants us to eat each other," Nick blurted.

"Why the fuck do you keep talking about eating people?" Victoria snapped.

"How are you not thinking about it?" Nick's eyes shone, bright with agitation. "After hearing that story, being this fucking hungry…how could you not consider it even a little? Maybe that's exactly what she wants. What she's expecting. Maybe if we just do it…she'll let us go."

Is he insane?

"Boy done lost his shit." Earl stood, the container of hemp milk dangling from his good hand, the angry red pincher fingers on the other twitching. "That boy didn't die 'cause someone ate 'im. He died 'cause he was sneakin' like a thug in the middle of the night. Serves him right."

Serves him right? "What is wrong with you?" Victoria said, struggling to keep her voice from shaking. "Why won't you admit that she trapped us down here on purpose and is picking us off one by one? There are two dead bodies down here for fuck's sake!" She was almost screaming through the gritty ache in her throat. "You can't keep pretending like this isn't happening!"

"You shut your mouth before—"

"You will not talk to my wife that way." Chad. Behind her. He literally had her back, maybe for the first time.

Earl dropped the open hemp milk onto the shelf and clenched his fists. The shelf… Someone had moved the unit back against the wall—how had she not noticed? What else was she missing?

"Son, you better—"

"I better nothing," Chad said, and stepped between Victoria and Earl.

Earl's spine went ramrod straight.

"You're the one without any sympathy for the people who've died. Who's only worried about the rations. More for you, right? You don't give a shit about anyone except yourself." Chad advanced, a steady aggression in his gait Victoria had never seen before. Ever. She had always been the one to fight with the water company or the insurance adjusters or the lawn service, while Chad was the one who'd pay unreasonable fees before he bothered arguing, even if he was in the right. Who was this man stalking toward Earl with his fists clenched? Whose voice was coming from Chad's lips?

"Maybe you'll kill us too," Chad said, "just to make sure you have enough to eat."

She didn't know her husband anymore. But she didn't know Earl either. Phillip's skin was in Earl's box, not Chad's. Earl had weapons, had known to bring them. Earl had cemented this room off from whatever escape might be hidden beyond the wall.

"I didn't do nothin' to y'all," Earl growled.

Heat rose through Victoria's chest, though she couldn't pinpoint what was triggering it in this moment. The heat was a whirlwind, burning in her throat and guts, but the hurricane of her emotions was worse, a delirious kind of confusion that destabilized the very foundation on which she'd built her world. Her rationality, the logic she clung to, none of it mattered here. Maybe it never had.

Earl advanced, two steps, and Victoria cried out as his fists connected with Chad's chest, half-punch-half-shove. Chad staggered back toward the ladder, tripping on his own feet and landing hard on his ass. And his eyes looked less angry now and more...hurt. That was the Chad she knew. But then the hurt melted away, his eyes hardening, and the man who stood...no, he was a stranger again, all cocked fists and hard jaw.

She stared, rapt.

Earl and Chad stood nose-to-nose, their faces flushed.

Nick put up his hands—*whoa, guys*—his gaze focused on Earl. "Just relax, okay? Don't get any...ideas." Eyes on Earl's leg. Where the knife was. "And we need to put all the weapons in a safe place, just in case—"

"I agree," Victoria said. But she had no intention of giving up the knife Windy had given her—didn't even want them to know she had it. That she'd been hiding it. *Maybe she* wants *us to kill each other*.

Earl backed off, his eyes on Victoria. "You can have my blade when you pry it out of my cold, dead hands, girl."

"Who the fuck are you calling girl?" Her chest was tighter with panic than with anger, but the words kept coming, forcing the fear from her body and out into the air where she might finally cope with it. "You can kiss my fucking ass."

"Tell him, sis," Phillip said, and laughed heartily.

Earl glared and opened his mouth, but Nick said, "Eh, we can just off him if he gets threatening." Nick cocked his head from his position on Victoria's right, suddenly taller—Chad had stepped back, behind her, of course he had. "We outnumber him, weapons or no. And then the rest of us will have one more source of food." Nick sniffed the air theatrically. "I bet he tastes like gator." There was a wildness in his gaze, a frenzied fire—madness.

Victoria's stomach rolled. She inhaled deeply—*I'm not here, I'm somewhere else, somewhere safe*.

"Ain't nothin' threatening down here but you," Earl muttered, shaking his head. "And nobody killed that boy, neither. He just ate somethin' bad."

"He ate something *poisonous* because she *put it here*," Victoria said, but it took so much effort. The words felt gummy in her brain, sticky, as if each one had no desire to emerge let alone form a sentence. "For the same reason she threw a dying man through that hole."

Earl pressed his lips into a tight bloodless line, his nostrils flaring. But for the first time, he actually looked worried. "And what reason would that be?"

"I…" But she didn't know. None of them did. *For fun? To see what we'd do?* There was no rational reason for that, none. And their little band of survivors had just been cut down once again.

Two down, five to go.

CHAPTER TWENTY

A KID. Carter was just a *kid*. None of them had had the heart to wrap him in plastic, though it was possible they were all in shock. Olivia most definitely was. She hadn't left her sleeping bag since they'd found Carter's body.

What was the point? What was the fucking point?

Victoria closed her eyes and tried to rest despite the blaring lightbulbs, but behind her eyelids she saw Nick drawing Carter's sleeping bag over the body on repeat; saw Ken's bloody hand lying palm up on the floor; saw the crust of vomit on Carter's mouth. A thin squealing like a whimper cut the air, too low to be Olivia...was Carter crying? "He's dead like I am," Phillip whispered.

No...that whimper was...it was...the hatch?

Victoria threw herself from the bag, exhausted muscles screaming, and scrambled to the base of the ladder, but the sliver of light did not appear. Nor did Windy. The sound... wasn't real.

Confusion. Delirium. Death. That's where they were headed. Dizziness wound around her, the room spinning, her grip on the ladder the only thing between her and face-planting against the linoleum.

As of today, her bottle of bleached bloody water was gone. A few tablespoons of orange urine stood between Victoria and death.

"She has to come back." Phillip's voice. Panic rose and settled. Victoria could climb the ladder, wait at the top of the hatch, and the next time Windy showed up to throw another human into the bunker...

But Windy didn't have to come back, and there was no reason to think she would. If the storms were over or weaker than anticipated, people weren't going to follow her down here. Not willingly.

"What kind of killer doesn't watch?" Phillip asked.

One who doesn't care what your death looks like so long as you end up a corpse.

And those last words didn't sound like Phillip—they sounded like...her. Had she said that out loud? Nick was frowning at her. She doubled down and said to the dark hole in the ceiling: "We should be up at ground level when she returns." *If she returns.*

In their weakened state just standing on the ladder would be agony, but what other options did they have? "We don't know when she'll be back, so we'll alternate," she said, forcing her voice to steady. "When we hear her coming, the rest of us can climb up behind the first—"

"What if she throws someone else down?" Chad.

She dropped her gaze and watched him blink, too slowly. His flushed face looked haggard, twenty years older, skin sagging around his cheeks. She probably looked awful too; her heart was racing and not just from the fear—dehydration.

Confusion. Delirium. Death, death, death.

"We might have to shove the new person between the lip of the door and the hatch to keep Windy from locking it, use the crowbar—whatever we can to keep her from latching it closed."

"But then," Chad said slowly, "she'll panic and slam the door on them."

"A few broken ribs are better than letting them fall in here to die. We should be able to overtake her." She locked her gaze on Earl's cold stare. "And if she has a new victim out there with her, that person will surely help once they realize she's a fucking liar."

VICTORIA TOOK THE FIRST WATCH. She climbed to the top of the ladder, crowbar clutched tight in her fist, but holding the position was tedious and painful—her knuckles kept hitting the side of the tunnel, and the escape ladder meant she constantly fought for her balance in the filmy dark. Dizziness tugged at her each time she switched positions. It reminded her of a vast cave, like in Ecuador, the last vacation she and Chad had gone on. Five years ago now? She'd wanted to hike up the volcanoes, smell the lava, feel it in her blood. He'd wanted to spend time in the villages, doing coin tricks for the children. They'd done both, and spent the night making love on the beach, sand be damned.

And look at them now. Just fucking look.

Her hollow guts clenched. Her starved thigh muscles ached. The ladder swayed. Her knuckles hit the cement. Pause. Repeat. "Hard to hold this position," she called down.

"We can anchor the ladder, maybe," Chad said, his voice slow and muddy through the tunnel. "Maybe use the shelving. It's the only thing heavy enough."

That could...work. She listened to the grinding as the men moved the shelving into position with not so much as one harsh word between Nick and Earl. Then she climbed down so they could secure the base of the ladder to one side of the shelf with strips of cloth. She was tying the last strip when she recognized the shredded smiley face. Carter's T-shirt. Earl—had to have been Earl. No one else would strip Carter's clothes from his body, dead or not.

Victoria glanced back at Olivia's sleeping bag—she was lying on the ground, eyes closed. The woman had fallen asleep.

"Just try not to stand on the shelf," Chad said as she ascended into the tunnel again. "Seems pretty unstable."

The shelving might have been unstable, but the ladder was better. This time it did not smash her knuckles against the sides, and the swaying was less angry hurricane, more gentle breeze. But it did not stop the tunnel from spinning around her like a black hole.

She stood at the top of the ladder, staring at the closed door, running the tip of the crowbar along the metal, waiting for the squeal of the handle, the shriek of the hatch. Through the hole beneath her, she could see Chad bracing the shelving in place to help keep the ladder steady—it really was a flimsy unit—Earl or Nick surely on the other side. Once she thought she heard a subtle scraping noise, and she put her hand up, pressing it to the cold metal, anticipation slinging electricity through her veins, but the sound vanished as fast as it had come. Had she imagined it? *Confusion.*

Time stretched. Paused. Stood still.

Nick was up next. He caught her eye as he climbed, that dark glitter in his irises vivid though his skin was sallow and waxy. How old was he? He knew how old she was, she remembered, knew she was *exactly thirty-four* when he had no reason to know that.

Victoria took her position at the shelving, her back stinging as she leaned against it, bracing the base of the ladder. Olivia slept. Time passed. Nothing.

Chad's turn. As he ascended, she noticed the wound on his leg, swollen again—it could be killing him and she had forgotten all about it. What kind of person was she? Was that pus? But he was gone too quickly for her to examine it.

Victoria clenched her fists and leaned her back against the shelf once more. The silence of the room was maddening. But then…a sound. A creak?

Earl hissed, "She's here! Go, *go!*"

Victoria leapt to standing, her muscles screaming, the room wavering, and stumbled against the shelf. Earl grabbed the ladder and climbed swiftly to the top shelf, but his weight was too much—the unit swayed. "Can't have all the weight on one side," Nick said, and Earl changed position, balancing in the middle, the muscles in his back so rigid they were visible beneath the cloth of his tank top. Had he always been wearing the tank top? He used to have a T-shirt right? Had she ever noticed? She couldn't remember. But Chad had said not to stand on the shelf—*seems pretty unstable.* Victoria gripped the shelving harder, ready to hold it steady should some violent force try to rip the boards from her hands.

Earl's knuckles were white on the ladder's rungs, his boots still on the top shelf. "As soon as she—"

"I know," Chad hissed from above, the word echoing down toward them from the darkness. Silence. Victoria held her breath. What was Windy doing? Did she know they were waiting for her?

Earl leapt onto his toes, up and down like he was dancing, the unit shifting even as Victoria and Nick held it fast, bracing from either side. The supports groaned. And then *rain*, the sweetest thing she'd ever seen, falling through the hole and splattering against the shelves, larger droplets than in the past, pebbling the tile with a staccato *tink, tink, tink.* Her lips burned. Rain spattered Victoria's face, and she opened her mouth trying to catch the drops, disoriented by the men's voices falling from above along with the steady rush of water. Something creaked—the hatch or the shelf? The men were shouting at one another or maybe at Windy, their voices muddled by the driving storm and howling wind.

"Fuck! Fuck you!" Chad, though the words sounded foreign on his lips. "There's no one here, she isn't here!"

"Grab her!" Earl screamed from the bottom of the tunnel, but Victoria couldn't see past his bulk to identify who he meant—Windy herself? Or someone new? "Dammit, boy, push—"

"I *can't*." Chad. "There's nothing—"

"The crowbar, use the crowbar! You have it for a fuckin' reason!"

The shelving brackets shrieked beneath Earl's feet and Victoria shoved against the shelf, bracing it, or trying to, but he was moving too much. The shelf shuddered. The unit swayed in Victoria's direction. She pushed again, Nick over-corrected. Earl planted his feet, trying to remain upright.

"Grab her!" Earl screamed. "Push—"

The brackets cracked with the *errrrrk* of groaning metal.

Earl's legs wavered like he was made of rubber, wobbling back and forth once, twice in slow motion, and before he could right himself, the whole unit collapsed, flinging Earl's legs into the air, and then Chad was falling after him, both men crashing through the shelving and landing on the tile in the midst of splintered wood.

"Now or never!" A voice—Windy's voice?—shouted over the rain, but it wasn't right, it was as if it were coming from down inside the bunker. And then Victoria couldn't hear anything at all over the noise of the shelving as the men tried to free themselves, over Chad's moaning and Earl's barking, and…Victoria's screaming. She was screaming.

Now or never. Her tattoo—Phillip's tattoo. *Now or never, now or never*. "What the fuck do you want from me?" she shrieked at the dark tunnel, the escape hatch that did not lead to any such thing. "What the fuck do you want?"

Earl extracted himself from the pile, kicking at Chad, tossing away busted shelving boards. Chad was rubbing his head, moaning—no, his eyes, he was rubbing his eyes.

"You sorry motherfucker! You killed us all, you coulda grabbed her, you—"

"There was no one there!" Chad yelled, hands still over his eyes. "You just started yelling out of nowhere!"

Was he right? But she'd heard the voice too, hadn't she? Victoria turned to the back wall where Olivia was now sitting on her bag, but she was staring off into space as if she hadn't even noticed them moving the shelves.

"Bullshit," Earl snapped. "I saw—"

"You didn't see anything!" Chad heaved himself off the floor and stumbled over the debris. "The door never opened, you're seeing—"

"You just killed us all!" Earl's eyes flashed fire, and he reared back, then slammed the full weight of his body against Chad, knocking him to the tiles near the wall where the shelves used to be. Chad scrambled to his feet, fists clenched at his sides. Face red. Eyes redder. And Nick...where was Nick? By the broken shelving? No, but...

The shelving. Around it, the floor glistened. *Wet.* It was wet. She threw herself into the rubble and put her mouth to the tile.

Her lips stuck to the dirty linoleum. There was nothing there but splintered boards, broken brackets, all dry.

No water. No Windy.

Chad was right.

She stood again in time to see Earl push Chad toward the base of the ladder. The ladder shimmied wildly, wrenching itself free of its busted wooden supports, and hit the side of the tunnel with the bright clang of metal on cement.

Earl ran at Chad again and Victoria leapt after them, trying to grab Earl's arm, but the forward momentum was too much. They all tumbled to the shattered pile on the ground, Chad on the bottom on his back, Earl on top of him, Victoria on top of Earl. She gripped his beefy forearm with her scrawny hands.

Earl shook her to the tile beside them. Blindly she kicked at what she thought was Earl, but then someone's arm or leg or head or fist slammed into her shin and she cried out. The noises of the men were deafening: the horrid gurgling of their breath, a thin wheeze, something that sounded like a growl, all the horrible feral noises of the uncivilized wild where man and beast were one and the same. Her eyes blurred. All she could see was Earl's back, his hard muscles, straining to...he was strangling Chad.

She heaved herself up and lunged at him. Her fingers brushed cloth...Earl, his muscles corded at the shoulder where she held his shirt. She yanked as hard as she could and a harsh ripping sounded in her ears. *Fuck.* She staggered back. "Earl, get off him, get off now!" She grabbed for him again.

Earl still didn't move. Now she only heard Earl's breath, panting—Chad had gone silent.

"Chad?" *Shit, shit, shit.*

Earl's muscles suddenly relaxed and he skittered away behind her, his pant legs making a raspy *shh* against the splintered wood on the floor.

Her heart slammed harder into her ribs. "Chad?" He was staring at the ceiling...no, he wasn't staring—his eyes had rolled back in his head, a thin line of foam at the corner of his lips. Like the crust on Carter's mouth. Poisoned? Victoria fumbled, touched his shirt, felt the shaking, convulsing; unsteady but violent muscle contractions. "Chad!" She drew her fingers to his face—jaw hard, skin on fire.

Victoria leapt astride him, trying to hold him still, and

when she blinked he was her brother, Phillip, cold and blue with his hair sticking to his clammy forehead. Was he breathing? What was she supposed to do? "Oh god, someone help!"

Earl tugged her arm. "You gotta get off him."

"Fuck you, don't touch—"

"Just back up, I seen it all before, just step back."

"Phillip, please don't die." Her brother did not answer, but he was moving, convulsing, and though that wasn't right, it wasn't normal, he was alive, still alive. The room around them felt like a soul sucking void into which her entire life was disappearing.

"Let me."

She jumped at Earl's hand on her arm, but her blood ran cold. "You killed him," she said. "You did this."

Phillip's movements eased. He stilled.

Earl was shaking his head. "He's having a seizure—the dehydration. It was gonna happen anyway." Behind Earl, Nick stood with his arms crossed, glaring like he wanted her brother to die.

But how could Phillip be having a seizure from dehydration? He had drowned, hadn't he? When they were kids or... no, recently too. He'd drowned and Windy had stolen his skin.

Victoria felt on the cold tile for Phillip's fingers. Still warm and supple covered in little half-healed cuts and scrapes. What had happened to his hand?

"You did this," she whispered again. "Please don't let him be dead, bring him back, bring him back, bring him back, you fucker." She didn't even know who she was talking to anymore, but she kept uttering the words in a voice that was more sob than speech. Nearby came the muffled sounds of crying. Or was that her? And why were Phillip's hands so big, why...

Not Phillip. Chad. Her husband, her husband was here and her brother was not and she was going fucking insane.

Victoria inhaled through her nose, out her mouth, trying to erase Earl's huffing and puffing, the meaty *thup* of feet on the floor. *I'm not crazy, I'm stressed and dehydrated, it's okay, it's okay.* But it wasn't okay and she was even crazier than she'd feared if she believed for even a moment that things were going to work out now. She was going to die here, alone in this room with strangers. Her chest throbbed with a violent raging ache, a pain that might have been a heart attack if she were just a little older, just a little less healthy.

Phillip was laughing. "You're not healthy right now. Your blood is probably sludge."

He's not real, he's not real. But Victoria's heart was in her throat.

And then Chad opened his eyes. Blinked at her. And groaned. "What happened?"

"You had a seizure." She touched his face. Tried to ignore the vibrant pink of his flesh.

Chad put one arm beneath him as if he were going to roll over, then collapsed back onto the floor. "I don't feel so good, Vicky. And my mouth tastes like piss."

She almost laughed, but the pain on his face burned through his forced smile. When had he taken his very last sip? Her eyes stung, hot like she wanted to cry, but no tears came.

CHAPTER TWENTY-ONE

THE KNUCKLES of Earl's right hand were bloody—the one with half his fingers gone. He appeared not to notice. Maybe he had nerve damage from whatever had caused the original injury. Or from… *Chad, he punched Chad*. She winced.

That was the last thing she registered before the lights clicked off.

She couldn't see a thing.

Olivia's arm felt warm beside her, but the subtle pressure was of little comfort. It was a reminder that they were all too hot, too thirsty. All dying.

She'd scrubbed Chad's wounds—infected, like she'd thought, but no streaks or mottled skin, no signs of sepsis that she could tease apart from the symptoms of dehydration. Her husband lay unconscious on his sleeping bag across the room from where she sat with Olivia. She wanted to say he was asleep, but she'd tried to rouse him without success, shaking his shoulders, calling his name. Dehydration—it had hit him faster, and with the infection… Probably why he'd been lethargic this whole time. Not lazy, just weaker due to the wound and a lack of fluids. He outweighed her by at least sixty pounds, he needed more water to survive, but he hadn't demanded one extra sip—he'd even given his water to her. That was probably the only reason Nick was still okay, big as he was. He'd kept all his water for himself.

"You could give him your pee," Phillip said, but she pushed the words away. She'd die too, if she did that. But she'd die soon anyway.

Olivia's breath came fast through the darkness. "Windy poisoned Carter," she whispered.

"I know."

"I think I know why."

Because she's insane? "You do?"

"She used to say that good guys finish last," Olivia said, voice quaking. "Said it to Carter once. Do you think she killed him because he was nice?"

Confusion. Delirium. Nonsense. She almost laughed out loud.

"No, being nice has nothing to do with this—she had no way to know who would eat the wasabi peas. She's just crazy." *But she knew I wouldn't eat them.* Victoria was suddenly certain Windy had known about her allergy. *She wants to kill me slowly.* The black world turned red.

"Nick told Carter to take the peas. Maybe Nick is…her friend."

Phillip laughed. "Some friend, locking him up with you fuckers."

"Hey, don't be an asshole," she snapped.

Olivia tensed.

"Oh, sorry. Not you. I just…I'm losing it a little." *A lot.*

"And here I thought you were talking to me," Nick said, sliding up to sit on Olivia's other side.

Olivia froze.

Victoria's mind drifted to the shelves, to Ken's body, to Phillip's torn flesh.

"You think Chad's dying?" Nick said.

Her breath caught. *Yes. And so are we.* But they weren't going as quickly.

"What a thing to say." Olivia didn't sound especially upset, more hollow than angry, as if she felt obligated to admonish Nick. But she scooted away from him, pressing into Victoria's arm.

"I blame Earl," Nick said. "I bet he's happy about Carter. Chad too. One less mouth, right?" He leaned closer and whispered, "If anything happens to Earl, I think we should eat him. He's such a dick I don't think I'd even mind, as awful as it is to say."

Victoria's chest ached, pain pulsing where her heart should be, so hard she couldn't get her head together, couldn't think of one single comeback.

Nick leaned back against the wall once more, voice so low she could barely hear him, too low to be heard from across the room. "Maybe Chad'll make it longer, you know? If something happens to Earl soon. Not like we can eat Carter if he ate poisoned shit—who knows what it'd do to us?"

Panic—blinding, racing through her brain, scrambling her thoughts. *Be logical.* But she couldn't. She wasn't logical, she was losing her husband and they were all going to die. What else was left?

A small click, and there was the flashlight, making the highlights and shadows on their faces sharper, harder, monstrous. Earl aimed the yellow beam at the floor

"The prodigal grandfather returns!" Nick chortled.

Stop fucking with him. Earl was unstable, seeing things, had already attacked Chad over it. But she didn't have the energy to say it out loud.

"Watch it, son." The light clicked off once more.

"Spooky," Nick said.

No response. Chad's breath across the room was too fast, panting—loud, so fucking *loud*.

Her heart thrummed, increasing to meet the rhythm of Chad's breath, the blood in her veins practically vibrating with it. "Is he in pain?" Victoria whispered.

"Dying by dehydration…it is peaceful," Olivia said. "The nervous system will dull the hunger and thirst. If he goes into a coma, it will be faster. And uh…softer."

Victoria's breath had evened, her heart no longer thundering so loudly in her ears. Chad, too, had quieted. Was he breathing at all? *Is he dead already?* Chest tight, she made her way back to her side of the room and lowered her ear near his face, feeling the shallow heat of air from his lips. Too slow now.

Too slow—he was dying too quickly. She'd just gotten him back and he was being snatched away from her before she could correct her errors. Before she could try to do it differently.

Would their bones at least end up together? What would the people who found them assume? *Lovers dead in each other's arms.*

Victoria stretched out beside her husband, her leg over his thigh, one arm across his belly. Her ear on his chest. Listening to his heartbeat. Listening to Phillip's voice, the stupid made-up song he used to sing in the closet while they were waiting for their father to stop throwing things.

"Don't worry today, there's still time to play…" Phillip's falsetto, off-key as always.

Thud. Thud. Chad's heart like drums marking the beat of Phillip's eleven-year-old voice.

"Tomorrow will come, we'll get up and run!"

Thudthudthudthud.

"Tomorrow's not here, be happy today, now or neeeeeever."

Thud. Thud. Thunkthudthunk.

From somewhere in the dark came another sound, a low growl, but it wasn't Chad nor did it sound like an animal—not as throaty, a higher, very human rattle.

Thud. Thud. Thunk, thunk, thunk. Footsteps?

A tall shape emerged from the shadows just beyond Chad's rising chest. She blinked at Phillip's gangly frame, so thin his arms almost looked like those of an insect—exactly as he was as a child, but taller. Seaweed dripped from his hair, off his outstretched arms, his blue skin almost translucent in the hazy lights, though she shouldn't have been able to see him at all. The hollows beneath his cheekbones were hidden in shadow. And dark or not, he definitely couldn't see her.

His eyes were gone.

CHAPTER TWENTY-TWO

"GET AWAY FROM ME, OLD MAN!"

Bright webs of lightning flashed across Victoria's vision. Her retinas burned. Oh, right. The lights.

"I'm not gonna let you cop a feel just because you're bored and horny." Nick's voice. She pushed herself to seated in time to see Earl advance on Nick, hands fisted at his sides, his pink claw-hand scrunched into a little ball of rage.

"I know you ain't right, son, and that girl"—he jerked his head at Olivia—"she said you told the black kid to take that bag of peas. Poisoned peas, ain't no other explanation. You killed him, sure as shit."

Hadn't Earl said it wasn't poison, that Carter had gotten greedy? When had he changed his mind? Olivia was climbing from her bag now, muttering something Victoria couldn't quite hear. At some point in the night, Olivia had moved her bag away from Nick and closer to Victoria and Chad, halfway up the wall; she didn't have anyone else, not anymore.

Nick threw his hands up in the air. "I didn't kill Carter! And I was just talking shit about the peas, I'm always talking shit."

Victoria got to her feet and stepped gingerly over her husband. Chad's face was flushed, hot, but there was an orange pallor underneath the pink. His organs were shutting down.

Earl was screaming, face as red as Chad's. "You told him to take—"

"It was a couple ounces of fucking *peas*. Even if I told him to take them—"

"You expect me to believe that you told him to hoard those peas for himself and didn't take nothin' for you?"

"We are alone," Olivia said to the wall. "Windy is not coming back."

Victoria blinked, her chest still aching—grief and terror—but at least her brain was clearer now, her thoughts lucid.

"I thought you just said I *knowingly* gave him poisoned food. Why the fuck would I take poisoned food for myself?"

"We're out of food now." Earl stepped closer, voice low and dangerous, his vowels hitting all the discordant notes of fury. "It's high time we looked at what else you got, son." Then he lunged and threw Nick against the wall, held him by the shoulders as Nick's tattoos undulated, the dragon scales on his forearm distorted by the muscle underneath, the R on his shoulder like a beacon in its frame of flesh tones—the only unadorned spot below his clavicle.

Olivia finally turned from the wall, face blank. Like she was stoned.

"Stop!" Victoria moved closer, but not close enough to actually get in the middle—she wasn't going to risk getting hurt for those two. "Both of you, enough!"

Nick shoved Earl, and Earl stumbled back, hitting his head against the metal ladder with a *clong*. The floor there was still littered with shattered pieces of shelving, dust, debris—streaks of deep, clotted brown that might have been someone's blood.

"If there is more food," Victoria said, "shoving him around isn't going to help. I'm sure he'll tell us." She leveled her gaze at Nick. "Right?"

Nick's jaw clenched.

Oh shit, he does *have food.*

"She is not coming back," Olivia said softly, eyes bloodshot, glassy. "She is not coming back until we starve to death, or die of poisoning, or lose our minds."

"I'm betting on insanity for that big gay bastard in the corner," Nick said, straightening his jeans, dusting off his shoulders—deflecting, changing the subject. Or had Olivia changed it? But Victoria recognized the tactic; Nick had turned on Victoria, too, lied about her knowing Windy, turned them all against her when she asked too many questions about Windy's past.

"This is what she wants," Olivia practically whispered, but the men did not seem to hear her.

Nick went on: "Waving that knife around, fucking with us, insulting us..."

"I don't need a knife to kill you, boy. And if you don't stop with the accusations—"

"They aren't accusations. Broo...I mean Windy told me about your man at home. How you take it up the ass every—"

"I ain't some fairy." But Earl's voice trembled, just a little. Because it was true? And Nick had almost called Windy "Brooke" again. Because...that's how he knew her. Windy had changed her name—h*er brother had too*. They hadn't wanted to be known as the Fossé cannibals.

Oh fuck.

Olivia's mouth had dropped open. Had she heard him call Windy "Brooke" also? Olivia sidestepped along the wall, reaching for Nick's sleeping bag—the only item he had down here—eyes narrowed. Yes, she'd heard. *She knows too.*

Nick was still watching Earl, shoulders rigid, a cocky smile fixed to his lips. The older man kept his gaze fixed on Nick though he clearly saw Olivia moving.

"Hey, we don't care if you're queer," Nick said.

"You close your mouth, boy, or I'll close it for ya."

Nick advanced on him, stepping barefooted over the splintered shelving.

Olivia's fist clenched around Nick's sleeping bag.

Nick smiled, not in a friendly way—a challenge. "Come on then, cocksucker."

Olivia yanked at the fabric. Nick whirled around, but it was too late—the sleeping bag flew open, and with it came the clattering thunk of…little squares. Oh shit. *Shit!* Were those Energy Blasts? Opened as they were they looked like tiny brownies, but Victoria had seen traveling partners use this brand in the past—super high protein, high fat. One square was enough for an entire meal.

And there were three of them on the floor.

Victoria fell to the ground, reaching, frantic, but Nick was faster, diving to his hands and knees, grabbing all of them in his fists, and Earl leapt on top of his back, the two of them scrabbling and clawing, Nick punching Earl in the face as Earl hooked an elbow around Nick's throat. But Nick was bigger, stronger, and he hadn't been starving the way the rest of them had—he'd been faking it. Nick kicked, launched himself forward into the bathroom and—

No.

"Stop!" Olivia shouted.

Victoria leapt for the men, but there was no room to get around them, no way to get leverage, and as she reached for Nick's legs to pull him backward she saw Nick's hand stretching for the toilet—the handle to open the bowl—then Earl's hand, his pink claw of a hand, and Earl's ankle coming up closer to meet his fingers.

Olivia was still screaming: "Stop, we have to stop, this is what she wants, this is—"

Earl's claw-hand shot out toward Nick once more, a blur of light, a burst of mirror-like glare. But skin didn't reflect light like that. Nick fell to his belly, drew his hands to his throat, wriggling—struggling—a sound like a gasp.

The lights clicked off. The room plunged into darkness.

But they had just come on, she was sure they had just—

"Nick?" Victoria's blood went cold despite the persistent heat in her cheeks.

Silence.

"Nick?" Victoria said again, louder, hitting her hands and knees, watching, waiting for Earl to come back, to punch her in the face, to push her away. Still Nick did not answer.

"Nick!"

"He threw them in the toilet," Earl said from somewhere to her left. "We try to eat them, sitting there in our shit... we'll die like Carter." Carter's name sounded foreign on Earl's lips. Had he ever used it before?

Victoria searched the floor, splinters pricking her fingers as she brushed broken boards and something small and cold that might have been a screw. "Maybe he has more stashed somewhere." The calm in her voice shocked her—her insides were trembling.

Something touched her ankle and Victoria whirled around, ready to strike, but Olivia said, "Do you see him?"

Victoria reached out once more in the dark—*there!* She grabbed Nick's elbow—no, foot—and shook him. "Hey, Nick!"

The icy kiss of linoleum chilled her knees and froze the blood in her veins. She crawled closer.

"Victoria, what happened? Is he okay?"

Victoria touched the hump of Nick's shoulder—on his side now, facing away—and pulled him toward her. He flopped onto his back. The tiniest shred of blue night-light glinted off the whites of his eyes—unmoving. Unblinking. But he was warm, he was so warm.

"Oh god, Victoria, what…is he…?"

"Shut up," she snapped. Because their words weren't the only thing she could hear—someone else was breathing heavily. Someone…

She drew her gaze to the back corner behind the bathroom, the nook, back in the pitch darkness where the light never reached. Where Earl slept. But the man wasn't sleeping now—she could feel his eyes burning a hole into her forehead.

"Victoria? Did he…?" Olivia's voice trembled so badly her teeth chattered—cold? Victoria felt the cold too. Actually… maybe it *was* cold. Had Windy lowered the temperature? But she'd felt no breeze the whole time she'd been here, no sign of a vent either…

Victoria felt along Nick's jaw for a pulse…hot. So hot. And wet? Her fingers slipped into something, a deep pocket…a gash, severed muscles and flayed windpipe on either side of her fingers.

Earl had slit Nick's throat.

CHAPTER TWENTY-THREE

OLIVIA'S HAND on her shoulder was a weight—heavy. Victoria wanted to slap it away, but her body was cold, her feet nailed to the floor. She didn't even recall standing up. And the *dark*. The velvet blackness felt alive and full of nasty, creeping things; she was certain her brother was there too, edging steadily closer, eyeless sockets gaping. And Chad, he was there in the dark—was he dead? He hadn't even shifted when Earl killed Nick.

But more than those things, she saw Earl, knife in hand, lips peeled back in a sneer, coming to finish them off.

"He…Earl killed him," Victoria whispered, and it almost sounded like Phillip's voice, but she'd said that hadn't she? But she *felt* Phillip too, his fingers on her back dancing like the many legs of insects, a game they used to play as children to freak each other out.

Olivia gasped. "No, that is—"

"It's true," Earl barked—too close. "And I'd do it again."

"Dark in here," Phillip said.

"For god's sake, turn on the flashlight." She hated the way

her voice shook, hated how loud and screechy it was, but her rage and panic had concentrated in her voice box.

The flashlight clicked on.

The air thinned. Nick's face was pale, mouth gaping like a fish, eyes glassy and staring. And below his chin, a river of crimson covered his bare chest, brighter even than his tattoos. Blood spattered the cement wall.

Earl emerged from his shadowed corner, coming toward them. No knife in his hand, not that she could see, just the light; he kept his blade at his ankle. *I have a knife too.* She could make it to her sleeping bag, maybe, but she had little chance of winning in hand-to-hand combat. Maybe if all three of them jumped on Earl at once, but Chad was still unconscious, maybe even in a coma, and Earl was more likely to hurt them than they were to overpower him—the risk was too severe. She licked her lips, dry and rough as the splintered boards beneath the tunnel.

Water. She needed water. Did Nick have a stash? The man wasn't even cold and she was worried about his rations—just like Earl. Maybe she was no better.

But she hadn't killed a man. Well, here anyway. And the man she had stabbed with her trowel, that mugger in India...

He had it coming.

Earl's footsteps sounded on the floor, soft. Barefoot. He stopped just outside the shattered shelf. "That boy wasn't no good."

"Nick hoarded food, I know, but so did Carter—would you have killed Carter too?" Victoria's fists clenched, leg muscles coiled, but they released just as quickly—too weak to remain rigid. Her shoulders sagged. She forced herself upright once more.

Earl's nostrils flared, and in the shuddering beam of the flashlight, he appeared all the more a monster, a human-bull hybrid ready to expose his horns and gore them. "Nick killed that boy."

When Phillip just laughed, Victoria said, "What makes you think—"

"You see that tattoo of the *R* on his shoulder? Windy has the same one." Was his voice shaking, just a little? Regret? The swatch of skin inside the metal box in Earl's pocket flashed in her mind. Her inner arm tingled, the tattoo itching, itching.

Nick had known Windy's name. Her *real* name. Right? And he had brought food because he'd known there wouldn't be enough, that they'd be down there longer than the rest of them believed. He thought he'd be walking out of there. And he'd been messing with them, talking about eating people, making accusations. Maybe Windy had expected them all to kill each other, with Nick there to stoke every flame of agitation. They were in the movie where the killer was in the room the whole time, like Olivia had said.

And now he was gone.

But there was still one killer left—the woman who had locked them down here to begin with. And Earl.

Iron clogged her nostrils, cloying at the back of her throat. Blood, Nick's blood. And god help her, she wasn't as disgusted as she should have been.

Earl set his jaw. "He wasn't no good," he said again. "He was the one she was mad at, the one she wants to punish!"

"But he had food, Earl, obviously he knew—"

"She tricked him too. Must've told him he'd get to be in on it." He jabbed a finger—his claw—at Victoria in the flashlight's beam and the shadows bounced around the walls like macabre finger puppets. "We all knew 'bout her daddy and the folks who saw those remains, those cuts…it wasn't just for food, girl. He tore his daddy apart. And he liked it."

"But you said—"

"When she and her brother came back for the funeral, he looked all smug about it. She was a mess of a baby though, couldn't stop cryin'. I tried to help her out—state let us foster her. Stayed with me and the wife 'fore the missus died, God rest her soul."

"So she was like...what? A daughter to you?" No wonder he'd been so tight-lipped.

Earl sniffed. "She was a girl in need. A few years back, when she got her inheritance, she helped me out—paid off my mortgage. Never told me it was her, but I knew."

"So why would she lock you down here?"

A pause. Then: "I ain't do right by her."

"What the fuck did you do?" They had a lake of blood at their feet, for fuck's sake.

"I stopped carin'."

"Not caring doesn't give her a motive to lock you up."

"I didn't see her for years, not until I started buildin' out this bunker for her. My son...he got killed by some gang-bangers for his phone, and I wasn't no good to anyone, even when she came 'round." He sniffed again. "She called one night, feeling guilty about the past, I guess, but I had guilt, too, over Ronnie, and I told her to go up to the church if she was after forgiveness. That I had nothin' for her. And she... well, she stopped callin'. Until last year."

I still don't get it. "Why wouldn't you just tell us this up front?"

"I think...I felt like maybe I deserved it. Figured maybe y'all had done somethin' too, like she wanted to teach us a lesson. But I didn't think it'd go this far."

Victoria watched the tight set of Earl's mouth in the glow of the flashlight's beam. "No, that's not enough, it doesn't explain how you...I mean, you took them in. You had Nick, or whatever his name was, living with you and you didn't recognize him?"

"He don't look the same as he did when he was twelve, now, and I ain't seen him since then. I let him go into the system. I didn't want no punk kid in my house, and the way she looked at 'im, her eyes all wide like she was terrified..." Earl shook his head and the flashlight wavered. "He hurt Brooke enough. He's the one she wanted dead, I'm sure of it. Even if he didn't have that food, I'd've killed him anyway."

Olivia's sobs echoed through the dark. Where had she gone? But Victoria could not drag her eyes from Earl's face. Even in the dim light, the white stubble on the right side of his face was pink. Blood?

"Say you're right," she said. "Why am I here? Or Olivia? I never met Windy—er, Brooke. Not once."

"We're a means to an end. And I'm not 'bout to die just because she cain't forgive him for trickin' her into eatin' her daddy. She told me that, cried to my wife about it. But now she can have her peace. Ain't no reason to keep us down here no more."

"There isn't even a camera, how would she know he's dead? He brought food, Earl! The rest of us will die before she comes back to get him, if she ever intended to. And if you're right, if she's punishing him..."

She'd never come back anyway.

Earl pointed at Nick's body, but Victoria could not bear to look "She wanted us to get rid of 'im. I know it. And I ain't sorry."

"He could have had information—"

Earl snorted. "You think he was gonna grow a conscience and tell us if he knew somethin'? After all this time?" He turned to Victoria, eyes flashing. "He was just as stuck as we are. And he was dangerous." His voice hissed over her eardrums like the subtle shake of a rattlesnake's tail.

Dangerous. But they were all dangerous, given the right set of circumstances. "If she wanted to get rid of Nick, she could have just locked him down here. Alone. She didn't need the rest of us."

And Phillip's skin. She took his *skin*.

Earl's brows furrowed. Olivia's quiet sobbing echoed against the cement.

None of them knew why they were there, not conclusively. But Windy had chosen them, and they could be pretty certain the cannibalism story was accurate. And now she was alone with Earl and Olivia and—

Oh shit.

She glanced over her shoulder. Chad hadn't moved from his spot on the sleeping bag. Panting again. Hanging on. *Please hang on, just a little longer, please don't leave me.* "So we're locked down here the way she was, locked up with the dead bodies—"

"—of our loved ones," Olivia finished, her voice whispering through the dark. Closer now. "Does she want us to… do what she had to?"

"Want us to…" *Eat the people we love.* But Victoria couldn't say it. The room spun.

Carter and Olivia, the doting ex and the unrequited lover. Windy had known about Victoria and Chad too, their issues —had known about Victoria's brother. And the woman had taken Victoria's foundation apart brick by brick, taken her trust in Chad, taken her brother, her logic, her sanity, until she had nothing left but herself…and her own survival.

Earl's face had paled. "I ain't nobody's puppet," he snapped, but he backed away, one step, then another. In the yellow flashlight beam, she could see blood splattered across his tank top, the strap on one side torn halfway through.

Victoria glanced at the bodies in the corner—Ken, Carter —then at Nick's corpse, the linoleum around his head dark with blood. Her stomach turned.

Phillip said, "They do look delicious."

CHAPTER TWENTY-FOUR

VICTORIA STARED at the ceiling from her spot beside Chad's still form, straining her eyes in the blackness. Exhaustion weighed on her, heavy and thick, but even with the blade hard beneath her sleeping bag, she couldn't rest. Earl was watching from his corner, and he was a killer. None of them should turn their backs on him.

Nick and Carter's absence was palpable, as was Ken's; their living, breathing energy unnoticed until it was gone, and the quiet they'd left ached like a wound dead center of her chest. But that wasn't nearly as painful as the hunger in her belly. Her guts flared again, hot, electric, and it spread like wildfire through her abdomen and charred her esophagus. She swallowed—dry, scratchy—but the burning remained.

Though they had searched, they'd found no more food in Nick's things, not even a single gelatinous bubble from an edible water bottle like the ones she'd seen traveling partners use. If they'd ever existed here, Nick had devoured them along with any hope for sustenance.

She kept her gaze away from the corner where she knew

Carter was still lying, covered by the sleeping bag. Where Ken's body was. Nick's. They should wrap them, but it was a fool's errand to try now. Touching the dead in the brilliant fluorescents was one thing, but in the dark... Her skin crawled.

Victoria passed the bottle of urine back and forth in her palms. Back and forth. Nick had been out of water too—and urine. As was Chad.

"Earl's going to kill you for your pee," Phillip warned.

Chad snorted as if he'd heard Phillip too, but it was weak. Thin. Victoria put her palm on his chest, waiting for Chad to say something, anything, but he just lay there, and she should have worried more, maybe—they were *dying*. Already half dead. This was when you were supposed to look at your life and evaluate it, see if you'd done right by the people you were leaving behind. Try to figure out who would miss you.

If it had...meant anything.

But she had no one who would care when she died. Phillip was dead—his skin was in a box for fuck's sake. And even if Chad wasn't locked in this dungeon, even if he lived, she'd given up on him. On them. He'd been the one who'd sacrificed for her. He'd given her his water.

Maybe Windy had known he would.

Victoria sat on the top of her bag, staring into the gloom. She'd imagined being without Chad in so many ways, in so many moments of frustration, and in every one she'd felt lighter, free. But now her heart cracked like a glass bottle someone had filled with pain and left in the freezer until all the desperation and hopelessness and grief expanded to break the form around it. He was dying. And there wasn't anything she could do about it.

Was this how it was for Windy when she'd been trapped in the basement, watching her parents die? It was like the woman was replaying her own trauma, but not just replaying —recreating.

"Her father," Phillip said. "She ate her fucking father."

She listened to the thin wheezing of Chad's breath—so fast.

Would she eat him to survive? No, he had an infection; dying like that would be even worse. And there was no point anyway, was there? With no way out, she was prolonging her own death, making her final hours more agonizing.

Chad's breath hitched, then steadied. She felt every exhale in the throb of blood in her veins.

Victoria laid her head against his chest. "Do you remember our first date?"

Inhale. Exhale.

"The Ferris wheel got stuck a million miles off the ground and I got so pissed. Started swearing. And you held my hand, thinking I was scared." She chuckled but it sounded like bees in her brain. He'd told her jokes until they'd gotten it moving again. Looked at her from under those hooded eyelids. He'd wanted to kiss her then, she knew it, but she'd waited until he dropped her at the door to press her lips to his. And then she'd led him into her apartment.

She'd been leading him around this whole time, because he needed leading and she needed control, control she'd never had as a child. All he'd wanted was for her to love him.

"You killed him, you know," Phillip whispered.

Guilt, hot and thick, flared in her chest. "I'm sorry," she said, but Chad did not answer.

Not that she'd expected him to.

SHE SQUINTED AT NOTHING. At the black.

She felt the hardness of the knife against her thigh.

The cement wall cold on her spine.

She listened for Earl.

She watched the dark. But even if Earl was staring at her right now, there wasn't enough light to catch his gaze—nothing to alert her.

Her guts seized, a cramp. Her belly was beyond rumbling. The bottle crinkled—her bottle, her bottle of piss. *Not yet.* Like their last meal, this last sip would start a countdown, a heavy trudge toward death.

Confusion. Delirium. Hallucinations. Now all she had to look forward to was oblivion. "Maybe you'll get lucky," Phillip whispered. Phillip, her brother who'd been brought back from the dead. His very life was a second chance.

She straightened.

Olivia gasped—*is she choking?*—then whimpered. Crying, she was crying. Nick muttered something to the woman, soft and low, and his kindness…he really wasn't a bad guy, talking to Olivia the way Phillip had always comforted Victoria.

Wait, *Nick* muttered something? Had she heard him talking? But that couldn't be right, he was—

"I can't just sit here," Olivia wailed through the dark.

"We should get some bags going." Earl. The flashlight clicked on once more, aimed at the sleeping bag that covered Carter. The broken shelving cast stark shadows on the back wall behind him. And Nick was there too, by the bathroom, wearing a beard of gore.

"Why does Earl get to have the light?" Phillip asked.

Because he has a knife and it's not worth fighting over. In another time, another place, she'd have attacked, at least screamed that him having the light was bullshit, but Chad was dying and everyone else was already dead except for Olivia and it was just one more reason for Earl to kill her.

And he has Phillip's skin in his pocket. He probably cut it off him. Earl was the killer in the room the entire time. *What am I supposed to do now?* "Just give it one more shot," Phillip said. "Now or never."

Victoria eased herself off the sleeping bag, groaning; she could barely move, but like Olivia, she couldn't just sit and wait to die. Anything to keep her hands busy, anything to keep her brain occupied. And there was that pesky sliver of hope...the hope that maybe she'd discover some way out.

The halo of light from the flashlight oozed through the gloom, landing on the sleeping bag that covered the student. He used to have a name...but Victoria couldn't recall it. Nick's bare toes were one step from where she stood. How long until she forgot his name? Gooseflesh prickled on her arms. She wrapped her fingers around the ladder's rung.

"Okay, let's wrap 'im up," Nick said, no, not Nick, he was dead. *Earl.* The man who'd killed Nick. Who had Phillip's skin. Who had the knife.

The only knife besides hers.

"You just have to use it right. Sneak up on him," Phillip said.

"Okay."

"Okay what?" Earl turned and bathed her in the yellow glow of the flashlight's beam.

She squinted. "All the death, all the bodies..." Her voice was not right, not at all. Too high. Frantic. A putrid, sulfuric stench hit her nostrils, then dissipated. She gagged. Stepped backward, away from the ladder, away from Nick's body, away from the weird patches of shadow that looked like cancer across Nick's bloody chest. His eyes were wide, blood-shot. Had someone opened them? They were half closed before, she could almost swear...

Phillip's lips were at her ear—she could feel his breath. "Earl's going to kill you too, he's going to—"

"Shut up!" she screamed, but it was more of a hiss. Her throat wasn't working.

The light swung away, back to the dead student under his sleeping bag turned burial shroud. Though she could see no more than a dingy mound against the wall, soaked in shadows and not blood, in her mind the mountain of flesh and bone was alive and leaking—wet.

"I'll take care of this," Earl said slowly. "You go back to sleep."

Sleep wasn't the issue. It was food. It was water. Phillip chuckled: "He probably wants you to sleep so he can kill you." Victoria took another step backward. She'd die anyway if she kept refusing rest. If she kept refusing to…*drink*. The bottle lay still in her hand, dark liquid—orange. Her mouth tingled. Her hands unscrewed the cap.

Time, it's time. It went down like water—tasteless.

Something brushed her arm and she would have jumped if she'd had the energy. Olivia was behind her. And Earl had moved too…beneath the tunnel now, where she'd been just moments before. He aimed the light up toward the hatch, but though she strained her ears, she heard nothing from above, nothing to indicate that Windy might have returned. He set the light on the floor in the midst of the broken shelving, a dozen inches from Nick's dead feet. Then he headed for the back wall, where the shelving unit used to be.

"Now's your chance," Phillip said. "Go get the light."

So he can slit my throat too?

Chad wheezed, and his breath hitched…oddly. Victoria's skin was itchy, like she wanted to climb out of her own flesh. And Nick…shit, he was the only one behaving normally. Just lying there like the dead man he was.

"You guys are crazy," Phillip said. "You're just going about your business, sitting there like this is *usual*." He laughed. "Just fucking *kill him*."

Earl grunted. The crowbar, he had the crowbar now. Victoria's heart thundered in her ears, but she swallowed hard and wrestled her nerves into submission. And when had she sat down? She didn't remember moving to Olivia's sleeping bag either, but there they were, sitting in the dark outside the halo of flashlight.

Olivia kept her face aimed toward Earl. "People do not want to believe the worst." Her voice was hollow. "When my husband died…I heard him in the house. For many days after. I thought the doctor had to be wrong, that he was still alive, and it kept me from…panic. Until it did not work."

Another sound rang through the space then: a clanging. Earl was pounding on the hatch—he must have climbed up the tunnel with the crowbar. And he was cackling, maniacally, a sound like a murder of crows all fighting over the same piece of meat.

"You said you'd come back, woman!" Earl screamed suddenly. "You promised, ya fuckin' bitch! I even gave you my watch!" His watch? Then another kind of banging, but not the bright clang of metal on metal—was Earl punching the door with his bare fists? A drop of something dark fell from the tunnel, just one, but Victoria could not take her eyes from it as it hit the broken shelving with a tiny splat and smeared from a period to a bloody comma. Because things weren't over yet—no this sentence wasn't done.

None of them would get out easy. She blinked and the comma vanished. The dark thickened over the wood once more.

The banging stopped and in its wake the sudden silence was just as jarring as the meaty thwack of Earl's fists on the hatch door.

"Is he…off his rocker now?" Olivia said. "Do you think he is okay?"

No, he was not okay. None of them were okay. Earl cackled again, long and loud and high and then whooped like his favorite team had just won the Super Bowl. Had he found a way out? Victoria listened for the squeal of the hatch, but he resumed banging with the crowbar again—harder than before. They were still stuck. He was losing his shit.

Chad's breathing hitched again—shallower. Surely not asleep, not with the cackling and the clanging above them. As if on cue, her husband shifted, moaned: "Hey, shut the fuck up!" Then he rolled over to face the wall, burying his head beneath the yellow cloth.

Victoria watched him for a moment, noting the stiff set of his shoulders, wanting to go to him, but her muscles refused to move. And...wait. He was still on his back. He hadn't rolled over at all.

Hallucinating. You're hallucinating. The hairs on the back of Victoria's neck prickled. Was someone watching her?

"Who is Phillip?"

Olivia? Victoria startled. How did she know about Phillip? *I said his name, didn't I?* "My brother."

"Does Windy know him?"

Yes, she took his skin, she killed him. Victoria opened her mouth to answer, then closed it again. She shrugged though it took far too much strength.

"Do you think we will get out of here?"

She met Olivia's gaze. Matter of fact. Realistic.

They both turned and stared at the tunnel, listening to Earl's frantic pounding.

CHAPTER TWENTY-FIVE

"THIS MACARONI and cheese is really good, isn't it?" Windy stabbed a bite onto her fork and forced a smile. But her eyelids felt heavy, her chest tight with exhaustion. Watching the video feed all night was taking its toll, and after the dim screen in the dark-paneled living room, the brilliant lights here made this room practically glow. Cement painted in white, so blissfully unassuming—sterile. No furniture besides the TV tray dead center, a television-VCR combo, her dad's, resting precariously on the top, and a single metal chair bolted to the floor. There used to be a bed too, before her new brother had tried to take it apart. Maybe he didn't like what he'd seen on the iPad? She hoped he'd settle enough in the future for her to bring the mattress back. She hated having to drug him into rest, but she'd need to give him something soon—better to sleep than sit in that hard chair all day, right?

Windy drew the fork toward his mouth. "Come on, you have to eat something."

He frowned, and pressed his lips shut. Not ideal, but preferable to her old brother's appetites. But was he okay?

Her new brother had a ripeness to him, sweat and rotting cheese, his dark brown hair lank and sticking to his smooth chin—no cuts. She'd gotten better at shaving, at least.

Windy grimaced and dropped the fork back into the bowl. She used to have lunch with her old brother every week, as prescribed by her therapist. Of course, the doctor hadn't known he was still sending her weird messages. Pictures of bodies, sacrifices from cannibalistic tribes. A coping skill, her brother had called it, but the joy on his face when he looked at those images, the fast way he talked when he got really excited…

He'd surely suggested it to the others in the bunker—he wouldn't have been able to help himself. He relished the suspense, the chase, and getting them to agree to eat another human would take more than a simple suggestion, so he'd have planted seeds early. Sharing that sin with others, that was his thing. The most exciting part, he'd once said, had been watching her chew. At least he'd died before he got that last little whiff of pleasure; they hadn't been ready.

"Maybe I can get you a soda?" she asked now.

The hollows of his cheeks were deeper, his bones sharper than they'd been just a few months ago. He'd hardly taken any convincing to stay with her in her little hilltop cabin when she'd hired him to work on the shelter, laying tile. He'd been trying to save enough to go back to school, get a degree —show his sister he'd turned over a new leaf. She'd only cuffed him when he tried to leave.

Windy bit her lip. Was this worth it? It was, right? If it helped. Already she was feeling more confident—one horrifying piece of her life had been resolved.

She set the macaroni dish on top of the television and picked up the iPad. Wishing she had audio. "Want to watch again?"

His nostrils flared as he glanced at her, then at the vibrant red door that led to the rest of the house, then behind her, at the gaping open doorway in the cement. She should have closed the wall up, maybe, but then the front door would have been the only way in or out, a thought that made her guts churn and her brain crawl with images of the blocked stairway from the cellar where her parents had died. One escape route was not enough. The other exit was a crawl space three hundred feet past the open archway—an old, but now clean, sewage pipe, secured with a metal grate that only she had the key to. Besides, the open wall allowed for some much-needed ventilation. If she were being honest, he really did reek.

His eyes dropped closed.

Windy hit play. Watched her old brother hit his hands and knees. Watched Earl leap on top of him. The ankle holster, the blade. She didn't see the blade go in, didn't see Jack—*no, Nick's*—face as he died because he'd been in the blind spot below the camera. The tiny hidden lens in the bell gave her a 180-degree view, and the painted over magnetic strip in the doorframe ensured the bell always landed in the right spot for her to see outward, but she couldn't see directly beneath it. She'd watched Nick pretend to examine it when the group had first searched—the others were unlikely to search for the camera again.

On the screen, Nick fell to his belly, and Earl reared back just far enough to be in her line of sight. He didn't even look upset, eyes hot and righteous, blood on his shirt. Then the screen went dim; she'd turned the lights out in a moment of panic. She was glad, sure she was, but she'd been as shocked as any of them when Earl had whipped out that blade. There was still enough with the night-lights for her to know what was happening, but not enough to see details, which was how she preferred it. The look on Earl's face had made her back tense. But now...a peace had begun to settle over her.

Her old brother was officially gone. And her new one…
"This is going to get better, you know," she said.

His eyes blinked open. "Let Victoria go. I'll do whatever you want."

"I just want a family." Nick hadn't given her that. Or Earl. Carter. Windy gazed into her new brother's eyes, trying to read his expression, but it was dull—tired.

"You don't need more family. I'm already your brother, sis, you know that."

She smiled, but he was lying, and this thought, that he didn't want her, was a crushing pressure, releasing a vicious wave of self-hatred. But soon it'd be the truth, wouldn't it? Soon he'd have no other family to run back to—isolated, the way she'd been with Nick. Even if he was angry for a while, she'd be all he had. And he'd be all she needed. She had told him her deepest, darkest secrets, and he'd said he understood, that anyone would surely forgive her. And then he'd asked the question that had set her world on its head: "If you were talking to your best friend and they told you this story, wouldn't you forgive them?"

In his eyes she'd seen the truth in that—that *others* were the key to forgiveness. If someone else acted the same way, might she finally find peace, knowing she wasn't alone? As for Nick, the man who'd turned her into a cannibal, who'd tricked her…she could trick him too. And when he was gone, she and her new brother could start over.

She had thought she'd have to take people by force, trick them into going down to the bunker. She'd even collected drugs and syringes to put them out, though Nick had given her whatever she'd shot into Ken. Nick…he'd had far too many ideas—the poisoned peas, the fake food—as if he'd been planning for something like this all his life. That's how she'd tricked him. She'd told him she had an idea, the perfect opportunity to get exactly what he'd been fantasizing about since they were kids.

But then the storms whirling in the Gulf had turned on their little town. Epiphany. She hadn't needed force at all, and isolating them down there, letting them wonder about their fates, about the storm... Windy knew better than anyone how being trapped could stretch the days until you were certain you should already be dead. Until you wished you were.

Until you felt you had to act now or there would be no tomorrow.

Her brother opened his eyes, blinking, glassy. The same shade as Victoria's.

She ran her fingers over the healed wound on his bicep—the tattoo, inked with love, was the other reason she'd been so certain he was perfect. Nick had gotten her tattoo—R for their last name, for Dad's last name—just to piss her off. He didn't want her to have anything of her own.

But now she did. She had a new brother. She had Phillip.

Phillip talked about Victoria as if she was the strongest, most amazing person he'd ever met—a survivor. Like Windy. Victoria had let Phillip drown, had almost killed him, and he'd forgiven her. A man who could forgive you for almost killing him had to forgive you for a past you hadn't chosen... and a few months in cuffs. So she'd severed Victoria from Phillip's flesh the way she'd severed Nick from her heart the moment he slid that blade over her father's arm.

What had Victoria thought when Nick called her house and told them Phillip was dead? It would make her more desperate now, knowing she had nothing left out there. It took a certain amount of surrender to become what you most fear—that tattoo should push her over the edge if all else failed.

Victoria would do the same as Windy herself had all those years ago, Windy was sure of it. She was a survivor. And she would survive just a little longer on the blood of the people she loved.

CHAPTER TWENTY-SIX

EVEN IN THE dark she could tell Earl was staring at her from his nook. Was he going to stab her to death in her sleep?

Nick, Nick's dead. It had been dark since Earl slit his throat, as if the room was in mourning, leaving Nick's blood to congeal—invisible—on her hands. But she felt it: sticky. Smelled the metal. Her mouth tingled, and then she was raising her hand, pressing her thumb against her lips and—

The lights clicked back on. Victoria dropped her hand, saw the brilliant red streaks on the bathroom doorframe, on the white cement—arterial blood—and looked back down, heart in her throat. Had she tried to lick her fingers?

"You did, sicko." Phillip laughed. "Do it again, you wuss."

Her belly heaved. She blinked. Was she asleep? Her body felt heavy enough as she scrubbed her fingers with alcohol and the last of the cotton balls, half expecting the wall to clear, for the blood to vanish. For Nick to be alive.

But the blood remained on the walls, crimson over the white. At least Earl had dragged Nick's body to the corner with the others. *Three down, four to go.* There were nearly as many dead bodies as there were living people here now, a thought that made the unease rise in her chest. She tamped it back down. Stomped it like a West Nile–carrying mosquito.

But it buzzed back to life when she saw Chad's face, his slack mouth. He wasn't snoring, and he hadn't stirred at all when the lights came on. Shouldn't he at least wince and pull the sleeping bag over his face?

"Chad?"

He did not stir. Did not move.

She touched his cheek—so hot. "Chad!"

Nothing. And she suddenly needed to see his eyes, to have him there with her—he couldn't be dying. Not in this moment. *Not yet, not yet, not yet.*

She grabbed his arms. Shook him, her own muscles aching, though she barely managed to make his shoulders move. His head flopped to the left.

Nothing.

"What is it?"

Earl. Did he know how to fix this? *Earl will bring him back, like they did Phillip, like they did me. Everything is fine.*

But the air had thinned. She lunged herself onto Chad's body, battering his shoulders, slapping his face, punching his chest with her fists, screaming his name.

He did not respond. And the orange pallor beneath his flesh…he was in a coma. She'd known it already, maybe, but she'd refused to admit it, because now she knew he wasn't going to wake up. They'd said their final words to one another. She'd blabbered on about their first date. She'd told him she loved him. And what was the last thing he'd said?

I don't feel so good, Vicky. And my mouth tastes like piss.

It was so ridiculously Chad that her chest seized. Her heart was not ready. *It can't be over. He's just sleeping, just lethargic.* She hadn't sent the divorce papers in, hadn't even shown them to Chad, hadn't taken that step because a part of her hadn't wanted to. She'd been ready to hate him, but she hadn't been ready to…lose him.

And now she had. Windy had taken that control from her too.

Fuck you. Fuck you. Fuck you. She slumped back onto her sleeping bag, her husband's shirt still fisted in her hand.

"Good guys do finish last," Phillip said. "No wonder I'm dead."

A sob wrenched itself from her guts, tearing through her throat.

"We have to give him something." Earl. Standing beneath the tunnel, hands behind him.

"Like what?" Her muscles ached and she released Chad's shirt and watched her hand slide onto the floor. Onto her bag. "There's no water, there's nothing to give him."

"Blood."

"Excuse me?"

"Nick ain't been gone all that long, you could—"

"You want me to feed my husband—"

"It's the only way." Earl approached her, pulling his hand from behind his back, holding…oh god. He had a bottle. Thick red liquid. Her mouth watered even as her stomach turned.

"We can't do this, we shouldn't—"

We can. We should. *I should.* Her eyes tingled though no tears came.

Olivia was on her feet, palms up in a *stop* gesture. "No, that is crazy!"

"It's liquid, woman—"

"Liquid with much salt. Drinking that will dehydrate him faster."

Earl's nostrils flared. Disappointed? He…knew that. *He's trying to kill Chad.* Her stomach roiled with disgust and starvation, thirst and horror as she stared at the bottle. Because she should have known that. Maybe she had. And she'd almost gone along with it.

"Why don't you drink it," she said. *He collected it, collected Nick's blood in a bottle like it was no big deal.* Had he been eating the others? Would he try to eat Chad?

She reached down near her thigh, seeking the hardness of the knife's handle through her sleeping bag. But she felt only the cement, warmed by the heat of her body.

The knife was gone.

Shit, no, no, no. She dropped her gaze, fumbling beneath the sleeping bag, shifting her hips, seeking the hard bulge of the handle or the leather casing, but felt only the smooth tiles. Earl narrowed his eyes. Had Earl taken it?

"Of course he took it, he wants to make sure you're defenseless," Phillip whispered.

I ain't the only one with a weapon, let's not get silly, Earl had said. She'd thought he meant the crowbar, but he'd known. Oh yes, he'd known about her knife.

She flipped the bag. The linoleum was glaring, shiny and empty, but she fell to her hands and knees, searching, scrabbling—something hard beneath her shin. A plastic water-bottle cap. Nothing more.

Earl was still staring at her, Olivia kneeling beside her bag now, too, concerned. Olivia dropped her hand from Victoria's shoulder—*when did she put a hand on my arm?*—and the sudden chill was a balm, a release from captivity. But they weren't free. This man had taken her knife. This man had drained Nick's blood without the rest of them even noticing.

Earl would bleed them too, if it came down to it.

Because he could.

CHAPTER TWENTY-SEVEN

CHAD LASTED the rest of that day, or at least what Victoria thought was the rest of the day. Day thirteen of the flood, said the hash marks—that was the day she lost her husband, and it did not escape her that she should have been dead too, dehydrated as she was. She sat beside him, wishing she could drip water into his mouth, but they'd been down here far too long —it wasn't only water anymore. He needed food. They all did.

When he finally slipped away, it was anticlimactic. His breath just...stopped. Quietly, discreet. Agreeable.

Olivia sat on the opposite side of the room, away from Chad's body, away from Victoria. Earl wandered, moving pieces of busted shelving that had been scattered around the room to the corner—the discard pile—stacking them around the bodies, the terrible jagged silhouette of the broken shelving like spikes ready to impale them. It was a constant reminder of their failure, a prelude to their own deaths.

Nice guys finish last. Every time she closed her eyes, she saw how nervous Chad had been with the ring in his hand, his smile when she said yes. Felt the steady hiss of his sleeping breath against the back of her neck. Their life hadn't been perfect, but it had been safe. It was that safety she craved now.

The ache came on softly as the night progressed, a chasm that widened sometime before dawn into a deep, sharp hollowness filled with all the things she should have done differently. Things she should have said to him. Regrets that she'd stayed. Anger that he'd kept Windy from her, that they'd ended up here. And through it all, the guilt, hot and bright. Even Phillip's voice had quieted, as if her grief were too much for him to bear. Olivia, too, left Victoria alone with her thoughts.

Had she wished this upon her husband? Wished that he'd just die? She'd imagined leaving him enough times, sure, imagined being free. Had she really, ultimately, wanted him gone?

And the answer was a mantra on repeat in her brain: *Not like this, not like this, not like this.*

But Chad was indeed gone—she'd pressed her fingers into the hollow at the side of his throat, seeking that low, steady throb of pulse, and there was nothing. She'd climbed inside Chad's sleeping bag in the pitch blackness too, clutched his still-warm hand, imagined he was only resting. Imagined, too, that the clink of Earl's blade from over near the bodies was him merely sharpening something. That the scraping and tearing she heard was just Earl kindly wrapping the people who had been trapped here with them. But he wasn't—it wasn't. The moist sounds from his mouth as he chewed was proof enough of that. He was eating them. Maybe he was the smart one, though the thought of it turned her stomach. And where had he gotten the extra water? He had to have some, eating all that salt, either through careful rationing or flat-out theft, but she couldn't do anything about it—he was stronger, and he had a knife and she didn't, not anymore. Earl had made sure of that.

When the cool of the tile finally seeped into Chad's skin and made his flesh go rigid, she skittered away into her own bag, telling herself it was just a doll, that it wasn't Chad, but she could scarcely breathe through the astronomical weight that was crushing her chest, trying to smash her heart beneath her rib cage. Her breath panted from her like a dog. She jumped at a hiss from the other side of the room, half certain she'd see Earl emerge from the darkness, ready to cut her throat, or maybe it was Windy, tired of playing with them and ready to do away with her for good. No...it was Phillip, staggering closer, eye sockets gaping, blood dripping off the ends of his fingers, arm stained red from his flayed tattoo, a needle in his other hand: "I'll take the pain away for you. It's okay." She stifled a scream and clamped her eyelids closed. *Just breathe, just breathe. It's a dream.* But it wasn't. She knew it wasn't. The panic in her chest clamped around her lungs again. Earl's moist chewing smacked against her eardrums—she stifled a gag. Her best chance of getting out, perhaps the only way she'd be able to survive, was if she...ate her husband. But she couldn't eat him, he was infected and she had no more water to help her digest anything—Olivia was right, the sodium content would be too high. But if she had water...

Her lungs hardened to stone. Wheezing filled her ears.

"Victoria?" Olivia, whispering. "Can I help?"

Victoria shook her head. No one could help. No one but Windy. She'd never understood prayer before, but if Windy had been there, that bitch she hated with every ounce of rage in her body, she'd have been on her knees in a heartbeat.

Clang, clang. The hatch.

She opened her eyes. The flashlight glowed beside the

ladder. "Earl's up there with the crowbar again," Olivia said from the wall opposite her. "I think he's—"

A guttural cry rang through the room. Cursing, then something unintelligible, then clanging, screaming.

Victoria slipped from her sleeping bag and crept to Olivia's side of the room, keeping one eye on the tunnel, keeping her eyes off the places where the bodies lay, cooling, decaying, dead, dead, dead. Maybe she should start wishing to die—or wishing it would just go faster.

Clang, clang.

Earl grunting.

Clang, clang, clang.

Victoria tried to keep her breath low and even, the way Olivia was, but her gaze was locked on the dark section of the room where Earl usually sat. She wanted her fucking knife back, but he wouldn't have left it down here, not when he'd taken the trouble to steal it—he'd probably shoved it in his holster, or his pocket.

Clang, clang.

Earl had the energy to bang on the hatch, to climb up the tunnel, to *scream* while she had trouble remaining upright. Because he ate Nick, *because he's eating other humans*.

"You should kill Earl before he comes after you." Phillip. And she could almost feel the steady pressure of his hand on her shoulder, but no, that was Olivia's hand. And though Victoria's brain raced with thoughts of Earl and his blade, the blood on the wall, her muscles remained limp. A gut-wrenching cramp tore a grunt from her lips and she frowned at the desperation in that noise.

Clang, clang, clang.

They needed food. They needed water more.

We're going to die.

"Seriously, can I help? I feel so…helpless."

Helpless. Hopeless. Sure, she could help—did Olivia have

a way out? *Chicago. I'll just wander out of here and go back to Chicago.* Victoria chuckled, swallowed it back down. Hysterical, she was hysterical.

"I am so sorry about Chad."

Chad. She'd have to call his mother. Chad's brother had died of a heart attack, slept right through that final shuddery beat. Maybe he was the lucky one.

Victoria stared at the dark tunnel, the yellow halo from the flashlight like a dirty spotlight on the ceiling. "I'm sorry about your husband too. And Carter."

Clang, clang, clang.

"I have been thinking..." Olivia whispered, though there was no way Earl could hear them—maybe she was just weak. "I am not afraid of dying down here. Is that strange?"

Victoria tried to meet her eyes in the dark. And shook her head.

Olivia raised her arms and unclasped her necklace. "I wore these on my wedding day. My Lenny...he was sick for the whole year before we got married, had so many bills. Later, I found out that he did not buy his insulin for months so he could afford these. Just because he knew I loved the sea." She lowered the pearls into Victoria's hand. "Bury them with my husband, yes?"

Clang, clang, clang.

"Why don't you do it yourself? If I find a way to get out of here, it isn't like I'll leave you behind."

"You have been here fewer days. I think...you are stronger."

She was giving up. But really, wasn't it better to go out peacefully? There were worse things.

Victoria's hands shook as she clasped the pearls around her own throat. They hung heavy between her breasts. She'd never get to bury them, she was never leaving here, but this was one final kindness she could offer.

"Victoria? Will you pray with me? Not even out loud, just...together?"

Victoria touched the pearls. Couldn't bring herself to look at Olivia. But she clasped her hands, hoping she was doing it right, doing what Olivia—her friend, maybe her only friend—needed to see. To know it was okay to let go.

Olivia bowed her head over her steepled fingers. "Thank you."

Victoria nodded in the dark.

CHAPTER TWENTY-EIGHT

PLIP, plipity-plip.

What the fuck is that? It sounded like water. *And someone has my knife.* But that didn't matter now; this whole thing was almost over. Was she dead yet? Chad's sleeping bag was down near her feet, pressed hard against the wall. Silent. She resisted the urge to touch him with her toe, make sure he was still in there.

Plip.

She sat up. Above the hissing of her breath, the steady *plip, plip* continued—water, dripping, dripping.

Plipplip, plip.

Hallucinating. She was hallucinating. But she could not ignore it. The sound tugged at her guts in a profound way, drawing her like a magnet from her sleeping bag, pulling her to her hands and knees, dragging her toward the middle of the room. Crawling.

Plip, plipplip.

The floor was covered in crimson, and when she raised her head she could see a dim shape in the gloom. Yellow light glittered off Olivia's eyes—upside down. Oh god, Olivia's body, hanging from her ankles, suspended from the hole in the ceiling, throat slit like a hog hung up for slaughter. Blood dripped over Olivia's cheeks, staining her flesh like the gore that had marred Ken's face.

Plip, plip, plip.

Soaking her hair.

Plipplipplip.

Earl was…draining her. Victoria couldn't breathe, frozen on her hands and knees, sure she'd see the knife, her knife, glimmering in Earl's fist—blackness, everything so black. But then how could she see Olivia? She blinked. The yellow light vanished. The tunnel was dark, empty in the hazy blue LEDs…no one hanging from it. Olivia was fine. It was a dream—a hallucination.

Plip, plipity-plip.

She resisted the urge to clamp her hands over her ears. The noise…it sounded so *real.*

The floor was hard beneath her knees. Cold. Her hands were cold too, cold and…

Her palms slipped.

Wet.

Something *wet.*

Was it blood? It was, she'd been right, Olivia was dead, and she was stuck here with Earl, Earl who would kill her the moment she fell asleep, probably with her own knife. But when she raised her hand from the floor, her fingers did not glare darkly in the dim night-lights. Her palms glistened, wet but *clean.*

She put her lips to the floor. Oh god. *Oh god.*

Water.

The sound in her ears was a sick sucking noise, her lips aching as she pressed them to the ground, her nose numb and cold and bruised from hitting it against the tiles. And she didn't care. She didn't care. Her lips were wet, her tongue was damp, and her throat, so sandpapery and harsh, now had fluid trickling over those parched surfaces, a cooling monsoon after a season of drought. Tiny little *plip*s hit the back of her head and she flipped over, opened her mouth and felt drops on her nose, on her cheek and—*there!*—into her mouth, on her teeth, down her throat. Earl...he'd broken the seal on the hatch. And if the seals could be broken, maybe the hatch could be opened. Maybe...

Oh, for fuck's sake, nothing else mattered, not now. Just the cool wet against her lips.

The others didn't know yet, or they'd be here too. She wasn't going to tell them. No, wait, she should tell Olivia. But her limbs, her legs, every muscle burned with the exertion it'd taken to get here in the first place. Water dripped into her mouth. She wanted to cry, laugh, scream. But she didn't dare move, convinced that if she did, the water would vanish like a mirage.

She lay on the floor, the linoleum hard against her spine, and let her mouth fill.

VICTORIA LAY there for what seemed like hours, her eyes and mouth open to the black hole in the ceiling, the liquid dripping down into her belly. Her arms and legs ached.

Someone was holding her wrists. Earl. He was there to kill her, and for a moment she saw him, his breath hot on her cheek, but when she blinked, only the water remained. Her arms were heavy from wasting muscle and exhaustion, nothing more. And...*oh*.

Her abdomen was distended with fluid. Sloshing when she rolled over. But the liquid in her guts would soon be absorbed—used. They needed reserves.

The bucket. The bucket. Near the bathroom door. Empty.

She crawled, crawled past Chad's body—still, lifeless—listened for Earl's voice. For his breath.

The plastic bucket grated against the linoleum. Her arms ached, every muscle burning, nearly useless.

Plip. Plip.

But not quite.

Plunk. Plunk.

She collapsed onto the linoleum tiles, listening to the steady dripping—*plunkplunkplunk*—of the water into the plastic container, life-giving water, feeling the vibrations from the pail, sinking, sinking, sinking beneath the waves.

TIME DRONED ON, minutes blurring into hours, moments marked only by the *plunk* of water in the pail, and the breathing of the other two. The other hostages, though that word didn't feel strong enough for their predicament—sacrifices felt closer. And once she'd thought it, the word filled every molecule of extra space in the air around her until they were all one enormous organism made of flesh and blood and pain and terror. She barely noticed when the lights blinked back on.

Earl had realized the water was dribbling in soon after she set the bucket up under the hatch. Olivia had clambered beneath the dripping rainwater too, trying to catch what she could, while Earl had done his damndest to get back up the tunnel—took longer than it should have, each step making him groan. Though he'd hidden it well, he'd clearly been weakening too. When Earl finally managed to reach the top, he had resumed his hollow clanging, and his cries had echoed down for what seemed like hours, the water flowing in faster with every grunt from above. But when he finally emerged from the tunnel in the ceiling, his eyes were red—starvation or exhaustion or crying, she couldn't tell. But she and Olivia knew from the defeated look on his face that even if he'd managed to break the seal, there was no way through the solid metal of the hatch door.

Her back was cold against the cement wall. Victoria pulled her gaze from Earl and locked her eyes on her husband, mere feet from her bare toes.

She should pull his sleeping bag off his face, he couldn't breathe, he'd suffocate. Her breath hitched—no, *she* was going to suffocate. The pail was nearly full already, even after Olivia and Earl had drunk their fill. It would soon overflow.

Plunk, plippity-plunk.

The cement room was going to flood. She would watch the water ooze slowly around her toes, then her ankles, closing around her calves, and she'd suck the liquid into her throat, into her belly, relishing every swallow even as she drowned drop by drop. Would she stay sane for that? Perhaps she'd slip mercifully into madness, blissfully unaware as the water crept over her nostrils. *Oh god.* Maybe Chad was the lucky one, slipping away before he had to suffocate. It was a wonder she hadn't lost her mind already.

"Oh but you have, sis. You have." Maybe Phillip's body was out there now, with his dripping hair falling into his eyeless sockets, his lips as purple as a bruise, floating around with that bloated cat. Everything out there dead. Rotting.

"Pessimistic, much?" Phillip asked. But sometimes it was wrong to hope. Yet still Victoria watched Chad's body, looking for signs of life, for a signal they'd been wrong.

Maybe he's okay. Maybe…

The sunny yellow sleeping bag over Chad's face, her husband just lying there, one arm out, it was far too close to the way he'd been all week. Sleeping. As long as he looked normal, she'd drive herself insane. She leaned over and ran her fingers along Chad's exposed arm. The skin felt oddly hard, cold, but her fingers were already tingling, electricity zipping through her nerve endings from nail bed to elbow to shoulder, then across her chest, and her belly... The ache there was suddenly unbearable, a molten, twisting void where nothing existed but that pain. Her fingertips burned as if they were on fire. Chad's skin seemed to vibrate, soft and supple and *tender*.

Her mouth watered. No one would see, no one that would care. Olivia was asleep, her back to the room. Earl would probably be proud.

Oh god. Ohgodohgodohgod.

What the fuck was wrong with her? But her belly was growling, rumbling so loud she could taste it, feel it all the way down her spine, and her mouth was squirting out saliva, *feed me, feed me*. She gagged. And glanced past Chad at the wall where the shelves had once stood...at the stacks of supplies on the floor.

She crawled to the garbage bags through grime and grit and smeared dried blood and returned to the body with the bags clenched in her fist, her knees aching. Not Chad. Just a body. An infected body. She could feel Earl's eyes on her back, boring a hole into her flesh. Maybe he was on his way to kill her now, but she was tired of being afraid. She ground her teeth and knelt beside Chad. So still. *I'll wait until Earl's asleep and I'll get one of his weapons. I'll slit his fucking throat*.

"I bet he tastes like gator." Phillip's voice. No...Nick. Nick had said that.

The bag over Chad's feet went on quickly, almost too easily, and she cinched it at the knees. She tore the bottom seam of the next bag and slid it under his legs and up past the first. It stopped around the thigh, the plastic stretching where she was trying to shimmy it beneath him. The edge of the plastic seemed to be...painted in something dark from beneath his body. Blood? Shit? Her sense of smell didn't seem to be working, but the blackness beneath him was like his soul had leaked out onto the floor.

His flesh beneath her fingertips was cool, but still pliable. Meaty. *That's why Windy gave me the blade. So I'd have no trouble severing flesh from bone.*

Her gut twisted, forcing bile and undigested water into her esophagus. She put her hand over her abdomen as if it would ease the oily sickness that was slithering around like a tapeworm in a dish. Her mouth—god, her tongue was so wet. Tingling with the promise of food. But she didn't have the blade. She'd have to saw at him with her teeth, tear him apart with her fingernails.

Footsteps sounded behind her.

"Lemme help."

Rage burned, white hot inside her chest. He'd killed Nick and he'd stolen her knife and he'd busted the hatch—she would have been dead by now, out of her misery without that rainwater, and instead she was stuck here with...with... Her fists clenched around the plastic bag. She whirled on him. "Fuck you. Get the fuck away from me."

And miraculously...he did. He backed up and turned to his corner, treading softer than she'd ever heard him before. Like he was tiptoeing. Unless she was having a hard time hearing his footsteps over her own panicked breath.

Chad was dead. *He's dead, I'm down here with a murderer, and we're all going to die.*

I'm going to die.

"You are," Phillip agreed.

Her hands shook as she tugged the bag into place. Then the next. Shimmying, tying, wrapping, rolling—just a heavy thing, not a person. Sweating. Muscles aching. Before she knew it, she was sitting with the last garbage sack in her hands, staring at a lump in the sleeping bag—Chad's head— the plastic clenched in her fist. She had to pull it over his face. Was she supposed to say goodbye? She should, surely that was a thing she should do, but she couldn't make her mouth form the words.

She closed her eyes, trying to avoid looking at the plastic, at Chad, Chad who was cold now, whose eyes might be glassy but maybe they still looked like him, looked like him enough that she was suddenly certain she heard him snoring from beneath the cloth. And then it was Nick snoring, blinking from his place with the rest of the bodies in the corner, his body free of worms and bugs and maggots, but soon it would bloat and split like Chad's. Carter's. Ken's. Chad's dead heart throbbed quietly in her brain and the *tic-plink, plunk-tic* of the water was so harsh in comparison that Victoria had to resist screaming. But there was another sound too—real or imagined? No, definitely real, a thin, hiccupping moan—Olivia crying. Again.

The pearls around Victoria's throat shifted with her breath, heavier now. Olivia knew she wasn't leaving this place, and yet, she'd still thought Victoria might. And Chad…he'd given her water. He'd wanted her to live, even at his own expense. She opened her eyes. Chad's shoes stared back at her from the corner behind her own sleeping bag—his favorite yellow Converse. Windy's smile flashed in her brain, and rage burned brighter than her hunger.

She wasn't giving up. She was going to get the fuck out of there.

And if she didn't, she'd wrap her arms around Chad's corpse and kiss his cold, dead lips and whisper her goodbyes into the silence.

CHAPTER TWENTY-NINE

VICTORIA DUMPED the alcohol down the toilet and sat next to the water bucket, filling bottle after bottle in the dark, listening to the dribbling, watching the level in the pail recede. But it would soon fill again. And then what?

When she was done, she sat facing the wall where the shelves had once stood, her forehead resting on the dark cement, her husband's filthy yellow Converse in her lap, tracing the gouges Chad had made with the crowbar—the jagged hole, the metal sheeting beneath it cold and unforgiving. Was his blood still there, staining the concrete where he'd tried so hard to find them an escape? Was this really all she had left of him, of them? She brought her fingertips to her nose, almost hoping for the faintest tinge of iron, as if she could inhale some semblance of what he used to be, as if it would help her feel less alone. But her fingers smelled of dust—of old, dirty water. And behind it all came the fetid stench of rotting meat and the gasses of the dead. Earl had wrapped the others, but not well enough. She gagged, and the reek vanished as quickly as it had appeared.

She drew her fingertips back to the wall, lightly at first,

then with her fingernails, grinding them over the surface like a claw, erasing the *tic, plunk-tic,* of the water. Each drop that fell into the bucket pushed another drip from the pail to the tiles. The floor was wet. She pressed harder against the cement, clawing with one hand, over and over and over, letting the jagged rock cut into her flesh.

One of Chad's Converse fell from her lap and onto the floor with a *thup.* Those silly shoes, something a child would wear. She'd never had a childhood, but Chad had given her that—quiet and meek, a grown-up boy-next-door and she'd fallen so hard for him. She'd forgotten that. Forgotten how they'd laughed. His shy fingertips on her spine the first time they kissed.

A sob escaped her throat as she clawed again, feeling the nail on her pinky split, and she bit her lip but did not cry out, just drew her hand down harder, faster, balling it into a fist at the base of the wall, driving her knuckles against the tile. The pain centered her. The frantic pace of her heart slowed. Her breath evened, dulling the ache in her fingertips.

Chad was the nice one, the softie. Victoria was the bitch. And if she ever got out of here, Windy wasn't going to know what hit her.

SLEEP CAME FAST AND UNCEREMONIOUSLY, sucking her under before she could object. Victoria's head was throbbing when she awoke in the blackness, her forehead still pressed into the corner between the tile and the cement wall. Her hands stung.

"Olivia." Earl's voice floated through the dark and set the hairs on the back of her neck pricking. Harsh. Angry? She held her breath—was he trying to find Olivia so he could hurt her? But if that were the case, he'd have done it while she was sleeping.

Shuffling rose from near Olivia's sleeping bag, but she did not answer Earl. Victoria pulled herself to standing, her knees groaning as the shelving had before it snapped.

Earl coughed. Then she heard his rubber soles on the tile —he'd put on his boots—and a faint *click*. The flashlight glowed. Victoria shrank back against the wall, as if at any moment he might change course and come for her, wielding her own blade in one clenched, murderous fist. But he didn't. He was crouched over Olivia, her friend sitting against the cement wall across the way; a barely audible squeak hit her ear. Was Olivia trying to scream?

Earl glanced back, saw Victoria, narrowed his eyes. *Guilty.* The light went out.

The room wavered, and Victoria put her hand on the wall, then staggered forward, one arm out to the side to steady herself, keeping her gaze on the place she'd last seen Olivia. Where she'd seen Earl.

"Hurry, he's going to hurt her," Phillip whispered.

She heard a steady tapping as if Earl were hitting the light against the meat of his palm. Unless he had the crowbar—

Olivia's face was suddenly bathed in yellow again. *The flashlight.* The deep shadows over her legs glared against the glow, and Earl was kneeling there, he was beside her, touching her—

"Get away from her," Victoria hissed. Her footsteps splashed—puddles, how the fuck was it still raining?—her heart throbbing in her ears, all the noises running together in a sick *whoosh* that reminded her of waves—a dark, vast lake, out to drown them all. And now she was close enough to see her friend.

To see the blood.

What had he done? Oh shit, what had he done?

"What he always does," Phillip said. "Kills people."

The shadows around Olivia's legs were not shadows at all, but deep pools of blood. Her hands were covered in it too, her shorts, a deep gouge on the inside of her forearm that could have been from a bear claw—as if she'd tried hard to fight him off. And beside Earl's knee, Windy's knife, the one he'd stolen from Victoria. Earl's eyes glittered meanly in the yellow flashlight beam.

He wrapped his hand around Olivia's throat.

Victoria gagged. There was so much blood—she was probably dead, she had to be dead, but then why was he trying to finish the job? Olivia's face stayed placid and still above Earl's meaty fingers. *Dead, oh god, she's definitely dead.*

Victoria backed away from him, but there was nowhere to go; one step and her shoulders hit the wall. Earl straightened. Olivia between them, Olivia and the knife. Should she lunge for the weapon? Could she get it before he did? This man had killed Nick, killed Olivia. And she was alone with him.

Alone.

His eyes landed on the blade too. Waiting. Her fingers twitched.

"How could you?" she whispered.

He raised his head. "That blade ain't mine, girl."

"No, it's mine. And you took it. You—"

"You go ahead and take back what's yours." Earl leveled his gaze at her.

Was this a trick? Was he going to stab her if she bent over to retrieve the blade? She did not move. "You're a murderer."

He nodded. "Yeah, I am. But I didn't have no reason to do this."

The room was so quiet, Victoria could almost hear the moist sound of Olivia's blood congealing on the floor. Even the dripping water had gone silent. Her muscles screamed with tension as she stared him down. Finally, Earl dropped his eyes...to the knife. He stooped to grab it, wiped the blade on his pants, and flipped it, just as Windy had done, holding the handle out to her. The leather was sticky in her palm. The flashlight retreated to Earl's little corner and clicked off.

The world was black around them now, but she could still see Olivia in her brain. Her bloody arms. Crimson stained clothes. And her face—peaceful. She wasn't worried about getting out of there anymore. She wasn't worried about her husband's death, about Carter's death, about drowning down here, about starving. Olivia was free.

And she'd given Victoria her pearls. That gash, forearm, wrist up toward her elbow—it wasn't a quick slash to the neck like she'd expect if it had been Earl. And she wouldn't have sat there quietly and just let it happen. No, Olivia had... done this. That was the most rational explanation. Victoria just didn't want it to be true. But she also didn't want to be locked in a cement box that was slowly filling up with water, alone with a murderer. *Tic, plunk-plip.*

The room spun. Her brain whirled in the dark and not just the dark of the room; it was as if a black hole had opened in her brain, a vast nothingness, pulling the last pieces of her foundation from beneath her, devouring the final threads of her sanity.

She was going to die. At Earl's hand, like Nick? At Windy's? Or at her own?

But she could only rule out one of those.

"You know what you have to do, sis."

Resolve wrapped her muscles. Steadied her hands. Settled her nerves.

SHE PASSED the time sitting on her sleeping bag near the middle of the room, where the water was shallower, listening to the patter of the droplets, a million tiny splashes. Trying to pretend that the wrenching agony in her belly was excitement. She stared into the darkness. If she didn't kill him first, he would slit her throat like he had Nick's. And then he'd eat her.

She was alone here, alone with a killer, and if she was going to die she didn't want to do it with someone watching her, ready to consume her if she went first. Was that logical? She couldn't tell anymore. Maybe she didn't care.

Earl's breathing was light, but from the duration of his exhales, he was asleep—asleep without a care in the world. And she had a knife in her palm.

"It's time," Phillip said.

The blade was heavy in her hand, still damp and sticky with Olivia's blood. Why had he given it to her? Did he want to die?

Her footsteps in the water should have made more noise, but the plinking from the pail helped some, and the darkness further masked her movements. She strained her ears, following the sound of Earl's exhales. She had to get the blade to his throat before he stopped her. Though what was the worst that could happen? He'd kill her? They were stuck in a room full of dead bodies. They had little to no hope of escape. Olivia had known that and chosen to end her own suffering—maybe she should take that control back, too, take her own life before she starved to death or drowned at Windy's hand. Or before Earl killed her on his terms. *No, him first*.

One more step.

The pain. Her hunger was eating her alive, gnashing teeth tearing at her insides.

She was there.

Earl lay on the floor just in front of where she stood, drier here even than her own spot, as if he'd known just where to put his bag. Her toes tingled with his body heat. She could just make out the lump of his sleeping form—barely there, but good enough. She exhaled once, silently, and inhaled deep. Then dropped to her knees and whipped the knife to his throat, the blade against his stubbled Adam's apple.

"I know I deserve it, girl, let's get it over with."

"You do deserve it, you fucking do." But the blade was frozen in her hand. She ground her teeth, trying to force herself to press it into his throat, pictured severing his jugular, slicing through his windpipe, the gore coating her hands...

"Just do it," Phillip said.

"Yeah," Nick agreed. "He fucking killed me, you're going to let him live?"

The darkness was a living thing, wrapping around her like a soaked towel, filling her lungs with musty wet.

"He's got my skin in his pocket, sis, in his little silver box."

"What're you waiting for?" Earl's throat vibrated against her hands, Adam's apple bobbing below the blade.

Her eyes burned, and in the dark she could see nothing but Nick's gaping throat, Phillip's dried flesh.

Earl shifted, as if trying to turn toward her, but he did not resist the blade. "You deserved better, you know," he said, softly—too calm. As if resigned to death.

"You don't know anything about me."

"I know 'bout your husband. Saw him at the diner one day, with her. Ain't nobody deserve to be cuckolded, and I told her so."

Victoria's hand shook. She pressed the knife harder into his flesh. There was no noise save her heart thundering in her ears. Had Earl's breath gone silent? She should kill him, she should.

Don't let her win.

"You stole water," Victoria said. Not a question.

"I had extra, came down with it in my boot. I wasn't 'bout to split it with people who were gonna die anyhow. I would'a split with you, after they was gone, but then…"

The water had come through the ceiling.

"You tried to kill Chad, giving him that blood."

"I wasn't trying to hurt him. I just wasn't thinkin'. Things got…confusin' for a bit."

Confusion she understood—she'd been arguing with her dead brother for days.

He exhaled, hard enough to jar the knife. Her hand wavered.

In Bali, a guide had told her, "The angel of death comes for us all, but we need not embrace him." Earl was death— Earl would kill her if she let him live. But while her logical brain ran through these thoughts, something far more primal and visceral was happening deep in her lungs, a clenching panic—*I can't be alone down here in the dark*. She had died like that once already, all alone in the dark water after she'd lost Phillip's hand. Both of them drowning—*drowned*—until they'd been fished out and revived. She didn't want to die like that again, no matter how much she hated this man. Dying down here without even this psycho to hear her cry was suddenly more frightening than anything she could imagine.

Her pinky was wet. Something warm dripped onto her thumb—she'd cut him. Bile rose in her throat. She could eat him. She *should* eat him. Her mouth watered. And suddenly the hunger was all-consuming, a twisting, vile thing writhing in her guts, cramping with a ferocity she'd never felt before. Saliva shot from the glands at the back of her mouth, tingly and painful, wetting her tongue. No. *No*.

She released the pressure on Earl's throat.

Olivia was already dead. Olivia had wanted a favor. Olivia had wanted her to *live*.

She pulled the knife away from Earl's neck with a shaking hand and stood. Her feet slid over the wet tiles with a moist splashing sound. Moving toward Olivia's little section of the room. The sleeping bag.

Warm. Was Olivia really warm or was it wishful thinking, as if that would somehow make it better?

The tile was so hard, so cold. Her knees were wet. Her belly was a living thing all its own, a monster slashing at her insides.

What part of Olivia to take? Did it matter? Her belly roiled and growled, the creature in her guts shivering with anticipation.

She put a hand on Olivia's bicep. Definitely warm. Oh god, she couldn't. *I can't do this.*

"You have to, sis, there's no other choice."

The shoulder, like pork shoulder, but it was so close to Olivia's face, hiding under her hair. She'd cried on that shoulder, hadn't she? Literally, figuratively, she couldn't remember, and it didn't matter. Bile rose in her throat. Images blinked behind her eyes: Olivia smiling; Olivia's face; Olivia fingering her pearls; the softness in her gaze when she'd talked about her husband.

She gagged, trying not to puke.

Olivia laughing.

Victoria's belly expanded, shrank, cramped, and she felt her way lower in the dark, brought the blade down near Olivia's bare calf—if she'd had to cut through pants she might have lost her nerve. Same if she could...see. *Maybe that's why Windy turned the lights off.* She paused, swallowed hard. And angled the blade.

The flesh cleaved like the outside of a peach. Nausea tightened her insides—*I can't, yes, I can*—and she pressed harder, dragged the blade down toward the base of the woman's calf, to Olivia's heel. Her dear friend's foot.

Olivia's voice: "Yes, Carter, why would singing to her lend a helping foot?"

Victoria moved the blade, flensing flesh from bone, feeling the wetness of it.

"I wore these on my wedding day."

A long, curved slice of flesh. She'd expected blood to pour from the wound, but it was just a drizzle, a tiny weeping trickle like you'd get from...

A steak.

The pearls were heavy around Victoria's neck, like a noose.

"Bury them with my husband, okay?"

She brought the meat to her lips. There was little flavor, just a bit of...rust. Didn't even taste like meat. But the taste was irrelevant—the monster in her abdomen wrapped itself around it with an almost religious zeal, worshipping that bite as if there would never be another as worthy. But there would. Many more bites—she'd eat until the monster in her belly was satiated. She shoved another slice between her lips, suppressing a moan, and the pleasure expanded upward through her ribs and down into her toes with a tingly fervor. Like an electrical current. Her heart slowed.

From the corner, Earl's eyes burned into her back—a killer in the shadows. Waiting.

All of them were capable of something terrible.

CHAPTER THIRTY

THE WATER CHURNED AROUND HER, the waves so dark she could not see the sky above. Her lungs screamed for oxygen, but if she went back up, if she tried to get to the surface to take a breath, she'd lose him. Phillip. Her brother's arm floated just beyond reach, his fingers limp in the tumultuous currents, undulating with the flow of the water. *He can't be dead, not yet, he can't be.* She'd only lost sight of him for a moment. How had he sunk so deep?

She kicked harder, her vision blurring at the edges, though Phillip remained sharply in focus. His index finger caught a current and crooked slightly as if beckoning her closer: "Come help me, help me, sis!"

Victoria kicked again, lungs on fire, and with one final burst of power, she broke through the space between them and wrapped her fingers around his wrist. And pulled, kicking her legs, trying to haul them both to the surface, though she was only half sure she was swimming toward the air—was that the bottom?

No, there! The sky solidified as her head broke through the surface of the water, and she gasped, inhaling great lungfuls of oxygen. "I got you, Phillip, I got you." She blinked water from her eyes to clear her vision and let go of his hand. Not Phillip. Chad floated beside her, his blue, bloated face almost unrecognizable, but she'd have known his eyes anywhere, milky as they were. He turned to her, his lips curling up in a smile as a giant slug emerged from his mouth and crept down his chin. "Miss me?" A death rattle emanated from his throat, low and harsh.

She bolted upright, trying to suck air into her lungs, but her body was frozen, muscles tight with panic. *Just a dream, just a dream*. Wait. No, she was actually cold. And wet—water dripped down her back from her soaked hair.

She scrambled to her feet, splashing ringing in her ears. How long had she been asleep? Water covered the tile, almost touching the bottom of the night-lights tacked to the walls. When the water reached those lights would they go out for good? Would she be stuck in the dark with a murderer, waiting to drown?

Rustling came from the far corner and then the flashlight clicked on.

Her stomach turned. The bodies, all wrapped up in plastic, were being slowly submerged, and Earl's wiry hair sprang from the top of the pile. Jesus Christ, he'd put his sleeping bag on top of them—a king sitting atop a mountain of corpses, the remnants of the shelving unit surrounding him like a military wall. *What the fuck kind of psycho does that?* Was that why he'd insisted on wrapping Olivia after Victoria had…finished with her? Her stomach rolled. At least Earl had left her husband alone. Chad's wrapped body was off to the side, his shoes on top where she'd left them. Like an offering.

Earl's eyes glittered, cat-like in the dimness. "This was the only dry place I could find. You might want to get out of it too…that water ain't kosher, if you know what I'm sayin'." He gestured to the wet floor with the flashlight.

Oh god, the fluids from the bodies...the blood on the floor...she was soaked in it. As if on cue, a drip sluiced from her hair down her spine, covering her flesh with goose bumps. "Why didn't you wake me?" Her voice was shrill. "You knew the water was coming in, why didn't you—"

"Same reason I slept up here—because if we want to have any chance, we need to be rested." Rested, because their other needs were met. Had he eaten pieces of Olivia too? But this no longer disgusted her and that itself sent a panicky tingle through her chest. Made her gut clench, full of acid and water and her friend's leg muscle.

Yet still her heart hitched—hope. "You have a plan? You know how to get out?"

"No. But you never know. She could come back any time."

No, she couldn't—wouldn't. Nick's voice echoed in her head: *Windy wants us to eat each other.* Victoria had done what Windy wanted. And it didn't matter—nothing mattered. They were stuck. Dying. Not starvation. Not thirst. Drowning. The water creeping ever higher—all the bacteria. She was wet, she was so wet, infected and filthy.

Her gut heaved. She staggered, fell, crawled for the bathroom, sloshing through the mess, and flung open the door, choking on bile, though puke was the least of their concerns —she could have hurled on the floor, but she didn't want to see it, didn't want one more disgusting thing to contend with. She emptied her sour guts into the toilet bowl. Nothing but acid, she'd been asleep long enough to digest her friend. *Olivia, fuck, I'm sorry.* She laid her forehead on the seat, panting.

I don't want to die down here, I don't want to die.

All the things she'd stressed over before, her divorce, changing jobs, seemed small—idiotic. Now, after a lifetime of being worried about Phillip, of being frustrated with Chad, of being angry and unfulfilled, she knew exactly what she wanted: to live. So simple. And she had no hope of achieving it.

She wiped her mouth and left the musty bathroom. Once the water hit the top of the bowl, the sewage would invade everything. And the water would keep rising. *Fuck*. They'd examined every inch of this place. Exhausted every option for escape. Unless they found a way out through the hatch, they were never leaving.

She paused at the doorway, staring out into the room, at the sheen of water glistening in the flashlight's beam like a moonlit lake. Ripples shuddered out from where her footsteps had disturbed the placid surface—Earl had left the light on for her. Her heartbeat steadied. Was she even afraid of death anymore or had she found peace, like Olivia? Her stomach heaved again and she swallowed hard.

Phillip answered: "No. You're still a giant wuss."

She stood a moment longer, watching the water ripple around her feet like the waves in the lake the day Phillip had dragged her under. Her throat constricted. She'd *almost* died then, but today...today she would drown. Or tomorrow. And this time no one was going to resurrect her.

She glanced down at the water covering her toes, dimly aware that this should have bothered her more than it did—she was going to die inhaling sewage into her lungs, why wasn't she screaming? But the vital bite of panic had waned, softened to a subtle ache that barely crested into agitation. Was this what surrender felt like? No. This was defeat.

Ripples tugged again at the skin of her toes. Her heels. But... Those ripples weren't coming from the movement of her feet. She wasn't moving at all, yet there was a distinct current beneath the surface. What was causing it? Was there a way for the water to get out and if so, if so...

Her heart thundered in her chest as she bent, squinting at the surface of the water. A rustling from the other side of the room made her look up. Earl aimed the light at her, the man now sitting on top of the bodies, stiff on his throne of dead flesh. She grimaced, but put up a hand. "Don't move. I think there's a place for the water to drain."

Earl sat straighter, aiming the light at the water near her feet. Now she could see the piece of shelving he'd laid on top of the plastic-wrapped bodies, like they were nothing.

Maybe in the end they were all nothing. Just flesh.

She scanned the floor more fervently. Fake cereal boxes floated against the wall. But with her view no longer obstructed by the shelving unit, the floor felt larger and she was looking for something so small, the tiniest crack, a barely-there fissure...

The difference was almost undetectable, but it was there. Perhaps in the overheads she wouldn't have been able to pick it out at all, but the angle of the low yellow lighting skimmed off the surface differently, illuminating the tiny, persistent ripples that covered a dinner-plate-sized area just in front of the wall, beneath where the shelving unit had been. She picked her way closer, keeping her gaze locked on that spot.

"What do you see?"

"I think...I'm not sure. Did you do the tile down here?"

"Nah, she had someone else do that recently, some druggie." Earl's feet splashed onto the floor.

She squinted harder. The flashlight's glare bounced from the surface of the water, but it was less like glass in the light, more murky. Adrenaline sang through her veins as she stooped down near the section where she'd seen the ripples. There was definitely something down here. The water here moved of its own accord, sucking harder, but subtly, at her toes.

She ran her fingers along the floor, the tile slick against her palms. But why was there linoleum here at all? Didn't these places usually have cement floors like the walls? Maybe…

Windy tiled over a drain. A drainage pipe, that might be all it was, but the water could at least escape—they wouldn't drown. Then maybe Windy would assume they were dead and show up in time to get tag-teamed, that fucking bitch.

She squinted through the dirty water, looking for the smallest glint of metal. Just the tiled floor, and they'd have seen a drain if there was one, but there had to be an opening here, there had to be. *Please let it be true, please don't let me be crazy.*

She hooked a corner of the tile with one of her fingernails and pulled, but the tile held fast. The split nail on her pinky stung.

"Victoria?"

She raised her head and her heart stopped as she stared at the shining edge of Earl's blade.

"Use this." He flipped it around for her. But she had her own. She whipped it from the back of her shorts—it wasn't leaving her side again—and ground her teeth together as she shimmied the edge of the knife under one corner of the tile and pulled, trying to work the glue free of the cement. Earl slid his blade beneath a tile to her right.

Crack!

She jumped and reeled back as her tile gave, but not all the way—a tiny sliver. It would take forever to pry the tiles up with the knife. She tried again, jamming the edge under the tile and heaving until her muscles felt like they might snap. The blade snapped instead. Her feet lost purchase and she careened backward, but a warm hand on her back righted her: Earl. She hadn't even seen him get up. The crowbar in his hand cast harsh lines on the watery floor in the haze of the yellow light.

He knelt beside her once more, the flashlight in his

injured hand, the crowbar in the other—offering it to her. Her lungs expanded as she clutched the metal. Her spine straightened. *If it is a game this bitch is playing, goddammit, I'm going to win.*

Her chest lighter, she pushed on with the crowbar, Earl using his blade. The crowbar made the work faster, but it was still slow going; the tiles were attached directly to the cement and cracked off in small pieces, one corner at a time. Beneath the ones they'd removed, the floor felt normal—cement covered with squiggles of glue.

Her stomach dropped. Maybe she was way off on this drain thing and the ripples she'd seen were from angry electrical currents running through this spot. Maybe she would hit the wrong place and zap the shit out of herself on a live wire. But electrocution was better than drowning—or just waiting to drown. The shadows rippled along with the water, all of them crooked like the beckoning fingers from her nightmare.

Fuck it, she'd pull up this entire floor, and at least she could die knowing she tried. *How are we just thinking of this?* But who would have thought to dig down when the world above was flooding? She jammed the crowbar under the next tile and heaved, a whooshing noise coming from beneath it, intensifying as she pulled harder. The water around her hands tugged at her skin. *It's being sucked away.*

Earl moved closer, jimmying his knife under the tile directly next to hers. She heaved again, then flew backward as the resistance gave way entirely. The tile landed on her chest, a fist-sized chunk of cement still attached to the back, the crowbar splashing into the water beside her. The light wavered.

"We've got something here." Earl's voice was high, excited. She scrambled to her knees and sloshed through the water toward him, looking through the murky liquid for the drainage pipe. The water was a tornado now, being sucked through a hole—the hole left by that chunk of cement. Not a drain, though, or at least it didn't have an open metal grate on the top. This was all cement. But unlike the smooth white walls, here the cement had been poured into some kind of metal grid—added on later? At the top left corner of the opening, a metal and plywood surround secured the grid to the rest of the floor. *What the hell?* She leaned closer, touching the edge. Circular—too large to be covering a standard PVC pipe. Only that one side was visible, one long, rounded edge, the rest of the hole hidden beneath the surrounding tiles. But if that edge continued to curve…

They hadn't found a drain at all.

They'd found a tunnel.

CHAPTER THIRTY-ONE

SHE JAMMED the crowbar under the edge of the next tile, Earl making quick work of the one adjacent to it, and the scraping of metal on cement, the slap of the water seemed to hit her in the gut. The rushing of the current flowed downward, fighting against their tools as if it, too, was in an exceptional hurry to escape. Her tile peeled back with a sickening *crriiiiiiick* and she tossed it behind her as Earl's gave way. More of the hole was visible now, jagged gouges in the gridded cement from their tools, all of it framed by metal brackets screwed into the surrounding cement.

Her fingers tightened on the crowbar. She sat up on her knees, raised the crowbar, and smashed it downward into the brackets. Cement fragments exploded around them, and she went again, harder, harder, the cement thunking, the metal bracing squealing, but the brackets held. Earl backed away and aimed the flashlight at the floor so she could see. She raised the bar again and brought it down as hard as she could, the clanging metal reverberating through the room and juddering up her arms—one corner of the support broke free. She attacked the next brace, then the next, her heart thundering in her ears, slamming and clanging and crashing, the whoosh of the water around her feet intensifying, trying to pull her under, into the tunnel. Last bracket. She raised the bar, then thought better of it—she hooked the already free side instead and pried the entire grid out of the way like a trapdoor. A trapdoor—escape. *Please be a way out.*

Water rushed through the hole like a waterfall down to some unknown end. How far down did it go? How large was the tunnel?

As if reading her mind, Earl snatched up a hunk of cement and aimed the light into the hole, the black shadows crawling along the floor like subterranean insects. He dropped the cement. They both leaned closer and watched it hit the surface of the black water beneath and sink, but it was like trying to peer through oil—they couldn't see the bottom. Victoria gagged as an old, rotten smell rose from the space below.

Earl grabbed two of the water bottles she'd filled—"one for each outta do it"—stuck them into the back pockets of his jeans, and took the crowbar from her. Miracle of miracles, she let him. "I'll go down first," he said. "You hold the light and pass it down and then—"

"I've got this." But her insides were quaking with fear as she squeezed her feet into her already wet boots. They could drown down there as easily as here. Maybe they'd die of sepsis before they got to an exit. But which was worse? She couldn't just wait to die here, watching her husband putrefy. She glanced back at the tunnel in the ceiling, the one that should have led to their freedom. Then at the plastic garbage bags in the corner, so unassuming until you looked carefully at the outlines of faces, hidden noses, barely concealed fingers. The bodies were surely putrefying by now. Her eyes landed on the last bag—the one topped with a pair of electric yellow Converse. The one she'd wrapped herself.

Goodbye, Chad.

Her nostrils stung. She took one final inhale, the putrid stench from the corner suddenly stronger against the musty water beneath them, but she didn't gag. Adrenaline thrummed in her aching muscles. She sat on the side of the tunnel.

And jumped down into the dark.

CHAPTER THIRTY-TWO

HER ANKLE SLAMMED into the ground, a sharp pain shooting up through her hip. But...the ground. They could touch the bottom. *Oh thank god.*

"You okay?" Earl's voice echoed from above.

"Yeah." She righted herself and peered down the dark passage, but she could see nothing outside the rippling yellowed halo from Earl's flashlight, still poised above the hole.

The water lapped around her thighs. The rest of her legs were invisible beneath the muck. What else was lurking beneath the surface?

"Not too deep."

Earl angled the light to the tunnel in front of her, then behind. Nothing behind, now that she looked. Nothing that passed beneath the bunker room. But ahead of her...

"I can't see the end of the tunnel, but..."

"Military tunnels have exits," Earl said. "I know these structures."

The room plunged into darkness as the flashlight, too, disappeared. Her breath echoed in the hollow chamber. *Did he leave me?* Was he really Windy's boyfriend and knew there was no way out and he'd sent her down here to die?

Then the light reappeared in the hole above her, but it seemed dimmer somehow, and more white than yellow. She inhaled sharply, trying to calm herself, but her heart rate continued its frenzied dance in her chest. Then the light was moving toward her. Falling.

She turned her head as Earl splashed down beside her, flashlight in one hand, the light wrapped in a garbage bag to keep it from getting too wet. He grunted and regained his balance, then aimed the light around them.

The tunnel branched out in two directions, one path at a ninety degree angle to her left, the other straight ahead, away from the cement room, into the unknown. Throughout, the ceiling was crosshatched with badly rusted metal braces and what might have been wood or filthy metal reinforcements, the edges crumbling—larger than the pieces of bracing that had held the cement and tile over the hole. But though these metal braces were larger, more substantial, they were far older; the entire thing looked at risk of collapse.

Earl followed her gaze down the tunnel to their left.

"That direction leads off toward the water." She considered the boat, the floating cat, the fence posts, then pictured the hill that stretched up, up, up. "We should have more luck heading this way, farther up the hill."

She turned and slogged off without waiting for him to agree. The stench of something old and foul permeated her nostrils, the gentle sloshing of the water licking at the walls and reverberating down the chamber like the cackle of a distant sea monster. Her nose stung. After weeks in a room full of dead things, she should have been used to it, but this was different—this wasn't the sweet rot of decay. It was thicker, the burning reek of fermented urine.

"That'll wake you up in the morning," Earl muttered, his

voice and the wet slapping of the muck echoing back to them —whispers from the dead. In front of them, the corridor seemed to stretch out forever. The sound of their breath was suddenly obscene. The quiet clawed at the base of her spine and squeezed the air from her lungs; drips of murky water raised the hair on her arms. Just a long, lonely hallway vanishing into blackness.

What if they never found an exit, or it was blocked? What if the water rose and they died trapped inside the tunnel? She'd thought she'd escaped from drowning—had she been wrong?

"How far do you think these tunnels go?" she asked, though there was no reason for him to know that. At least it broke the silence. And her voice bouncing off the tunnel walls jarred her nervous system into action. She pressed forward, hands shaking—suddenly exhausted. *I wish Chad were here*.

"One way to find out. But bunkers…military tunnels…if there's a tunnel, there's another exit."

She stumbled, her big toe throbbing as her foot connected with something hard but slippery, unseen beneath the water.

"Don't look, sis, don't look."

She kept on. Pushing harder, faster. *Now or never*.

The walls on either side of them had morphed from the metal-braced cement into dirt held back with larger pieces of metal sheeting. But there was a space in the sheeting at about chest level, a space that had once contained the packed dirt of the tunnel, now empty, the earth eroded away. This entire place was falling apart. And with the storms, the soaked earth above the tunnel was probably pressing down even now, heavier every minute, straining the ceiling joists.

Around her legs, the water splashed more violently as she picked up her pace, but she didn't get far—a fork in the tunnel loomed. Which way? To the left, the walls appeared more solid, arching up slightly, reinforced with cement pillars and topped with metal braces and…was there cement on the ceiling too? The tunnel on the right was similar to the one they were in, dirt sides, all of it shoddily reinforced with rusted metal sheeting.

Left *seemed* like the right way, but still she hesitated, standing thigh-deep in the nasty water, staring into the dark. The flashlight cast harsh shadows on Earl's face. Not more than a hundred feet off, half of the right tunnel was blocked by dirt—partial collapse.

Victoria stepped toward the cement tunnel. "It seems sturdier here."

Earl nodded. And followed.

The water level lowered slightly—calf high—as they stepped up and made their way past the first cement pillar and into the tunnel. The walls here didn't bounce the sound back in the same way; instead of the brighter slapping sound of water on metal, this tunnel absorbed half the noise, reducing their panting to a muted *shh, shh, shh* and their steps to the moist thwacks of sloshing water. Almost the same wet meat-on-meat sound as fists on flesh, and suddenly, all she could think of was Chad's breath as Earl fought him, and then…silence. Chad's cold hands. The slippery fluids leaking from his body and pooling on the tile beneath him. She could almost imagine that his body had somehow fallen into the hole and was floating after them—*What happened to us, Vick? Don't leave me here, I love you!* But Chad had been screaming that inside his head for months, hadn't he? Maybe years. Chasing her while she pulled further away, and she'd never noticed. Her heart twisted, grief widening the hollow place in her chest, but her chest didn't ache—the hollow had gone numb.

But other parts hurt. Her eyes. Her head. The water was at her knees, slightly easier to wade through than when it had been at her thighs, but not by much—her muscles burned with every step, and the tendons in her feet were on fire. Above them, the metal and cement ceiling loomed, shadowed and hulking like it might at any moment lunge downward and trap them. If the tunnel filled with water, they'd never get back to the hole in time to catch a breath. The only way to escape was through.

TIME PASSED IN A DARK, bleary fog, her heart an agitated flutter in her throat, but her breathing had slowed even as her legs burned with the effort of slogging through the black water. The smell had eased, or at least she wasn't as aware of it, but her lips tasted like salt. She clamped them together to make sure she didn't swallow anything nasty. Her clothes were soaked through now, and for the first time in days, she had to pee, her swollen bladder pressing against the waistband of her jean shorts with every step. But it was distracting. She needed distracting.

"You remind me of my son," Earl said suddenly, and if she wasn't so damn exhausted she would have jumped. "Brave. He had that about him too."

The sound of their splashing was the only reply—she had no idea what to say. She'd never had a father who had called her anything like brave. Little shit, maybe. She was more comfortable with that, truth be told.

"My boy…he would've done good in this world," Earl continued and his voice cracked. She glanced over. She couldn't tell if he was crying with the layer of wet and filth on his cheeks, but the sorrow in his gaze…

Her heart. Phillip. Chad. Victoria drew her eyes to the ceiling—the tunnel felt tighter than it had earlier. "Is it just me, or is the tunnel getting smaller?"

Earl drew the light up above his head, eyes on the walls, then on the ceiling. "I believe it is."

If the tunnel was changing, maybe they'd found a way out. Or would there be an intact ladder leading to another bunker like the one they'd just escaped from? Even if a higher room didn't have an exit door, it would be a dry place to rest a moment, out of the murky water. Her muscles ached as though she'd run a marathon.

At least you're moving, sis.

Yeah, because I ate Olivia.

A low groaning rumbled through the space and now she did jump. *Shit.* She grabbed Earl's bicep as the earth shifted beneath her feet, water rippling on both sides of them, like standing on a tectonic plate. *Oh fuck, oh fuck, oh fuck.*

The tunnel was collapsing.

CHAPTER THIRTY-THREE

HER FINGERS ACHED against Earl's skin but she gripped him harder, not sure which direction the collapse was coming from. Would it move like a wave, the brackets tearing loose from their mounts and showering them with dirt before the cement ceiling crashed down and forced them beneath the inky water? *No, we've come so far, not now, shit, just give me a fucking break!*

The earth trembled once more, then stilled. Rocks shook from the infrastructure overhead and splashed into the muck, from back the way they'd come. The tunnel behind them was falling in. Should they run ahead? Would it even help?

But her feet were already moving, sluicing through the water, the nastiness splashing up against her arms, soaking her chest, dripping into her mouth. She barely noticed. The rumbling faded behind her though her feet were still vibrating with it.

"I think it's over," Earl said, and she slowed but didn't stop. He was right—the only vibration she felt now was the quivering of her own abused muscles as she slogged through the water. More difficult than before.

She looked down. The water was at her hips now. Creeping higher.

Keep going, sis, now or never. She ground her teeth and continued on.

SHE WASN'T sure how long they'd been walking. The water level had crept steadily upward, over her hips, up past her belly—surrounding her ribs. Swimming might have been faster, but stopping to breathe, trying to keep the muck out of her mouth, out of her face… Was there even another way out, or was it an illusion? Maybe they'd get to the end of this passage to find another wall of cement.

Pinpricks of light bounced around her, tricking her brain. She'd let her bladder loose hours ago in desperation and the rush of warmth had been almost relaxing against the chilly muck. But she was still trapped. Claustrophobic. And with every step, the water rose.

She pushed on, her feet on the ground, and spat rancid water from her mouth. Her eyes burned.

But wait…what was that? Tiny lights still danced in her vision like fireflies, but was there really something…glinting? Earl stopped beside her and aimed the flashlight at the ceiling. She blinked dirty water from her eyes. Maybe she'd imagined it, a trick of her feverish brain as her body prepared for death. But, no, there it was again, a tiny flicker of something—*A latch? A handle?*—in the ceiling overhead, a foot off the right wall. And as they drew beneath it, she could see the tiny squares mounted above the flat of the ceiling—a large grate, wide enough for them to fit through…if they squeezed. A metal handle protruded from either side.

The ceiling here was a little more than seven feet, still too high for her to reach. Her gaze dropped to the water's

surface, mercilessly black. *Don't think about it. Just be logical…
and jump.* With one final glance at the ceiling, she let herself
sink beneath the inky surface, and when her feet were
securely against the floor, she shoved upward, her hands
straining toward the grate, breaking the water, brushing the
metal—but she hadn't made it high enough to wrap them
around the handle.

"I can lift ya," Earl began, but she ignored him. The black
water filled her ears as she sank, then sheeted off her as she
flew out of the water again, and this time her fingers touched
the handle. Slid. Found purchase.

She put her boot on the wall, and it slipped, but she held
onto the grate with one hand, the other wrapped firmly over
the handle, the rusty grit making it easier to grasp though it
bit into the pads of her fingers. *Righty tighty, lefty loosey.* But
no matter how hard she pulled, it would not turn. *Fuck.* She
tried wrenching it the opposite direction—nothing. Her
shoulders burned. She wouldn't be able to hold herself up for
much longer.

Something grabbed her legs.

"Hey!"

"Oh stop, child."

Earl lifted her, fingers gripping her thighs, her butt on his
shoulder, and aimed the flashlight at the grate. She shifted so
her head was off to the side instead of beneath the handle in
case it lowered into her forehead. *Better.* With the light it was
easier to see the problem—rust coated the entire locking
mechanism.

"Let's try the other."

This time when she tugged on the handle, a thin grinding
noise shuddered from above her— rust flaked off the metal
and landed on her cheeks. Some movement, but not much.

She pulled harder. The latch gave way with a horrible
sound like the grinding squeal of a car wreck. *Finally!* She

dropped the handle and pulled the grate—if she yanked hard enough would the other side give way? But all she was able to do was worm her fingers into the space between the lip of the hatch and the warped metal grate—only a few inches of room, barely enough for her fingertips. Not nearly enough for good leverage.

But they had the crowbar. She'd handed it to Earl before they jumped. Earl pulled it from his belt loops now and passed it up, the flashlight casting new and eerie shadows as she raised the crowbar to the grate and wedged the end into the crevice. And pulled. The metal groaned, moved...her hand slipped. The grate snapped back. She heaved again, but it did not budge. "Fuck."

"Lemme try."

Her arms weighed a thousand pounds. She let go of the grate and moved beneath it so they could trade places—she should be able to prop him up for a minute. But when her feet landed on the ground, she stumbled. The water had risen, and quickly. At the top of her rib cage now. *We have to hurry.* She traded the crowbar for the flashlight and slipped the flashlight cord around her wrist— almost all bone.

Earl raised the crowbar and hooked it between the grate and the lip. But instead of letting her support him, he pulled himself up out of the water and swung his legs front to back, using the full weight of his body to twerk the metal, the crowbar clanging against the lip each time he swung. The metal groaned under his weight. But it didn't snap open.

Victoria frowned. "Maybe we can hammer it apart."

His first blow landed squarely, but the latch remained intact. The second one snapped the handle off. And still the grate remained fused shut aside from the little sliver she'd managed to bend apart. At least his swinging had wrenched the steel grate open a bit farther—the size of her fist now.

We've got this. We can do it. Now or never. The water was

higher, at her chest, at her *fucking chest,* lapping at Olivia's pearls. Her muscles vibrated with anticipation. Earl was grunting. Out of breath.

"My turn," she said.

He hooked the crowbar back under the lip of the grate, and boosted her up. She grabbed the grate and the crowbar as best she could, tugged on the grate, but as before, the slippery metal didn't allow her to gain much traction even with Earl's support below. The flashlight swung wildly from her wrist. She took a breath and tried again, and when Earl let her go, she swung her legs the way he had. The metal remained rigid, only shifting slightly with her efforts. She dropped once more, her muscles on fire.

Earl grabbed the bar and pulled himself up to the grate itself. His scarred hand rested on the top part of the crowbar —she'd almost forgotten about his injured hand. He walked his feet up the wall, but his boots slid and he lost the grate and splashed into the water beside her. The waterline was above her nipples, rising, still rising, and when she drew her eyes back down the tunnel the way they'd come, there was a definite ripple of current. The water was flowing in. Toward them. It was this or nothing. It was this, or drown. *I'm not going to drown again, not here, not after all this.*

Her mind cleared.

Earl came up grumbling and tried again and this time his feet stayed on the wall. "All right, on the count of three. One..."

She grabbed the bar beneath his hand.

"Two."

She tightened her grip.

"Three."

The groaning metal was like music echoing through the empty tunnel, Earl moaning as he pulled against the top of the bar, but it was nearly impossible to find purchase on the slime-covered walls or on the floor beneath the chest-high water. Her hands slipped. The grate stayed.

"This isn't going to work." Earl dropped again, shaking his head.

"It has to work. Fuck you if you want to give up, but I will not die like this." She met his eyes. "I thought you knew these structures."

Earl frowned at her, pursed his lips. Then he whipped around, snatched the crowbar from the grate and waded for the wall with it held above his head, his jaw set in a tight line as if he were about to attack.

Her heart rate ratcheted up.

She clenched her fists as he smashed the bar into the wall with a dull crashing sound. Cement broke. He went again. A piece of cement flew by her ear. She turned her face away, the echoes filling her head and rattling her brain. He was going to cause another collapse, or open up a new way for the water to get in, and that would be far worse than going quietly beneath the waves. Dying with hope was worse than surrendering because you had to acknowledge that you had a way out and you had failed. But she didn't care. She'd go out swinging.

I'm not dying now.

Earl was gasping. The crowbar had broken through one of the seams in the cement, and a piece of metal glowered dully beneath, similar to the metal under the cement walls in the bunker, but this wasn't solid, not sheeting—just bracing. Earl grimaced, heaving on the crowbar, and the piece of bracing split. Then he hoisted himself up so both legs were off the earth and slid one foot, then two against the wall—hooking his toes under the metal support bar. Finding purchase. Leverage.

The water was past her biceps now.

"I'm going to pull with the bar," he said. "You push as well as you can."

He did. She did, lifting herself out of the muck, swinging as well as she could. The metal grate groaned, and then something gave, a crackling like lightning snapping through the tunnel as the grate edged down, but not far enough— they'd need another foot before it'd be wide enough for a person to squeeze through, even a half-starved person.

They both released the grate and dropped into the water. Shoulder height now. *Oh god.* This was it. This was how it ended.

But goddammit, she'd tried.

She was still trying. For a moment she swore she saw Phillip's head, his eyeless sockets approaching from upstream, but instead of panicking, she tightened her fists into hard knots.

Windy had killed her brother.

I am not going to let you take both of us.

She eyed the grate, then lowered her head. Earl met her gaze. "Let's go again."

He inhaled deeply and retook his position with his feet against the wall. She grabbed the bar, her muscles shivering with exertion, the water lapping against her waist, then her hip as she pulled herself higher, one hand on the ceiling, shoving with all her strength. Earl grunted, moaned, and the grate growled back at them. The latch held, but the grate bent. Farther. Farther. Almost there. But the water…she was barely swinging. She was floating. Over her head now. Her fingers tightened on the metal.

"You need to climb!" Earl said. "When I say, you climb through the hole, and put your feet on the top of the grate once you get through." She did not question him; she pulled harder but she was floating, *floating*, and he let out a guttural

"Ahhhhhhh" that she barely heard over the splashing of the water and the moan of the metal. One inch more. Two.

"Climb! Now!"

"Now or never!" Phillip screamed.

She hauled herself through the opening, wriggling, the rusty metal slicing the skin on her belly, the lip of the hatch shearing flesh from her spine. Her thighs were out of the water.

Below her, Earl moaned, louder this time. "Hurry... can't...hold..."

She kicked, feeling the tightening on the backs of her thighs—if he let go, she'd be trapped half in and half out of this hole. Her fingers found the tunnel wall at a ninety-degree angle to the grate, the dangling flashlight bouncing light around at...metal. *A ladder.* She grabbed the lowest rung and pulled as hard as she could, hauling herself through, her injured skin screaming. Then she was in. Her feet were safe. The grate snapped back. Earl peered up through it, his fingers wrapped through the square holes as if he were trying to pull downward. The water was higher now—a foot below the ceiling.

She shifted the light. Above the grate, the metal rungs in the tunnel were damp but solid. She curled her fingers around one of them, bracing her feet against the grate, and shoved downward, trying to push the grate open from above —with the rusted latches, she had no hope of pulling it upward, even if she had been able to avoid standing on it. She kicked harder, glancing down for Earl's fingers. Why wasn't he helping?

"Go," he said.

"What?" Uncomprehending. She fumbled for the light. Above her, the tunnel stretched out, a heavy black void.

Earl unhooked the crowbar and fed it through the space in the grate. "Something's opened up down here, another collapse, a busted water line. Your tunnel's gonna fill next, and it's smaller than this one. You ain't need to be in there when it happens."

She was supposed to…leave him here? And suddenly she was ten years old, hiding in the closet with Phillip because he'd refused to leave her by herself; then she was twenty, calling the PI, refusing to let go of Phillip, unwilling to leave him out there alone. She grabbed the crowbar from Earl —"Move!"—but instead of climbing she raised it to shoulder height, then brought the curved edge crashing down on the grate's rusty latch. The *clong* rang in her ears, the vibration sang through her bones, but the grate did not move. She leapt, jumping, feeling the bit of give under the soles of her boots. The grate held fast.

"I'm sorry," Earl said from his spot beneath her feet. But she wasn't sure for what.

"Pull, goddammit!" He was all she had left in this moment. The worst thing was being alone.

Alone.

She met his eyes, keeping one hand on the rungs of the ladder. There had to be another way. She frantically searched the edges of the grate, looking for anything that might allow her to open it from this side, but the rusted latches were even more gnarled looking from above.

She drew the crowbar up again, watched him slide out of the way, and smashed it down.

Clong!

Earl's face reappeared below her feet. "Stop, girl. Stop and listen. Once this water reaches the ceiling, you ain't got no chance of climbing out before it drowns you." He spit water from his mouth—at his jawline now, oh god, she was going to watch him drown the way she'd watched Phillip drown.

"Get outta here, girl! Climb!" His upper lip trembled.

But she couldn't fail again, couldn't fail someone else

who'd helped her survive—she'd failed Phillip, failed Chad, failed Olivia, and that was already too much to bear. "I can't, I have to—"

"Go," he said more quietly. "Climb, now, or it was all for nothin'."

Hot tears slipped down her cheeks. The sound of the rushing water stole her breath. Earl pressed his nose through the grate—at the ceiling, the water was at the ceiling. He spluttered, spat water from his mouth.

She slid the crowbar down the back of her shirt, hooking the curved edge on her bra and letting the bottom rest inside her shorts in case it came loose. She kicked at the locking mechanism again, again, her foot aching, muscles screaming.

"Go!" Earl yelled, voice choked with water, gurgling.

"I…" *I can't leave you.*

"Get out of here, girl!"

She stopped kicking, the bones in her foot throbbing. He was right. It was logical. Pragmatic. No matter what she did, she was going to fail him. He blinked, but his face was underwater, and she could no longer see the blue of his eyes. He resurfaced—his mouth, just his mouth—coughing, choking. Like Phillip had. He let go of the grate.

Her heart hammered in her throat. Beneath the shadows of the grate, Earl went hazy, a ghostly figure in the dimness. The rushing water whooshed in her ears. *Get out of here, girl! Go!*

She grabbed the rungs of the ladder with both hands and climbed. The next time she looked back, the bottom of the tunnel had descended into rippling blackness and the only sound she could hear was her own hoarse screaming.

CHAPTER THIRTY-FOUR

SHE CLIMBED, climbed as fast as she could, muscles burning, chest aching. The *ting, ting, ting* of the flashlight against the rungs of the ladder sounded in time to her frantic breath. What would she find at the top of the tunnel? Another grate? This time, if the latches refused to budge, she'd have no one to help her pry them open.

She'd die like Earl.

"Climb faster, sis!"

She could still hear the rush of water from below, but more distantly now—had a water main broken, like Earl said? Was Chad underwater now? Her lungs were on fire.

Would she die too?

What would she think about in her final moments? The tendons in her ankles felt as if they might snap.

Above her…the tunnel ended. No grate. A ceiling, cement —gray and *dry*.

She climbed over the top lip of the tunnel. Miraculously, wonderfully, blissfully dry and her eyes burned with unshed tears.

"Don't get cocky." This time it sounded less like Phillip

and more like her. *Run*. There would be time to rest when she got out of there.

She swung the light around her—brighter than before?—ah, she'd lost the bag somewhere below. Off to her right, the tunnel ended and there were no other paths that she could see. *Fuck*—the more paths, the more places for the water to go should it rise this high.

Her legs wobbled as she hooked left and staggered down the cement tunnel, listening to the sick squelch of her boots and the thundering throb of her heart. Her gait evened. And then she was really running, flying down the hallway, stumbling, nearly sobbing with exhaustion, her breath panting from her, adrenaline surging through her muscles. She should have taken one of those water bottles from Earl, why hadn't she?

Vaguely she heard the back of her shorts tearing where the tip of the crowbar rested, and she let it; the dry air on her left hip was better than the sticky chafing of the rest of her clothes. Ahead, the tunnel came to an *X*, four branches at right angles. Which way? She tried to remember which direction she'd entered from—was this tunnel parallel to the one beneath? But it didn't matter. Even if she knew which direction she was headed, she didn't know which way was out.

Choose. *Now or never*.

She hooked another left. The world went dark. Blackness, nothing but blackness. The flashlight had gone out.

She tapped it against her palm, her wrist raw against the cord, and it blazed to life once more. Either it had been damaged during her escape from the flooded tunnel or it was just running out of batteries. She had to hurry if she wanted to be able to see.

She ran faster.

Swung the light to get rid of the excess water.

Her heart was in her throat.

Her breath was too fast, too hard.

Her mouth was dry.

And the smell...was that her? God knew what kind of horribleness had made its way into her flesh through the gouges in her back and along her thighs. If she made it out of here but died from some infection, she was going to be fucking pissed.

Csssshhhh. She froze. The sound came again, a harsh scratching from somewhere up ahead, then a *thunk* that sounded like a footstep.

She wasn't alone.

CHAPTER THIRTY-FIVE

SHE LOOKED BACK DOWN the hallway behind her. Should she run for it? But the person at the other end of the tunnel had surely heard her approach—if they were working with Windy, they'd come after her, kill her, anything to prevent her from escaping. And she'd rather face them head-on than have them sneak up from behind.

Was that logical? It didn't sound logical.

"You lost logical a long time ago, sis."

Victoria pulled the crowbar from the back of her shirt and held it in both hands like a softball bat—like Chad had taught her—the flashlight swinging, turning the world into a half-assed strobe. She steadied it. Steadied the weapon, too, crowbar poised and ready to strike should they come closer. Movement, someone shifting against the wall, sitting, but everything was blurry, cast in the yellowed haze of the flashlight and the filmy spots that could only be coming from her eyes. Why was the world so hazy all of a sudden? Was starvation making her lose her eyesight? Probably that shitty water from the tunnels.

She stepped closer. "Hello?"

No response, but definite movement, though it was an odd sort of moving, she realized, a twitching. And...was someone laughing? She blinked hard. *What the—*

She screamed. A rat. A fucking rat. Victoria staggered back as the creature emerged from the shadows near the side wall and scurried into the darkness back the way she'd come, straight across the fork in the road, down one of the other paths that branched from the main tunnel.

"You're alone, sis. You're going to die alone, just like last time."

"I'm not going to die, and I'm not alone!" Her voice echoed through the chamber. Bile rose in her throat as she stared back down the hall after the rat. If rats could get in, they must have a way out, right? Rats didn't just appear.

"No, they fucking live here, sis. You want to live here forever too?"

She followed the rat anyway, crowbar in her fist, tracking the flashlight side to side, straining her eyes for signs of the rat or for other things trapped here with her. She saw nothing but the cement tunnel.

But she heard...laughter.

Hallucinating, still hallucinating. She couldn't swallow. Then she heard Nick's voice in her ears: "This side is completely smooth like a dead baby's ass," and she saw him smile almost as clearly as she heard the words, and then the memory of the laughter from their little group came again, raucous and loud.

Wait...no one had laughed that hard at his jokes, especially not that one. She paused, listening. A murmuring sound, not Nick, and then the laughter again, the laughter, the canned laugh track of a television sitcom.

Coming from the ceiling.

CHAPTER THIRTY-SIX

THERE WAS NOTHING ABOVE HER—JUST cement. But even if she wasn't near the exit, she was not alone. Someone was up there watching shitty TV.

Unless the laughter was in her head.

Her heart in her throat, she blinked at the corridor in front of her, flipped off the flashlight, and rested the crowbar on her shoulder. If she came across someone who wished her harm, at least she'd have the element of surprise if she approached in the dark. She snuck down the corridor, following the sound as best she could, telling herself that the squelching of her boots was near silent, that whoever was watching TV couldn't hear her.

The sitcom noise suddenly stopped.

She pressed herself against the wall, the surface grainy and freezing against her damp back. Then an advertisement clicked on, and she exhaled and pulled herself off the cement, followed the drone of an auto salesman, then the low growl of someone pushing fast food as the black of the tunnel went on and on. She grasped the crowbar so hard her knuckles ached. But was it getting lighter? Yes, definitely lighter, and then she saw the source: a fuzzy white haze glowed from a narrow opening in the left wall of the tunnel. Did this tunnel lead to the exit, or was the sound a ruse, a trick? Maybe she'd find Windy waiting. But it wasn't like Victoria could stay here.

Now or never, just go. She ran on her tiptoes, paused at the opening, and then peered cautiously around the corner...and straightened. Not a tunnel at all. *Stairs.* Lots of them, and narrow as hell, like those she'd once seen in an underground crypt. The television was louder here, too. Was that Mr. Belding she heard? *Saved by the Bell*?

She stepped onto the staircase. Listened to the canned laughter, bracing for another set of footsteps or someone else's breath behind her. The sitcom went on.

Up the second stair. The fourth, sixth, eighth, the ceiling leaning closer with every step, the walls threatening to close in. Her knuckles sang, the crowbar hot against her palms.

Four more. Four more to the hallway at the top of the steps. In front of her, the flat wall glowed blue from what had to be the television. Louder now.

She couldn't breathe.

Three more steps.

Her thighs shuddered.

Two more steps.

Electricity zipped up her spine.

One.

She paused, trying to catch her breath, lips cracked and burning with every staccato exhale. A chill breeze passed over her skin. Air conditioning? No, that couldn't be right. She peeked her head around the corner into a hallway, narrow, but wider than the steps. To her right, thirty feet away, a craggy arched doorway made of the same cement as the tunnel, as the stairwell, led to a room. Brilliantly white walls. And there was the television, sitting in the middle of the room on a small tray table. The tunnel branched off to the left and right of the arched door, but no sounds came from either direction. No other lights. Probably dead ends.

She padded toward the room as quickly and quietly as she could, straining her ears, certain that at any moment she'd hear the thunk of someone else's shoes on the tunnel floor behind her—*almost there*—but the only noises were the TV and her own labored breathing.

She paused just outside the arch, listening hard. Nothing but the drone of the TV.

Closer, her neck muscles tightening, aching as she peered inside the room.

Not Windy.

In a chair in the corner, facing the television—facing her— sat a scrawny man with long dark hair the same shade as hers, his eyes closed. *So blurry*. She blinked hard, squinting, and the room solidified. The man was shirtless. Stained jeans. A thick strip of angry pink bisected his upper arm where …his tattoo should have been.

Phillip.

Her heart stopped.

He's alive? Was he breathing? He wasn't moving. Then he did—his pinky twitched. Silver cuffs glinted from just above his wrist bones. The chair was bolted to the floor.

What did she do to you?

"Get me out of here, sis!" She heard his voice clear as day, but his mouth remained slack. Victoria scanned the room, searching for Windy…no one else, silence except for the canned laughter, and even that had dulled.

Victoria slid the crowbar down inside the back of her shirt again and ran to her brother. "Phillip," she whispered. His eyes fluttered, but he did not awaken. "I'll get you out of here, just hang on."

In the glow of the television, the white walls looked slick

just like the bunker. No cameras. To her left, a single door gleamed, red as blood, a tiny little convex circle at eye level— a peephole.

Was that the way out? Probably. Windy wouldn't have left Phillip here if he could wander away through that door or into the tunnel, but she'd bolted him down—maybe she hadn't been as cautious with the red door since Phillip was incapacitated. Maybe they'd get lucky.

"Yeah, because we've been so lucky so far?" Phillip whispered without moving his lips. She was hallucinating. He was still unconscious.

"Phillip, you sorry shit, get up!" She shook him. His head lolled to one side. He moaned.

She pushed herself to standing, muscles twinging painfully. *Fuck*. Was the door wood or metal? With the paint it was impossible to tell, and if she went at the door with the crowbar, Windy would surely arrive with a weapon. Though if that bitch thought she was weakened from her ordeal... maybe Windy'd let her guard down. One moment, that's all Victoria needed.

Everything hurt. *But I will fuck her up despite the pain.*

Music on the television cut through her thoughts then vanished again. Her eyes burned with unshed tears. Her brother's cheekbones were sharp as blades, his skin sallow and wasting.

She'd let go of his hand once.

She'd be damned if she would let him go again.

CHAPTER THIRTY-SEVEN

"INTERESTING."

Victoria whirled around. Windy stood behind her, though she was certain the woman hadn't been there moments ago. There was no door back there, nothing but the mouth to the tunnel—how had she gotten in? Oh shit, had she seen the crowbar?

But if Windy knew she was armed, she didn't show it. She smiled. "Just amazing. I never thought you'd find a way out, not in a million years." She raised an eyebrow. "You bring Earl with you?"

Phillip moaned, and Windy narrowed her eyes at him. Victoria stepped in front of her brother, blocking Windy's view. In Victoria's peripheral vision, the television droned on. Laughter echoed through the room.

"Earl didn't make it...Brooke, is it?"

"Please, call me Windy. Brooke was...someone else. Someone I used to be." And when she straightened her shoulders, she looked...confident. It was a mad kind of confident, but a righteous confidence all the same, the insanity of a zealot.

"Why am I here?" Victoria kept her feet planted on the floor, watching Windy's hands. Why didn't she have a weapon? Oh...but she did. A little black box: a Taser. Aimed at Victoria.

Windy's face shone in the ghostlike glow of the TV. "I needed to see if you'd do it—I thought it'd be Chad, not Olivia, but..." Her eyes filled. "Thank you."

Fucking lunatic. Her husband's name in this woman's mouth was repulsive, as if Windy were perverting his memory—vomiting a pile of maggots onto his coffin. And...*she knows*. Windy knew what Victoria had done to survive. She had to have a camera down there somewhere, had to, and they'd missed it. Not that it mattered now.

The television laughed. Victoria's head throbbed. "You're welcome. Can I go home now?"

"What kind of lame thing is that to say?" Phillip said from his chair behind her, but when she glanced back at him, his eyes were still closed, his tongue limp and useless against his bottom lip.

Victoria's jaw hardened. Windy was making him suffer. Windy had killed Chad, killed all those people, just because she wanted to assuage her guilt about some shit she'd done twenty fucking years ago? She clenched her fists, aching to reach for the crowbar that had gone cold between her shoulder blades. "I still don't know what you want with me."

"I want to hear about it."

"I don't know what—"

"How do you feel?" Windy touched the trigger on the Taser with her thumb. Caressing it. *Probably the only thing she's ever fucking loved.*

"I feel...awful. Guilty." It was true, but fury had charred every ounce of guilt and reformed it into a hard ball of electric rage.

Windy nodded, a slow, sad smile spreading across her

face. "We're alike, you and I." She stepped closer, Taser aimed at Victoria's chest. "Our families fell apart. But we stayed strong through it, survived long enough to build new families, didn't we?"

Victoria's jaw dropped. "What? I wasn't building a new family, I moved down here looking for my broth—"

Windy put up one hand, still caressing the Taser trigger with her other thumb. "I wanted to be better, Victoria, you have to know that."

Victoria's mouth went dry. Her vision tunneled. The crowbar sat heavy against her spine. What had happened to the knife? Earl—he probably still had it secured in his ankle holster, deep in the bowels of Windy's dungeon. *Shit.*

Windy was still watching her, eyes shining—there was sorrow there, a yearning. Cautious questioning. And grief, definitely grief. Victoria had thought Windy wanted to see if others would have done the same to survive, but staring into her eyes... *It's more than that.* Windy wanted to be absolved.

"I get it," Victoria said slowly. "We all want to be better, but sometimes we have to do things we don't want to. It's a matter of life and death." Chad. Olivia. Carter. Earl. Victoria cleared her throat. "A matter of survival."

Windy's eyes widened, nostrils flaring. "You *do* understand, don't you?"

"Of course." Victoria nodded. "And what could I possibly have done differently? What could you have done?"

Windy's lip trembled. She tried to peer around Victoria at Phillip again, and when Victoria sidestepped to block her once more, the trembling stopped and Windy's jaw hardened, spots of pink rising in her cheeks. "He's mine now, you know."

"Your what?"

"My *brother*." Windy stepped closer, toward the droning

television—five feet away, tops, well within range of the Taser.

Victoria's muscles shrieked with tension. No windows. All cement. *You are not locking me up in here, you bitch.*

Windy was still staring as if expecting Victoria to respond to a question she hadn't asked. The television laughed. Phillip moaned.

"Olivia stole my last brother. It didn't turn out well for her, did it?"

Olivia's bloody wrist. Olivia's slack mouth. And that knife…

Victoria shifted backward, the pearls around her neck suddenly heavier—she'd forgotten all about them. The flesh on her back tingled, burning. *I will just stay away from you and stick with Victoria*—Olivia had said that to Earl when she found out about his knife. Olivia had known about her blade from the start.

"You told Olivia I had a knife. Before you sent her down."

Windy nodded. "I think…sometimes you only need to plant seeds without knowing what will grow. Makes sense, right?" She cocked her head as if she actually wanted an answer.

Crazy. She's fucking crazy. Victoria's adrenaline was rising, the cells in her body popping like fireworks, edging her brain toward explosion. Phillip shifted—the metal cuffs clanked.

"Phillip will be happier with me, Victoria." Windy grinned and tapped the Taser button with her fingernail.

Rage boiled in Victoria's belly, spreading into her chest, her face, as it used to when she was small, a rage without logic, a rage without consequence. *Don't talk about him, you motherfucking cunt.* Victoria was opening her mouth to say it out loud when she heard a tiny sound—off-key humming. Phillip?

Don't worry today, there's still time to play…

Windy's face did not change. The television droned on, but Victoria could no longer see it—she was watching Windy through a tunnel of black as if the passages below had burned themselves into her retinas. Could Windy hear him humming? Maybe, because Windy stepped to her left, toward the red door. "I'm disappointed that things have to end this way, but Phillip doesn't need two sisters."

The low humming continued, so quiet Victoria was half certain she was imagining it.

Tomorrow will come, we'll get up and run!

Windy took another small step backward—six feet away now. Three steps from the door. "Like you said...we do what we have to. To survive."

But this wasn't about survival. Guilt had driven Windy—and revenge. Windy had wanted to fuck with people the way she thought life had fucked with her.

Tomorrow's not here, be happy today...

"So you and I...we're special?" Victoria said, trying to keep her voice even. "We could be allies after this storm passes." *You little twit.*

Windy frowned. "Do you think I'm stupid, Victoria?"

"No. But you don't know everything. You've forgotten what strong people do in a crisis—the most important thing."

Windy slid one more step closer to the door, the Taser twitching in her hand. "What's that?"

Now or neeeeever.

Two things happened at once: Victoria lunged at Windy, the television cord catching on her ankle, the TV toppling off the tray; Victoria snatched the crowbar from the back of her shirt and swung it as hard as she could, and for a moment she was on the sand at home plate, a wooden bat in her hand, hearing Chad yell her name, but the crunch when the bat collided was not that of wood hitting a softball—it was denser, wetter. Everything went dark. The room erupted in a sick crackling sound—electricity—and Victoria leapt back, tripping over the television, landing on her ass with a thud, waiting for the current to catch her wet clothing and fry her.

Threadlike bolts of blue-white lightning arced up from behind the downed television; the thin crackling continued, piercing the air. But she felt no electric jolts running through her muscles, felt no new pain aside from the dull throbbing in her tailbone. Then the sound and sparking ceased. But everything else was still black—had the only light been from the television? It had been so bright after the dim of the tunnels that she hadn't even noticed.

She adjusted her grip on the crowbar and reached for the flashlight—gone. *Where the fuck...?* She climbed to her knees, seeking the television cord in the darkness, feeling for the wall, the outlet, her eyes never leaving the spot where she had last seen Windy.

There. Victoria shoved the cord into the socket and the screen flickered to life—white haze, aimed at the ceiling. She froze, crowbar-bat poised on her shoulder. The spot where Windy lay was shrouded in shadows beyond the reach of the TV. But she could see enough.

The television screen was splattered with blood. Gray matter clung to one edge of the crowbar. And the lightning... Windy's hand lay on top of the Taser. Unmoving. A dark puddle was widening around her head.

Victoria turned to the chair, to her brother. His skin was cold and clammy, like the day they'd drowned, but she pressed her fingers to his throat...he had a pulse. And he was *breathing*.

"Phillip." Her muscles weren't working right—so tired. Suddenly so tired.

He moaned. His head lolled. Then he opened his eyes. "Did you hear me?" And he smiled the way he used to when they were children, playing the whisper game, him in the treehouse, her on the ground. "Did you hear me, sis?"

"I'll get us out of here." Her throat prickled—hot. She stood, slowly, slowly, the room spinning. She'd have to find the keys for those cuffs; hopefully they were somewhere in the house, but she should call for help too…if she could. Phillip was in bad shape, and there was no way she'd be able to carry him out alone.

Victoria dropped the crowbar and stepped past Windy's lifeless body toward the red door, sure she'd not get that lucky, sure she'd have to search the limp woman on the floor, but the knob turned. She stepped through the door into a hallway. In front of her was a sitting room with dark paneling, dark wood floors, leather couch, so normal and unassuming, as was the photo on the wall: a much younger Windy and two older people, probably her parents. Smiling for eternity. Living forever in Windy's twisted reenactments. And to Victoria's right…a door waited at the end of a narrow foyer. Huge. Gray. Metal? A knob like a foot long ship's wheel in the center. She approached on autopilot, expecting it to open to another black tunnel, a hallway to nowhere.

Her hands shook as she grabbed the doorknob. She took a breath. And turned it.

Tears sprang into her eyes as she stumbled into the gray morning. The sky above was a hazy white, the outlines of the treetops muddled and fuzzy, like lines of black mold. Around the expanse of hills she was standing on, the world was a lake.

It was the most beautiful thing she'd ever seen. Victoria sat on the slippery earth, face up toward the sky, letting the water cleanse her.

"What do people do in a crisis, Windy?" She almost laughed.

They survive, you fucking bitch.

EPILOGUE

"YOU WANT COFFEE?"

Phillip's eyes glittered in the brilliant Chicago morning that filtered through their apartment window, his cheeks ruddier, fuller than they'd been when she found him. He shoved a bite of toast in his mouth and leaned back in his seat. "That stuff will kill ya."

"Very funny." Victoria grabbed the pot from the middle of their little bistro set, rolling her eyes. Across the table, Phillip grinned. To think she'd almost lost him. Almost lost herself too.

Six months in therapy had done him well, helped him with his guilt; he said he'd vanished because he was ashamed of himself, because she was better off without him around to get her into trouble. He still felt bad about her childhood trip to the emergency room, her broken rib. Deeply rooted shit. But they'd kill those roots together—that's what family was for.

Phillip finished the toast and shrugged into his jacket, then ran a hand through his short dark hair. "I get out of class at seven…Mexican for dinner? That place up the road has good vegetarian fajitas."

"Deal."

The vegetarianism thing had come as a shock, even to her. But something about the way they kept the animals locked up, listening to the mournful cries of their friends being led to slaughter, smelling the blood…it hit too close to home.

But not this home. This home meant freedom.

It didn't stop Chad's voice from coming to her sometimes. Didn't stop her from smelling the iron or the stink of decay, as if the reek of death had imprinted onto her sinuses. The things that had driven her and Chad apart seemed so small now, and sometimes she thought she might have tried again, tried harder, if he hadn't died. If Windy hadn't killed him.

Or maybe Victoria was at fault. Was there anything she could have done to keep him alive? If Chad had escaped into the tunnel with her, would they all have gotten out? Would he have let Earl die alone in the dark?

These were the questions that kept her up at night. That, and the way Olivia's meat tasted on her tongue. It only took the tiniest tinge of metal in the air to bring it all back, probably the other reason she was now meat-free. But weirdly, she thought Olivia would have been okay with the choice she'd made.

Eating Olivia had let Victoria kill that bitch. And she hadn't forgotten about the pearls.

Phillip smiled at her now, smiled like he always had when they were small. Like she was the best thing that had ever happened to him. She wasn't, he had better things ahead, she had to believe that, but right now they were working together. They'd even picked out their new furniture as a team: a suede couch, a glass coffee table with metal legs, a tall wooden bistro set, each of them gloriously new. New furniture, new jobs, new lives.

Nice guys didn't finish last, not always. Everyone wanted to believe they were kinder, better than most other people. But sometimes, when you dropped the front, when you were forced to lose yourself, you found a new way to survive.

～

HUNGRY FOR MORE?
READ ON FOR A SNEAK PEEK AT *FAMISHED*,
the first book in the Ash Park series!

～

Join Meghan's reader group at
MEGHANOFLYNN.COM, and get a
FREE SHORT STORY!
You'll also be first in line for
new release information.
No spam, and you can
opt out anytime.

PRAISE FOR THE ASH PARK SERIES

"Dark, gritty, and raw, O'Flynn's Ash Park series will take your mind prisoner. This series will keep you awake far into the morning hours."
~Kristen Mae, bestselling author of Red Water

"Haunting...the Ash Park series should be everyone's next binge-read."
~NYT bestselling author Andra Watkins

"Visceral, fearless, and addictive, this series will keep you on the edge of your seat."
~Bestselling author Mandi Castle

"Cunning, delightfully disturbing, and addictive, the Ash Park series is an expertly written labyrinth of twisted, unpredictable awesomeness!"
~Award-winning author Beth Teliho

"Intense and suspenseful...captured me from the first chapter and held me enthralled until the final page."
~Susan Sewell, Reader's Favorite

SNEAK PEEK AT FAMISHED

AN ASH PARK NOVEL (VOLUME 1)

Sunday, December 6th

FOCUS, or she's dead.

Petrosky ground his teeth together, but it didn't stop the panic from swelling hot and frantic within him. After the arrest last week, this crime should have been fucking impossible.

He wished it were a copycat. He knew it wasn't.

Anger knotted his chest as he examined the corpse that lay in the middle of the cavernous living room. Dominic Harwick's intestines spilled onto the white marble floor as though someone had tried to run off with them. His eyes were wide, milky at the edges already, so it had been awhile since someone gutted his sorry ass and turned him into a rag doll in a three-thousand-dollar suit.

That rich prick should have been able to protect her.

Petrosky looked at the couch: luxurious, empty, cold. Last week Hannah had sat on that couch, staring at him with wide green eyes that made her seem older than her twenty-three years. She had been happy, like Julie had been before she was stolen from him. He pictured Hannah as she might have been at eight years old, skirt twirling, dark hair flying, face flushed with sun, like one of the photos of Julie he kept tucked in his wallet.

They all started so innocent, so pure, so...*vulnerable*.

The idea that Hannah was the catalyst in the deaths of eight others, the cornerstone of some serial killer's plan, had not occurred to him when they first met. But it had later. It did now.

Petrosky resisted the urge to kick the body and refocused on the couch. Crimson congealed along the white leather as if marking Hannah's departure.

He wondered if the blood was hers.

The click of a doorknob caught Petrosky's attention. He turned to see Bryant Graves, the lead FBI agent, entering the room from the garage door, followed by four other agents. Petrosky tried not to think about what might be in the garage. Instead, he watched the four men survey the living room from different angles, their movements practically choreographed.

"Damn, does everyone that girl knows get whacked?" one of the agents asked.

"Pretty much," said another.

A plain-clothed agent stooped to inspect a chunk of scalp on the floor. Whitish-blond hair waved, tentacle-like, from the dead skin, beckoning Petrosky to touch it.

"You know this guy?" one of Graves's cronies asked from the doorway.

"Dominic Harwick." Petrosky nearly spat out the bastard's name.

"No signs of forced entry, so one of them knew the killer," Graves said.

"*She* knew the killer," Petrosky said. "Obsession builds over time. This level of obsession indicates it was probably someone she knew well."

But who?

Petrosky turned back to the floor in front of him, where words scrawled in blood had dried sickly brown in the morning light.

> Ever drifting down the stream—
> Lingering in the golden gleam—
> Life, what is it but a dream?

Petrosky's gut clenched. He forced himself to look at Graves. "And, Han—" *Hannah*. Her name caught in his throat, sharp like a razor blade. "The girl?"

"There are bloody drag marks heading out to the back shower and a pile of bloody clothes," Graves said. "He must have cleaned her up before taking her. We've got the techs on it now, but they're working the perimeter first." Graves bent and used a pencil to lift the edge of the scalp, but it was suctioned to the floor with dried blood.

"Hair? That's new," said another voice. Petrosky didn't bother to find out who had spoken. He stared at the coppery stains on the floor, his muscles twitching with anticipation. Someone could be tearing her apart as the agents roped off the room. How long did she have? He wanted to run, to find her, but he had no idea where to look.

"Bag it," Graves said to the agent examining the scalp, then turned to Petrosky. "It's all been connected from the beginning. Either Hannah Montgomery was his target all along or she's just another random victim. I think the fact that she isn't filleted on the floor like the others points to her being the goal, not an extra."

"He's got something special planned for her," Petrosky

whispered. He hung his head, hoping it wasn't already too late.

If it was, it was all his fault.

∽

GET *FAMISHED* AT MEGHANOFLYNN.COM.

∽

"Fearless, smart writing, and a plot
that will stick with you."
~*Beth Teliho, award-winning author of* Order of Seven

SNEAK PEAK AT SHADOW'S KEEP

FOR WILLIAM SHANNAHAN, six-thirty on Tuesday, the third of August, was "the moment." Life was full of those moments, his mother had always told him, experiences that prevented you from going back to who you were before, tiny decisions that changed you forever.

And that morning, the moment came and went, though he didn't recognize it, nor would he ever have wished to recall that morning again for as long as he lived. But he would never, from that day on, be able to forget it.

He left his Mississippi farmhouse a little after six, dressed in running shorts and an old T-shirt that still had sunny yellow paint dashed across the front from decorating the child's room. *The child.* William had named him Brett, but he'd never told anyone that. To everyone else, the baby was just that-thing-you-could-never-mention, particularly since William had also lost his wife at Bartlett General.

His green Nikes beat against the gravel, a blunt metronome as he left the porch and started along the road parallel to the Oval, what the townsfolk called the near hundred square miles of woods that had turned marshy wasteland when freeway construction had dammed the creeks downstream. Before William was born, those fifty or so unlucky folks who owned property inside the Oval had gotten some settlement from the developers when their houses flooded and were deemed uninhabitable. Now those homes were part of a ghost town, tucked well beyond the reach of prying eyes.

William's mother had called it a disgrace. William thought it might be the price of progress, though he'd never dared to tell her that. He'd also never told her that his fondest memory of the Oval was when his best friend Mike had beat the crap out of Kevin Pultzer for punching William in the eye. That was before Mike was the sheriff, back when they were all just "us" or "them" and William had always been a them, except when Mike was around. He might fit in somewhere else, some other place where the rest of the dorky goofballs lived, but here in Graybel he was just a little...odd. Oh well. People in this town gossiped far too much to trust them as friends anyway.

William sniffed at the marshy air, the closely-shorn grass sucking at his sneakers as he increased his pace. Somewhere near him a bird shrieked, sharp and high. He startled as it took flight above him with another aggravated scream.

Straight ahead, the car road leading into town was bathed in filtered dawn, the first rays of sun painting the gravel gold, though the road was slippery with moss and morning damp. To his right, deep shadows pulled at him from the trees; the tall pines crouched close together as if hiding a secret bundle in their underbrush. Dark but calm, quiet—comforting. Legs pumping, William headed off the road toward the pines.

A snap like that of a muted gunshot echoed through the morning air, somewhere deep inside the wooded stillness, and though it was surely just a fox, or maybe a raccoon, he paused, running in place, disquiet spreading through him like the worms of fog that were only now rolling out from under the trees to be burned off as the sun made its debut. Cops never got a moment off, although in this sleepy town the worst he'd see today would be an argument over cattle. He glanced up the road. Squinted. Should he continue up the brighter main street or escape into the shadows beneath the trees?

That was his moment.

William ran toward the woods.

As soon as he set foot inside the tree line, the dark descended on him like a blanket, the cool air brushing his face as another hawk shrieked overhead. William nodded to it, as if the animal had sought his approval, then swiped his arm over his forehead and dodged a limb, pick-jogging his way down the path. A branch caught his ear. He winced. Six foot three was great for some things, but not for running in the woods. Either that or God was pissed at him, which wouldn't be surprising, though he wasn't clear on what he had done wrong. Probably for smirking at his memories of Kevin Pultzer with a torn T-shirt and a bloodied nose.

He smiled again, just a little one this time.

When the path opened up, he raised his gaze above the canopy. He had an hour before he needed to be at the precinct, but the pewter sky beckoned him to run quicker before the heat crept up. It was a good day to turn forty-two, he decided. He might not be the best-looking guy around, but he had his health. And there was a woman whom he adored, even if she wasn't sure about him yet.

William didn't blame her. He probably didn't deserve her, but he'd surely try to convince her that he did, like he had with Marianna...though he didn't think weird card tricks would help this time. But weird was what he had. Without it, he was just background noise, part of the wallpaper of this small town, and at forty-one—*no, forty-two, now*—he was running out of time to start over.

He was pondering this when he rounded the bend and saw the feet. Pale soles barely bigger than his hand, poking from behind a rust-colored boulder that sat a few feet from the edge of the trail. He stopped, his heart throbbing an erratic rhythm in his ears.

Please let it be a doll. But he saw the flies buzzing around the top of the boulder. Buzzing. Buzzing.

William crept forward along the path, reaching for his hip where his gun usually sat, but he touched only cloth. The dried yellow paint scratched his thumb. He thrust his hand into his pocket for his lucky coin. No quarter. Only his phone.

William approached the rock, the edges of his vision dark and unfocused as if he were looking through a telescope, but in the dirt around the stone he could make out deep paw prints. Probably from a dog or a coyote, though these were *enormous*—nearly the size of a salad plate, too big for anything he'd expect to find in these woods. He frantically scanned the underbrush, trying to locate the animal, but saw only a cardinal appraising him from a nearby branch.

Someone's back there, someone needs my help.

He stepped closer to the boulder. *Please don't let it be what I think it is.* Two more steps and he'd be able to see beyond the rock, but he could not drag his gaze from the trees where he was certain canine eyes were watching. Still nothing there save the shaded bark of the surrounding woods. He took another step—cold oozed from the muddy earth into his shoe and around his left ankle, like a hand from the grave. William stumbled, pulling his gaze from the trees just in time to see the boulder rushing at his head and then he was on his side in the slimy filth to the right of the boulder, next to...

Oh god, oh god, oh god.

William had seen death in his twenty years as a deputy, but usually it was the result of a drunken accident, a car wreck, an old man found dead on his couch.

This was not that. The boy was no more than six, probably less. He lay on a carpet of rotting leaves, one arm draped over his chest, legs splayed haphazardly as if he, too, had tripped in the muck. But this wasn't an accident; the boy's throat was torn, jagged ribbons of flesh peeled back, drooping on either side of the muscle meat, the unwanted skin on a Thanksgiving turkey. Deep gouges permeated his chest and abdomen, black slashes against mottled green flesh, the wounds obscured behind his shredded clothing and bits of twigs and leaves.

William scrambled backward, clawing at the ground, his muddy shoe kicking the child's ruined calf, where the boy's shy white bones peeked from under congealing blackish tissue. The legs looked…*chewed on.*

His hand slipped in the muck. The child's face was turned to his, mouth open, black tongue lolling as if he were about to plead for help. *Not good, oh shit, not good.*

William finally clambered to standing, yanked his cell from his pocket, and tapped a button, barely registering his friend's answering bark. A fly lit on the boy's eyebrow above a single white mushroom that crept upward over the landscape of his cheek, rooted in the empty socket that had once contained an eye.

"Mike, it's William. I need a…tell Dr. Klinger to bring the wagon."

He stepped backward, toward the path, shoe sinking again, the mud trying to root him there, and he yanked his foot free with a squelching sound. Another step backward and he was on the path, and another step off the path again, and another, another, feet moving until his back slammed against a gnarled oak on the opposite side of the trail. He jerked his head up, squinting through the greening awning half convinced the boy's assailant would be perched there, ready to leap from the trees and lurch him into oblivion on flensing jaws. But there was no wretched animal. Blue leaked through the filtered haze of dawn.

William lowered his gaze, Mike's voice a distant crackle irritating the edges of his brain but not breaking through—he could not understand what his friend was saying. He stopped trying to decipher it and said, "I'm on the trails behind my house, found a body. Tell them to come in through the path on the Winchester side." He tried to listen to the receiver, but heard only the buzzing of flies across the trail—had they been so loud a moment ago? Their noise grew, amplified to unnatural volumes, filling his head until every other sound fell away—was Mike still talking? He pushed *End*, pocketed the phone, and then leaned back and slid down the tree trunk.

And William Shannahan, not recognizing the event the rest of his life would hinge upon, sat at the base of a gnarled oak tree on Tuesday, the third of August, put his head into his hands, and wept.

～

GET *SHADOW'S KEEP* ON MEGHANOFLYNN.COM.

～

"Masterful, staggering, twisted...and completely unpredictable."
~*Wendy Heard,* Hunting Annabelle

SNEAK PEEK AT THE JILTED

ABRAM SHEPHERD, PRESENT DAY

THE MAN WRITHES, his body twisting against the mattress, fists clenched, face shadowed beneath the low-hanging beams of the roofline. His olive-skinned chest seeps blood from wounds I cannot heal. He licks his lips like a nervous animal, and then cries out, high and piercing, as if someone were running him through with a blade, such a guttural incantation it sounds almost inhuman. And it may be, for who's to say what is mortal and what is not? From the moment humans emerged from Earth's womb, we have carried a thread of sharpness within us, a fury that expands when we allow even the slightest hint of that agitation to catch our gaze. Because we focus there, you know, fascinated by the wickedness we see laid bare like the flesh of a lover.

That madness becomes our own. And soon it is all we see.

I clench my pipe harder between my teeth, the smoke circling my head like an herbal fog.

The man's eyes snap open and focus—for an instant only —but in that moment I see his humanity concentrated there, fixed in that tiny glint of light around the iris. "Please, Father

…" he croaks in a strong Spanish accent, and his head snaps back, his spine contorts—"Father, save me, help me"—and then his words degenerate into glottal, hopeless blubbering. "Perdóname, Padre, perdóname."

Forgive me, Father, forgive me.

I cough once, trying to clear the putrid, meaty stench from the back of my throat, but it remains despite the smoke from my pipe, the air heavy as the cross around my neck. Perhaps if I truly wore the Roman collar as I'd once intended, I would be better equipped to fight this. But even if I were a priest, no one is remarkable enough to be granted forgiveness; my deeds here are but a physical prayer of repentance.

The man moans, froth forming at his lips and dripping down his cheek to the bed like the ooze of raw egg white. I have seen this surrender before, oh so many times, but they do not all go so easily; the skin on my left leg still burns with my most recent wound. *Helen.* She fought harder than most, crying out in prayer as she fled over the lawn, red scarf flying behind her like blood spurting from a neck wound. Afterward, I could almost feel the quivering nerves beneath her flesh as if they were mine, the sharp agony as The Dark bound her in coils of hate that tore her soul from her body and dragged it to a place I cannot begin to name. It was over quickly, as endings so often are, and though I hurled my prayers into the night, I was soon alone, my only response the bitter howl of the wind.

The man bucks off the mattress now, spraying spittle against the pillow, wetting the stained green blanket. It will not be long. He has gone so much faster than the others, perhaps because the evil is thicker since Helen was taken; I can feel the violence in the air, seeping from The Dark like pollutants into a water supply.

I can practically hear the good doctor, my only friend, whispering, "You're obsessed, Mr. Shepherd. Delusional."

The doctor would tell me I should stop this madness. "Go back to your wife," he'd say. But I've spent far too much of my life ignoring my calling—the past looms full of abandoned things, wasted moments I could have used more wisely.

The man's arms and legs still, though his chest heaves with the rapid inhales of a panting dog—much too fast. Then he screams again, loud and long, and this time it is wholly and poignantly human, and my own humanity responds with a painful tightening of my rib cage. Staring at the glitter in his wild eyes, watching him go from madness, to horror, and back, my heart vibrates with such savage intensity I think it might stop altogether; I fight against this, for I am not ready to be tossed into the fiery pits with my ancestors. I know what they did—I found the journals in this old house, hidden beneath a floorboard, the pages tattered and worn. How I wish I had not read them. Because now I see fully the wickedness I am up against—see The Dark for what he is. He's been tormenting these grounds for eons, spreading malevolence like a virus, and far more will be sacrificed unless I find another strong enough to help me, someone who can lure The Dark out, so I might expel him from this place. And if I cannot weaken his hold here, I will not have the slightest chance of salvation.

The doctor may believe he can ease my burden, soften the pain of the cancer, but he cannot ease the suffering of my soul—he does not believe there is anything to fear. But he will believe. Soon he will see it too.

I can feel The Dark even now in the coldness whirling around me, though there is no open window, no earthly source for such a breeze. The man in the bed shudders then stills, his breath a thin wheeze, his shirt covered in crimson, so steeped in his own pain he cannot not see beyond the tip of his nose. So many exorcisms, and every one ends in defeat.

I still hear those lost souls crying sometimes—or the wails of angels, admonishing me for my failures. Or perhaps that is my own soul, crying out in the night, reminding me that my faith is not strong enough to heal anyone.

Yet healing is not the goal. Expelling The Dark requires far more unusual methods than exorcism or mere summoning; and something far more dangerous. The demons here must be allowed to roam free and all those near will feel their presence even if they are not perceptive enough to identify that barbarous clawing at the base of their spine. I do not know what it will do to those who are able to see the evil. Perhaps they'll go mad with it, too.

I sit on the edge of the bed, and the man's eyes snap open, the fear reflected there deeper and more harrowing than the malignancy that tightens the air around us, the breeze suddenly hot as campfire smoke. The Dark is messing with us, trying to confuse me. It will not work.

"The Light or The Dark?" I ask him.

"The Light, The Light ..." Blood bubbles between his lips. I press a rosary into his hand—his mother's, his most prized possession, and it is the last bit of comfort I can offer. "Go now, my son."

"No, no, Padre, no ... help ... help ..."

I lean close to his ear, whispering, the stink of his sweat ripe in my nostrils. "I cast thee out." He coughs, and his eyes flutter closed, still and silent as if in death. Then his back arches and he shrieks—even the walls vibrate with the intensity of his screams.

I spread my hands in the air above his forehead, his fevered skin already writhing, like a nest of snakes is wriggling beneath his flesh, and though my rings do not touch him, the skin sizzles—the smell of burning fat seeps into my sinuses. My wedding band, and Justine's band on my pinky, warm, the engraved crosses inside them brighter, hotter, than the rest. It does not matter that Justine no longer recognizes me—evil remains, but love lingers too, even if it is harder to spread.

I close my eyes, feeling the room shrink and expand, the entire house breathing with me. "I cast thee out," I whisper again. "Into The Light." I lean closer and whisper the final words, once, twice, thrice.

The man shudders. I lower my hands, the flesh on the young man's head still sizzling, burning, then extinguishing itself with a staccato sucking sound. My rings are still warm against my palm. And as the breath leaks from him in one final exhale, I feel it, the thread of insanity, the demon beneath his flesh, squirming at my nearness, gnashing its horrible teeth. I know precisely how to recognize it—I brought it here. And I will send it back.

The room seems to waver, contracting once as if birthing the evil from the atmosphere. Then it is over, the vestiges of spirit vanishing like the dew evaporating from the grass in the rays of dawn.

I push myself to standing, bones aching, and hobble to the window, to that pane of glass as perfectly round as the moon outside, and I am struck with a coldness in the gut, as if I've stepped into someone else's shoes. Is this what my ancestors saw looking out this window? Tonight I peer out at another world from the one I strode through this afternoon— the front yard is empty, the grass a dusky greenish-gray beneath the towering oak, and the earth is no longer sodden with spilled blood. But my heart hammers against my breast- bone, and I see Helen's red scarf in my mind's eye, hear her screams in my ears, and the *snap* of her spine, see the way it appeared as though every bone in her body was being crunched to dust, blood spurting from the ruptured shell of her chest.

Then the scene returns to normal—quiet, gray-green, empty.

But it isn't really empty. I feel the energy there, lingering in the shadow of the porch, waiting for the next soul to be lured by the force that emanates from this place.

For every slight, there must come a balancing blow. Every dark deed done must be repaid in blood.

The girl, that unfortunate girl, red scarf billowing behind her, screaming, screaming … Helen saw the madness of this world, the evil that must be quelled. Everyone does.

But never soon enough.

～

GET *THE JILTED* ON MEGHANOFLYNN.COM.

～

"RELENTLESS SUSPENSE THAT WILL LEAVE YOU QUESTIONING EVERY ELEMENT OF REALITY."
~*WENDY HEARD*, HUNTING ANNABELLE

ALSO BY BESTSELLING AUTHOR
MEGHAN O'FLYNN

STAND-ALONE THRILLERS
The Jilted
Shadow's Keep
The Flood

THE ASH PARK SERIES
Salvation
Famished
Conviction
Repressed
Hidden
Redemption
Recall
Imposter

SHORT STORY COLLECTIONS
Aftertaste
Listeners
People Like Us

DON'T MISS ANOTHER RELEASE!
SIGN UP FOR THE NEWSLETTER AT
MEGHANOFLYNN.COM!

ABOUT THE AUTHOR

Meghan O'Flynn is the bestselling author of *The Flood*, *The Jilted*, *Shadow's Keep*, and the Ash Park series, which includes *Salvation*, *Famished*, *Conviction*, *Repressed*, *Hidden*, and *Redemption*. She also writes creepy short stories, some of which are inspired by her husband, a man whose continued willingness to sleep beside her with the lights off—even after discussions about cannibalism—is downright disconcerting. Her quirky and amazingly hilarious children have not been privy to these discussions, but her hundred-and-seventy-pound beast of a puppy would probably eat Earl if given the chance. He just doesn't seem like a dog person.

If you want to find out about new releases and freebies, join Meghan's reader group at meghanoflynn.com, and get a **FREE SHORT STORY**. Guaranteed spam free. And if you have a few minutes, pop over to your favorite book site to leave your review. It's a great way to avoid getting eaten by…guilt.

64627595R00194

Made in the USA
Middletown, DE
29 August 2019